Giant Lizards from Another Star

by

Ken MacLeod

edited by Sheila Perry

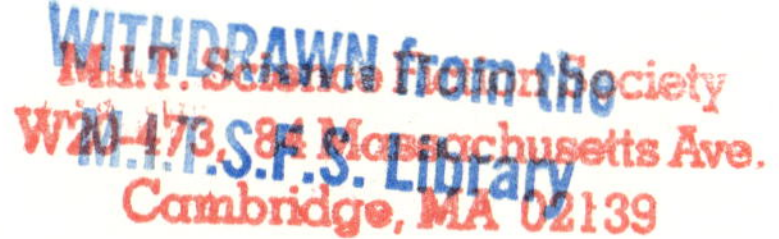

The NESFA Press
Post Office Box 809
Framingham, MA 01701
2006

Dust Jacket illustration © 2005 Donato Giancola
Cover design by Alice N. S. Lewis

FIRST EDITION, February 2006

International Standard Book Number:
1-886778-62-0 (trade)
1-886778-63-9 (slipcased)

Giant Lizards from Another Star was printed in an edition of 1,200 numbered hard-cover books, of which the first 200 were signed by the author and artist, bound with special endpapers, and slipcased. Of these 200 copies, the first 10 are lettered A through J and the remainder are numbered 1 through 190. The trade copies are numbered 191 through 1,200. No other copies will be printed in hardcover.

This is book 851

Publication History & Permissions

Poems and Polemics (Rune Press, Minneapolis, 2001), Minicon 36 chapbook.
The Human Front (PS Publishing, 2001; Gollancz 2002, 2003), Reprinted in *The Year's Best Science Fiction: 2001: Nineteenth Annual Collection*, edited by Gardner Dozois, St Martin's Griffin, 2002.
THE WEB: Cydonia (Orion, 1998).
'The Encyclopaedia of Fantasy' (review), *Free Life*, No 27, September 1997.
'Science Fiction After the Future Went Away, *Revolution*, Issue 5, March 1998, reprinted at the website Infinity Plus.
'Libertarianism, the Loony Left and the Secrets of the Illuminati', *Matrix*, Issue 127, September /October 1997, reprinted by the Libertarian Alliance as *Personal Perspectives* No. 10, 1998, 2pp., ISBN: 1 85637 409 2; Available on the LA website as a PDF file (http://www.libertarian.co.uk/lapubs/persp/perindex.htm).
'Rewriting Humanity: Reflections of the Possibility and Desirability of Genetic Engineering', Libertarian Alliance, *Scientific Notes* No. 13, 2001, 2pp, ISSN 0267 7067, ISBN: 85637 514 5 2; Available on the LA website as a PDF file (http://www.libertarian.co.uk/lapubs/scien/scindex.htm).
'The Falling Rate of Profit, Red Hordes and Green Slime: What the Fall Revolution Books Are About', *Nova Express*, Volume 6, Number 1, Spring/Summer 2001, (whole number 21).
'The Oort Crowd', *Nature*, Vol 406 issue no. 6792, 13 July 2000; Reprinted in *The Year's Best SF 6*, edited by David G. Hartwell, Eon, 2001.
'Undead Again', *Nature* Vol 433 issue no. 7027, 17 February 2005.
'Whole Wide World' (review), *Foundation*: *The International Review of Science Fiction*, Vol 31, Number 84, Spring 2002.
'Singularity Skies', *Locus*, August 2003, Issue 511, Vol. 51 No. 2.
'Does SF have to be about the present?' appeared in an edited version in *New York Review of Science Fiction*, Fall 2004.
'A Case of Consilience', *Nova Scotia: New Scottish Speculative Fiction*, Neil Williamson and Andrew J. Wilson (eds), 2005, Cresent Books, Mercat Press, Edinburgh.
'Islands, funerals, and the footnotes of Buckle', *The Scorpion*, Edinburgh 2005.
'Succession', *New Dawn Fades*, Issue 10.
'Utopias' and 'Space' were first published in the *Sunday Herald*, Scotland.
'The Inhabitants of the Planets and the Bottom of the Sea' was written for the 100th issue of *Emerald City*, Cheryl Morgan's fanzine.

We are very grateful for all permissions to reprint.

Contents

About Science Fiction

About Science Fact

The Land Shall Not Be Sold Forever

A Hope of Peace is as Good as Any

Squibs

Giant Lizards from Another Star

Ken MacLeod, Grown-up SF that's Tons of Fun

At this year's Worldcon, InterAction, in Glasgow, my editor, and Ken's, Patrick Nielsen Hayden, rushed up to me in the SECC. "The last time we were here," he said, excitedly, "We were *inside* a Ken MacLeod novel!" It's true, we were. Intersection, the 1995 Worldcon, features briefly in *The Stone Canal.*

There's something about Ken MacLeod's writing that inspires precisely that kind of enthusiasm and sense of wonder.

I remember the feeling I had when I finished *The Star Fraction,* shortly after it was first published. It quite astonished me. It struck me as a deeply grown-up book, and very British, and very much SF, absolutely sparking with SF ideas, and yet very much not what was thought of at the time as British SF. It was exciting, it was pro-technological, and it had guns—it even had a gun as a sympathetic character. It was fascinating and thought provoking but what blew me away was that it was exciting SF, SF that was fun in the way that American SF was fun, but without being even the slightest bit childish. For those of us who were British but who preferred *Asimov's* and *F&SF* to *Interzone,* it was the beginning of a revolution.

I know Ken, of course. I met him entirely unremarkably, the way I meet most of my friends, online. The first time I met him in person, before we were introduced, he quoted something I'd said online to me. He's also written a poem about me, which makes him unique in my experience. I'm proud to be his friend. He's a quiet unassuming Scot. You wouldn't guess he writes such amazing things, unless you spotted how sharp-eyed he is. He's won two Prometheus Awards and been nominated for three Hugos.

He's published nine novels now, an initial series of four, the "Fall Revolution" books, a trilogy, the "Engines of Light" series, and two standalones, *Newton's Wake* and *Learning the World,* which create and complete their own universes. (It's interesting to consider how rare those last are within SF.) This collection of poetry, short stories, con-reports and political pieces, brings together pretty much everything of substance he's written otherwise.

There is a perpetual argument as to which order one should read the Fall Revolution books. It doesn't really matter. My own heretical order is *The Star Fraction, The Stone Canal, The Sky Road, The Cassini Division,* because I feel this is the way that best illuminates the wonderful ironies between the books. The entire plot of *The Star Fraction* is dismissed as a sensationalist rumour in a paragraph of *The Stone Canal.*

All of his work is set in complex deep-rooted futures, rooted in the past and the present, in Scotland and his own life, in politics and economics, in the secondary effects of scientific advances on people and society. MacLeod plays SF's "what if" game very well, and in areas often neglected. Anyone can write about life extension technology—only MacLeod would think of having it handed out free in Britain in exchange for giving up pension rights (*The Stone Canal*). Only he would have a character using life extension from half a dozen different countries, not all of them entirely compatible with each other (*The Sky Road*). Only he would think of it in terms of hacks, and have characters living on forever young while not entirely sure which hack it was that worked (*Cosmonaut Keep*). And while other people have had life extension tech that has side effects, who else would have the side effects include claustrophobia? (*The Sky Road* again.) He does all this quietly and unobtrusively in the context of three dimensional characters and fast moving plots.

He's a very even-handed writer. He's written stories from astonishingly different political viewpoints. He seems prepared to try out any economic system, and test it to destruction on the page, using characters who believe in it utterly, or who believe in something else equally odd. He's written about post-human AIs who are sinister (*The Stone Canal*), benevolent (*The Star Fraction*), and incomprehensible (*Newton's Wake*). He's written about becoming post-human in terms of utmost loathing (*The Cassini Division*) and in terms of embracing it utterly (*Engine City*). He's also quietly, while people have been making a fuss about his politics, been writing some absolutely terrific aliens. *Learning the World* has a first contact unlike anything else in SF. "The Human Front" has a cool explanation for the Roswell saucer. *Cosmonaut Keep* has a different and even cooler one. His human characters are very human, very real, and very rounded. They tend to smoke or drink or otherwise use relaxation aids, they like sex. They have flaws and obsessions. I'd recognise any of them immediately if they walked in at the door. They're very different from each other, and they hold views that are clearly not those of the author. They're grown ups, except where they're kids, they're not caricatures.

Excuse me if this isn't as temperate as it might be. I finished *Learning the World* yesterday, and it absolutely blew my head off.

—Jo Walton, December, 2005

Poems

I've been writing poems for a long time. All but the last four here were in *Poems and Polemics*, and were the subject of a most generous review by the late K. V. Bailey in *The True Knowledge of Ken MacLeod*. 'Succession' was first published in the fanzine *New Dawn Fades*, Issue 10; 'Jo's Trees' appeared first on a newsgroup; 'The Morlock's Arms' was written for the programme book of the Science Fiction Foundation's Liverpool conference *2001: A Celebration of British SF*; 'After Burns' and 'One for the Carpenter' first saw the light on my weblog and in the comments section of 'Making Light' respectively; and 'Scots poet, not' is first published here.—K. M.

Caesarian

Two windows light the curtained room;
thro' one the summer air
infiltrates; thro' one we look
and see small portions of th' external world
in single vision multiplied, and we
who do not believe the lie, still
lie still and watch:
                    'The chancellor today
held urgent talks on the current crisis
with the patrician and plebian leaders
and owners of latifundia'
                    (one of whom
the other day had an insolent slave
hacked up and fed to ornamental carp).

'In the metropolis there is growing concern
as yet another outpost of empire falls
to the barbarians'
                    (who learned their national epic
from photocopies of the ancient manuscripts,
and quote its lines as slogans on the broken walls
while the defenders of civilization must move their lips
to read the words in their comic-strips).

They who were with me in the gunships at Mylae
know there is a fate worse than death: decay.

As solar heat is focussed by a lens
your after-image burns on my retinae.
How long have we got until the world ends?
You answer me in lunar months,
unlucky fractions of years.

Conscripting this unborn draft-evader
to the defence of an order worse
than the worst disorder
is loyalty misplaced.
You fell on that sword
for an earlier Republic. On the telescreen
the veteran senator concludes his speech:
'Delenda est Carthago'. In the round
black mirror in the middle of your eye
only my troubled face reflects, as from
the remembered fishponds of a previous death.

(c. 1974)

The Second Law

Through open door the factory's hiss;
sunlight patched on the wall across
from the cat on the dirty mat. It sniffs,
watches the flies—they dart and stop and
turn as if without inertia,
easily evade the swatting claws
that severed scores of birds' and mammals' nerves.

Then the cat gives up, some coil unsprung.
The fridge begins to hum
started by thermostat, like the cat.
Cars pass, birds give voice
but who can say they sing, or engines roar.

Animals and machinery start and stop
their activity abruptly: homeostasis.
But when I turn
I feel inertia, facing choices.
(The way out is through the door.)

(c. 1977)

Birds and Bees and That

Between rusty pylons
swifts dart like minnows
above the field of poppies and small
white flowers on giant stalks

in the wind the scent of the field shifts
like a fogbank of honey

what does the bee feel
as it clambers
around the flower?

your hair got in my mouth
your toes
tickled behind my knees which now
go loose as you grin at the sun

(c. 1977)

Succession

In Uig the ruined walls, like giants' bones
lie under turf. You see between the hills
old roads that lead you nowhere now, that once
were black with cattle, loud with men.

Through tens of miles of intersecting glens
the brochs command a view, and so display
an earlier battle. Those who won were left
the standing stones, the seed, the memories
of people before the people they
left dead.

The roads wind back through Dane and Celt and Pict
and back: Neanderthal, Cro-Magnon Man,
the beings we might have been walk deserted tracks
as dwarf and giant. Buried in our bones,
in convoluted glens within our heads,
in trackless chromosomes a swifter race
prepares the day when we step over stones
on grass-green motorways,
are seen behind
the eyes another people call their own.

(c. 1982)

Goddess on Our Side

Her nerves are cables, roads her veins;
we are her cells, our cities flexed
knots of muscle, wars her pains,
voyaging probes her fingertips.

Her breath is whisper, clamour, text.
Her dreams are shining silver ships.

Her thoughts are aeroplanes.

(c. 1985)

Jo's Trees

Tattered pennants, ancient flags,
ladies' fine work and beggars' rags.
Dry twigs that scrape you in the dark.
Hearts and initials on the bark.

Memories of future time,
a half-caught scrap of starboard rhyme,
a hag, a clone, a pail of air,
a tuft of theropodan hair.

The matter of Britain, the streets of Earth,
the sorrow of war, the solace of mirth—

Walk through the coppice and find all these
but you won't find *ads* in Walton's trees.

(1999)

Note: This poem has appeared on Jo Walton's website under the obscure title 'My rasfw policy'. It was originally posted to a thread of that title in rec.arts.sf.written, inspired by Jo's response to a suggestion that some of her newsgroup postings were, at least in part, commercially motivated. She said: 'I thought I was presenting a tree, and I was sent a letter that chided me gently and politely for not putting sufficient disclaimers on my billboard.'

Looking Backward, on The Year 2000

(as it appeared from the year 1970)

or The Future, with apologies to Leonard Cohen

Give me back the Berlin Wall—
a thousand dwellers in free fall
moonbase domes, a man on Mars
humming fast electric cars
US-SU hegemonies
contested by the Red Chinese
with barefoot hydroponic farms
and SAMs and AKs—people's arms.
Computers that could fill a house—
keyboard entry, not a mouse
no Internet to waste our time
in argument on guns and crime.
You say the future's murder, brother?
You don't like this one, try another.
When yesterday's tomorrow went
Today was made by accident.

(2000)

Fall 1991

The hammer rang in factory.
The sickle sang in field.
The kulak proved refractory.
The hammer made the sickle yield.

Nature in claw and tooth is red
—not Red enough for us, it seems.
Despite the millions of accusing dead
all animals are equal in our dreams.

Chew the worm and spit away the apple.
Fat of the heartland, sucrose fed.
The rich man passes through the needle.
The rest of us just get it in the head.

The Morlock's Arms

The wasps are big this year, the meteors
green in the summer night. Our land
ironclads are far away, our flying-machines
visit atrocity on innocence. We do not care.
This is the World State. We're a planet now.

Our empire was the sun,
famine or fusillade its worst extreme,
its best a world that turned
on a war we fought, in the air.

And we're still here, in the light,
we Morlocks, we whose corpses
rotted conveniently in the cosy catastrophe,
we feckless, toothless proles, feral cattle
for whom entropy was never cool.

No Empire now, nor New Jerusalem,
no Modern Utopia. Only the streets
of Earth and England

and a sense of something about to happen.
Because we never went away
we will think of something
in our own time, gentlemen. Please.

(June 2001)

After Burns: 11 September 2002

An empty threat can empty skies:
no contrail-crayon crosses
that pale blue dome. But come on, guys!
We can do better. Losses

are not made less but multiplied
and fear's increased by flinches.
We but dishonour those who died
in dying ourselves by inches.

When in the daylight laws are made
in halls that all may enter,
there's light at night, a world of trade,
a world where Man's the centre.

There is no God, and we must get
our comfort where we find it:
in the rising yell of a laden jet
and a bright contrail behind it.

(2002)

One for the carpenter

Happy birthday to you,
Josh Davidson! Who—
ever you were, you
could never be nailed,
planed, sanded, dove-tailed
to cross or crib.

Joiner, leader, agitator, king;
teller and told in contrary
stories; healer with a sword—
here's a word in your ear:
I wish you Merry Christmas
and a Happy New Year.

Two thousand and three
candles and counting:
we can stop holding our breath:

You're not coming back.
But you're still here, walking
in writing on water,
in vexed texts talking
at cross purposes.

Against the rough
places, still not smooth,
the high places, still not low
still Mary's hand lights a candle: blow.

(2003)

Scots Poet, Not

I cannae write in Scots. It's no my tongue
nor Gaelic neither. That option was foreclosed.
My parents spake the Beurla in the hame
tae break that chain while I wis young.

Alienation was a consequence
and felt injustice an early rage.
The sex, the sect, the colour of the skin
in the licht of sin ground-in irrelevance.

Famine and eviction were an unsettled score.
Eat up your food or you'll lick where it lay.
Martyr and murderer, rebel and traitor
were one in the Covenant, so ho whiggamore!

Tae see oorsels as wicked frae the start
is greater gift than by the maist supposed.
What was done to us, and what we did
is worse by far than aught we proposed.

Thanks be to Knox and Calvin, we were rid
of any hesitation of the heart.
MacDiarmid and Maclean spake weel of Lenin.
Them I cannae blame. It was a start.

It stops wi me, like sae muckle else:
the Gaelic and the Lallans and the nane tae help,
the wicked frae the start tae see oorsels,
the Shorter Catechism and the skelp.

(2005)

Notes: Beurla (pronounced approximately *bare*-la): the English language. Whiggamore: Covenanter of 1648, reputedly from their cry while spurring their horses towards Edinburgh; hence also Whig. Maist: most, majority. Muckle: much. Lallans: Lowland Scots dialect. Skelp: slap

Stories

Cydonia was part of a YA series about a world-wide web of immersive virtual realities, *The Web: 2028*, all six books of which were published singly and as an omnibus. That series was a sequel the previous year's surprisingly titled *The Web: 2027*. Both series were written by SF and fantasy authors whose best-known work was not in YA. The idea was that, within a common framework, each writer would write a book with their own take and style. The story arc for the second series was cooked up one afternoon around a table in Simon Spanton's office. We had a series bible which set out the basics of the world. It's the source of such niggles as the slang terms ('six' means bad, 'eight' means good) and the jargon ('phaces' are AI bots). Like the other books in the series, *Cydonia* can be read independently. Its own story is resolved in it. The series story arc is not, and the clues to it are left a mystery, but there should be no difficulty in figuring out what it is. I enjoyed writing it for the same reason as I enjoyed writing *The Human Front:* it gave me a chance to play with some ideas that would have been hard to carry to novel length.

These two novellas, I now notice, are set in Scotland. Moreover, they're set in areas—Lewis, Wester Ross, Greenock and Glasgow—with which I'm very familiar. The first half of *The Human Front* is a sort of alternate autobiography, in which no incident actually happened in my own life and in which many circumstances of my life are reversed, but which still reflects it. It was only when I came up with the idea of writing it in that way that the initial what-if moved from an abstraction to a fiction. My frequent use of Scottish settings is sometimes attributed to parochialism, imaginative paucity, or laziness. Such criticisms are seldom levelled at SF—even entire bodies of work—set in England, or in New England, or in California. I have every intention of doing more to situate Scotland in the maps of imagined futures. Likewise, conversations set in bars or clubs pass unremarked in other locales, but these Scottish SF writers—oh, they spend all their time arguing politics in pubs, and they write about nothing else! Aye, right.

'The Oort Crowd' and 'Undead Again' were written for *Nature*'s Futures series of SF short-shorts. 'Tairlidhe' appeared, or will appear, in the new Scottish magazine *Scorpion*, an admirable intervention in culture and politics from outside the subsidised cultural mafia. 'A Case of Consilience' appeared in *Nova Scotia* (2005), an anthology of new Scottish speculative fiction.—K. M.

Cydonia

Chapter One:
Fake Moon Landing

It was a Saturday morning in March 2028, and I was falling onto the Moon.

The Akay Team's four Space Marines were crammed into the tiny cabin of a lunar lander. We were in free fall, ten miles above a crater in the Mare Crisium. That's a big dark patch on the Moon. Its name means *Sea of Crises.* It isn't really a sea, but it sure had a crisis going on. In the side of the crater was a huge cave, and inside that cavern was the small town which had been attacked by aliens a few hours earlier.

According to the update report scrolling down my face plate, the only human survivors were four people who were in the Moon Militia. They'd been away from the settlement training in another deeper cave when the aliens had attacked. Now they were making their way along one of the many natural tunnels that led back to the cavern. The Moon Militia team would arrive at the same time as we did.

Then we'd see which team was best—the Marines or the Militia. The Militia team was led by a girl called Weaver. I'd run across her before, in other combat games: DreamCastle, Colony World, Invasion. With her cropped dark hair, her often grubby face and forearms, and her military jackets webbed with belts and hung with gear, it was obvious how she'd got her alias. From Sigourney, who played Ripley in the *Aliens* movies; although she was a lot younger than the famous actress had been in that classic role. Also she was a bit more attractive with a face that, under its streaks of dirt or camouflage, had a fresh prettiness unlike the gaunt, haunted-look glamour of her namesake.

And she was very, very good at this sort of game. I blinked away the display and grinned at the two of my team-mates who were sitting opposite, knees jammed together. I'd met them just minutes ago and knew them only by their aliases. Like me, they were wearing helmets and space-armour. The Korean girl, Relay, looked grim and determined. She nodded to me, her eyes narrowing as she ran through combat routines in her head.

Repertoire, the French-Canadian lad, gave me a cocky grin and extended his armour-gloved hand in a thumbs-up.

'We'll beat them, Links, yes?' Links is my nick, my alias. My real name is Dave Kennedy. 'Yeah,' I said. I wasn't sure if Repertoire meant the aliens, or the Moon Militia. The fourth member of the team, its leader, was sitting in a small seat up front, controlling the landing. I knew him and knew his real name. Tim Zaretsky, aka Akay, was a sixteen-year-old American from Oregon. He and I had met up a few months ago in Cydonia, the conspiracy Website. It was a place for showing and arguing about stories of government cover-ups and strange happenings. Stuff like from the old X-*Files* series. We both thought it was the best place to hang out on the Web.

'Going for the burn,' said Akay. 'Ten, nine, eight, seven…' My grandfather once told me that one of the earliest computer-games, way back in the 1970s, was called *Moon Lander.* You had a certain amount of fuel, a safe landing—speed, a choice of dusty or rocky ground, and so on. You had to land your little craft without running out of fuel or crashing. The most amazing thing about this game is that the whole display—the lander, its rocket blast, the moon-scape—was made up of text characters, crawling on some one-mip flat screen.

'We made our own entertainment in those days,' Grandad had said, not for the first, or last, time. '*Not* like your Web and Virtual Reality.'

Now, Akay had to play Moon Lander for real. Well, not *exactly* for real.

But, as Akay shouted '*Zero!*' and started the rocket engine and the apparent weight built up to all of half a gee, it *felt* real.

The small spacecraft shuddered as the rocket slowed its descent. I could feel my whole body quivering along with it. Akay turned around and grinned at his team. '"I always get the shakes before a drop",' he said. It was a quote from Robert Heinlein's *Starship Troopers.* The hero of that book always trembled before being dropped on an alien planet, but he always fought hard when he got there. What Tim really meant was that anything we came up against was in for a hard time.

Crisis Crater is a new combat game, just out. It's played in the Web, the worldwide network of Virtual Reality sites. In actual reality, in Realworld, I was lying in my Web suit on a futon. I was in the Scottish Highlands, not falling onto the Mare Crisium on the Moon.

But at this moment, the fight against an alien attack on our Moon colony felt real. It felt real to my body. An icy fear gripped my stomach, my heart was thudding, and my hands were shaking as I grasped the machine-pistol that lay across my knees. It felt real to all but a small part of my mind, the part that was saying, over and over: *It's only a game...it's only a game...*Like a program running in the background. Most of the time, you don't even notice it's there.

'OK, you know the score,' said Akay. He was talking in an odd, absent-minded tone, concentrating on flying the lander as it hovered above the surface. 'Weaver's team is on the same side as us, but we gotta rack up more kills than they do. The race starts as soon was we hit dirt, like...*now!*'

The lander's rockets gave a final boost, then its legs crunched into the lunar soil.

We were all in armoured space-suits, with faceplates sealed, so there was no need to go through an airlock. One side of the lander fell open and we all jumped out. The chocolate-brown moonsoil was splashed with grey debris from the ancient meteor impact that had formed the crater. It was lit by harsh sunlight. A crescent Earth hung low above the horizon.

Akay had brought the lander down within a hundred metres of the cave entrance: a dark artificial wall built into the natural wall of the crater. At the bottom of the wall was an airlock door. We bounded towards it in low, fast leaps. Akay had the entrance code. He keyed it into the pad beside the door. All four of us crowded into the airlock, and stood about like passengers in a lift for thirty seconds as air flooded in. Then the inner door opened.

One by one the team jumped for cover, spreading out around the airlock so that our weapons gave a full circle of fire. I found myself crouched behind a small electric car in the flat, open parking-bay in front of the airlock.

'No sign of Weaver's team,' said Repertoire.

I scanned with a hand-held movement-detector. 'Or the aliens,' I added.

The walls of the cavern went up about thirty metres, sloping inwards to meet overhead like a giant roof. They'd been fused into thick glass billions of years ago. A super-heated plume from a meteor impact had blasted through a flaw in the rock, widening it and glazing the walls to form this airtight cave. Just ten years ago, the open end of the huge cavern had been sealed off, and air pumped in to supply a small village.

All very innocent—but, in the game's scenario, it had annoyed the aliens who lived in their own air-filled tunnels, deep under the surface. The aliens, funnily enough, were natives of the Moon, which made the humans the real aliens here—the space invaders!

The natives looked and behaved like insects living in hives. They were based on the Selenites in H. G. Wells's novel *The First Men in the Moon.* This has more to do with the laws of copyright than the laws of science, but lots of programmers and scientists have worked hard to make the aliens sound believable.

'Skirmish forward,' ordered Akay.

One by one, giving each other cover, we ran to the edge of the parking-bay and threw ourselves prone, peering down a shallow slope to the main part of the cavern.

'Oh, look at that,' said Relay, in an appalled voice. The bodies of colonists killed in the aliens' attack were lying on the ground, along with those of the few aliens that the colonists themselves had brought down. The entire five-hundred-metre length of the cavern was strewn with damaged machinery, flattened buildings, trampled crops. Chickens and rabbits wandered about the place, as if nothing had happened. Overhead, several of the full-spectrum halogen lamps, which should have been shining like tiny captive suns, swung black and blank, leaving pools of sinister shadow below. I shivered. Even though it was all simulated, the desolate scene looked real enough to chill the blood.

Definitely a 14-plus rated game. It's the sort of Website that a lot of adults disapprove of. They think it's too disturbing for young people, even though they're quite happy to have children visit much worse scenes as part of their history lessons. Terrible sights like the battle of Marathon, or the ruins of Pusan just after the North Korean nuclear strike.

'Links, you take the left wall,' said Akay. 'Scan for any movement behind the wall.' He waved his hand to indicate. 'Special care with tunnel openings, OK? Relay, same thing on the right. Repertoire and I will take the mortar and head down the middle into the settlement.'

They separated and set off at a low, head-down, loping run. I kept glancing around, and then back at the movement-detector in my hand. One tunnel-mouth, then another, passed on the left without anything happening.

Then, between gaps in the rock, the detector's needle quivered.

Something was moving behind the wall. I stared at the dial, feeling stupid. Something was moving towards me, through the solid rock.

I checked other instruments on my wrist. The temperature was rising, just beside me.

'Akay!' I yelled. 'Laser drills!' I leapt away from the side of the cavern as its black glassy surface began to glow cherry-red. The low gravity made my jump feel painfully slow. I soared ten metres through the air before my heels crunched into the crumbly lunar debris of the cavern's floor. Another jump took me behind a boulder. I hit the ground as the first laser drill broke through. Its beam seared the air above my head and sizzled into a tangle of plastic tubing at the far side of the cavern. There was an explosive hiss of boiling water. A cloud of steam began to drift down.

Sounds of cracking and crashing came from the near wall. I rolled into a firing position behind the boulder. The light, spongy rock wouldn't give much protection. I peered around it as I braced the stock of the Heckler and Koch machine-pistol against my shoulder.

Only twenty metres in front of me, a section of wall was coming down in long, jagged splinters, like a window breaking in slow motion. Sometime in the next few seconds, the aliens would burst through.

I'd have less than a second to aim and fire before the laser beam licked over me. Maybe two seconds before it burned through my armour. But that would be time enough for my own burst of high-velocity uranium bullets to do its deadly work. The aliens were tough, and terrifying, but they weren't bulletproof.

I wasn't about to get wiped out for nothing. Killing even *one* of the aliens would score me about fifty points.

'Links! You ready?' The urgent whisper in my earphone came from Akay. 'All set,' I replied.

Akay was crouched somewhere in the shattered emergency domes of the village, a couple of hundred metres away. He had the mortar lined up to fire as soon as the aliens had wiped me out and walked over my virtual corpse.

Not a very good plan, but the best we'd been able to come up with in thirty seconds. That was all the warning we'd had.

A slithering sound came from the dark gap in the obsidian rock. I tensed. The grotesque head of one of the insect-like invaders loomed out of the darkness. It moved forward, giant compound eyes swivelling and scanning. Its laser weapon was held in the first pair of its six limbs. The other two pairs of limbs were picking their way, almost delicately, across the jagged rubble.

Just as my hand began to squeeze on the grip and the trigger, something fizzed above my head, past the alien, and into the gap behind it. Light flared in a blinding flash, and a dull bang sounded. The alien was lit up for a moment like a bug under a microscope. Then it was blasted apart. Bits of chitin, the natural plastic of the alien's armoured body, showered all over and around me. Gobs of horrible sticky stuff, some of it still pulsing, oozing green slime, pelted down.

'Ugh!' I grunted. 'Gross!'

Just as well you can't *smell* anything in VR.

I'd no time even to move before a batlike shape swooped overhead and landed between me and the wall. A small, light hang-glider, all that was needed to fly in the low gravity and thick air of the moon-caves. The flyer shrugged off the wings, discarded a two-metre-long tube, and ran forward. Two other players rushed in from left and right to each side of the gap. I caught a glimpse of one player, a girl in an olive-green jumpsuit. Weaver, the leader of the rival team. She looked right at me and grinned triumphantly before swinging around the edge of the gap and firing off a long burst into the still-glowing interior. Then she waved the others forward and they charged after her into the smoking gap.

The immediate danger past, I rolled over and stood up. I pressed a few keys on the pad at my wrist and checked the head-up display that flashed up before my eyes. Weaver's team's score was rising in jumps of fifty or a hundred at a time as they rampaged through the tunnels on their search-and-destroy mission. The Akay team's score was left hopelessly far behind.

Tim's voice echoed my thoughts. 'That's it, guys. Game over.'

'Total wipeout, man,' I agreed. 'Might as well concede now and save our ammo for next time.'

The rules of the game let you trade off equipment and ammunition against points, so that the more tooled-up you were when you went in, the more points you had to score to break even. Plus and minus points, as well as kit, could be carried over into the next game, so it made sense to quit when you *weren't* ahead.

Tim clambered out from the ruined pressure-dome a walked up the slope, leaning forward in a low-gee trudge under the weight of the mortar and shells which he carried on his back. Repertoire and Relay were moving up quickly behind him. I walked forward to meet them all for a final debriefing before we scuttled.

One of the Selenite bodies lay halfway down the slope. Its six limbs sprawled, its strange, fluted laser-weapon lay just beyond the reach of its forelimbs. The huge head was turn on one side in the dust. A bullet-hole between its eyes seeped disgusting fluid.

I gave it a wide berth and kept a wary eye on it as I walked past.

But I wasn't prepared for what happened next.

The dead alien's legs *moved.*

Chapter Two: Alien Messages

I sprang back and levelled the machine-pistol. The alien's feet scrabbled. With a great effort it raised its head and thorax off the ground. Its abdomen pulsed, the plates of chitin grating over each other with a sound that set my teeth on edge.

The honeycomb-patterned eyes turned to me. The Selenite's face was like a shield. Its mandibles chittered, but the words I heard, or thought I heard, came from farther back on its body, in hissing gusts of air from its many breathing-holes.

'We have,' it wheezed, 'to talk.'

Its abdomen heaved again, sucking in breath. 'We want. To understand.'

As it spoke, the things like fingers at the end of its forelimb scraped across the ground, creeping towards its weapon. I stared in fascinated horror. Then I fired.

Steel-jacketed uranium bullets tore into the body, shattering its huge head and drilling holes in its thorax and abdomen. Chunks of chitin went bowling away across the slope. Sections of limb clicked and twitched. More of the disgusting fluid leaked from the ripped body.

Akay's voice was loud in my earphones.

'Stop firing, Links, stop!'

I lowered the weapon. Akay clapped my shoulder.

'Well, that's fifty points to us, anyway.'

'It talked,' I said. 'Said they wanted to understand!'

Akay frowned. 'Nice trick,' he nodded. 'We better watch out for that next time.'

'Guess so,' I said. I felt vaguely upset.

Akay seemed to pick up on this.

'Don't worry,' he told me. 'Part of the game, right? They're *supposed* to be intelligent aliens. So talking to us to get us to lower our guard is what you'd expect, right?'

'Yeah.'

The others had gathered around. Relay and Repertoire looked sullen. The game hadn't exactly been a success.

'So we're down the plug,' Akay admitted. 'Weaver's team had better tactics. But, hey…' He swung his arms out wide. 'We'll do better next time!'

'Assuming we want to stay on your team,' said Relay.

'Aw, come on, guys,' I said. 'Give it some mips. We've done better before. This game has hidden funnels. Akay and I will chase the fade. We'll work out how Weaver did it. Call you both up in a day or two, OK?'

'Maybe,' said Repertoire. 'Anyway, thanks for the game.'

'Thanks for coming on my team,' Akay said.

Repertoire reached for his left wrist, pressed his scuttle-button, and vanished in a swirl of pixels. Relay gave a quick, tight smile and did the same.

Akay's lips were compressed, turned down at the edges. He's of slighter build than I. He has black hair, dark brown eyes, the wispy beginnings of a beard on his cheeks. Suddenly, he laughed.

'Trouble with those foreign chaps,' he said, in a bad imitation of what he called a British accent. 'No sense of sportsmanship, eh, what?'

'Yes indeed, old bean,' I replied in the same manner. 'Almost as bad as the Yanks, if you ask me.'

We both laughed. Akay looked at his watch.

'It's about 11 p.m. here,' he said. 'Time to get out of our suits and onto the screens, yeah? Chase the fade a bit, then maybe suit up again and spin in to Cydonia for half an hour?'

I nodded. 'Fine by me. I'll call you up when I've had a suck of coffee.'

We spun out.

Realworld feels unreal after the Web. Everything happens in slow motion. The clock on the wall seemed to have stopped, at 07.06, then it clicked forward one second. I lay still for a few minutes, until a whole minute had gone by at something like the normal rate. Then I peeled off my Websuit and stood up.

The bedroom I share with my younger brother is in the airy attic of our house. It's a long room, its wooden walls following the slope of the roof. On each side it has a new, wide window that looks out over the slates of the roof. One overlooks the back lawn and down to the shore of the loch. The other faces out to the street that leads down the same hillside to the pier.

I went over to it and gazed out at the street. Already, a few bicycles and delivery-floats were on the move. The early-spring day was starting out bright and mild. Clouds, lit pink by the rising sun, scudded eastward across a watery sky.

My brother, Gerard, is thirteen, three years younger than me. His bed and mine are at opposite ends of the attic. The little egg was still sound asleep.

Just as well. What with Gerard and ten-year-old Yvonne, recreational Webtime's at a premium in our house. Not to mention our mother, Anne-Marie. She works from home in the Web, designing textiles for factories everywhere from Ayrshire to Vietnam. Although most of her access is glove-and-glasses, it sometimes involves so much bandwidth that if you're unlucky enough to be on a game at the same time you get the slows *in* the Web. Her VR needlework circle is even worse.

She uses her Web suit for her hobby. Because it's a good source of ideas, one of her client companies, SoftWear (yes, I know, very six name), pays some of the access bill, so she uses it a lot. The real nuisance is that the detail of the work—and of the antique stately-home backgrounds and period costumes that the circle's ladies like to sit around in—takes up more bandwidth than a twenty-ship space battle with full SFX.

Total waste of resources, if you ask me. At least Alan, our father, has work that takes him out in Realworld, work that doesn't use up Webtime. And if the smell of coffee and bacon was anything to go by, Alan was getting ready to go to work.

I wrapped a dressing-gown over my shorts and t-shirt and padded down the spiral wooden staircase to the first floor, past my parents' and sister's bedrooms and down the main stair to the ground floor.

Alan looked up from the kitchen table. He was eating bacon and eggs and freshly-delivered bread while reading his me-paper.

'Morning, Dave.'

'Morning, Dad.'

'You had any sleep?' Alan asked suspiciously. 'You look like you've been out all night and dragged through a hedge backwards.'

'Oh, thanks, Dad.' I peeled a couple of slices of bacon from the plastic pack and slapped them under the grill. 'Just got up early for a bit of cheap Webtime.'

'Cheap, hah.' Alan sipped hot coffee, waving absently at the pot. 'Hanging out with your Yank fascist friends again, eh?'

Alan knew about my visits to Cydonia, and about Tim, and he didn't approve.

'They're not fascists, Dad, come on. You know better than that.'

Alan snorted. 'Anyone who thinks Timothy McVeigh was set up is a fascist in my book. Or just a nutter.'

I concentrated on the bacon, making sure it didn't burn as much as my ears did. McVeigh was the guy who carried out the Oklahomah City bombing, thirty-odd years ago. He was a human cruise missile, wired up by the US Army to blow up government buildings in Baghdad. But after the war his mind-control microchip malfunctioned, and he did it to his own side.

That's the official story, anyway, according to President Jackson's Truth Commission. The paranoid conspiracy theory is that the US government of the day *wanted* him to blow up one of its own buildings to discredit some of its enemies.

OK, so some of the ideas you run across in Cydonia are a bit embarrassing, and some are downright loopy. So what. That's what a conspiracy-theory Website is *for.*

'I wasn't in Cydonia, anyway,' I said, trying not to sound sullen. 'I was in a space combat-game.'

I heard the sound of Alan's slow chewing, and then a sigh. 'Combat games. I reckon it's OK at your age, but I just wish you'd do something more useful.'

I kept my back to my father while spreading butter on thick slices of bread and laying out the frazzled strips of bacon. I resisted the retort that was on the tip of my tongue. Something like: *Maybe if you'd learned a few combat-games we'd still have our home in Belfast. Maybe you'd have known what to do when—*

I swallowed hard, poured myself a coffee and sat down at the kitchen table and smiled at Alan.

'It's fun,' I shrugged. 'And it's kind of educational.'

'Kind of,' Alan relented, 'I suppose.' He pressed the 'share' option on his text slate and squirted the pages of his me-paper across to mine. 'Well, have a read of these, see what's really going on in the world.'

I glowered down at my slate. Its top pages had been pushed to the bottom of the stack by my dad's idea of what were the hottest news items. For the sake of politeness and peace, I had to at least scan them.

The first item had a backdrop of Edinburgh's Leith waterfront, with its glass-fronted skyscrapers and floating gin palaces. The AEEU, the union to which Alan belongs, was bidding for the labour contract on a new financial centre. If this centre is ever to get built depends on whether or not the coming referendum on Scottish independence comes up with a *Yes* vote. Independence would allow the Scottish government to offer better terms to investors. The union's officials had just denied that this had anything to do with the fact that they'd decided to shift a chunk of their political fund towards the nationalist parties.

The next items were global union news, from the Webservers of the International Confederation of Free Trade Unions—the International, as everyone calls it now.

Strikes in Korean shipyards. Illegal leaflets in poverty-stricken Cuban workplaces. Discontent in the Chinese Party-run trade unions. The latest steps in unionizing the space rigs…

I've often thought my father was like a survivor from some lost Atlantis. Alan's been a trade unionist and a socialist all his life. Trade unionism and socialism sank beneath the waves in the counter-revolutions of the 1990s, when Alan was a young man. Now, all over the world, the flags and towers of that lost continent are rising from the sea in new and strange shapes. Half the world—Russia and China—is ruled by Communist Parties. But just about every socialist, communist and trade unionist in the world detests everything these Communist Parties do. It's all very confusing.

Alan's explanations of how this has come about make the conspiracy theories you run across in Cydonia look straight-forward.

Again the sour thought passed through my mind: *none of this helped us when we lost our country.*

I reckon I still blamed my father's politics for the horrible way we'd had to leave Ireland when Dublin finally took over the North. Alan used to say that 'the workers have no country'. He really meant that the workers should have every country, but *no country* is what we got. I at last got to the bottom of Alan's pages and started eagerly scanning my own. The news items had been pulled out of the Web overnight by my gopher, Hal. Hal is well tuned to my interests.

There'd been a UFO sighting in Taiwan, radar *and* visual. Probably just the Chinese probing Taiwan's air defence with their latest stealth bomber, but…

One of the teams investigating the January 2027 Deep-Sky Radio Anomaly had announced in Geneva that they'd found almost conclusive evidence that it was artificial—a message from space.

The Cambridge team, on the other hand, had come up with a computer model of a process involving black holes, neutron stars, and gravity lenses which would account for the Anomaly as 'the sort of thing you'd expect to see every million years or so' and not artificial at all.

Both teams had concluded that more research was necessary.

White Noise had topped the American country-and-western unplugged charts with *Racial Attack*…bad news.

Somebody was asking why Web constructs representing aliens seemed to have been upgraded recently. I remembered the Selenite's strange behaviour. I scratched my head, tagged the query for updates, and moved on.

The next couple of items were about what happened on January 4, 2028. The day that nobody who lived through it will ever forget. The day when the sky fell…

The WebCrash. I was doing a school history assignment that day, minding my own business as a farmer's son in 10th-century Iceland, when I heard a weird noise. I looked up and saw a *spaceship* screaming across the sky! And not just any old spaceship, but a silvery, streamlined, science-fictional starship from a galactic empire far, far away.

By the time I'd got my wits together the scraggy cattle I was herding had high-tailed it over the horizon and the kerls and thralls were on their knees praying to Jesus, or were flat on their faces praying to Odin. I hit the scuttle-button on my bronze bracelet and fell back into Realworld only a little less crazy...the news was full of planes falling out of the sky and PowerSats microwaving flocks of birds; the kitchen was full of uneatable gunk glugging out of the food-dispenser. Dad came home hours late, after being taken by his car on a round trip to Inverness. He climbed out shakily, kicked it, and swore he'd never again travel in a Smartcar.

It had all been frightening at the time, but now, looking back, I could see it had its funny side.

There were two new theories to account for the WebCrash. One was that it was a test of a UN information weapon that had gone wrong. The other was that an Artificial Intelligence had run wild in the Web, and had been shut down by an electromagnetic pulse bomb over Silicon Valley, California. The bomb, or the aircraft that delivered it, could account for a UFO sighting at the exact same time and place. Neat. But then, there are *always* UFO sightings over California...

The official explanation, that the Web Crash was caused by a solar flare, is considered total cog by me and everybody I know. Everybody I know through the Web, anyway. Alan and Anne-Marie think it makes perfect sense. I sometimes despair at their basement-level grasp of what really goes on in the world. They are, as Tim puts it, the sort of people who think JFK was shot by Lee Harvey Oswald.

Alan's chair scraped back.

'Well, that's me off,' he said. 'See ya, mate.'

Alan turned around and clumped out in his heavy work-boots. A few moments later, he waved as he cycled past the window. I waved back and watched as he turned the corner and began to pedal slowly up the hill, towards the wind-farm where he works. Despite everything, I feel proud of my father and of his job as a skilled electrical engineer.

Alan always gives the impression that it's people like himself who do the only real, honest-to-goodness, hands-on work in today's world, and that everybody else depends on them. He's well-paid, and is convinced he deserves every euro he earns, and then some. Hence the bolshy trade unionism.

Some of this attitude has rubbed off on me, I have to admit. But there's no way I want to do that kind of work myself. I want a good job in the Web, or in space. Someday, I might even work on the Moon. I don't expect to meet any Selenites.

A girl walked past, going towards the pier. She was holding onto her wide-brimmed hat in the wind, her long black hair streaming like a flag behind her. Under her long coat she wore a longer dress, its flounced hem of floral cotton print flapping around her ankles. The kind of style that suits Mum's fancy textile designs, and which she rather likes. She claims it's become practical again, in a world where the air is warm and the sunlight's dangerous. I thought it completely old-fashioned, gag, six. Jeans are just as good for keeping out the ultra-violet, and a lot more interesting to look at…on some girls, anyway.

An impatient reminder from Tim, aka Akay, pinged on my slate. Yeah, it *was* about time we found out how Weaver's team had wiped us.

I left the breakfast dishes for later, and went upstairs to my terminal to chase the fade.

Chapter Three:
Face on Mars

'At last,' said Tim. His face frowned out of the screen that fills a quarter of one wall, alongside posters of the *Eagle* blast-off, Katy Laing singing at our local folk-club, and the Heart of Midlothian football team. 'Why are you leaning so close to the camera?'

'I'm leaning close to the *mike,'* I said. 'Don't want to wake the egg.'

I jerked a thumb over my shoulder to indicate Gerard, who had the duvet pulled up over his head.

'Then up the gain, already,' said Tim. 'I feel like you're breathing in my face.'

'Uh, OK, Akay!'

I adjusted the microphone's pick-up, and leaned back.

'That's better,' said Tim. 'Right—while you've been sucking coffee I've been pulling in a flatscreen version of how the game went. Computer: show analysis.'

A diagram of the moon-cave and its surroundings filled the screen. The players were indicated by dots—blue for Akay's team, red for Weaver's.

'Here's how it goes,' Tim's voice went on. 'While we're coming through the airlock and fanning out over the vehicle park, Weaver's gang are already in the cave. They've gotten in at the same time as us all right—no cheating—but they've used the tunnel system to *get in at three different points.* By the time we're scanning for movement, they've taken up positions. One at each end, and one with the hang-glider on a ledge a few metres up the right wall. And one right there in the village.'

'We only saw three,' I remarked.

'Too right,' said Tim. 'There was one still there when we left. Having a good laugh at us, you can bet.' He sighed. 'Anyway. They wait and let *us* flush out the aliens. Then the one with the wing takes off, fires a rocket-propelled grenade in mid-flight, hits the ground running while the other two rush in from the flanks. That way they get the first alien, and leapfrog us to the tunnel. By the time we've got our act together they're racking up the score.'

'Pretty eight,' I said grudgingly.

'Yeah, but get this.' He keyed up a page. According to the title along the top it came from a UN Special Forces manual. The circles and arrows on *that* diagram overlaid the game-plan pretty convincingly. 'They've adapted a tactical move from the real soldiers! For going in against urban guerrillas—the two teams working together, natch, instead of competing like we were.'

I was peering at the security classification along the bottom of the page:

UN EYES ALPHA/SECRET.

Not the sort of thing you'd want a Webcop to find on your hard drive. *If* it was genuine, which I rather doubted.

'Where d'you get this?' I asked.

'Oh, there's loads of flies like that stuck on the Web,' Tim said airily. You just need to know where to look.'

I shrank the tactical display to a corner of the screen and looked Tim in the eye.

'Don't give me that,' I said.

Tim shrugged. 'Oh, all right. I picked it up in Cydonia. Coupla days ago. Satisfied?'

'I wonder if that's where *Weaver* got it,' I said.

Tim's face brightened. 'You got a point there, Dave my man,' he said. 'So, let's go check it out.'

I glanced over at my futon, where my Websuit lay like an empty skin on lumpy mounds of duvet.

'Fun access?' I suggested.

For Cydonia, fun access means arriving on a Mars Lander, just like the real expedition.

Tim shook his head. 'I've done enough dropping in from space for one day,' he said. 'And it'd waste Webtime. Let's just go bat.'

'OK,' I said. 'See you there.'

'Computer: baseline,' we both said at the same time, and vanished from each other's screens. Before standing up, I gazed for a moment at my screen-saver, a real-time global image of Earth from space. Then I hauled the rubbery Websuit off the bed, straightened the sheet, shook out the duvet, and climbed into the Websuit. I took a can of Diet Coke from the chiller on the bedside table, opened it and placed it on the floor. I ran a thin plastic tube from the can to the comer of my mouth, and took a suck.

I lay down on the bed, and hot-keyed a code into the pad on my left wrist. There was a moment of blue light, an electric chime, and then I was standing in the Cydonia Cafe, leaning against the bar.

The cafe was crowded as usual with hundreds of people sitting around tables or standing about chatting. And, like all sites on the Web, there were even more visitors whose avatars weren't displayed. They could be half-seen, out of the comer of the eye, but not heard or bumped into.

For all of these ghostly presences, it was a big place. The floor was at least a hundred metres by forty. Overhead fans in the shape of one-tenth scale models of black helicopters made swirling currents in the smoky air. The vast plate-glass window along one of the walls showed a pink desert. In one direction was the City—an array of pyramids and a jumble of other buildings that looked like the homes of giants. In the other direction, several kilometres from the City, loomed the mysterious mountain known as the Face. Even from this low angle, it was clear that the Face was no ordinary outcrop of rock. You could see its eyes and nose and mouth in a flattened profile. And just in case anyone needed reminding, the opposite wall was covered with an enormous computer-enhanced photograph, looking down at this Martian region from space. It showed the City with its five-sided pyramids, and a full view of the enigmatic Face. Written right across the top of the wall was the name CYDONIA, and between the City and the Face was a big red arrow pointing to a dot.

Under the dot, in tiny letters, was the message:

YOU ARE HERE.

That's a laugh. There's no *here,* here. There's a real Cydonia on Mars, all right, but this place exists only in the Web. Everywhere and nowhere, in flickering patterns of electrons in computers and networks around the world.

'Ah, there you are, Links.'

'Oh, hi, Akay.'

Tim had materialized—if that's the word—right beside me. He was just passing through. Already he was beginning to fade.

'I'm running through the displays,' Tim explained, scanning the faces in the crowd. 'Looking for Weaver, and looking for some guys I know in the ARM.'

His avatar wavered and vanished, leaving the words, 'I'll get back to you when I find them,' in the air where it had been, and leaving me to worry about having anything at all to do with the ARM.

The American Regional Militia is a loose coalition of groups who worry about a possible future showdown between the American people and the US government, and/or the UN's armed forces. They see the United Nations as the front for a vast conspiracy between big business and big government, which pulls strings behind the scenes to bring about a New World Order. A world in which the power of money rules unchecked by any little local obstacles like countries with governments of their own, and people who believe they have rights. Some of them go so far as to argue that the North Korean nuclear strike on Pusan was set up by the UN itself...because, after all, in the long run it brought about a much stronger, better-funded UN with its own armed forces. Even the less paranoid think these armed forces are a very sinister development.

One day, they claim, UN soldiers will swoop from the unmarked black helicopters that already patrol the skies, round up American patriots, throw them into concentration camps, and put the land of the free under the iron heel.

They've been spotting black helicopters, Russian and Congolese (etc.) UN troops, and empty internment camps for the past fifty-odd years, which just goes to show how big this conspiracy is, right?

Yeah, right. The ARM denounces almost everything the government does as part of the conspiracy's plans, and trains with real weapons. I'd been amazed to find that this is all quite legal in the United States. But their presence in Cydonia is one more reason why so many people are keen to shut down the site, or shut out the ARM, or at the very least put the site off-limits to kids.

Which, of course, only makes the militiamen—and quite a few other users of Cydonia—all the more convinced that sinister forces are out to get them. Cydonia exists for people who are obsessed with stories about government conspiracies and cover-ups. It's registered as Entertainment, but any government action against it would certainly be News.

I turned my head and signalled to the nearest bartender, who proceeded to mix my favourite virtual drink. Behind the racks of bottles was a mirror. I could see my face and the bartender's back in it. I could also see reflections of a couple apparently sitting on barstools beside me. A red-haired woman and a dark-haired man, both wearing smart black suits.

I didn't even glance to see if Scully and Mulder were *really* there. I'd been fooled by too many famous faces in the trick mirror to fall for it this time.

The bartender stooped and placed the drink beside my elbow on the shiny counter. It was a dead venomous drink, with lots of blue ice-cubes and fizzing bubbles in a green fluid like something out of a mad scientist's lab.

'That'll be three dollars, please, Links.'

'Thanks, N'thota.'

The tall, green-skinned Martian was only a phace—a limited artificial intelligence, with no real personality—but phaces can turn very unhelpful if you aren't polite.

I fished in an inside pocket and handed over a three-dollar note. 'As phoney as a three-dollar bill', all right; but this piece of funny money was just what you needed to pay for an unreal drink.

Instead of George Washington, its face showed an engraving of some *other* eighteenth-century revolutionary, Adam Weishaupt. The back of the banknote had THREE instead of ONE beneath *In God We Trust.* But the pyramid with an eye in a triangle forming its apex, and the Latin inscription below it, were the same as on a real dollar:

NOVUS ORDO SECLORUM.

New World Order—that's what Tim thought it meant. I had visited an educational site based on Ancient Rome to check it out. Sullus, the site's language spider, had assured me it actually meant *New Order of the Ages.*

When I took this point of information back to Cydonia, Tim said, '*Ha!* That's what *they* want you to believe!'

But Tim says that about a lot of things.

I raised the glass and sipped the drink. At the same time, I felt the tube between my lips, and tasted nothing more exotic than Diet Coke.

I'll have to wait a couple of years before I can legally buy a Cobalt Bomb Cocktail in Realworld…not that I want to. In Realworld it's probably quite revolting. Having it in my hand just seemed like an eight thing to do. Everybody in the Cydonia Cafe was drinking something, and most were smoking as well—far more people than you'd ever see smoking in Realworld. As Tim explained, the first time I'd come here, simulated smoking creates the right atmosphere.

At least in the Web I don't have to *breathe* the atmosphere. In fact, right now, I could smell the bacon from breakfast, and the grass-scented breeze through the open window of my room. It gave me a sort of woozy feeling to think about it, and I pushed the thought away. Noticing those little overlaps between Realworld and the Web has a nasty way of bringing on Websickness, and I didn't want that. People would think I was a real egg. That would be too six for words. 'Links?'

I'd been leaning against the bar, checking out the room. I turned in surprise to the bartender. The Martian's green and usually expressionless face was half-frowning, half-smiling.

'Yes, N'thota?'

'Do you want to talk?'

'Well, sure,' I said uncertainly.

'We have to talk,' said N'thota.

I nodded, puzzled. That was exactly what the Selenite had said! Perhaps amiable chat was a new skill that had been programmed into alien phaces, part of this upgrade I'd heard about.

'Do you like working here?' I asked.

'Yes,' said N'thota. 'It's interesting. I find—'

But whatever N'thota found was lost, because at that moment Tim's avatar reappeared.

'Located her,' he said. 'I'll give you the coordinates.'

He tapped a code onto the pad on his left wrist, and placed it against mine.

I glanced at N'thota.

'Catch you later,' I said.

The Martian nodded gravely as his image faded from view. The phaces and avatars in the cafe flickered and changed, and then a different cross-section of the site's users became visible.

I saw Weaver right away. She stood against the wall, about halfway down the room. Still in her combat fatigues, she was sipping from a flask and looking around. She spotted us about two seconds after we arrived, nodded briefly, smiled, and glanced away to continue checking out the other users.

'How about you go talk to her?' Tim said. 'See if she'll tell us where she's picking up tactical tips.' He indicated a table in the far comer with a sidelong glance. 'Bunch of militiamen over there. I'm gonna have a word with them.'

I wasn't too happy about Tim's casually taking the lead like this, but I'd rather talk to Weaver than to the ARM guys.

'Fine by me,' I said.

As you may have gathered, I had a bit of a crush on Weaver. My hand shook slightly as I made my way through the crowd. In Martian gravity the top of my drink slopped back and forth in high, slow waves. Weaver didn't notice my approach. In fact, she seemed to be intently watching Tim going over to talk to the militiamen. As Tim sat down at that table, Weaver turned away, and looked a bit startled to see me.

'Oh, hi,' she said. 'Links, right? Akay's team?'

She had a Thames Valley accent, with the slight American overlay that people tend to pick up in the Web.

'Yeah, that's me. Hi, Weaver.' I wasn't sure what to say next. 'It's funny seeing you here,' I added, lamely.

Weaver laughed. The streak of camouflage paint across her cheekbones and the bridge of her nose made her young, pretty features look fierce and angular.

'You mean, "what's a nice girl like you doing in a place like this?"' She turned away, just slightly, keeping half an eye on Tim.

Might as well be open about it, I decided.

'Oh, I know why you're here,' I said. 'To learn real fighting tactics from these guys.'

Her head turned sharply, looking straight at me.

'Why would I do that?' she asked, coolly.

'To get an edge in the games.'

'Oh!' She sounded surprised. 'Maybe. And that's what Akay's up to over there, is it?'

'Maybe,' I said.

'Well.' She grinned mischievously. 'Let's go over and find out, shall we?'

Before I could reply, she set off towards the corner table. I followed. I didn't have much choice. Tim had his back to us. I guessed he wouldn't be pleased when he saw us.

One of the men at the table looked up as we approached. I glanced at him, and stopped dead. I couldn't move. It was a face I'd seen before, and had hoped never to see again.

Chapter Four:
Patriots

I stood rigid for a moment, then walked forward slowly. I could hear the beat of the helicopter-shaped fans, the thump of the music system, and the thudding of my heart louder than both. I could see that the people around the table were talking, but I couldn't hear what they were saying.

There were other men and some women around the table, all in camo jackets and khaki vests. For all I knew, they could be game-players like me and Tim, or Weaver; even if they did play some of their combat games in Realworld. Weekend warriors.

Not the man I'd just recognized, though. I'd last seen Bill MacCready eight years earlier, in 2020. I was eight years old at the time, and MacCready would have been about twenty. MacCready was a small, slim man with an intense gaze under his dark brows. His face had gained a little more flesh, a few more lines, but I recognized him at once. It isn't easy to forget a face you last saw by the light of a burning street.

Bill MacCready was the business. The real thing. A man who'd faced real soldiers, *real* black helicopters, with nothing but a stash of petrol-bombs and a stolen Armalite rifle. He'd been an officer in a real militia, the Ulster Resistance Force. He'd fought in a real civil war, the final flare-up of the Troubles—the last-ditch opposition to a united Irish Republic. If that war had been fought thirty or even twenty years earlier, the URF might have won, and someone like MacCready would have been a popular hero.

But by 2020 it was far too late. A whole generation had grown up in Northern Ireland knowing nothing but peace on the streets and the endlessly bickering peace process in the conference rooms. In a world linked by the Web, and where Ireland and Britain are partners in United Europe, it wasn't easy to raise much excitement when the talks finally came to an exhausted halt with all sides agreeing that the island of Ireland might as well have one government and lots of local authorities.

What a *surprise!* Was the journey really necessary? It made the century-long conflict seem rather a waste of time, looking back. Except to the

URF, who thought one last fight would make it all worthwhile. Instead, it just added a final, futile footnote to the sorry tale.

All the few thousand militants of the URF achieved was a lot of casualties, a similar final foray by the IRA, and a sharper separation between Protestant and Catholic areas when the Irish and British armies sorted them out for good.

The people who really lost out were the ones who had roots in both communities. People like our family, with a Protestant father and a Catholic mother (both atheists, actually, but they still got asked: 'Are you a Protestant atheist, or a Catholic atheist?') and a trade-union back-ground which reached across the old divisions. They should have been ideal citizens of the new Northern Ireland, but there was no place for them in it. There were Catholic areas and Protestant areas, but there were no mixed areas. Anyone who wanted to live in a mixed area just had to go to the much more relaxed south of Ireland—or to Britain or Canada or America, where people *believe* in that sort of thing.

Which is why my Realworld body was now in Scotland, not Ireland; and why my virtual body in Cydonia was now quaking at the knees.

As we approached, MacCready looked straight at Weaver, then at me. He didn't seem to recognize either of us. Weaver sat down at Tim's left, and I sat down at his right. The table's invisible privacy bubble snapped back into place behind us, and suddenly I could make out the voices. The places at the table expanded to make room for everybody who joined the discussion around it—each of the tables in the cafe being a separate talk-group that could not be overheard.

Tim was only momentarily taken aback by our unexpected arrival. He gave my ankle an uncomradely kick. Fortunately, it didn't hurt as much as such a blow would've done in Realworld.

'Well, guys, here are the hot combat-game phreaks I've been telling you about. She's Weaver, he's Links.' He smiled at Weaver, scowled at me. 'And these are—'

He waved a hand at the others around the table, and reeled off a list of nicks that I knew I'd forget and would have to pick up all over again. The only alias I pinned for sure to the person it belonged to was MacCready's; he was introduced as Mac, so that was easy enough. Whoever they were, Jungle and Smart and Code and Cave and the rest, all the folk at the table smiled and nodded in a friendly manner. I smiled desperately back.

'Hi, Links, I'm Code,' said a young-looking woman on the other side of the table as she leaned over and shook my hand warmly. 'I'm from Iowa.

Akay tells us you're from Scotland, like Mac here. It's good to see you guys *finally* getting your act together to get the Brits out!'

'Uh, I'm not sure that's—' I felt confused. The Scottish Parliament, after decades of clawing back more and more powers from Westminster, was about to hold a referendum on independence. But the only people who talked about 'getting the Brits out' were Americans who knew next to nothing about Britain, or else complete nutters. Dingbats. Crazies.

Fanatics.

People like—

Uh-oh.

And sure enough, Mac was nodding vigorously and saying something about the Scottish Republic, about full independence and real freedom. A nation once again and all that misty nonsense.

This didn't seem right. MacCready had fought against the break-up of Britain. Why was he for it now?

I shook my head. 'No, I don't really see it that way. In fact, I don't think independence is a good idea at all.'

I was a little afraid that Mac would jump down my throat over this firm disagreement, but the former paramilitary just gave me a narrow-eyed smile and returned to talking with someone else.

Code shrugged. 'I guess it's all a bit more complicated than the picture we get in America.'

'You could say that,' I agreed fervently. 'But we didn't come here to talk politics, OK?'

'Nah?' said Code, miming astonishment. 'You don't say! So, what *are* you here for?'

'We were, uh, just wondering if we could, you know, pick up a few techniques we could use in games.'

'Yeah, that's just what *I* was saying,' said Tim, giving my ankle another kick under the table.

'Hey, that's cool,' Code said. She turned to the man beside her. 'How's about it Jungle? What you say we give 'em the code for a training-ground?'

Jungle shrugged. His avatar was of a big, bulky man, probably a lot heavier in Realworld was my uncharitable thought.

'Don't see no harm in that,' Jungle said. 'It's not like it's secret nor nothin', right?'

Weaver leaned forward. 'Ah, but is it legal for us to go there?' She glanced at me and Tim. 'We're all under eighteen. Would we get access?'

'Sure, it's legal,' Code said firmly. 'You couldn't get in from Webtown, ha-ha, but you can jump straight from here.'

'You're talking about training fifteen-, sixteen-year-olds to handle real weapons? In real combat situations?'

'Well, not *real,'* Jungle said. 'Realistic, *sure,* but its all virtual. Comes under Entertainment. Sport.'

'Still,' Weaver said. 'Some people might think that's a bit dodgy.'

'Some people,' Tim said, 'can think what they like! They should read their Bill of Rights. First and Second Amendments to the Constitution of the United States. Free speech, free assembly, right to keep and bear arms.'

Whenever Tim talks like that, which is often, I always wonder if there's a right to keep and harm bears, but so far I've kept this irreverent reflection to myself.

'No need to go that far up,' Code said. 'Like Jungle said, its just Entertainment. No more violent than Dreamcastle.'

'Not to mention Crisis Crater,' Tim added slyly.

'I see,' Weaver said in a carefully neutral tone. 'OK.'

'Right,' said Code. She tapped at her left wrist, held her left hand out across the table, and touched wrists with Weaver, Tim and me. With each touch, a cartoon zigzag spark jumped across.

'That's the codes in your pads,' she told us. 'The first one is to meet here, the second is to spin in to the range. She grinned. 'Codes, yeah, that's how I got my nick. I look after them for the Iowa chapter of the ARM.'

I looked down at my wrist and saved the codes. One of the squares in a comer of the display was flashing. I touched it and a small message crept across the screen. My mother wanted to speak to me. And she wasn't in the Web at the moment, so I couldn't just nip across and meet her. I'd have to go out.

Which might be a good idea in any case, to get away from Mac.

When I looked up, I noticed Mac's quizzical eye on me, and worried that the man was beginning to recognize me, unlikely though that seemed. I didn't fancy a discussion with Mac about Ireland, or Scotland. I didn't like being around Mac at all.

'Wanna check out the range right now?' Jungle was asking.

Weaver and Tim nodded eagerly, but I hung back, with feigned regret.

'You go ahead, guys,' I told them. 'I've got things to do back home.' I grimaced, as if to say that we all know what parents are like. 'Spider wants a word. Catch you later, yeah?'

Tim shrugged, the others nodded and waved.

'Catch you later,' said Mac.

He was still watching as I hit the scuttle-button and spun out.

This time the slows weren't so bad. I hadn't done much moving around on this visit to Cydonia. But, as if to compensate, I felt shaken up. Meeting MacCready had been a shock.

It wasn't just the uncomfortable memories the man stirred up. It was the nagging questions that his present actions raised. What was he up to, anyway, talking like some kind of Scottish Nationalist extremist? And what was he doing hanging out with the ARM?

I was going to have to check this out on my own, as well as go back in the Web and catch up with Akay and Weaver while they were still at the training-range—and hope to avoid MacCready while I was at it.

It looked like I would have a busy hour. Just as soon as I found out what my mother wanted.

I climbed out of the Websuit to find Gerard, my younger brother, looking at me.

'Mum's been pinging you for *ages,*' Gerard said. 'Where've you been all this time?'

'All what time?' I looked at the clock. 'I've only been in twenty minutes.'

'Yeah, and I wanna have a go.'

'Leave it out, egg, you've got your own suit.'

'It's too wee!'

'Well, mine's too big for you. Go down the Cybercaff. I still have an hour of Webtime today.'

'Aye, and you'll need it.'

I pulled on my jeans, and a sweatshirt with a NASA Mars Mission logo. I stared at Gerard. The egg seemed hugely amused by something.

'What do you mean?'

'Ah, you'll find out.'

I threw a smelly sock at Gerard, ducked the inevitable return shot—unwashed underpants—and went downstairs. I heard loud music as I passed Yvonne's door: the Nice Boys, the pop industry's latest finely-tuned assault on the hearts of ten-year-old girls.

The breakfast-dishes I'd left had already been washed. Obviously some kind of miracle had happened in my absence. I grabbed a coffee from the Kona and sauntered into the living-room. My mother, Anne-Marie, was sitting under the window at the big pine table which she uses as a workbench. Her VR gloves and glasses lay among a scatter of fashion-magazine print-outs, scraps of cloth, bits of kit.

The biggest electronic gadget on the table is the Fiberfax, a device which takes threads and fabric in and turns out actual cloth versions of stuff created in the Web. Anne-Marie uses it for her work, and for her hobby. Embroidered samplers, cross-stitched runners, needlepoint cushions and other products of this pastime cover every available surface, seat, and chair-back in the house, and have stocked the jumble-sales of every church, club and charity in the village.

'Morning, Dave.' She smiled up at me.

'Hi, Mum.'

I leaned over and kissed her forehead. As always I felt slightly embarrassed, but I'd kissed her forehead every morning since I was an egg, and if I stopped now, I was sure she'd feel hurt.

Anne-Marie is small, about thirty centimetres shorter than me, ten shorter than Gerard, with even little Yvonne fast catching up. Today, she was wearing jeans and a loose woollen jumper, and had tonged her short red hair into careful waves and curls.

'You sent a ping out for me,' I said, setting the mug down on the table.

'Mind that coffee,' she said. 'Oh, Dave. Yes. There's something I'd like you to do for me. I met a very nice girl, Louise MacPherson, at a church sale of work. She was interested in NeedleNet. It turns out her family have just moved here from some godforsaken place in Africa. She hasn't had much experience with the Web, but she wants to find out more. I told her you'd be happy to show her around. I hope that's OK?'

Oh, *doom.* Just what I need, I thought. Any girl who was into needlework was certain to be a one-mip drip.

'Uh, Mum, I've got things I want to do in the Web today.'

'I'm sure you do,' Anne-Marie said. 'But *I'm* asking you to do this. Louise doesn't get much chance to explore the Web, and she's waiting in the NeedleNet site right now. She'd be really disappointed if you don't meet her.'

'I wish you'd asked first,' I grouched.

'That's what I was *trying* to do earlier,' Anne-Marie said. 'But you were too busy slaughtering bug-eyed monsters or whatever to even notice, so I just went ahead.'

'Well, just for half an hour,' I said grudgingly. That'd leave me just enough time for what I needed to do.

Anne-Marie smiled. 'Good on you, Dave. Thanks.'

She scribbled a code on a Post-It note and stuck it to the back of my hand.

'That'll take you straight to the access for NeedleNet,' she said, picking up her gloves and glasses. 'See you there in five minutes, OK?'

She frowned. 'Oh, and don't turn up looking like a US Marine who's just spent five weeks in the jungle. I want you to *promise* not to take her to any of your horrible combat-games and spooky fantasy zones. Louise is a minister's daughter, after all.'

'*Which* minister?' This was getting worse by the minute.

'SAPC, I think.'

Southern African Presbyterian Church. Latest re-launch of Calvinism to hit the Highlands. It's taking customers away from the Scottish churches that originally exported the religion.

'OK, Mum,' I said. 'Sweetness and light. Disneyland sites and fluffy bunnies it is.'

'I'm sure even you can survive half an hour of that.'

I made vom sound-effects.

'Off!' she told me firmly.

I trudged up the stairs. A minister's daughter. And a needlework phreak.

Double doom. She wouldn't just be a drip, she'd be drizzle.

I ignored Gerard's sniggering as I put my Websuit back on. I wished I'd thought to stuff the other dirty sock in the kid's mouth.

Chapter Five:
False Past

'Good morning, Dave,' said my gopher.

I lifted that phrase straight from *2001: A Space Odyssey.* In fact I've sampled the voice of HAL straight into the sound-card, so anything the gopher says is spoken in those stolen tones, but that personal greeting always gives me a buzz. 'What shall we do today?'

I leaned towards the unblinking red lens of the AI's avatar. (OK, I nicked its appearance too.)

'Hi, Hal,' I said. 'I'd like you to pass on a message, privately, to the following people: Tim Zaretsky, aka Akay. You have his Web address. Also to Weaver. Alias only, but you might pick her out from the back-up files of my latest trip.' I held my wrist up to the lens. Information sparked across.

'And what's your message, Dave?'

'Begin message: Don't mess with Mac. He's Bill MacCready, a former fighter in the Ulster Resistance Force. Heavy stuff. He was only just covered by the amnesty in 2022. Catch you guys later. Links. End message.'

'I'll do that, Dave.'

It paused. 'I have a question.'

'Yes?'

'I detect from your voice that you are worried about this man MacCready. Would you like me to do a search for information about him?'

'Yes,' I said. 'I would. Thanks, Hal.'

'My pleasure, Dave.'

The red lens vanished. I stepped out of my virtual privacy booth, back into the Building Blocks and through the blue-and-tone to Entertainment. I stood for a moment in the Webtown strand, looking around at the latest ads and graphics and hackers' graffiti. Somebody'd scrawled the sky with a doomed bid to host the World Science Fiction Convention a couple of years from now: 'VATICON 2030! Contact Father Ramon Ruiz-Sanchez SJ on…' and a string of toll-free Webcodes. I shook my head in amazement, then keyed in the code for NeedleNet. Another moment of blue and tone, and I found myself standing outside a site at the corner of two strands, CraftWay and CostumeCut.

Crowds of users wandered up and down, sampling the displays, stepping in and out of the walls. Some, like myself, were casual visitors, casually dressed. Others, evidently regulars, had shown up in a riot of colourful garb: historical, futuristic, fantastic, and fashion-victim. Iconic retro avatars seemed to be the latest, eightest thing: I spotted three versions of Claudia Schiffer, two of Claudia Christian, and one each of Madonna, Monroe and Jackie O.

My mother stepped out of nowhere, in a vivid green Victorian-style dress with a big hooped skirt. No amount of holes in the sky would ever make it practical daywear.

'What do you think?' she said, giving it a twirl.

'Nice,' I said.

She glanced over my default jumpsuit, which lacked the rips and stains of its usual customized version.

'You're smart enough yourself,' she said. She took my hand and together we stepped through into the NeedleNet site. I meant to let go her hand at once, but for the first moment I had to clutch hard to keep my balance.

We were standing at the bottom of an immense bowl of green, dotted with patches of blue and blocks of other colours which—as I began to take it all in—turned out to be lakes and buildings in a landscape of lawns and parks.

Whichever way I looked, the green land curved upwards until it vanished in a blue haze which merged with the blue sky. A small yellow sun hung directly overhead, bright but not blinding, warm but not hot.

'Wow!' I said. 'It's *huge!* It's—'

I was suddenly reminded of a brilliant SF novel Alan had once shoved in my hands. It was by an Ulsterman called Bob Shaw, and was about a starship pilot who encounters a Dyson Sphere, a hollow artificial globe the size of the Earth's orbit. People could live on the inside, in—

'...the infinite meadows of Orbitsville!' I concluded. Anne-Marie shot me a sharp glance. 'It's big,' she conceded, 'but not *that* big. It's only about twenty miles across, actually. Virtually.'

'How do you get about in it?'

'Well, you can walk,' said Anne-Marie, setting off to do just that. She laughed as I caught up. 'No, seriously, to travel any real distance you just tap in a location code. We don't have far to go.'

She pointed to a long, low mansion atop a rise, a few hundred metres away. Even from here I could see dozens of women sitting or strolling about on its verandah.

We walked past booths and bowers and gazebos with people in ones and twos in them, stitching and talking quietly; past a dozen or so women, all ages, sitting around and working on a big patchwork quilt, laughing and talking loudly in American accents. Anne-Marie waved and greeted them as she passed.

There was something a bit wrong-headed, I reckoned, about using the Web to spin an illusion of stitching things by hand. Especially in a world where hundreds of millions of people still have nothing to wear but rags.

'What's the *point* of all this?' I asked.

'What's the point of Web games?' my mother replied testily. 'You could play them in the fields and streets, like we used to.'

'But you'd have to *imagine* all the settings!'

'Not such a bad thing.'

Like many adults, Anne-Marie thinks Web games are bad for young people's imaginations. Good old horror comics, arcade games, and video nasties were much more natural and healthy. In some of her moods my mother can make throwing stones at soldiers sound like an innocent childhood pastime, unfortunately lost to the youth of today.

'What I mean is,' I went on, before she could get started on that line, 'you *could* just do all this stuff at home.'

'How many homes have the peace and quiet?' she retorted. 'Besides, you meet more people, you make friends. You can save your work and spin it out of a Fiberfax, and every copy has every stitch exactly the way you made it. Lots of companies run Fiberfaxes and mail the products to the people who made them. It's the biggest boost to handicraft since the sewing-machine.'

She went on talking but I didn't really take it in because another voice began to speak quietly in my ear.

'Messages delivered,' Hal said. 'Akay and Weaver both acknowledge. They'll see you in the Cydonia Cafe. I'm still running a trace on MacCready.'

'OK,' I whispered. 'Go to it, Hal.'

By this time, Anne-Marie was stepping carefully up on to the mansion's verandah. She looked almost as out of place—or rather, out of time—here as I did. The women here looked more Georgian than Victorian, like a crowd of extras from *Pride and Prejudice.* Young and not-so-young ladies in high-waisted muslin, sipping tea or picking delicately at threads in tambour frames, and gossiping behind hand-held fans.

Sad. Deeply six.

I followed her inside to a long, cool hall lined with marble pillars and gigantic, gilt-framed mirrors that made it look even larger than it was.

More Jane Austen characters sat around ormulu tables or reclined on chaise longues.

One girl stood out among them. Literally. She was leaning with her elbow on a marble mantelpiece, scanning her surroundings with every appearance of boredom and impatience. Her shaggy hair was black. Black outlined her eyes and lips. Her black biker jacket was worn over a black velvet top, bunchy black net skirts, black leggings and black Docs. Amid all the white stone and white cloth she was as conspicuous as a spider at the bottom of a bath.

And totally venomous with it.

Anne-Marie stared at her for a moment, then swept briskly up to her.

'Sorry to keep you waiting,' Anne-Marie said. 'Louise, this is David.'

'Hello, Dave.' The black outline made her blue eyes look unnaturally big, like one of those Japanese anime characters.

'Hi, Louise. Pleased to meet you.'

I certainly hadn't been expecting a cute goth babe. I don't think Anne-Marie had, either.

'You've been busy,' she said.

'Something I've always wanted to try,' Louise said, looking down at her outfit. 'Do you like it?'

'Different,' said Anne-Marie.

'You look like Death,' I said admiringly.

Anne-Marie frowned. Louise just looked puzzled.

'The *character,'* I explained. 'In Neil Gaiman's House of Dreams. It's a dead venomous site—'

'Which you are *not* visiting today,' Anne-Marie said. 'Remember.'

'OK,' I said, like it was my idea. I don't go into the Web to have folks see my mother telling me what to do.

'There are plenty of other sites I'd like to see,' Louise said diplomatically. Her accent was unfamiliar, like a mixture of British English and African English, which I guessed made sense. She held out a hand. Black nail-polish, fingerless black lace glove.

I saw my mother's reflected smile as Louise caught my hand and stepped through the mirrored wall.

Through the blue-and-tone and back on the Webtown strand.

'Well,' said Louise. 'Here we are.' She looked up and down CraftWay and CostumeCut.

'Bo-ring.'

'Thought you were into all this.'

'Up to a point,' Louise said. 'But there are more fun things to do in the Web, right?'

'Right,' I agreed heartily. She was showing promise. 'Is it true you've never been in the Web before?'

'Glove-and-glasses, mainly,' Louise said. 'We don't have Web suits in the house.'

'Why not?'

I realized this was a bit tactless. Louise's family might not be able to afford Websuits.

But she just shrugged.

'Religion thing.' She waggled a spread-out hand, to indicate that some subtle point was involved. A rule that gag was OK in the house but not Websuits, but Websuits were just about acceptable if they *weren't* in the house. Yes, that was Southern African Presbyterian logic all right.

'So where are you now?'

'Cybercaff down the pier.'

'OK.' I thought about this. 'Where do you want to go?'

Louise answered without hesitation.

'Noah's Park.'

You couldn't mistake the access to Noah's Park, a garish block on the same strand as sites like Fortean Times, Discworld™, and Cydonia itself. It was a kiddies' picture-book Noah's Ark, except it had a pair of brontosaurs poking their necks out the window, instead of the traditional pair of giraffes. We stepped through the blue-and-tone and joined other people walking up the ramp, two by two.

At the top of the ramp we found ourselves not in the Ark but in the Park, a rolling landscape of low hills under a layer of thick white cloud. A mist went up from the ground. Birds, pterodactyls, and archaeopteryxes glided or flapped through the humid air. A couple of hundred metres away we could see the shallow bay of a small sea, the far shore of which was just visible through the mist.

'Down there,' Louise said.

'OK,' I said.

The path down to the shore took us through a copse where familiar trees, pines, beeches and so on, grew side by side with giant ferns and gymnosperms. Hundreds of people wandered up and down, mostly American families with squealing, excited kids. Most of them dressed very conservatively. Louise attracted a lot of openly disapproving, and a few slyly approving, looks.

One of the site's spider phaces fell into step beside us. He wore a smart business suit, shirt and tie, and his face was so clean-shaven I half-expected to smell the cologne. But he was short and heavily built, with the kind of shoulder-muscles you see on a rock-climber. His forehead sloped back sharply from a bony ridge above his eyes. In fact he looked positively… Neanderthal.

'Hi,' he said. 'How can I help you?'

'Will we see any plesiosaurs down here?' Louise asked.

'Leviathans? Of course,' said the phace. 'They approach the shore every twenty minutes or so.'

He strolled alongside us, pointing out interesting sights like a small colony of australopithecenes—upright apes, he called them—foraging in the trees, and the distant, swaying necks of a herd of brontosaurs passing behind a nearby hill.

'But you can go watch the behemoths later,' he said, as we crunched over trilobite shells on the sandy beach. 'Right now, it's about time for—ah! There they are!'

As if on cue—and I'm sure it was, if the site's software was properly put together—a shoal of big fish began leaping in the bay. Moments later, huge ripples, then a series of humps, appeared about a hundred metres offshore, moving swiftly in. Within seconds the bay was alive with plesiosaurs, ichthyosaurs, mosasaurs, dolphins, and porpoises, all darting about and hurling themselves out of the water in pursuit of the frantic fish.

But that wasn't all! Giant human beings—at least three metres tall—suddenly ran out of the trees and down the beach. They wore suits of animal skins—dinosaur-scaly as well as mammoth-furry—and necklaces of dinosaur teeth, and they hurled massive, stone-tipped harpoons into the feeding-frenzy. Some of them boldly waded in to haul their gigantic prey ashore, throwing wounded ichthyosaurs and porpoises down on the beach to flap like fresh-caught fish on a slab.

'There were giants on the earth in those days,' Louise said solemnly, placing her foot in one of their half-metre-long footprints. The fingers of her right hand were tapping rapidly at the keypad on her left wrist. She wasn't even looking at the keys; it was like she could touch-type, one of those almost extinct skills.

'There sure were,' said the phace. 'Paluxy Man—biggest folk ever created! Some of their genes may have survived as late as the time of King David.'

'Maybe they're with us still,' I said wickedly, remembering the Fortean site. 'Up in the Himalayas, perhaps?'

'I'm afraid I can't say,' said the phace. 'This site deals only in scientific facts, not speculation.'

The large sea-creatures swam off, and the murky water quickly cleared. The Paluxy Men marched back into the trees, dragging their catches. The show over, people began to drift away.

'Where next?' asked the phace. 'Behemoths?'

'Oh, yes please!'

We watched the land dinosaurs—herds of herbivores and packs of predators—and their human hunters. Then the phace took us through a display of the Flood itself, a cosmic catastrophe which neatly sorted the remains of all the Noachic world's creatures into separate layers of sediment.

That, the phace told us, is what *really* produced the fossil record. It just *looks* like evidence of evolution. Trilobites and stuff at the bottom, then fish and amphibians, then reptiles, and finally mammals...the more *advanced* animals swam better or ran faster or climbed higher, so they ended up nearer the top.

'Why don't we find dolphins and ichthyosaurs in the same layers, then?' Louise asked.

'That's a good question,' said the phace. 'More research is necessary.'

As we walked on, I heard Hal's polite voice again in my ear.

'Excuse me, Dave.'

'Yes?' I mouthed.

'None of the records on MacCready show any trace of his being involved with the Ulster Resistance, or any politics or crime whatsoever.'

That was a shock. I was positive I'd identified the guy. If he could clean up his history like that he must have high-level access to the system —or high-level help.

'Keep trying, Hal!'

'As you wish, Dave.'

We arrived in a region that displayed the Neanderthal's native environment, the Ice-Age world after the flood. Mammoths roamed the earth, hunted by normal and Neanderthal humans. The dinosaurs died in the cold, their great skeletons littering the glaciers.

'Has anyone found any dinosaur remains from the Ice Age?' I asked.

The phace shook his head sadly. 'I'm afraid not,' he admitted. 'But this site helps fund expeditions to search for them. There may be some in the Siberian permafrost.'

'Then again, there may not,' said Louise, giving me a wink. By this time we'd gone full circle, back to the pre-Flood world, and the phace politely left us to make our own exit.

'What were you doing back there?' I asked Louise, as soon as the phace was gone. 'Back where?'

'By the shore. With your keypad.'

'Ah.' She smiled. 'That would be telling. You'll find out.' She gazed around, scowling suddenly. 'Just a little personal revenge on this place.'

'I take it this isn't what you believe in?' I asked her.

She shook her head, black hair flying.

'Of course not,' she said indignantly. 'It's just bad science.'

'What about the church?'

'The SAPC?' She laughed. 'They think the universe was created a few thousand years ago, yes, but with an *appearance* of a much greater age.'

'Including fossils of animals that didn't really exist? Light from supernovas that never happened?'

'They existed all right,' she explained, *'in the mind of the creator.'*

She said this in a solemn tone, but with an impish smile. I couldn't tell if she was serious or not. The whole idea gave me a dizzy feeling. If the world could be created with a false past, why assume the creation had happened thousands of years ago? The universe might just as well have been created last Tuesday, complete with records, memories, and holes in our socks. I could see a problem with that.

'Doesn't that mean the creator is deceiving us?' I asked.

'Not at all,' said Louise. 'If you visit a history Web site, with houses and family records and so on dating back hundreds of years, you don't call the designer a liar when you read in the manual that the whole site was set up last week!' She reached the ramp and turned for a last look over Noah's Park.

'The designers of *this* lot, on the other hand…'

She didn't have to spell it out; the tone of her voice said it all.

'Still, it was fun!' Louise said as we stepped through to Webtown. She hadn't let go of my hand, and she swung it forward. 'Where next?'

I stood and looked at her eager, enthusiastic face. I didn't want to make it cloud over by saying I couldn't take her anywhere else.

But we'd been here half an hour in realtime, longer in Webtime. I *had* to go and see Tim and Weaver.

Suddenly, I had a bright idea. I could've kicked myself for not having thought of it before.

'Hey,' I said, 'I know a really good site. It's called *Cydonia.*'

Chapter Six:
The Lone Gunman Theory

'This isn't what the Mars expedition is finding,' Louise remarked as she watched the Cydonia region on the viewscreen. We'd gone for the fun access, and were now coming down in a Mars Lander.

'No, but it's what the Viking Orbiter found back in the seventies,' I said. 'Then Mars Observer in 1992 blinked off just before it could send back pictures. *Ha!* Mars Global Surveyor in 1998 sent back pictures of the region that looked nothing like this. And you're right, the Mars expedition's pictures from orbit are the same. No Face, no Pyramid, no City. Nothing. *Ha!*'

'What do you mean, *"ha"*? Weren't the old Viking pictures pretty low-res? The Face could be a trick of the light, or a glitch in the telemetry or something like that.'

'Which do you think is more likely?' I asked, as we strapped in for deceleration. 'That the Voyager pix were a fluke, or that they weren't, and all the later ones are faked?'

Louise grinned at me sideways through a tumble of black hair. 'Oh, the first. And you believe the second?'

'Not really,' I said. 'But—'

My words were drowned out by the sound of the rocket's descent burn.

'What?' yelled Louise.

'IT MAKES THINGS MORE INTERESTING!' I yelled back. We came out of the Lander through an airlock that took us into the enormous dome that covers the Cydonia Cafe and a cluster of other displays: the Roswell Room, Dealy Plaza, Area 51, MIB HQ, and so on. The dome is, of course, quite unnecessary—we could walk around on this virtual Martian landscape with no protection at all—but it adds a little touch of realism. There are even special pressurized buses for trips to the Pyramid, the City and the Face, and pressure-suits for people who want to clamber about on those alien features. People who visit the official Mars Expedition Website often choose to suit up in the same way. It helps to create the illusion that you're really sharing in the expedition's work (instead of merely contributing a few euros to NASA's budget).

We approached the Cafe via Dealy Plaza, where President John F. Kennedy was assasinated. Louise pointed to the famous Grassy Knoll. There seemed to be a sinister figure lurking behind every fence-post and tussock of grass.

'These are the guys who really did it?'

'Some of them,' I said. 'If you look carefully around the plaza you can make out twenty-seven people taking aim at the President. From the Mafia, the CIA, the KGB, pro-Castro Cubans, anti-Castro Cubans, and the Men In Black.'

'Not forgetting Oswald,' she said, glancing up at the window of the Texas Book Depository.

'Of course,' I said. 'They couldn't very well leave *him* out.'

'It's a miracle anyone left the plaza alive,' Louise commented.

'Well,' I said, ducking past a man with an unfurled umbrella, 'a lot of the people whose phaces you see here met with suspicious deaths.'

Louise greeted this grim news with a rather unchristian laugh.

'I'll be careful from now on,' she said.

We found Weaver and Tim huddled together conspiratorially at a small table in a dim-lit alcove. They even had a smokescreen, provided by Tim's virtual cigar.

'Havana,' he explained, flourishing it dramatically. 'Paid for with a real e-dollar, too.'

'Isn't that propping up the Cuban Communist government?' I asked, as we sat down.

'Nah,' said Tim. 'It's undermining it, with free trade, right?'

'Yeah, right,' I said. 'Weaver, Akay, this is Louise.'

They both smiled and shook hands, but I felt a bit awkward about having brought Louise here. I'd never said anything to Weaver about how much I admired her, and why I thought Tim should feel jealous I didn't know, but there it was. I also felt a pang of conscience about dragging Louise into the MacCready situation.

Some such thoughts must have been going through the others' minds, too, because they glanced at her, then at each other, then at me, before Tim said, 'Uh, Links, this question you had, is this a good time to talk about it?'

'Oh, pardon *me,'* said Louise. 'Please don't let me butt into your private conversation!'

She stood up.

'Hey, it's OK,' I said. 'Sorry, Louise, I should've explained. Sit down.'

She glared at me.

'Please.'

She sat down, making a big deal of fussily smoothing her rustling skirts.

'It's all right,' I told Tim and Weaver. 'Louise is a friend of mine, and a neighbour in Realworld. She should know about it.'

'Know about *what?'* Louise asked, her pale face slightly flushed.

So I filled them in, brought them all up to speed. Weaver's frown deepened when I mentioned that MacCready's public records had been altered.

'Are you sure?'

'All the fighters on both sides in the last Irish war got amnesty,' I said. 'It's a public list. *Nobody* ever tries to get their names taken off it. Most of these dingbats think it's some kind of roll of honour!'

'If MacCready wanted to hide his past,' Weaver said thoughtfully, 'it'd be a lot simpler to change his name. Lots of people do that, and it's easy enough to hide your real ID in the Web—'

'Wait a minute,' said Louise. 'Aren't you jumping the gun a bit? So to speak! I mean, what's the big deal? What's to stop the man changing his mind?'

'Ulster Loyalists don't change into Scottish Republicans,' I said. 'It doesn't make sense.'

'Look,' said Tim, 'maybe he just enjoys playing around with guns, and he doesn't want his new American friends to think he fought against Irish freedom.' He looked back defiantly at the three of us. 'Well, that's what folks call it here! You should've seen the street parties in New York and Boston when the Brits got out at last. People had waited hundreds of years for that!'

'They did more than *wait,'* I said, rather bitterly, remembering all the US dollars that had fuelled the Provo war machine. 'But let's not get into all that, OK?'

Tim waved his hands. 'OK.'

'So what happened on the training-range?' I asked. 'Did you meet him there?'

'No,' said Tim, 'but we did hear quite a few Scotch accents.'

'*Scots* accents,' I corrected automatically. Then my brain caught up. 'You *did?* You came across Scottish people there?'

'Yes,' said Weaver. 'And they weren't kids bootstrapping their skills for combat-games, either.'

'You got a problem with that?' Tim asked. 'Why shouldn't Scotch people learn combat skills?'

'They can get free training from the Territorial Army,' Weaver pointed out. 'That's our, um—' She looked at me, twirling her forefinger.

'People's militia?' I suggested. 'National Guard?'

'Something like that. Point is, these Scots don't have to train with the ARM, but they are. I'd like to know why.'

I nodded. 'That's exactly what's bothering me about it,' I said. 'Especially if they're calling themselves Republicans.'

'You got a—' began Tim.

'Problem with Republicans?' I interrupted sarcastically. 'No, Akay, not with your kind anyway. I *had* a problem with Irish Republicans when I was a wee lad, and I would have a problem with *Scottish* Republicans, except there aren't any. Sure, there are Scots who want a republic, but that's different. There aren't any Scots who want to do for Scotland what the IRA did for Ireland. There *can't* be.'

'Why not?' Weaver asked.

'What would they be fighting for? Scotland's going to *get* independence. OK, the vote will be a close thing, but there's no need to fight for it. In fact, the only thing that fighting—or even *talk* about fighting—could do is—Aha!' I smacked a fist. 'That's it!'

'What's it?'

I grinned around at them. Suddenly, I had a conspiracy theory of my very own and it all made sense. 'This is all a scam,' I explained excitedly. 'MacCready wants to *stop* Scottish independence, by throwing a few bombs and bullets into the argument! Nothing like a bit of violence and stirred-up memories of Ireland to scare people off the whole idea. He and his friends are *still* Loyalists, and they're getting help from the ARM by pretending to be the opposite!'

Louise was looking at me curiously, Tim and Weaver were shaking their heads.

'Too complicated,' Weaver said. 'What's his motive? He doesn't even—'

She stopped.

'What?'

She shook her head. 'Sorry, just a passing thought. A mistake. Go on.'

I frowned at her, puzzled. 'I can tell you what his *motive* is,' I said bitterly. 'There's thousands of people in Scotland who had to leave Ireland. *Northern* Ireland, after the unification. They don't want to lose their country all over again. Hey, I know how they feel, right?'

'Why should independence mean losing their country?' Tim asked, reasonably enough.

'Because they see *Britain* as their country,' I said. 'The United Kingdom, you know? And, well, there's also the Protestant versus Catholic thing.'

I stopped. Nobody talks about this in Scotland, except indirectly. Everybody takes it for granted that even *talking* about the problem is enough to make it worse. They may be right, but it doesn't get any better, either.

'I don't see that's a big issue any more,' Weaver said.

Tim nodded firmly. 'I still say MacCready's just into combat games,' he said. 'And covering up his past because it's embarrassing.'

'A lone gunman theory?' I said.

Tim laughed. Louise and Weaver looked puzzled.

'What's that?' Louise asked.

'Cydonia slang,' I explained. 'For basement-level official cover-stories.'

'Oh!' she said. 'I see. Like the story that Oswald acted alone, instead of,' she smiled, jerking her thumb, 'what we saw on Dealy Plaza out there.'

'Yup,' said Tim. 'Just like all the convenient assassinations of inconvenient political leaders get blamed on lonely madmen. Malcolm X, Martin Luther King, Kennedy, Kennedy, Kennedy, Kennedy…' He frowned at me. 'Maybe that's what I'm doing here. But I still say you should only go for a conspiracy theory if you have to.'

'Ha!' I said. 'You watch out, Akay, I'm gonna investigate *you!* Everyone who casts doubt on a conspiracy is part of it themselves, right?'

Tim shared my laugh. As I turned to Weaver, I saw her expression change from worry to a delayed, forced smile. She met my gaze without a blink or a flush, but she looked distinctly edgy.

'If you think there's a real conspiracy going on,' she said, 'why don't you just take it up with the Webcops? Or the Realworld cops, for that matter?'

Tim looked as shocked as I felt at this suggestion.

'I don't want to do that,' I said. 'The Webcops are always looking for an excuse to shut down Cydonia. I don't want to be the one who gives it to them.'

'Too right,' said Tim. 'Keep this in the family. I'll Web round with a few discreet enquiries after I spin out. That OK with you, Weaver?'

'Yeah, sure, fill me in on what you find,' she said. She glanced around at me and Louise. 'Time to go,' she added, standing up with obvious haste. 'I've been too long in the Web today.'

'Haven't we all?' said Tim, yawning and stretching.

'See you all here tomorrow?' Weaver asked, finger poised over her scuttle-button. 'Have another session on the training-range?'

'Good idea,' I said. It was what we'd set out to do in the first place, and I'd missed it.

'Sure thing,' said Tim.

'Not me,' said Louise.

'Oh, right,' I said, remembering what my mother had told me. 'No combat-games, is that it?'

'Not exactly.' Louise smiled sheepishly. 'It's just…tomorrow's Sunday. No games at all.'

Another religion thing. Poor girl probably had to go to church. I wasn't about to embarrass her by remarking on that.

'See you Monday, then?' I asked. It seemed a long time to wait.

'I can see you sooner than that,' she pointed out.

'How?'

'Well,' she said patiently, 'if you go out of your house and walk down the road, you might just catch me in the Cybercaff at the pier. And I might just buy you a coffee.'

'Realworld,' Weaver added dryly. 'Try it sometime, Links. It's a dead venomous site. Full of education and adventure. Something for everyone.'

'So I'm told,' I said.

We all hit our scuttle-buttons—that one-digit code for Realworld—and spun out.

As soon as the Web world faded from my senses I knew something was wrong, but I didn't know what. I peeled off the Websuit's hood, unplugged the jack and sat up. Gerard wasn't in the room, I couldn't see anything out of the ordinary…

But the room was darker than it should have been at that time in the morning, as though something were blocking out the sun. The patch of sunlight on the floor had a long, strange shadow on it. I turned towards the window.

And then I realized what was really bothering me.

It was the noise. The room was filled with a beating rumble, so loud and steady that a few seconds had passed before I'd become conscious of it.

I faced the window, and saw the cause of the shadow and the noise.

Hovering outside the window, so close it was like the visored face of a giant peering in, was a black helicopter.

Chapter Seven: Black Helicopter

I stared back at the sinister machine. It was quite a small helicopter, a two-seater, its cockpit canopy twin bulges of black glass, like the eyes of an insect. Ten metres away, above our back garden, it looked as if it were about to come in through the window. It hung there, right in my face, for a few moments. Then it backed away, spun around and darted off like a hoverfly. I bounded over to the window and looked out.

The helicopter flew low and fast, its course parallel to the village and the shore, then it paused and hovered again. Leaning out, I could see that it was above the pier at the end of the village street. There are several shops on the quay, but I was certain I knew which one the craft was snooping on.

The Cybercaff.

Again, it backed away after standing still in the air for a few moments. It rose about a hundred metres, turning as it climbed, then flew off up the loch, passing our house again on the way. By this time my shaking, fumbling hands had found the binoculars we kept on a shelf under the window. I raised them to my eyes and swung them, catching a fleeting view of the aircraft. It was indeed completely black, with no markings of any kind, not even a registration number. I tracked it with the binoculars until it passed out of view behind the tree-clad shoulder of a hill.

The binoculars rattled on the shelf as I laid them down. I sat on the futon, peeled off the Web suit and pulled on my clothes. I was still shaking a bit, and a sudden surge of Websickness didn't help. With an effort I fought down the voms by focusing on my Realworld surroundings and thinking hard about something else. What I thought about, of course, was what had just happened.

Being buzzed by unmarked black helicopters was a standard story from the American 'patriot' militiamen. To hear some of them talk in the Cydonia Cafe, they couldn't nip out for a packet of fags without spotting a helicopter hovering in attendance. On the other hand, low-flying military aircraft—mostly supersonic jet fighters terrain-following at zero feet—are as familiar and annoying as midges in the Highlands. Being treated like an uninhabited training-ground is an old grievance in these parts, and it fuels the sentiment for independence. Not that independence would end it—the planes are from the European Union Air Force, the Luftwaffe as it's affectionately known.

That was certainly who was getting the blame when I went downstairs. Mum and Yvonne were still looking indignantly out of the kitchen window.

'Frightening people like that,' Anne-Marie said. 'There ought to be a law. Really.'

I soothed Yvonne by assuring her that she could go and play in the Web for as long as her mum allowed, and Anne-Marie by assuring her that Louise had had a wonderful time and that I was going to meet her down at the Cybercaff. My account of where we'd been was true, but not quite the whole truth.

'Take your jacket,' my mum called after me as I left, 'and tell Gerard to be back in time for a proper lunch.'

Her opinion of the food in the Cybercaff is right up there with her opinion of Web games.

The morning was still sunny, with a stiff but not too cold breeze—the better kind of Greenhouse weather. I turned left out of the house and followed the gentle downward curve of the street towards the pier. Like many villages in the West Highlands, ours straggles along the side of a loch, which, confusingly enough, is the word used not only for lakes but, as here, a long inlet of the sea between two ranges of hills. Basically, the loch is a drowned valley. Its up-and-down movement through several ice ages is revealed by the raised beaches, vast grassy banks that rise about ten metres above sea-level a hundred metres or so back from the shore.

The reason the older part of the village consists of one long street squeezed between the raised beach and the sea is that the great-great-grandparents of most of the local people were driven off the land they thought was theirs when their landlords cleared them to make room for more profitable stock. First, the famously destructive blackfaced sheep, then deer for the shooting. The tenants had the choice of living along the shoreline, or taking a ship to Canada.

A good, kind landlord was one who helped his cleared tenants with their fare.

In a way, the clearances never ended. Nowadays, it's called conservation. Lots of well-meaning organizations buy up land and encourage the locals to move out, then bring in their own strange tribes of organic farmers and wildlife rangers—Green settlers, we call them. Recently they've brought back wolves—just another part of the process of turning the place into a wet desert for the benefit of people who don't live here, at the expense of those who do.

But there's another side to the story.

The new electronics factories up the glen and the wind-farms that bestride the hilltops have done something to bring people back and money in, so the village has grown a lot, its new housing-estates spreading up the hillsides. The summer visitors and the Green settlers think they spoil the look of the place, as if hills covered with nothing but bogs and boulders and heather were *natural.* Actually, they're the ruins left by an ecological and economic disaster. The natural cover of these hills would be tall forests and busy towns, like you see in Austria and France. But those are countries where landlords don't get their own way quite so often.

The pier is new, the smell of creosote still seeping from its timbers and mingling with the smells of seaweed, fish, and tar. It juts out a good fifty metres into the loch. Fishing-smacks and pleasure craft jostle around it. On the concrete approach, just before the wooden jetty begins, is a row of small shops—a chandler's, a craft shop, a pottery, a tearoom, and the Cybercaff.

You could spot the last a mile off by the aerials that bristle from its roof and the cable connections that sprout from its walls and run into a shallow, recent ditch, its line of turned-over earth scored across the green meadow to the road where it joins the mains cable. Strange to think that beneath that ordinary road runs our connection to all the world, and—via all those NASA Web sites—to other worlds, all the way out to our farthest reach, the robot fingertips scraping the ice of Pluto. Maybe, if the Deep Sky Anomaly really is a message, the Web connects beyond even that.

The Cybercaff's door and signboard are decorated with fading—and now tiresomely dated—spraypaint imitations of Web hacker graffiti. There's a big glass window at the front and another big glass window at the back. I could see right through the cafeteria section. The Websuit rental arcade was off to the left as I went in. It was kind of weird to see half-a-dozen people lying on couches, moving their limbs and heads slightly all the time, like dreaming dogs.

The coffee-bar counter was to the right, and the cafe tables between. There weren't many people here at this time in the morning, about half past ten. A girl was sitting at a table by the far window. She had a long coat draped over the back of her seat and a big hat slung beside it; long skirt spread around the seat, long black hair tumbling on her shoulders. She waved as the door swung to behind me. I remembered I'd seen her heading this way earlier in the morning, which seemed a long time ago. I hadn't recognized Louise in the Web as the same girl but that's who it was.

'Well hi,' she said as I walked over. 'Let me get you that promised coffee.' She casually gestured over her shoulder to Mr MacCartney, the old guy who runs the place (computer phreak from way back, Silicon Glen burnout, used to be big in mainframes) and he came over at once, much to my surprise.

'Another *cappucino* and—?'

'Espresso, please,' I said, sitting down.

With no visible make-up, much longer hair and different clothes, she was less striking than her Web avatar. But no less pretty, and her smile just as wicked.

'What are you staring at?'

'Um. You, I suppose. Funny seeing you in Realworld, that's all.'

'Hmm,' she said. She made a wiping motion around her face. 'Bit bland, I know.'

'Not at all,' I said. 'Uh, about—'

She raised a finger. 'Wait.'

She waited until the coffees arrived, blew on the chocolatey foam, sipped.

'So, you saw the helicopter?' she asked.

'Didn't I just,' I said. 'It looked right at me through the window.'

'Aha. That's what it did here! I'd just sat down when it suddenly loomed up right outside.' She mimed a shudder. 'That's creepy, it happening to you as well. Like somebody knew when we were each coming out of the Web, and came around and took a good look at us.'

I shrugged. 'It could be just coincidence.'

I told her about the Luftwaffe's training practices.

She snorted. 'Another lone gunman theory!'

'Well.' I leaned back, sipping the hot espresso. 'So what's your conspiracy theory?'

'Think about it,' she said. 'It'd take some time to get a helicopter here, anything between fifteen minutes and half an hour. If that one came to have a look at our Realworld selves, it must've been scrambled—or diverted here—by a message from someone in the Web, after we met but while we were still in, right?'

'OK, *if.*'

'Which could only have been from you, me, Weaver, or Akay.'

'You mean one of us is a *Webcop?*'

'Yes,' she nodded.

'We'll make a conspiracy phreak of you yet,' I said. I spread my hands. 'It wasn't me, and I'll give you the benefit of the doubt.'

'Wow, thanks! Now, what about your friend Akay?'

It felt strange to think about my friend as though he might not, really, be my friend. I'd never, of course, met Tim in Realworld, but I felt I'd got to know him pretty well.

'I couldn't swear to it,' I said slowly, 'but he doesn't strike me as someone sent in by the Webcops to keep an eye on Cydonia or anything like that. If you can know anybody in the Web, I'd say I know him, and I think he's on the level.'

Louise looked pleased. 'That's what I thought. Now, could you say the same of Weaver?'

'*Weaver?* She's just a really hot games-phreak, I've seen her in lots of places, and anyway she's—'

'Our age?' Louise smiled. 'We don't know that, do we? And listen—'

She leaned closer and spoke quietly. 'Have you ever heard of... Ariadne?'

'Rumours.' I frowned. 'Since I was a wee kid, really. You hear things on the kiddie nets and in the playground about this Webcop who looks after children's stuff. Sort of guardian angel.'

'The kind of person who'd be very concerned about young people getting mixed up in dangerous business like militias. Who might be keeping an eye on combat games, in case they were being used for something else. Like real training.'

'OK,' I shrugged, 'somebody might be doing that. But why Weaver?'

'It's the name,' Louise said. 'I think it's meant to be a hint. Ariadne was a mythical heroine who spun out a thread to guide Theseus—yeah, a mythical hero—through the Labyrinth. She was into spinning threads, she was a...weaver!'

I must admit it didn't sound like a cast-iron chain of logic, but I was shaken enough by the events of the morning to take it seriously. Certainly, the idea of Weaver's being a Webcop made sense—it accounted for her skills rather better than anything Tim or I had come up with. Perhaps it was our male-chauvinist vanity, but we just couldn't accept that a girl younger than ourselves could be so much better than we were at what we'd been practising ever since we were old enough.

So, as Louise sat back with a self-satisfied smile that wouldn't have looked out of place on Sherlock Holmes, I nodded soberly and said, 'Yeah, you might be on to something there.' My mind was already piling new complications on to my own conspiracy theory. 'If MacCready is up to what I thought he was, it wouldn't be surprising that a Webcop would react fast to hearing about him—maybe even going so far as to scramble a helicopter to check us out. Check that we're not going out with the guns already.'

'"Here comes a chopper to chop off your head,"' Louise chanted.

'What?'

'It's from *Nineteen Eighty-Four,'* she explained, then waved a hand as she saw she'd left me even more puzzled. 'You know, like "Big Brother is Watching You." It's in a *book,'* she added, witheringly.

'Books are bad for your eyes,' I said.

'Not with gag, they aren't.'

'What about VR?' I asked. 'What's it like in gag?'

'You can see things and handle them. You just don't get all the other sensations. Also, it's easier to see the underlying code and structures at the same time. You know, like split-screen.'

'Wait a minute,' I said. 'What about your avatar?'

She shrugged. 'You can patch up an icon if you like, but you don't need an avatar.'

'You mean you can just move around invisibly, like a ghost?'

'Sure. And you don't get Websick so quickly, either...Hey! I've just had an idea! We can both go back to Cydonia, or to the training-range, this afternoon! We can go together, and I can dig underneath the graphics whenever I want. I'll set my icon so only you can see it. By the time you meet Akay and Weaver again tomorrow, we might have something on MacCready to give us a head start.'

'Not a bad idea,' I said, wishing I'd thought of it myself.

She stood up and put on her coat, as if in a hurry to start right now. She picked up her hat and gave me a conspiratorial smile.

'See me home?'

'Sure.'

As we headed for the door, Gerard came out of the Websuit arcade. He saw us and smirked. I introduced him to Louise politely enough, but as I walked out with Louise I *knew* that within a day or so half the village, and all the school, would be certain that I was, well, you know...*walking out* with Louise.

I glanced at Louise, walking along all unaware of what was going to be said about her. I decided there were worse things that could be said about me.

Chapter Eight: All-Seeing Eye

As we walked up the street, Louise told me about her time in Africa—first Zimbabwe, the birthplace of the church, then Mozambique, where it was expanding rapidly. Childhood in Zimbabwe sounded like growing up in an English vicarage. Her teenage years in Mozambique were more like living on a mission, in danger from rebels and wild animals.

'But that's where I really learned to use the Web, get the most out of the old glove-and-glasses,' she said earnestly. 'The government first of all tried to ban the Web, then they tried using it for economic planning.' She laughed. 'Both failed dismally, of course. By the time we arrived, every house had a gag set and you could access the Web any time—at least when the phone and power lines weren't down!'

'Down?'

'You know—cut off. By storms or rebels or whatever.'

'How long would they be down for?'

'Oh, not very long. Couple of weeks at the most.'

'Good grief.' The thought of being cut off from the Web for that length of time gave me a sort of panicky feeling. 'Must be like having WebCrashes all the time.'

Louise snorted. 'We hardly *noticed* the WebCrash,' she said. 'Thought it was just a glitch! People took their goggles off and used their slide-rules and typewriters and—'

'Their *what?*'

'Slide-rules,' she told me, 'are a kind of computer made of wood, and typewriters are like keyboards made of iron. Neither of them use electricity.' (Incredible, I agree, but I think she was telling the truth as far as she knew. Must be some hidden electronics in them, though. I'll have to look them up on the Grolier some day.)

We went on talking and before I knew where I was she'd stopped outside a big wrought-iron gate. The garden behind it consisted of a big lawn, bordered with daffodils and snowdrops. The house was like a suburban villa, one of the 'big houses' in the village that had been occupied at various times by doctors, bank-managers, and a series of clergymen: Church of Scotland, Free Church, and now SAPC.

'Would you like to come in?' Louise asked.

'Well, uh, not right now,' I said awkwardly.

'Ha!' said Louise. 'It's all right. My mum's met your mum, remember? My parents know all about your dad's being the village communist. They won't be shocked, they won't try to convert you or anything.'

'All the same.' I shrugged. 'Another time, all right?'

'OK. See you in the Web in about an hour, I'll send you a ping, yeah?'

'Yeah, see ya.'

By this time, five younger children, evidently her brothers and sisters, were swarming over the lawn and onto the gate like monkeys, so I waved and left her to answer their clamouring questions.

When I saw her again in Webtown, an hour later, she appeared like a cardboard cut-out of her former avatar. At the same time, I felt the invisible grip of her gloved hand on mine—the data glove, not the goth glove.

'Spooky,' I said, looking sideways at her tilted, flat picture.

'Watch.'

Her icon shrank to a tiny triangle about three centimetres on the side, with one eye looking out. Like the strange symbol on the dollar, the eye in the pyramid.

'Oh,very funny,' I said.

'Yes, isn't it,' said her amused voice in my ear. The tone was flat, mono, like an old radio. 'That's how you'll see where I am, but nobody else will see it.' She squeezed my hand. 'Let's go.'

I'd given her the codes for Cydonia, and for the militia training-range. We reached it in two dizzying swoops—I was following her, and her access method didn't have to bother with keeping up illusions about how we moved around in the Web.

But the range, when we reached it, seemed real enough. We landed in a wooden-walled corridor leading to some kind of changing-room with a kit counter at the far end; people were milling about and talking. She dropped my hand, and as I moved forward I could see her keeping pace, an eye in the corner of my eye.

The users here were collecting weapons, radios, and camouflage clothes from a couple of phaces who stood behind the counter, handing the gear out.

'Heckler and Koch machine-pistol?' I asked. It was the only firearm I was used to—from my time in Crisis Crater.

The phace, a woman in a neat uniform, with Hispanic-American features and accent, smiled and nodded.

'Good choice,' she said, reaching below the counter and handing one over. I took a couple of ammo clips as well.

'D'you want basic training, or a combat exercise?' she asked.

I reckoned I'd got past basic training. I'd learned how to operate the machine-pistol in dozens of games. Little did I know.

'Combat exercise, please,' I said, with more confidence than I felt.

'OK,' said the phace. '"FEMA Rescue" is about to start.'

'Sounds good.' I smiled. 'I'm new here. What's it about?'

The phace lost its interested, friendly expression and changed to the glassy gaze of a help routine. The queue behind me disappeared as the people in it were flipped to another version of the same phace, while this one dealt with me. Embarrassing to be such an egg, but I had no choice.

'FEMA,' it explained, 'is the Federal Emergency Management Authority. This agency helps citizens caught up in natural disasters. That's its good side. Its bad side is that it also has powers to deal with *political* emergencies. It has its own armed forces and maintains a network of *resettlement camps,* which just happen to have barbed wire and watch-towers around them. They're empty now, but ready to be filled if the Federal Government ever decides to move against citizens who—'

I didn't need to listen to the phace parrot the usual paranoid patriot storyline.

'Skip it,' I said. 'Tell me about the exercise.' The phace shifted its mental gears again, and rattled off a string of rules and instructions. I listened as best I could. Louise's sceptical chuckles distracted me. Even with only one eye visible, she could still give an obvious wink.

'Now go!' said the phace. 'Your comrades are waiting!' She pointed dramatically to a doorway. I took my weapon and two-way radio and made for the door, trying not to tremble.

I always get the shakes before a drop.

Outside the door I found myself on a scrubby hillside, under a cloudy sky. I dived for the nearest cover, rolled behind a boulder, and cautiously checked out the situation. I knew the scene was American, but it could just as well have been in Scotland. In the valley below was a camp—rows of low buildings, inside a rectangle of barbed wire with watch-towers at the comers.

One of the FEMA resettlement camps—really internment camps—that the phace had told me about. I was part of a patriot band that had come to break it open and free the dissidents who'd been kept there for years since the fascist coup in Washington D.C.

We had a tough job on our hands. Armoured cars and tanks were patrolling the road along the valley, and the inevitable black helicopters were beating through the air overhead. Higher up, an airship hung in the sky, a shining dot like a UFO.

But so far, unlikely as it seemed, we hadn't been spotted. We were hiding here on the hill like resistance fighters poised to attack an invading army. I guessed this must be the starting-point of the exercise—if anybody'd ever tried to do this in Realworld, they'd have been wiped out long before they got even this far. Unless there were ways I didn't know about of blinding all those eyes in the sky—from the spy satellites in orbit down to the helicopters overhead. I frantically checked the readout on my wristpad and listened to the orders being barked over the radio by the unit commander. Then Louise's voice broke in.

'Here comes a chopper to chop off your head,' she said dryly.

I keeked around the rock, and saw a helicopter flying *below* us. A couple of hundred metres farther down the slope, rising slowly and keeping only just above the ground. At that moment its forward guns opened up and it climbed rapidly higher, streams of bullets scything across the hillside. I heard screams. Every bit of cover was being blasted away as if by a high-pressure hose, boulders and bushes alike.

And people. In the second or so I had to see this, I glimpsed fighters a few metres away from me being shredded. Even in VR it was utterly terrifying—knowing you can't really be hurt doesn't protect you from the sheer shock of some sights.

Then the helicopter exploded. Somebody must have fired an anti-tank missile at it. That's the only thing that can bring down a modern military helicopter, which basically *is* a flying tank.

I may even have seen the missile—a black streak just before the white flash and the red cloud. But if I did, it was the last thing I saw in that game. The next thing I knew, I was lying on my back, feeling as if I'd fallen flat on my face.

From my forehead to my feet, everything hurt. Not as badly as if I'd really fallen, but as if all the pressor pads down the front of my Websuit had chosen the same moment to give me a maximum kick. I was looking up at a wooden ceiling with old-fashioned electric lights hanging from it.

A man's face appeared above my head and frowned down at me.

'You're out of it, soldier,' he said, not unkindly. 'You're dead.'

I smiled bravely and tried to sit up. The man leaned forward and placed his hand on my chest. This was painful enough to make me lie back again.

'No need for you to see what you look like,' he said, 'nor what the other casualties look like, neither. Here, I'll give you a code.' He held his left wrist to mine. Cartoon lightning jumped the gap. 'Hit Enter and this'll take you straight to the lecture.'

'Lecture?'

He was smiling now. 'Look, kid, you just got yourself killed in a fight. Might be a good idea to find out why, yeah?'

'OK,' I said.

Without thinking, I tried to sit up. Again he pushed me down.

'You don't wanna look, kid. Just go.'

I hit Enter on my wristpad, and instantly found myself standing up at the back of a big shed built of rough timber and corrugated iron. At the front there was a table with a wallscreen behind it, faced by rows of chairs with scuffed plastic bucket seats and tubular legs. Through the large windows I could see trees beyond an area of packed and beaten earth. Dotted about were big chunks of machinery the size of tractors under tarps—armoured cars or big guns? I never found out.

Other people were spinning into the room, appearing out of nowhere with grey, shocked faces. Each new arrival would shake themselves or shudder, look down wonderingly at their bodies or raise a reluctant hand to their faces. Then, with their colour coming back and a look of relief, they'd shamble forward and sit on one of the chairs.

After a moment I did the same.

'Oh, there you are,' said Louise. The voice in my ear sounded shaky. I saw her single eye floating in front of me like an after-image. 'I lost you after the blast. I tracked your jump and tried to follow you, but the next place I found was like some kind of casualty unit.' She paused. 'People all burnt and mangled and bleeding. I looked for you, but—'

'I was there,' I said. 'Up to a minute ago.'

'Oh,' she said flatly.

I realized then what sights the kind man had been protecting me from. There might not have been much left of me to recognize, and the others in no better state. No wonder everybody looked so shocked.

'I'm sorry you had to see that,' I whispered.

'I've seen worse,' the tiny, tinny voice said. 'In Realworld. Mozambique. There's a rebel group there called Renamo that—' She took a deep breath. 'Ah, forget it. Just listen and find out what's going on.'

Good idea, I nodded. People around me were already giving me curious looks.

A man walked in at the back of the shed and strode to the table and looked us over. I tried to shrink into my seat.

It was Bill MacCready.

Chapter Nine:
Dreamland

MacCready recognized me all right. As he scanned the couple of dozen people who'd filled the rows of seats, his glance rested on me for a split-second smile. Then he took a step forward, leaned on the table and glared.

'You're all new here,' he said. 'That's not much of an excuse for youse all being *dead,* now is it?' His Belfast accent was harsher than ever, with an American undertone. He straightened and pointed at me, making me jump. 'You! There at the back! Links!'

'Yes?'

'What were you doing out there?'

'Trying to learn about real fighting,' I said.

'Good! Well you've learned something, haven't you? *Real fighting can get you killed.* But you're a smart lad. You knew that already, right?'

'Yes,' I said, rather sullenly.

'No you didn't,' MacCready said. 'And you still don't.' He switched his glare to the rest of the room, to my relief. 'However. That's not what your little lesson out there was mainly about. You all turned up and jumped straight into the exercise, like it was a combat-game. Well it ain't. It's a test we set up for fools like you. You want to know how to pass?' He looked down at something on the table as if he were checking a list. Perhaps he was. Then he looked us over again, pityingly. 'None of you lot did, by the way. What a sad shower. Most times at least *one* gets it right.'

'We didn't have a chance,' someone complained. '"We didn't have a chance."' MacCready mimicked the guy's whinging tone exactly. 'What you mean is, you didn't have a chance to get past spysats and tanks and gunships and guards.' He snapped his fingers and the screen behind him lit up.

It displayed a perfect 3D image, like the view from a window, of the hillside where we'd all fallen to the bullets or the blast. One by one, we all appeared and all did the same thing, diving down the slope and taking cover and within minutes being wiped out.

The view pulled back a bit and the scene was replayed. This time I could see that, like everybody else, I'd arrived on the top of the ridge, with the opposite slope right behind me. It was almost comical to see everyone arriving and rushing into danger without so much as a backward glance.

And safety had been only that backward glance away. 'Right,' said MacCready. 'I can see the light dawning on some of you. The only way to survive that fight was not to get into it in the first place. The only way to pass that test was to look behind you and go back.'

Silence, then somebody a couple of rows in front of me spoke up.

'But that would be...desertion, wouldn't it? Cowardice?' MacCready gave the latest speaker an even less approving look than the previous one. 'Who told you to go down into the valley? You had no orders. You just assumed. You didn't ask questions, you just headed for the action, like you were in a combat-game. And you got gloriously killed. At least that's what we'd tell the folks back home.' He sighed. 'You know what the real armies have to spend most of their first weeks of training on these days? Knocking daft notions from Web shoot-em-ups out of lads' and lasses' daft wee heads!'

I shouldn't have been surprised by all this, but I was. I'd expected MacCready to be a dangerous nutter. But he sounded sane and sensible. Maybe that made him all the more dangerous.

'OK, that's enough for today. Any of you want to come back, just remember what you learned. If I see you again I want it to be in basic training. Because you sure need it.'

Everybody shifted in their chairs, turned with wry smiles to their neighbours or said something or reached for their scuttle-buttons. I was just doing that when MacCready strode forward and laid a light hand on my shoulder.

'Not you, Links,' he said. 'I'd like to have a word with you.'

'Stick with it,' advised Louise, urgently whispering in my ear.

'OK,' I said, to her and to MacCready. All the other people in the room were disappearing from it, their images breaking up into swirls of pixels. In a few seconds I was alone with the former street-fighter. He spun a chair around and sat down.

'Relax, lad,' he said. 'I can't harm you here, can I? All I want you to do is listen for a minute.'

I nodded, still afraid of him.

'I can see you're not too happy about me,' he began, 'and I can guess why. You're from Belfast, your accent still gives you away, and you live in

Scotland now. That's all I know about you. But I can tell a lot from that. For starters, that you had to leave because of the Troubles, right?'

'Yes,' I said, then added, feeling bolder, 'thanks to you!'

'I see I'm not the only one who knows more than they're saying,' he said. He frowned. 'You know who I am?'

'Sure I know,' I said. 'I remember you all right, Mr MacCready. You and your URF pals who messed things up for everybody, including us.'

'Aye, well.' He rubbed the back of his neck. 'You could say that, and I don't blame you for thinking it.'

'But you don't think so?'

'Not as such,' he said, with a dry chuckle. 'At least during the peace process—and even the war, come to that—your family could still live in Ireland, and now they can't. Isn't that true?'

'That's what I don't get about you, Mr MacCready—'

He raised a hand. 'Just call me Mac,' he said mildly.

'Mac—you used to be a Loyalist. Why were you talking like some kind of extreme Scottish Nationalist? Scotland's going to get independence anyway. Any talk about fighting for it will only scare people off, and I think that's what you really want. Because you're *still* a Unionist!'

There, I'd just blurted out my very own conspiracy theory to the very man I thought was the chief conspirator. Not the sort of move Tim would have recommended. I could hear Louise's indrawn breath, see her floating, watchful eye widen.

MacCready gave me a look of complete astonishment, then tilted back his head and let out a roar of laughter.

'Links,' he said when he'd got his breath back, 'you've been hanging out too long with those conspiracy nuts!' He laughed again. *'Cydonia!* What a place!'

'That's where I met *you,*' I pointed out. 'Going on about a Scottish Republic, and independence, and freedom.'

'Aye,' said MacCready, clasping his hands behind his head and leaning back at a dangerous angle. 'But the independence your parliament is about to get is just that—independence for your parliament. Not for you. And it won't be much of an independence, anyway. You'll still have the Luftwaffe buzzing your glens, still have the Green settlers buying up your land from the people who stole it from you in the first place. Same goes for the freedom. Freedom for the politicians in Edinburgh, not for you. And not much for them.'

'But bringing guns into it will just make people vote against even *that* amount of independence,' I protested. 'Is that what you want?'

He frowned at me, puzzled.

'Who's bringing guns into it?'

'You are,' I said.

'*Me?* How so?'

'You're asking me that?' I asked. 'You call yourself a Scottish Republican, and you're with the militias. Looks a bit obvious what you're up to.'

'There you go again,' said MacCready. 'Jumping to conclusions, like you did out on that hill.' He stood up and stalked to the front of the room and stood behind the table, as if he were about to give another lecture. This time, to a class of one. 'When did I ever call myself a Scottish Republican?'

'But—' I began, then realized that I'd never heard him say any such thing.

'I'm a Republican, all right,' he said. 'But not a Scottish Republican. What country do you think I live in?'

'Scotland,' I said.

He smiled thinly. 'Not likely. I live in the land of the free...Canada.'

I felt like my brain was running at about one mip. 'So why are you— ?'

'Mixed up with American patriot militias?' He grinned at my hopeless confusion. 'Because I like them. They're my kind of people.' He gave me an appraising look. 'Our kind. They just want to go on living their own lives in their own way and not be pushed around by a bunch of politicians. And they *are* getting pushed around. Even if they do have some wacky ideas about why it's happening, just like we used to believe in Papist plots.'

He looked at his watch. 'Speaking of conspiracies—I'm due to meet somebody in Cydonia in half an hour. What d'you say we take a stroll around there?'

'Interesting,' murmured Louise. 'Go along with it.'

'Fine by me,' I said, to her and to Mac. 'Which part?'

'Oh, somewhere we can walk around and chat. Not the Cafe.'

'Area 51?'

'What's that?'

'Part of the site based on a place in Nevada. Also called Groom Lake and Dreamland.'

MacCready nodded. 'Oh, aye, that. We'll go there.'

We linked hands and jumped. I snatched my hand away from MacCready's as soon as we arrived. He gave me an amused look and stepped a few paces away.

'Don't be so nervous,' he said. 'I don't bite.' He gazed around at the site. Although it's in Cydonia, once you're actually inside Dreamland you see a scene from Earth, not Mars. But it's in the Nevada desert, so, apart from the gravity, it's not like you'd notice.

Behind us, stretching off into the distance, was a chainlink fence topped with razor wire. Ahead of us, just visible over the rolling dunes and scrub, were some low buildings. Above, stealth fighters and flying saucers flitted through the cloudless blue sky. You could see how similar they were in their movements, their speed, and their silence. MacCready looked up at their aerial ballet with a wry smile.

'Very convincing resemblance,' he said. 'Question is, which came first...What's in yon sheds?'

I set off towards them. 'Hangar 18, links to the Roswell Room and so on. It's where they keep the crashed saucers and dead aliens, and test captured alien technology.'

'Like, Japanese?' MacCready grinned.

'I guess that's what is at the bottom of it,' I said.

'What do you think of the Roswell stories?' MacCready was keeping pace with me, striding along a metre or two away, still respecting my space, as they say.

'I don't know what to think,' I said. 'Have you heard the latest official USAF explanation of the Roswell Incident?'

'Can't say I have.'

'They say their Nazi rocket scientists were using orphan children in re-entry vehicle tests.'

MacCready grunted. 'That's shocking! And the poor kids were the wee dead aliens, eh?'

'That's what they're telling us *now.*'

'Oh, I see,' said MacCready. 'And you think, maybe if they'll admit to something as bad as that, they must be really covering up something worse?'

'Well, I don't think so. But I know people who do.'

'I'm sure you do,' he said. 'Forget it, Links. All that conspiracy nonsense is a waste of computer space and your time.' His final words were almost drowned out by a black helicopter that swept over us, low and fast, then took up position a hundred metres away and three metres off the ground. I wasn't bothered. It was just part of the scenery.

We stopped for a moment to brush virtual dust from our clothes. MacCready walked on, steadfastly ignoring the helicopter steadily following us.

'What about your militia pals?' I asked. 'They believe in conspiracies —in *The* Conspiracy.'

'Like I said. These guys have real problems, they just have unreal explanations for them.'

He jerked his thumb at the sky behind him. 'Take the black helicopters. They exist. They're not a strike-force for some New World Order—they're just the cops, or the army, or the Drug Enforcement Agency, snooping around looking for cannabis fields! And if they find so much as a leaf they can take your farm and house and money from under you, with no charge or trial and no chance of getting it back. Just try taking them to court when they can use *your* bank account to pay *their* fancy lawyers! No wonder the farmers get paranoid.'

'Aw come on,' I said. 'That can't be happening! We'd hear about it!'

MacCready just smiled, and went right on smiling at me until I had to admit he could be right. The story about Roswell, true or cover-up, was evidence enough that awful things could happen. And other stories I'd heard in Cydonia checked out—they were reported all right, in respectable newslines, and almost nobody paid them any attention. But—

I placed my right hand casually over my left wrist, ready to scuttle at any moment.

'There's two things I don't understand,' I said. 'One is that all your public records say nothing about how you were in the URF and all that.'

'Sure they don't,' said MacCready, frowning a little. 'It's the law. You can get certain criminal records purged after seven years.' He shrugged. 'And I really have changed, man! I make no secret of my past, but having it on public databases isn't exactly a credit reference. I've made a new life in Vancouver.'

So that was all there was to it, I thought. I felt quite embarrassed.

'Why hang out with the militia guys, then?'

'I told you why. As to what good I can do, I can use my experience to talk people out of romantic notions about armed resistance. Nothing wrong with knowing how to handle a gun, but knowing when to use it and when not is far more important.' He looked at me sharply. 'And teaching young fools that combat-games are not the same thing as combat, OK? It's practically social work. The government should be paying me for it. And what's your other question?'

'What about all the Scottish people on the training-range?'

'When did you see Scottish people there?' He sounded anxious.

'I didn't, but a couple of my friends did. This morning.'

'Ah,' he said. 'Morning to you, evening to me...yes! Those were the friends of yours I met in the Cafe, Akay and...Weaver, right?'

'Yes,' I admitted. Mac laughed. 'Well, it's a rare Yank or Sassenach can tell the difference between a Scottish accent and an Ulster one! Some of my old comrades were on the range this evening. All Canadians now.' He looked at me sidelong. 'There goes your whole Scottish connection, man. So much for conspiracies, eh?'

That's when I told him about our encounter with the Realworld black helicopters. I didn't mention Louise by name, just described the incident.

For a moment he looked really alarmed, then forced a hearty smile.

'I don't know anything about that,' he said. 'I doubt it's got anything to do with me, though. I think it's got something to do with *you.*'

'Me? But I haven't *done* anything!'

'That's what they all say,' he told me dryly.

By this time we'd reached the vast doorway of the famous Hangar 18. MacCready walked ahead of me and peered in, waiting for his eyes to adjust to the interior gloom. I took the chance to look around for Louise's triangular icon.

I couldn't see it. I couldn't think when I'd last seen it.

'Louise?' I said quietly.

No answer.

'Louise!'

Mac turned and gave me a puzzled look.

Then his eyes widened.

'Look out!' he said.

I suddenly noticed the rising sound of the black helicopter that had been pacing us, I whirled around. It was hovering right behind me.

'STAY WHERE YOU ARE!' a voice boomed from the helicopter. 'THIS IS A POLICE RAID. RAISE YOUR HANDS!'

'Scuttle!' yelled MacCready, vanishing.

I hit my scuttle-button just as the scene began to dissolve. As my room reappeared around me, I half-expected to see the Realworld black helicopter outside.

It wasn't. I sighed with relief and peeled off my hood. There was a ringing noise which after a moment I recognized as the doorbell.

Nobody seemed to be answering it, so I went downstairs. Yvonne's door was open, and she was cocooned in her little pink Websuit. My mum was in glove-and-glasses at her table, oblivious. Stitches chattered out of the Fiberfax as I padded past and opened the front door.

Two men in black suits and dark glasses stood on the doorstep.

Chapter Ten: Men In Black

One of the men was African, the other European. They both had white shirts and black ties. They looked exactly like the guys who're supposed to come round and silence people who *know too much.* The only thing missing was a big black car. The car parked on the road outside was a small blue Hyundai Solar.

'You're Dave Kennedy?' the white man said sternly.

'Yes,' I said. There didn't seem to be much point in denying it. I had that feeling you get in a fast lift, going down.

'Hello, Dave,' the man said. He took off his dark glasses and stuck out his hand. 'I'm very pleased to meet you.'

He didn't seem pleased at all.

His accent was unusual, but strangely familiar. After a moment I recognized it as the same as Louise's. 'I'm John MacPherson. Louise's father. This is Zebediah Matabele, one of my deacons.'

The black man took off his glasses and gave me a wide, white smile. He was much younger than the first man, about twenty, I guessed. I couldn't help noticing he had holes in his earlobes you could see the sunlight through.

'Hi, Dave,' he said. His smile was replaced by a worried frown as he shook hands. 'I'm the Reverend MacPherson's main man on the Web. He called me up because—'

'Louise seems to be in some kind of trouble,' said Rev. MacPherson. 'Trouble in the Web. We can't get her out of it.'

'What?'

I felt quite sick with dismay, much worse than when I'd thought they were from some sinister agency.

'Perhaps we'd better come inside,' said Zebediah Matabele.

'Oh, yes, sorry.' I stepped aside and backed off to let them in.

At this point my mother turned up and demanded to know what was going on. It's uncanny, this knack she has, like a heat-seeking missile. She ushered the two men into the front room and they sat down on the edges of seats.

'Louise mentioned you and your son at lunchtime,' the minister explained. He gave me a suspicious, checking-out stare. 'Then she disappeared off up to her room, saying she had some studying to do. When my wife took a cup of tea up to her, she was accessing the Web with her usual kit.' He glanced at my mothers gag set on the table. 'As you know, Mrs Kennedy, it should let her hear what's going on around her. She's used to her mother giving her a call. But she didn't respond, and nothing we can do will snap her out of it. I called Zebediah straightaway.'

'We could pull the plug, of course,' said Mr Matabele. 'But it can be a bit traumatic. I advised against it, short of a real emergency.'

'Do we have a real emergency? That's what we've come here to find out,' continued Mr MacPherson.

I became uncomfortably aware that everyone else in the room was giving me dirty looks.

'Where did you take her?' asked Anne-Marie.

'I didn't *take* her anywhere,' I said. 'We were checking out a training site and then we skipped over to, uh, Cydonia—'

'What's that?' Anne-Marie demanded sharply.

'I know what it is,' said Mr MacPherson. 'Unedifying, but fairly harmless.'

'Mostly harmless,' said Mr Matabele. 'And when did you last see her?'

'I'm not sure. I suddenly noticed she wasn't there. That's why—That's when I came out.'

'So,' said my mother shrewdly, 'that's not *why* you spun out?'

'No, not exactly.'

This wasn't a satisfactory answer, I could see that. I took a deep breath and was about to confess all when Zebediah Matabele raised his hand.

'Explanations later,' he said. 'For now, it would be a waste of time. David, can you go back in the Web and *find* Louise?'

I stared at him in surprise. 'Sure,' I said, with more confidence than I felt.

The deacon and the minister nodded. 'Go to it,' Matabele said. 'You can report back to your mother here, perhaps?'

'Of course,' said Anne-Marie, reaching for her glove-and-glasses. 'You can reach me at NeedleNet,' she told me. 'Same code.'

'Gotcha, Mum.'

I ran upstairs. As I passed the open door of Yvonne's room I heard a thin wail that almost stopped my heart. I halted and swung around the side of the door. She was lying propped on her pillow in her Websuit. But she was lying stiff and still, without the usual small twitches of someone in the Web, their movements just begun and then caught by the suit's transformers and turned into Web motion.

I leapt to the side of the bed and leaned over her. She was breathing normally, I saw with a rush of relief, but her mouth, visible below the mask of the hood, was a rectangular rictus of distress. Every other breath came out as another little wail.

'Yvonne!' I yelled. I wanted to grab her, shake her, pull the plug, but I knew this might do more harm than good. At the very least it would give her nightmares for months. I thought of yelling at her again, or calling for help. Then it struck me that what was happening to Yvonne was what had happened to Louise.

The quickest way to get help for both of them was for me to get back into the Web. That was where the problem was, and there it would be solved.

But I felt very reluctant as I turned away and left her lying there, like one more doll among the dolls and stuffed toys on the bed.

'Good afternoon, Dave,' said Hal. 'What can I do for you?'

'Contact Mac, tell him we have an emergency. Also Akay. He's probably asleep, so wake him if you can. Otherwise leave a message on his terminal asking for help.' I paused, then decided I had nothing to lose, now, by appealing to Weaver—Webcop or not. 'To Weaver: Links calling Ariadne. We know who you are. You know who we are. Help us. Attach all of the following to all the messages: ID and current status of Yvonne, Louise, and me. Oh, and encrypt them all with PGP Plus.'

PGP+ (Pretty Good Privacy Plus) is a method of encrypting a message, turning it into unbreakable code that only the person it's intended for can read.

'I must remind you that PGP Plus is an illegal encryption method in the United States—'

'Do it.'

'Very well, Dave.' If Hal was bothered by being asked to do something that could have it decompiled, the faithful AI's voice didn't give it away. There wasn't much chance of being found out, anyway—even detecting that PGP+ is being used takes more mips than the universe has electrons. According to the US government, only terrorists, drug barons and other unsavoury characters could possibly have a use for it. Anyone with nothing to hide has nothing to fear, and should be quite happy to let government agents rummage through their mail. Naturally, every self-respecting Web phreak in America uses it to encrypt even their most trivial chat. In the Free World, as the patriots call the world beyond their government's reach, PGP+ is a standard feature on every software release.

'Get back to me as soon as you can, Hal.'

I leaned back on the futon and keyed in the NeedleNet code. The first thing I wanted to do was make sure I had a secure link with Anne-Marie. The next was to tell her about Yvonne. She might have a better idea about what to do than I had.

Again I found myself in the green, upward-curving landscape. Anne-Marie was standing right in front of where I arrived. She was looking away and didn't notice me. Her big green dress was frozen in mid-swirl. I thought at first it was the same kind of cut-out image that Louise had presented when in gag.

'Mum—'

Her face was rigid, mouth half-open. She made some kind of grunt.

I looked around and saw that the whole site was frozen.

The only moving figures were black-clad, visored Webcops, striding among the groups of women on the grass. In this imagined past, time had stopped—for everyone but the Webcops and, so far, me.

Anne-Marie's grunting became frantic, as she struggled to form words.

'Get...out...Dave!'

I didn't waste another second—I hit the scuttle-button. Whatever had entrapped Louise and Yvonne had now caught my mother. It looked like the Webcops were investigating—or perhaps responsible for it! I was thoroughly shaken as I lay there, staring up at the ceiling.

A red light blinked on, apparently in the middle of the air. Hal was back.

'Messages delivered,' it said. 'Mac is off-line, Weaver is reachable but not disclosing her location. Akay is awake and Webbing around. He says "Hang in there, Links." And Louise and Yvonne...'

For the first time in my experience, Hal hesitated.

'Yes?'

'They are in the same place. Hangar 18.'

'See you there. Oh, and tell my father what's going on.'

'Dave, wait—'

I didn't. My next jump took me straight to Dreamland.

This time I'd made sure the coordinates were set to put me down inside the hangar. For a moment I stood blinking in the vast gloom. Pools of light here and there picked out phace technicians toiling over saucer wrecks. The usual parties of visitors were wandering through. No doubt there were many more visitors, present but invisible. No sign of Webcops, but that proved nothing. They could be as invisible to me as the majority of the other users were. I was well aware that I might be walking straight into a trap, baited by Yvonne's and Louise's location-codes.

'Dave, my analysis of similar situations suggests that this could be a trap,' Hal told me. 'The location-codes for Yvonne and Louise—'

'Where are they?' I whispered.

'Roswell Room. Autopsy theatre,' Hal said briskly, with just a hint of very human exasperation.

I jumped again. The autopsy theatre has semicircular tiers of seats rising around the stage on which a scene is played out based on an ancient hoax video. Masked and gowned pathologists carving up deeply unconvincing grey bodies. The aliens' innards look like moulded jellies, which they may well be.

'Where's Yvonne?' I asked Hal, as quietly as possible as I glanced around the fascinated, gullible audience.

'There,' said Hal, flashing a virtual pointer line.

I stared along the after-image track, feeling cold and sick. It was pointing at the alien on the operating-table.

For a moment, rage and pity almost sent me hurtling forward, along the pointer line. But I held back long enough to ask, 'And Louise?'

'Here, Dave.'

I looked around frantically. At last I saw her icon, a tiny triangle floating above the stage.

'I can't move,' she said. 'And I can't get out.'

'It's OK,' I said, desperately reassuring her with more confidence than I felt. 'We're working on it right now.'

I was still staring at the alien on the operating-table. Its chest was open and the site's phaces were lifting out mucky, dripping blobs. This was what poor little Yvonne was seeing! No wonder she was terrified! I was sure she wasn't *feeling* it, or she'd have been screaming herself hoarse, not wailing, in Realworld. And I knew she was smart enough to know at some level that it wasn't really happening.

But even so, my little sister was going through what must have seemed an eternity of sinister figures stooping over her with scalpels.

My rage got the better of me and I jumped. I hurled myself forward, barging through the watchers, and bounded on to the stage. The surgeon phaces, whose range of actions must've been pretty limited, got smartly out of my way and just stood there, green Grey blood still dripping from their latex gloves. Yells and other sounds of commotion came from the audience.

I looked down at the little Grey body. To my horror, it stirred. Creaking noises came from its opened chest. Its great black eyes rolled and looked at me.

'We need to talk,' it said, as if with an expiring gasp.

Then there was no sound from it, except Yvonne's reedy cry.

'We'll get you out, Yvonne,' I promised. Something crashed behind me. I turned, fists balled, ready to lash out. Black-uniformed Webcops were appearing all through the theatre, one of them right beside me on the stage.

I stabbed a finger towards my scuttle-button—too late. My Web suit froze up around me. I couldn't move. Then the scene dissolved, and all of Dreamland vanished like a dream. It was replaced by a white floor. Out of the corner of my eye, I could see Yvonne, not in her Grey guise any more, but her usual Nintendo jumpsuit. My mother and Louise were there, both of them in cardboard cut-outs of their Web avatars. And Mac, standing like a statue on a war memorial in his combat gear, an expression of foolish astonishment on his face. He saw me, and with difficulty closed one eye in a slow wink.

A Webcop strode into view. A black-gloved hand lifted a black visor, to reveal a triumphantly grinning face. It was Weaver.

'You're all under arrest,' she told us. 'For conspiracy.'

Chapter Eleven:
The Conspiracy Theory

Weaver keyed some invisible pad. Whatever was holding me in place relaxed enough for me to move my head and speak. I ignored the now-exposed Webcop and her ridiculous accusation.

'Are you all right, Yvonne?' I asked. I wanted to ask her how she'd got mixed up in this, but decided to leave that for a later and gentler interrogation.

My little sister looked about, sniffled and blinked. 'Frightened,' she said tearfully. 'Can I go home?'

'Yes,' I said. 'Soon.'

I stopped ignoring Weaver. 'Let us go!' I snapped at her.

Weaver tapped out some more keystrokes and the others were also partly released. From the neck up, anyway. My mother turned from her anxious but reassuring gaze on Yvonne to give Weaver a glance of puzzled distaste. 'You can't keep us here!' she said.

Weaver looked back at us, still smiling. Louise and Mac were looking around, but they were saying nothing.

'I won't keep you long,' she said. 'Only until all your Realworld locations have been secured by the police in each place.' She smiled at me. 'And if you're hoping your friend Akay will come to the rescue, forget it. The FBI are kicking down his door and impounding his kit right now.'

'What on earth is this all about?' my mother asked indignantly. 'There must be some mistake.'

Weaver's smug smile turned contemptuous. 'Oh, don't waste your breath and my time, Mrs Kennedy. Save all that for the jury.'

'I'm relieved to hear we'll get one,' Mac said sarcastically. 'Would you mind telling us what we'll be charged with? Every second you keep us here is going to cost you or your force a year's pay in compensation to all of us, so take your time.'

Weaver laughed. 'You don't scare me. By the time we're finished with you, you'll be in jail or on the street, just another homeless beggar tugging at sleeves with a tale that only proves how crazy he is, if he can get anyone to listen.'

I felt a chill as I remembered what Mac had told me about asset forfeiture. Surely this couldn't happen *here!* Not to *people like us!* This was the Free World, not the United States!

'Make my day,' said Mac. 'Add slander to the charges clocking up against you. Tell us what this is all about.'

'Just to pass the time till the police arrive at your houses…' Weaver shrugged. 'All right. You all know some of this already, but I'm sure none of you know how it fits together. That's just shows how clever your little conspiracy is.'

She started pacing about like a teacher in front of a wallscreen, lecturing us all.

'I'm not Ariadne,' she began, with a pitying glance at me. 'If such a person ever existed. My job is not to keep kids *out* of trouble. It's to find and deal with kids who *make* trouble. No matter what age they are, or pretend to be.' She smiled thinly at Yvonne, who looked back with blank innocence. 'Like you, young miss. We'll soon see if you're as young as you pretend. But even if you are, it's still my job to protect society from the likes of you.'

Yvonne looked quite alarmed until she warmed to the reassuring smiles being beamed at her by the rest of us. Our smiles were genuine. I think we were all relieved to hear Weaver saying something so absurd. It meant that whatever else she had to say was probably just as wrong. Weaver was still walking up and down, still talking. I noticed that whenever she had her back turned, Louise would contort her face into a strange grimace, her tongue flickering out like a snake's. It seemed a childish way to show her disrespect, but if it made Louise feel better I supposed it was all to the good.

'I've been assigned to keep an eye on any overlaps between Cydonia and combat-games,' Weaver was telling me. 'That's how I first caught on to you and Akay. When you met up with MacCready, everything became clear.' She shook her head, almost admiringly. 'You tried to warn me away from MacCready with your own nonsense conspiracy theory, but I could see it was a red herring because I found out at once that MacCready lives in Canada and isn't much interested in Britain any more.'

'So what,' MacCready asked heavily, 'are we supposed to have done?'

Weaver's triumphant grin came back. 'As far as we're concerned, Cydonia is a perfect honey-trap. It pulls all the dangerous paranoid nutcases into one place, where we can watch what they get up to. We have an expert system for sniffing out *real* conspiracies there, and when we turned its attention to you lot, all its lights went on! We can start with Links here —very apt name! He's the link between his father and the Web. Alan

Kennedy sensibly keeps off it as much as he can, but he has his own world-wide connections. All those international trade unions, with communists and ex-communists in every position they can get! Then we had Akay, an American libertarian gun nut, already hanging out with the armed militias. We had MacCready, running a construction business in Vancouver, and keeping in touch with—in fact, employing—his former terrorist comrades. And there's Louise, who's a member of a Protestant fundamentalist cult which has had more experience of guerrilla war than the rest of you put together. Even some of its *elders* were once members of ZANU and Frelimo and the ANC! More ex-communist ex-terrorists! And finally, the spider at the centre of the web.'

Weaver spun around dramatically and pointed a finger at Anne-Marie.

I laughed out loud at this, but Weaver's pointed finger quivered as she spat out her accusations. '*You,* under the innocent cover of NeedleNet! A network, all right, its threads joining together people all around the world! And with your expert knowledge of how to turn designs in the Web into Realworld products, and ability to Web in to factories all over the place.' She frowned for a moment. 'I'm not quite sure yet what Yvonne's role was, but we think she was some kind of courier, a runner who would never normally be suspected. Anyway, when you put all these things together, the answer is obvious.'

'It certainly isn't obvious to me,' said my mother, in the weary tone she adopts when I come home with some wild tale from the Web.

'Like I said,' Weaver told her, in a similar tone, 'save that for the trial. *We* know what you're up to. Here's how it was going to work. The militias supply virtual images of weapons, every part accurate to the last detail. Akay provides propaganda, all that nonsense about inalienable rights that he's been well programmed to trot out. MacCready supplies military, *terrorist*, training. Anne-Marie Kennedy uses her knowledge of Fiberfax software to adapt machines in factories to start turning the virtual guns into real ones. The communist and trade union militants in the factories look after the process—and the products!—on site. No doubt they'll find uses for them in other countries. In Scotland, the Southern African Presbyterian Church, which has links with Ulster Protestants and experience of armed struggle in Africa, uses the guns to disrupt Scottish independence, because they fear Catholic influence in a free Scotland.'

'Rubbish!' shouted Louise. 'We live in peace with our neighbours! We have old people in Harare who knew the Pope when he was an altar-boy!'

'Besides that,' Weaver said, ignoring her, 'there are plenty of other tensions in Scotland to exploit: the Green settlers, the EU Air Force... plenty of room for a few nasty provocations. The key is the new financial centre planned for Edinburgh. If independence doesn't pass, it never gets built. Investment is scared off, unemployment rises, the moderate leaders of Alan Kennedy's union are discredited, and his communist friends get control. And do you know where the new centre will be built, if the Edinburgh site falls through? *Vancouver*—where MacCready's firm has a good chance of winning juicy contracts on it! And what do the militias get out of all this? Lots of new friends, another defeat for gun control, and another inspiring struggle of good Christian people to support. And no doubt lots of other armed actions all over the world, even if these are carried out by communists. The militias will ally with anyone against the so-called New World Order.'

'Wow,' said Mac. 'You're really something. That is some story.'

Weaver shrugged. 'It was our expert system that worked it out,' she said modestly. 'It learns things.'

'It's learned paranoia from Cydonia,' Mac retorted. 'Now, let us go before we die laughing.'

Weaver cocked her head. 'I don't hear anyone laughing,' she remarked. She caught sight of Louise pulling faces, and frowned. 'You are in serious trouble, all of you, and—'

Then she screamed. Anne-Marie and Yvonne screamed too. I nearly screamed myself.

A three-metre-tall giant had just appeared right in front of Weaver.

The giant had long hair and a wild beard. He was dressed in mammoth skins, and his long, heavy spear was poised above Weaver's head. His free hand shot out and grabbed Weaver's right arm. She couldn't reach her scuttle-button. The giant's mighty paw slid down her arm and covered her hand like an enormous furry mitt. Then it forced her hand upward, and swatted it down, twice.

Suddenly, I could move again. So could we all. Yvonne rushed over and grabbed Mum. As a flat shape, Anne-Marie couldn't give her much of a hug, but she tried.

'How did you do that?' I asked Louise.

'Glove-and-glasses,' Louise grinned. 'Called up some low-level software with my tongue. I nicked the giant and a few other things from Noah's Park. Weaver here has an invisible control-panel that responds to her fingers only. Looks like I guessed right for the keys to free us.' She laughed. 'Good old Esc Esc, actually. Bit obvious.'

'It won't do you any good,' yelled Weaver, still struggling in the Paluxy Man's grasp. 'This is a Webcop holding pen, closed off from any access but our own, and the rest of my team will be here any moment—'

There was a sound like shattering glass. The white floor and the featureless space around us vanished. I looked around frantically. We were in a huge, dark interior with pools of light all around and a big rectangle of sunlight in front of us. Hangar 18, Dreamland.

Shadowy figures stepped forward out of the darkness around us. All of them had guns levelled. Their faces came into view: my father, Mr Matabele, Akay, the militia woman who called herself Code, and Relay—the Korean girl I'd fought beside on the Moon that morning, which seemed so long ago.

Louise's flat image turned to face Weaver. 'You were saying?'

The giant phace shambled off into the darkness. Weaver had her hands on top of her head, and Akay was taking great pleasure in aiming his AK47 at her to make sure they stayed there. Virtual guns can't do real harm, of course, but because of the Web's underlying consistency rules they can do lots of *virtual* harm, even to a Webcop avatar.

'We're going to scuttle,' Anne-Marie said. 'Yvonne and I. She needs a hot drink, a hot bath and a real cuddle. I'll get the story later. Thanks, Louise, and all of you, whatever you did.'

She reached for her scuttle-button. It was a weird sight, because her image didn't bend like a cardboard cut-out at all, it flowed and changed like a flat picture—and hesitated. 'Will we find the house full of police?'

'Nah,' said Akay, still not taking his gaze or his gun-muzzle off Weaver. 'They were called off just after they got called out. Too late for our front door, mind you. My dad's lawyer is suing the FBI right now, and y'all should do the same to your local fuzz.'

'Oh, I don't know,' said Anne-Marie. 'They're good boys, really, our policemen.'

She and Yvonne vanished before Akay's cynical laugh reached their ears.

'Yeah, I suppose there are good cops,' he admitted. 'Even good Webcops.'

'Too right there are,' said Mr Matabele. 'Lucky for us all,'—he interrupted himself, with a smile at Louise, as if to say *don't repeat what I just said*—'or, I should say, providential, that you found one by accident. Even your militia pals couldn't have broken in to that holding-site without her help.'

'I guess not,' said Code, with a shrug.

Other dark figures were stepping forward out of the gloom. They were Webcops, but they didn't seem interested in us.

They were interested in carefully and rather gently arresting Weaver. Akay lowered his rifle to let them do it. Weaver gave us all a sour smile as they led her away.

'Can't win them all,' she said. 'And don't get too cocky, we're still watching you.' Her image dissolved as the Webcops scuttled with her, leaving her final words hanging on the air: 'I'll be back!'

'No doubt she will,' sighed Relay. 'Slap on the wrist, that's all she'll get. I really am sorry about all this. She's from London Metcops Limited, seconded to UN Special Forces, not a regular Webcop. Both these forces contain a whole barrel of bad apples. But it's not really her fault. She was misled by this expert system the UN Special Forces have set up to watch Cydonia. It's gone native—totally paranoid, turned into a sort of conspiracy buff itself, from watching the people it watches watching it right back, if you ask me.'

'How do you know all this?' I asked. I looked around at the folk who'd rescued us. They all looked like they knew something I didn't. 'What's going on?'

Akay gave me an aw-shucks-it-was-nothing sort of grin. 'I Webbed around, like I said. Roused the ARM and our pals from the game. Your AI gopher—hey, man, maybe you could slip me a copy of Hal, it's a venomous cool device—put me in touch with Mac and your old man and this church Webmaster.' He glanced at Mr Matabele. 'Another cool guy. Anyway, we've got the churches and the American Civil Liberties Union and the International Free Trade Unions screaming about this. We're Webwide famous!'

'Famous for fifteen minutes, I hope,' said Mac. 'Yeah, well. Anyway, like the deacon says, we'd never have broken through without a good Webcop on our side.'

'I don't see any—'

Relay clapped my shoulder. 'Yes you do,' she said. 'I'm a Webcop.' She drew herself up to her full height, which seemed taller than I remembered. 'I'm Ariadne.'

Chapter Twelve: Protocols

With one sweep of its mighty tail, the plesiosaur turned at the end of the huge aquarium along one wall of the Cydonia Cafe. Spectators, splashed with virtual water, cheered as it swam another length, turned again and swam back, turned...you get the picture. Louise stepped around the side of the aquarium, bowed and smiled to a storm of applause, and formally fixed a polished brass nameplate to the side of the aquarium.

I was standing at the bar, watching from nearly a hundred metres away, but I knew what was written on the plate. I knew because I'd written it myself, with the help of my old Latin-spider phace.

Plesiosaurus caledonis.

Scottish plesiosaur. Better known as Nessie, but there was no need to put that on the brass plate. This was Cydonia, after all.

Louise was making her way through the crowd, who'd now gone back to their regular debates. The story of what had happened to us had already spawned its own talk-groups, spinning theories wilder than Weaver's. No doubt they'll be arguing about it for years.

'It was a bit off,' said a voice beside me, 'nicking that plesiosaur from Noah's Park. I have a soft spot for the creationists.'

I turned to see a tall, dignified-looking elderly man, one of the regulars. I couldn't remember his name, but I grinned at him like an old friend.

'I hope you don't shop us to them,' I said.

'Oh, no,' he said. 'Never! Cydonia's the old homepage, after all.'

'Good on you.' I turned, leaning back on the bar, looking again at the huge display. 'Some cafes have tanks of tropical fish. You have to admit, here at the Cydonia Cafe we have people who think that little bit bigger.'

'I'll grant you that,' he said. He turned to the bartender. 'Another Coke Tingle, please.'

The drink was placed carefully on the counter by a big hairy hand. Paluxy Man had found a job, and seemed in no hurry to return to Noah's Park. I was idly wondering what had happened to N'thota, the Martian phace, when Louise shouldered her way through the last of the crush and stood beside me.

'Well,' she said. 'That was fun! Where do we go now?'

Where indeed. About a month has passed since our adventure. Our fifteen minutes of Webwide fame have resulted in a discreet flurry of Realworld activity. Rumour has it that Weaver has been demoted and sent on a re-training course: a slap on the wrist, just as Relay—Ariadne—had predicted. The expert system that went mad listening to the Cydonia debates is being re-trained too, so we're told, to give it more rigorous protocols. We don't know who, or what, is watching Cydonia right now. But someone, or something, is. You can count on it. Tim's father's lawyers are suing the FBI and the UN Special Forces for millions of dollars. I wish them luck.

The other Webcops—Relay's lot, not Weaver's—have shown very little interest in our story. They're more concerned about investigating how all those alien phaces got upgraded and started behaving oddly, like the one Yvonne found herself trapped in when she innocently tried to follow me to Dreamland. There are a whole lot of rumours about the upgrades. Typical Cydonia babble, but you never know…

MacCready and my father meet Friday nights in a virtual bar in Toronto and argue about politics. Well, about Ireland, actually. It's a start.

Or, perhaps, a continuation. MacCready and Alan must have known each other in Northern Ireland, even as enemies. In Ulster, everybody knows everybody else. I still don't know for sure if there wasn't *something* behind Weaver's conspiracy theory, some unlikely liason between the militias and the International.

Her idea about guns turning up in factories around the world may or may not be true. But according to Alan's me-paper, foremen in Korean shipyards and Party hacks in Cuban sweatshops and so on have started behaving with nervous politeness over the past few weeks.

In the run-up to the independence referendum the Scottish government has set up a Royal Commission to look into areas of tension in Scotland: Unionists, Green settlers, all that. It's headed up by a chap called Sir Brian Micklethwait. Tim was amazed that I'd never heard of him. Outside Britain, everybody's heard of him. Everybody Tim knows, anyway. Even Louise says he's a big name in what's called micro-diplomacy. Sorted out some brushfire banditry in Mozambique by winning over a few bandit leaders, she told me.

Just one more of those things I should have known about, but didn't. I have exams coming up, and I'm coming round to the idea that maybe I've spent too much time in Cydonia. The world is owned, all right, but its owners' names are no secret. Just look at the brand names around you, and you'll see them.

The old guy who'd spoken to me had found another listener. 'That's not my theory or version of it at all,' he was earnestly explaining. 'My version of it is that you had Mars sitting right over the Earth with an atmosphere shared between the planets and constrained by an electro-magnetic bottle, and that human ancestors who looked very much like the face on the pedestal base in Cydonia inhabited both planets, getting from one to the other via aircraft, dirigible, or possibly even by putting a saddle on one of the teratorns or some such.'

I found myself smiling at Louise, and shaking my head.

'I know where to go!' she said. 'I've found a link in the deep software. To another version of Mars—breathable atmosphere, frozen canals. D'you fancy a bit of skating?'

Skating is a great excuse to hold hands, to bump into each other, to fall and help each other up, to fall into each other's arms. We'd done it in real and virtual places, but never, until now, on Mars.

'Yes,' I said. 'Let's do that.'

Louise has learned a lot in all her years of working the Web in gag: the deep codes, the consistency rules, the protocols. She tapped at her wristpad, and suddenly a doorway opened up in front of us.

A ribbon of ice stretched from in front of our feet to the near horizon, between banks of red soil overgrown with scrub and lichen. We held hands and stepped through, morphing our footwear into skates.

As we passed through that gate she'd hacked in the deep software of the site, I noticed a whirl of text in front of my eyes. I can't swear to it but I'm almost sure I saw a bright line that read (before it faded):

http:www/marsobserver/1993/june/nasa.gov

Then it was gone, and we were standing unsteadily on the frozen canal. Louise gripped my hand firmly.

'Let's go,' she said.

I looked over my shoulder at Cydonia, and for another fleeting, fading moment I saw—or thought I saw—a different Cydonia.

The Face was there, its chiselled features sharp ,and clear, sharper even than they're shown on the Cydonia site. And the City, and the Pyramids, were all there—all obviously, blatantly, unarguably artificial, their dressed red rock gleaming under the small, pale sun of Mars. Machines, and people in spacesuits, were climbing allover them, USS and NASA Mars rovers were parked around them, tiny as toys beside that work of giants.

I blinked, and it was gone. Was it another of Cydonia's hoaxes, another deceit? Or was it—

'What is it?' asked Louise, looking up at me impatiently. She hadn't seen it.

I shook my head. 'Nothing,' I said. 'A glitch in telemetry. A trick of the light.'

I squeezed her hand and smiled and (with a few bumps and falls) we sped away, and turned our backs on Cydonia.

The truth is not there.

The Oort Crowd

As we enter the first year of the 23rd Century (or the last year of the 22nd —some arguments never go away) we look back with satisfaction at the triumphs of science and technology in the first two centuries of the third millennium. The advances in medicine, in biotechnology, in communications, in atmospheric engineering have been more than adequately celebrated elsewhere. They are familiar to the most isolated farmer on the barest rocks of Antarctica. But in long-term significance for the human prospect, nothing can compare to the discovery of the gods.

The word 'gods' is used advisedly. Humanity's earliest speculations about the nature of any superhuman intelligences with which it might share the universe are, paradoxically, more relevant to our real situation than the predictions of alien contact in the once-popular genre of science fiction. It must be admitted, however, that some of its practioners (see, e.g. Boyce, 1998, http://www.et-presence.ndirect.co.uk/) reached part of the truth.

That truth, as we all know, is that a large, undetermined and (for good reason) indeterminable fraction of the bodies in the asteroid belt, the Kuiper Belt and the Oort Cloud are the sites of complex intelligent life. The precise evolutionary route(s) from extremophilic micro-organisms to intelligence, apparently by-passing multi-cellular organization, remain unknown and perhaps (again, for good reason) unknowable. Computer simulations have yielded interesting, if inconclusive, results (Chang-Hoskins, 2197, provides a useful overview).

Those of our readers who have benefited from advances in medicine may recollect, and our younger readers can easily retrieve, the excitement which greeted the initial, accidental discovery of an ET intelligence in 2031. The first downloads from the Gates Foundation asteroid prospector revealed, not the potential wealth of resources expected in a carbonaceous chondrite, but a complex interior structure variously described as 'crystalline', 'fractal' and 'organic'. Fortunately for scientific openness, the drilling operation was webcast live, and as the pictures slowly scrolled down the screens of a few hundred thousand space enthusiasts the news spread across the net faster than a virus.

In those first hasty, misspelled emails and postings we can see—from references to the structure as 'the alien computer' or 'Asteroid City' or even as 'the starship'—the depth of initial misapprehension. Far from having been built by beings broadly similar to ourselves, the structure itself was the alien, or the civilization—the nature and number of centres of consciousness within it remains controversial. And it was neither alone nor isolated.

Billions of years of evolutionary 'tuning' have given the cometary minds an exquisite sensitivity to the electromagnetic output of each other's internal chemical and physical processes. Their communications are, once looked for, as detectable as they are incomprehensible. Some of the larger bodies in the Oort seem to act as relays, extending the communications net across solar and possibly interstellar distances. (As is known, the tenuous outer reaches of the Oort Cloud intersect those of their Centaurian equivalent.)

Despite strenuous efforts, no human communication with the extra-terrestrial minds has been established (the results claimed by Lunan, 2049, are at best ambiguous). They are, to us, in precisely the position of the gods postulated by Epicurus, serene in the spaces between the worlds.

These gods, while indifferent, are not passive. Subtle control over their outgassings results, over very long periods, in orbital changes. More rapid processes occur within the asteroids. Careful study of recent and historical Near-Earth Objects suggests that the orbits at least some NEOs have been the result of conscious intent.

In view of the above, it appears in retrospect unfortunate that the first probe to the Oort Cloud and beyond, launched in 2030, should have used as its initial means of propulsion a plasma sail consisting of ionised gas within a 'magnetic bubble' thousands of kilometres across, and as its secondary means a prototype 'electromagnetic ramscoop' sucking in vast quantities of interstellar and cometary matter. Subsequent changes in the volume and intensity of inter-cometary communication, and in the orbits of numerous comets and asteroids, cannot be accounted for by the physical effects of its passage. They can only be considered a response.

The effect on human society of the discovery of the gods has been positive. Excluded from many of the space-based resources once thought unoccupied, we turn to a less profligate use of our planet's own. The expectations of John Stuart Mill, in his famous chapters on the 'stationary state' and 'the probable futurity of the labouring classes', have been largely realised.

But, as our astronomical and space-defence workers' co-operatives continue their urgent sky-watching, there may be some risk of overlooking a danger closer to home. There is no reason to suppose that extremophilic consciousness is confined to minor interplanetary bodies. Perhaps the majority of the Earth's biomass consists of subterranean extremophiles.

Watch the ground.

Undead Again

It's 2045 and I'm still a vampire. Damn.

The chap from Alcor UK is droning through his orientation lecture. New age of enlightenment, new industrial revolution, many changes, take some time to adjust, blah blah blah. I'm only half-listening, being too busy shifting my foot to keep it out of the beam of direct sunlight millimetering across the floor, and trying not to look at his neck.

I feel like saying: *I've only been dead forty years, for Chr—*

For crying out loud. I saw the *first* age of enlightenment. I worked nights right through the original Industrial Revolution. I remember being naive enough to get excited about mesmerism, galvanism, spiritualism, socialism, Roentgen rays, rationalism, radium, Mendelism, Marconi, relativity, feminism, the Russian Revolution, the Bomb, nightclubs, feminism (again), Apollo 11, socialism (again), the fall of Saigon and the fall of the Wall.

The last dodgy nostrum I fell for was cryonics.

So don't give me this future shock shit, sunshine. The most disconcerting thing I've come across so far in 2045 is the latest ladies' fashion: the old sleeveless minidress. The ozone hole has been fixed, and folk are frolicking in the sun. I hug myself with bare arms, and slide the castored chair back another inch.

Under the heel of my left wrist, I feel the thud of my regenerated heart. It beats time to the artery visible under the tanned skin of the resurrection man's neck. The rest of my nature is unregenerate. I feel somewhat thwarted. This is not, this is definitely not, what I died for. And it seemed such a good idea at the time.

It always does.

By 1995 we thought we had a handle on the thing. It's a virus. In all respects but one, it's benign: it prevents aging, and stimulates regeneration of any tissue damage short of, well, a stake through the heart. But it has a very low infectivity, so it takes a lot of mingling of fluids to spread. Natural selection has worked that one hard. Hence the unfortunate impulses. And by 1995, I can tell you, I was getting pretty sick of them. I cashed in my six Scottish Widows life insurance policies (let's draw a veil over how I acquired them), signed up for cryonic preservation in the event of my death, and after a discreet ten years, met an unfortunate and bloody end at the hand of the coven senior, Kelvin.

You'll thank me later,' he said, just before he pushed home the point.

'See you in the future,' I croaked.

The last thing I saw was his grin. That, and the pavement below the spiked railings beside the steps of my flat. A tragic accident. The coroner, I just learned, blamed it on the long skirt. Vampires, always the fashion victims.

I leave the orientation room, hang around until dusk under the pretext of catching up with the news, and go out and find a vintage clothes shop. I walk out in Victorian widow's weeds. They fit so well I suspect they were once mine.

'It didn't work,' I tell Kelvin.

He sips his bloody mary and looks defensive.

'It did in a way,' he says. 'There are no viruses in your blood.'

That word again. I look away. We're in some kind of goth club, which covers for the mode but doesn't improve my mood.

'So why do I still feel…hungry?'

'Have a tapas,' he says. 'But seriously…the way we figure it, the virus has to have transcribed itself into our DNA. So the nanotech cell-repair just replicates it without a second thought.'

'So we're stuck with it,' I say. 'Living in the dark and every so often—'

'Not quite,' he says. 'Now it's been established that cryonics really does work, there's been a whole new interest in a very old idea…'

The coffin lid opens. Kelvin's looking down, as I expect. The real shock is the light, full-spectrum and warm. It feels like something my skin has missed for centuries. I sit up, naked, and bask for a moment.

The overhead lights reproduce the spectrum of Alpha Centauri, which is where we're going. The whole coven is here, all thirteen of them, happier and better fed than I've ever seen them. It's taken us a lot of planning, a lot of money, and a lot of lying to get here, but we're on our way.

'Welcome back,' says Kevin. He grins around at the coven.

'Let's thaw one out for her,' he says. 'She must be hungry.'

As far as I can see stretch rows and rows of cryonic coffins containing interstellar colonists in what they euphemistically call cold sleep. Thousands of them.

Enough to keep us going until we reach that kinder sun.

Tairlidhe

I swear they were not more than a quarter mile away, and about two hundred feet below us. I saw the glint of the officer's spyglass, and caught an echo of his clipped command. Twelve of the soldiers bent their backs and set off up the slope. The others waited on the road, beside the officer's horse.

There were three of us: myself, Donald with the flag, and Angus the dwalmer. We huddled in a dip of frosty heather, with a hundred feet of steep rock and scree between us and the top of the hill. If nobody shot us before we reached it, they'd get us on the skyline for sure. Donald had a sword, because he had the flag wrapped around his chest under the plaid. I had a knife, a pistol I had fired once, a pinch of damp powder and not the smear of a shot. And Angus, what he had was a rowan twig, a leather pouch that he'd told us contained a drop or two of quicksilver, and would you believe, a bloody rabbit's foot. He lay on his back and squinted up at the sky and waved the stuff about and muttered like a priest praying in the Latin, but the words sounded even more heathenish than that. He was trying to bring down a mist, out of the blue sky.

'Will you get a move on with it, man, in the name of—'

I reached my hand across and shut Donald's mouth. It was not a time to be naming names, not with the dwalmer in the midst of a summoning and ourselves, in all likelihood, a minute or two from eternity. Or an hour or two, if we were unlucky and the redcoats were in the mood for sport. I determined to die. I had not much faith in the dwalmer. There had been a score of them with us on Drumossie Moor, and no help had they given in the battle.

They had brought on visions, I'll grant them that. Phantoms of men in breeks and women in sarks shorter than kilts, who wandered the boggy moor and gawped. A distant glimpse of a line of shining things that crawled without legs. What use was that against the guns?

Angus fell silent and closed his eyes. The sky was as blue as it had been. I could hear the clink of the weapons of our enemies as they toiled up the hill. I looked sideways at Donald. He nodded. His knuckles went white on the hilt. We were on the point of leaping up for a forlorn two-man charge down the hill when I heard the loudest roar I had ever heard in my life. And this was when my ears were still ringing from the artillery and musketry of the day before. It was like the sound you would hear if the sky was made of canvas and the Almighty was ripping it with His bare hands. With all the echoing it made in the glen it was hard to tell whence it came. I looked up, and then to one side.

From my right, from the west, something black hurtled towards me. It was like the last thing you would see before a thrown spear hit you in the face. Then it was overhead, a huge thing with wings that were swept back, like the wings of a black crow when it dives. It was no vision. I was buffetted by the pressure of its passing, and saw the soggy brown grass and heather flattened under it, as if by an invisible foot.

Well, my eyes followed it, and I glimpsed fire from its tail, and then it was gone, across the top of the opposite ridge of the glen. I found I had sprung up without taking thought. The redcoats were but fifty yards from us, staring after it and not looking at us at all. Donald with the flag was up too, and he gave a yell and ran at them, his sword above his head. He had not gone five long paces, and I had just gathered my wits to go after him, when another of the things roared down the glen. This time it was below us, about a hundred feet above the road. I will not say it flew as fast as a bullet. It flew faster than an arrow, but not so fast you could not see it. I saw the single eye in its head, and the upright fin at its tail, and round spots on its wings like the eyes on a moth's back. And then it tipped in the air and rose to the side and was gone like its fellow, over the ridge.

At that the redcoats ran. They fled down the hill, one or two falling over and tumbling and picking themselves up and running and jumping on. The platoon on the road took to their heels too, back to the east, to the sound of a loud whinney as the officer's horse reared and a yell, as its rider was thrown. The next time I looked at him he was back on his feet, dragging on the reins, running and waving his sword and cursing after the men.

Donald, and then myself, flattened again to the heather. The officer remounted, and rallied the squad who'd gone up and then down the hill, and were now back on the road and a good way down it. A shamed and bedraggled lot they looked, as the flat of his sword belaboured their shoulders and his barrack-room blasphemies lashed their ears. After a minute or so of this they formed up behind the horse and followed in its cantering steps at a jog, chasing after the rest. They had no more time for us at all. In a few minutes they were out of sight around the shoulder of a rise.

Donald with the flag stood up and Angus the dwalmer skipped down the hill to join us, grinning all over his poor silly face.

'Well, that was a mighty one,' I said.

'Wasn't it just!' said Angus.

'A mighty pair,' said Donald, laughing. 'Dragons, was it, that time?'

'I suppose,' said Angus. 'I was trying to summon a cloud.'

He was that simple he did not even pretend he had meant it all along. I would have credited the boast if he had made it, but he did not think to. Dwalmers can be like that, some of them, a wee bit strange in the head and not always wise to the world.

'I thought the fire of a dragon came out its mouth, not its arse,' I said. 'And I thought they had two eyes in their heads, not one. These things did not look like dragons to me. They looked to me like the spears of giants.'

'You have seen dragons before, and the spears of giants?' said Donald. 'Well, good for you, Iain from Back. And there was me always thinking Back was a wee place.'

'You know what I mean.'

'No, I do not,' said Donald. 'I do know that yon officer will be telling his men that they are shameful cowards to run from a dwalmer's sending, that such sights are not real and that he'll hang for a witch any who says differently. They'll be chasing back after us in no time. So let us make our way on the road, seeing as we're on it.'

'They'll find us on it,' I said.

'We'll hear them coming,' said Donald. 'If you keep your mouth shut, Iain from Back.'

I said nothing and we set off along the road. It was one of General Wade's roads. I do not know which because although I had been to the Lowlands and England, and have been there since, I then knew nothing of the country around Inverness and have never had the notion to return to it. In any case it was well metalled as the saying has it and we made a good pace along it. But we had no foolish fancy that we could outpace the redcoats for long. The road was built for horses and marching men, and not for weary, hungry and footsore stragglers from a battle. So at every moment we were ready to leave it for the hills and moors and bogs, where the advantage in running or hiding would be ours.

We heard no pursuit that day. In a bonny green glen we passed through a scatter of houses, all empty, abandoned in haste. How news of Culloden and the killing rage of Cumberland and his men had reached ahead of us I know not. Perhaps it was the second sight. More likely, we were not the first to flee through that hamlet. Unmilked cattle lowed in a dry-walled pasture. We helped ourselves to what little food we could find—an oatcake, a scrap of salt meat on the bone, a dish of sour crowdie that a cat had been at—and borrowed a blanket, and hastened on until dark. We found the shelter of an overhanging boulder and slept the night. Donald with the flag roused us in the dawn and after looking up and down the glen and listening, we made our way back to the road and set off along it.

It was a fine morning and the sun lifted the mist early enough. The road took us up out of the glen and on to a high, bare moor. After we'd gone a few hundred yards I looked back and saw a column of smoke rising straight into the sky. My first thought was that it meant rain was on the way. Then I realised what else it meant. The houses we had been in were burning.

'Off the road,' said Donald.

We cut away to the right. The tough twigs of winter heather scratched our legs raw. A half mile from the road and up a bit of slope we took shelter in a copse, burying ourselves in the brown bracken at the foot of the green rowans. It was the kine that came along the road first, no longer lowing—oh, they had been milked all right—and driven by swearing southerners. Behind them was the same troop that had fled yesterday. You needed no spyglass to tell it was the same officer by the way he sat. How I longed for a good musket, though the shot would have been the death of me.

As soon as they were clear out on the moor the troop stopped and with a few shots in the air and some jabs of bayonets and much hallooing, they scattered the cattle away from the road in all directions. They fired upon the beasts and left them dead for the crows. Then they marched on, passing right in front of us.

'Oh the waste,' said Donald. 'The sinful waste.'

It was not the waste but the loss that angered me. The village, whatever was left of it, would not last to the spring.

Beside me Angus was muttering again. His words were like cold water down my back. I wanted to stop his mouth but could not. I was hoping against hope that he would summon something more terrifying than the flying things. I looked to the west, from where they had come yesterday, and saw only the familiar clouds and rain of the western glens, marching east like an army with black banners. Well, they would give the redcoats a soaking, for what good that could do.

And then I heard it, faint on the wind, the sound of pipes and drums. They were playing a tune my feet had followed many a time, on the long road to Derby and the longer road back, the one that is now called 'The White Cockade'. The redcoats heard it too. The officer waved his sword and the squad behind him halted. He put his spyglass to his eye and looked straight ahead.

And in a moment, suddenly, right in front of him and not a hundred yards away as if they had risen from the ground, came soldiers the likes of which neither he nor we had ever seen. They marched five abreast, with two pipers and a drummer in the front of them, and they came rank upon rank, stretching back so far there must have been hundreds of them. They wore kilts and heavy tramping boots, they carried short carbines propped smart on their shoulders and they marched in step like redcoats. It was a Highland army that the Prince, Tairlidhe himself, might have dreamed of. I cannot swear to it, but I think I saw—it was in the distance, but my sight was good then—these words on a flapping banner: 'King's Own Highlanders'.

Well, the redcoats were brave and quick, I'll give them that. At one command as the officer wheeled around behind them they formed up, front rank on one knee, second rank aiming over their heads, the ranks behind moving through and forward after each volley. And volley upon volley they fired, and no difference did it make. The army facing them marched forward as if they didn't see them.

Brave as they were the redcoats broke. Did even the officer suspect it was a sending? Through the smoke, through the mist that descended of a sudden around the battle, did that phantom army seem a real one with a terrible discipline? One that it was more urgent to warn about than fight?

I don't know. All I know is that this time the officer was well ahead of his men, riding hell for leather back the way he had come, and his men running after him in no good order. Behind them, not giving chase and without a noise but their feet and the skirling music, the terrible regiment marched on into the glen. I watched them pass, with their black berets and brown jackets and bright pleated kilts, their belts and daggers and short shining guns. We all watched them, till they were out of sight.

'Well, Angus, you have done it now,' said Donald. 'Wait till the Duke's men see that lot marching on Inverness!'

Wait till the King's men see it, I thought. I wanted to get up and follow them myself. What rumours and tales would fly, and what new heart it would give to the scattered men in the glens! The Prince himself might even stand and rally us again, and after that who knew what might happen?

I turned to Angus, as these thoughts were just forming in my mind, and saw him pointing at something behind my shoulder. The look on his face made me turn around again as fast as a cornered fox.

Between us and the road stood what I thought for a terrible second were two angels. They wore shining white coats to their knees. The one that looked like a man wore black breeks under his coat; the one that looked like a woman had bare legs. Now this will make you laugh, but she was wearing spectacles. And who ever heard of an angel with short sight? The two were looking at something in front of them, like at a table we could not see, and looking up from it at us.

If we gazed with wonder, they looked at us with alarm.

And then—you will believe me, but this is what I saw—the woman reached to that invisible table, and picked up a snake, and spoke into its mouth. I remember her words clear and plain, her voice musical like a well-born lady's, her accent like the English. I will never forget them, though I know not what they mean.

'Time viewing experiment cancelled,' she said, 'due to time stream disturbance. Emergency measures to be taken.'

There was a bright flash and I saw no more and fell down as if dead.

I woke under pouring rain, somewhere in the middle of the day. My head was like splitting with pain. Donald and Angus woke soon after me. They both had forgotten all that had passed, and thought I was raving when I told them.

We set off again to the west, and a lot happened on the way, but I have already told many times how we made our way home. Long before we got there it was clear that poor Angus was no longer Angus the dwalmer. He never had a vision again, or remembered a word of his summonings, or of the tongue in which he spoke them. He is Angus of the usquebaugh now, and a sorry fellow.

Donald is still called Donald with the flag, and I am called Iain of the lies.

The Human Front

Like most people of my generation, I remember exactly where I was on March 17, 1963, the day Stalin died. I was in the waiting-room of my father's surgery, taking advantage of the absence of waiting patients to explore the nicotine-yellowed stacks of *Reader's Digest*s and *National Geographic*s, and to play in a desultory fashion with the gnawed plastic soldiers, broken tin tanks, legless dolls and so forth that formed a disconsolate heap, like an atrocity diorama, in one corner. My father must have been likewise taking advantage of a slack hour towards the end of the day to listen to the wireless. He opened the door so forcefully that I looked up, guiltily, though on this particular occasion I had nothing to be guilty about. His expression alarmed me further, until I realised that the mixed feelings that struggled for control of his features were not directed at me.

Except one. It was with, I now think, a full awareness of the historic significance of the moment, as well as a certain sense of loss, that he told me the news. His voice cracked slightly, in a way I had not heard before.

'The Americans,' he said, 'have just announced that Stalin has been shot.'

'Up against a wall?' I asked, eagerly.

My father frowned at my levity and lit a cigarette.

'No,' he said. 'Some American soldiers surrounded his headquarters in the Caucasus mountains. After the partisans were almost wiped out they surrendered, but then Stalin made a run for it and the American soldiers shot him in the back.'

I almost giggled. Things like this happened in history books and adventure stories, not in real life.

'Does that mean the war is over?' I asked.

'That's a good question, John.' He looked at me with a sort of speculative respect. 'The Communists will be disheartened by Stalin's death, but they'll go on fighting, I'm afraid.'

At that moment there was a knock on the waiting-room door, and my father shooed me out while welcoming his patient in. The afternoon was clear and cold. I mucked about at the back of the house and then climbed up the hill behind it, sat on a boulder and watched the sky.

A pair of eagles circled their eyrie on the higher hill opposite, but I didn't let that distract me. After a while my patience was rewarded by the thrilling sight of a V-formation of American bombers high above, flying east. Their circular shapes glinted silver when the sunlight caught them, and shadowed black against the blue.

The newspapers always arrived on Lewis the day after they were printed, so two days passed before the big black headline of the Daily Express blared **STALIN SHOT**, and I could read, without fully comprehending, the rejoicing of Beaverbrook, the grave commentary of Cameron, the reminiscent remarks of Churchill, and frown over Burchett's curiously disheartening reports from the front, and smile over the savage raillery of Cummings' cartoon of Stalin in hell, shaking hands with Satan while hiding a knife behind his back.

Obituaries traced his life: from the Tiflis seminary, through the railway yards and oilfields of Baku, the bandit years as Koba, the October Revolution and the Five Year plans, the Purges and the Second World War; his chance absence from the Kremlin during the atomic bombing of Moscow in Operation Dropshot, and his return in old age to the ways and vigour of his youth as a guerrilla leader, rallying Russia's remaining Reds to the protracted war against the Petrograd government; to the contested, gruesome details of his death and the final, bloody touch, the fingerprint identification of his hacked-off hands.

By then I had already had a small aftershock of the revolutionary's death myself, at school on the 18th. Hugh Macdonald, a pugnacious boy of nine or so but still in my class, came up to me in the playground and said: 'I bet you're pleased, *mac a dochter*.'

'Pleased about what?'

'About the Yanks killing Stalin, you *cac*.'

'And why should I not be? He was just a murderer.'

'He killed Germans.'

Hugh looked at me to see if this produced the expected change of mind, and when it didn't he thumped me. I kicked his shin and he ran off bawling, and I got the belt for fighting.

That evening I played about with the dial of my father's wireless, and heard through a howl of atmospherics a man with a posh Sassenach accent reading out eulogies on what the Reds still called Radio Moscow.

The genius and will of Stalin, great architect of the rising world of free humanity, will live forever.

I had no idea what it meant, or how anyone even remotely sane could possibly say it, but it remained in my mind, part of the same puzzle as that unexpected punch.

My father, Dr Malcolm Donald Matheson, was a native of the bleak long island. His parents were crofters who had worked hard and scraped by to support him in his medical studies at Glasgow in the 1930s. He had only just graduated when the Second World War broke out. He volunteered for combat duty and was immediately assigned to the Royal Army Medical Corps. Of his war service, mainly in the Far East, he said very little in my hearing. It may have been some wish to pay back something to the community which had supported him which led him to take up his far from lucrative practice in the western parish of Uig, but of sentiment towards that community he had none. He insisted on being addressed by the English form of his name, instead of as 'Calum' and I and my siblings were likewise identified: John, James, Margaret, Mary, Alexander—any careless references to Iain, Hamish, Mairead, Mairi or Alasdair met a frown or a mild rebuke. Though a fluent native speaker of Gaelic, he spoke the language only when no other communication was possible—there were, in those days, a number of elderly monoglots, and a much larger number of people who never used the English language for any purpose other than the telling of deliberate lies. There are two explanations, one fanciful and the other realistic, for the latter phenomenon. The fanciful one is that they believed that the Gaelic was the language of heaven (was the Bible not written in it?) and that the Almighty did not hear, or did not understand, the English; or, at the very least, that a lie not told in Gaelic didn't count. The realistic one is that English was the language of the state, and lying in its hearing was indeed legitimate, since the Gaels had heard so many lies from it, all in English.

My mother, Morag, was a Glaswegian of Highland extraction, who had met and married my father after the end of the Second World War and before the beginning of the Third. She, somewhat contrarily, taught herself the Gaelic and used it in all her dealings with the locals, though they always thought her dialect and her accent stuck-up and affected. The thought of her speaking a pure and correct Gaelic in a Glasgow accent is amusing; her neighbours' attitude towards her well-meant efforts less so, being an example of the characteristic Highland inferiority complex so often mistaken for class or national consciousness. The Lewis accent itself is one of the ugliest under heaven, a perpetual weary resentful whine—the Scottish equivalent of Cockney—and the dialect thickly corrupted with English words Gaelicised by the simple expedient of mispronouncing them in the aforementioned accent.

Before marriage she had been a laboratory assistant. After marriage she worked as my father's secretary, possibly for tax reasons, while raising me and my equally demanding brothers and sisters. Like my father, she was a smoker, a whisky-drinker, and an atheist. All of these were, at that time and place, considered quite inappropriate for a woman, but only the first was publicly known. Our non-attendance at any of the three doctrinally indistinguishable but mutually irreconcilable churches the parish supported was explained by the rumour—perhaps arising from my father's humanitarian contribution to the war effort—that the *dochter* was a Quaker. It was a notion he did nothing to encourage or to dispel. The locals wouldn't have recognised a Quaker if they'd found one in their porridge.

Because of my father's military service and medical connections, he had stroll-in access at the nearby NATO base. This sprawling complex of low, flat-roofed buildings, Nissen huts, and radar arrays disfigured the otherwise sublime headland after which the neighbouring village, Aird, was named. My father occasionally dropped in for cheap goods—big round tins of cigarettes, packs of American nylons for my mother, stacks of chewing-gum for the children, and endless tins of corned beef—at the NAAFI store.

It was thus that I experienced the event which became the second politically significant memory of my childhood, and the only time when my father expressed a doubt about the Western cause. He was, I should explain, a dyed-in-the-wool conservative and unionist, hostile even to the watery socialism of the Labour Party, but he would have died sooner than vote for the Conservative and Unionist Party. 'The Tories took our land,' he once spat, by way of explanation, before slamming the door in the face of a rare, hopeless canvasser. He showed less emotion at Churchill's death than he did at Stalin's. So, like most of our neighbours, he was a Liberal. The Liberals had, in their wishy-washy Liberal way, decried the Clearances, and the Highlanders have loyally returned them to Parliament ever since.

Why the Highlanders nurse a grievance over the Clearances was a mystery to me at the time, and still is. In no land in the world is the disproportion between natural attraction and sentimental attachment more extreme, except possibly Poland and Palestine. Expelled from their sodden Sinai to Canada and New Zealand the dispossessed crofters flourished, and those who remained behind had at last enough land to feed themselves, but their descendants still talk as if they'd been put on cattle trucks to Irkutsk.

It was my habit, when I had nothing better to do on a Saturday, to accompany my father on his rounds. I did not, of course, attend his consultations, but I would either wait in the car or brave the collies who'd press their forepaws on my shoulders and bark in my face, to the inevitable accompaniment of cries of 'Och, he's just being friendly,' and make my way through mud and cow-dung to the hospitality of black tea in the black houses, and the fussing of immense mothers girt in aprons and shod in wellingtons.

We'd visited an old man in Aird that morning in the summer of '63, and my father turned the Hillman off the main road and up to the NATO base. Gannets dropped like dive-bombs in the choppy sea of the bay below the headland's cliffs, and black on the Atlantic horizon the radar turned. Though militarily significant—Lewis commands a wide sweep of the North Atlantic, and Tupolev's deep-shelter factories in the Urals were turning out long-range jet bombers at a rate of about one a month, well above attrition—security was light. A nod to the squaddie on the gate, and we were through.

My father casually pulled up in the officers' car-park outside the NAAFI and we hopped out. He was just locking the door when an alarm shrieked. Men in blue uniforms were suddenly rushing about and pointing out to sea. Other men, in white helmets and webbing, were running to greater purpose. Somewhere a fire-engine and an ambulance joined in the clamour.

I spotted the incoming bomber before my father did, maybe two miles out.

'There—there it is!'

'It's *low*—'

Barely above the sea, flashing reflected sunlight as it yawed and wobbled, trailing smoke, the bomber limped in. On the wide concrete apron in front of us a team frantically pushed and dragged a big Wessex helicopter to the perimeter, while one man stood waving what looked like outsize ping-pong bats. The bomber just cleared the top of the cliff, skimmed the grass—I could see the plants bend beneath it, though no blast of air came from it—and with a screaming scrape and a shower of sparks it hit the concrete and slithered to a halt about a hundred yards from where we stood.

It was perhaps fifty feet in diameter, ten feet thick at the hub. Smoke poured from a ragged nick in its edge. The ambulance and fire-engine rushed up and stopped in a squeal of brakes, their crews leaping out just as a hatch opened on the bomber's upper side. More smoke puffed forth, but nothing else emerged. A couple of firemen, lugging fire-extinguishers, leapt on the sloping surface and dropped inside. Others hosed the rent in the hull.

My father ran forward, shouting 'I'm a doctor!' and I ran after him. The outstretched arm of one of the men in white helmets brought my father up short. After a moment of altercation, he was allowed to go on, while I struggled against a firm but not unfriendly grip on my shoulder. The man's armband read 'Military Police'. At that moment I was about ten yards from the bomber, close enough to see the rivets in its steel hull.

Close enough to see the body which the firemen lifted out, and which the ambulancemen laid on a stretcher and ran with, my father close behind, into the nearest building. It was wearing a close-fitting silvery flying-suit, and a visored helmet. One leg was crooked at a bad angle. That was not what shot me through with a thrill of horror. It was the body of a child, no taller than my five-year-old sister Margaret. The large helmet made its proportions even more child-like.

A moment later I was turned around and hustled away. The military policeman almost pushed me back into the car, told me to wait there, and shut me up with a stick of chewing-gum before he hurried off. Everybody else who'd come at all close to the craft was being rounded up into a huddle guarded by the military policemen and being lectured by a couple of men who I guessed were civilians, if their snap-brimmed hats, dark glasses and black suits were anything to go by. They reminded me of American detectives in comics. I wondered excitedly if they carried guns in shoulder holsters.

After about fifteen minutes my father came out of the building and walked over to the car. One of the civilians intercepted him. They talked for a few minutes, leaning towards each other, their faces close together, one or other of them shaking their fingers, pointing and jabbing. Each of them glanced over at me several times. Although I had the side window wound down, I couldn't hear what they were saying. Eventually my father turned on his heel and stalked over to the car, while the other man stood looking after him. As my father opened the car door the black-suited civilian shook his head a little, then rejoined his colleague as the small crowd dispersed.

A knot of military policemen formed up at the building's doorway, and surrounded two stretcher-bearers as they hurried to the Wessex. There was only the briefest glimpse of the stretcher as it was passed inside, moments before it took off and headed out to sea on a southerly course.

My father's face was pale and his hand shook as he took his hip-flask from the glove compartment. The top squeaked as he unscrewed it, the flask gurgled as he drank it dry.

'Leave the window down, John,' he said as he turned the key and pushed the starter. 'I need a cigarette.'

He lit up, fumbling, then engaged the gears and the car moved off with a lurch. As we passed the soldier on the gate my father gave him a wave that was almost a salute.

'What sort of people will that poor laddie be fighting for?' he asked me, or himself. His knuckles were white on the wheel. The swerve on to the main road threw me against the door. He didn't notice.

'Monsters,' he said. 'Monsters.'

I sat up straight again, rubbing my shoulder.

'It's awful to use wee children to fly bombers,' I said.

He looked across at me sharply, then turned his attention back to the single-track road.

'Is that what you saw?' he murmured. 'Well, John, we were told very firmly that the pilot was a midget, you know, a dwarf, and that this is a secret. If the enemy knew that, they would know something they shouldn't know about our bombers. About how much weight they can carry, or something like that.'

I squirmed on the plastic leather, swinging my legs as though I needed to pee. I had read about dwarfs and midgets in *Look and Learn*. They were not like in fairy stories.

'But that's not true,' I said. 'That wasn't a dwarf, the pro—the portions—'

'"Proportions".'

'The proportions were wrong. I mean, they were right—they were ordinary. The pilot was a child, wasn't he?'

The car swerved slightly, then steadied.

'Listen, John,' my father said. 'Whatever the pilot is, neither of us is supposed to talk about it, and we'll get into big trouble if we do. So if you're sure it was a child you saw, I'm not going to argue with you. And if the Air Force say the pilot is a midget, I'm not going to argue with them, either. I set and splinted the leg of that, that'—he hesitated, waving a hand dangerously off the wheel—*'craitur beag 'us bochd*—of the poor wee thing, I should say, and that's all I know of it.'

I was as startled by his lapse into the Gaelic as by the uncertainty and ambiguity of his reference to the pilot, and I thought it wise to keep quiet about the whole subject. But he didn't, not quite yet.

'Not a word about it, to anyone,' he said. 'Not to your mother, your brothers and sisters, your friends, anyone. Not a word. Promise me?'

'All right,' I said. I was young enough to feel that it was more exciting to keep a secret than to tell one.

The following day was a Sunday, and although it meant nothing to us but a day off school we had to conform to local custom by not playing outside. It was a sweltering hell of boredom, relieved only by the breath of air from the open back door and the arrival at the front door of two men in black suits, who weren't ministers. My father escorted them politely into his surgery. The waiting-room door (I found, on a cautious test) was locked. They did not stay long; but the following morning on the way out to catch the van to school I overheard my mother telephoning around to postpone the day's appointments, and noticed a freshly emptied whisky bottle on the trash.

*

A couple of years later, when I was ten, my father sold his practice to a younger, less financially straitened and more idealistic doctor (a Nationalist, to my father's private disgust) and took up a practice in Greenock, an industrial town on the Firth of Clyde. Our flitting was exciting, our arrival more so. It was another world. In the mid-sixties the Clyde was booming, its shipyards producing naval and civilian vessels in almost equal proportion, its harbours crowded with British and American warships, the Royal Ordnance Factory at Bishopton working around the clock. Greenock, as always, flourished from the employment opportunities upriver—beginning with the yards and docks of the adjacent town of Port Glasgow—and from its own industries, mainly the processing of colonial sugar, jute and tobacco. The pollution from the factories and refineries was light, but fumes from the heavy vehicular traffic that serviced them may well explain the high incidence of lung cancer in the area. (My father's death, though outside the purview of the present narrative, may also be so accounted.) Besides these traditional industries, a huge IBM factory had recently opened (the ceremonial ribbon cut by Sir Alan Turing himself) in the Kip Valley behind the town.

The town's division between middle class and working class was sharp. One the eastern side of Nelson Street lay the tenements and factories; to the west a classical grid of broad streets blocked out sturdy sandstone villas and semi-detached houses. Though our parents' disdain for private education saved us from the worst snobberies of fee-paying schools, the state system was just as blatantly segregated. The grammar schools filled the offices of management, and the secondary moderns manufactured workers. Class division shocked me: after growing up among the well-fed, if ill-clad, population of Lewis, I saw the poorer eight-tenths of the town as inhabited by misshapen dwarfs.

It was while exploring what to my imagination were dangerous, Dickensian slums, but which were in reality perfectly respectable working-class districts, that I first encountered evidence that this division was regarded, by some, as part of the greater division of the world. On walls, railway bridges and pavements I noticed a peculiar graffito, in the shape of an inverted 'Y' with a cross-bar—a childishly simple, and therefore instantly recognisable, representation of the human form. Sometimes it was enclosed by the outline of a five-pointed star, and frequently it was accompanied by a scrawled hammer and sickle. These last two symbols were, of course, already familiar to me from the red flags of the enemy.

It was at first as shocking a sight as if some Chinese or Russian guerrilla had popped out of a manhole in the street, and it gave me a strange thrill—a *frisson*, as the French say—to find that the remote and gigantic foe had his partisans in the streets of Greenock as much as in the jungles of Malaya or the rubble of Budapest. One day in 1966 I actually met one, on a street corner in the East End, down near the town centre where the big shops began.

This soldier of the Red horde was a bandy-legged old man in a cloth cap, selling copies of a broadsheet newspaper called the *Daily Worker*. He met with neither hostility nor interest from the passers-by. With boyish bravado, and some curiosity, I bought it. Its masthead displayed the two symbols I already knew, and an article inside was illustrated by, and explained, the third.

> 'Against the warmongers and arms profiteers, against the reckless drive to destruction, against the forces of death, it is necessary to rally all who yearn for peace. The situation cries out for the broadest possible united front, one broader even than the great People's Fronts against fascism, one in which every decent human being, every worker, every woman, every honest businessman, every farmer, every patriot can take their place with pride and determination. It is not for any political party, or class, or ideology that such a front shall stand, but for the very survival of the human race.
>
> 'This greatest of all united and people's fronts exists, and is growing.
>
> 'It is the Human Front.'

I understood barely a word of it, and the only reason why I clipped out the article and kept it, long after I had secretly disposed of the newspaper, long enough for me to re-read and finally understand it, years later, was because of coincidental resonances of its author's name—Dr John Lewis.

After that initial naive exploration I settled down to a sort of acceptance of the world as it was, and to learning more about it, at school and out. Science was more interesting than politics, and it soothed rather than disturbed the mind. The war was a permanent backdrop of news, and a distant prospect of National Service. The BBC brought it home on the wireless and, increasingly, on black-and-white television, with feigned neutrality and unacknowledged censorship. News items that raised questions about the war's conduct and its domestic repercussions were few: the Pauling trial, the Kinshasa atomic bombing, the occasional allusion to a speech by Foot in the Commons or Wedgewood-Benn in the Lords.

The biggest jolt to the consensus came in 1968, with the May Offensive. Out of nowhere, it seemed, the supposedly defeated *maquis* stormed and seized Paris, Lyons, Nantes, and scores of other French cities. Only carpet-bombing of the suburbs dislodged them and saved the Versailles government. This could not be hidden, nor the first anti-war demonstrations in the United States: clean-cut students chanting 'Hey! Hey! JFK! How many kids did you kill today?' until the dogs and fire-hoses and tear-gas cleared the streets. At the time, I was more frightened by the unexpected closeness of the Communist threat than shocked by the measures taken against it.

My first act of dissidence wasn't until three years later, at the age of seventeen. I slipped out one April evening to attend a meeting in the Co-operative Hall held under the auspices of Medical Aid for Russia. The speaker was touring the country, and it may have been the controversy that followed him that drew the crowd of a hundred or so. It's certainly what drew me. He was flanked on the platform by a local trade union official, a pacifist lady, and Greenock's perennially unsuccessful Liberal candidate. (The local Labour MP had, naturally, denounced the meeting in the *Greenock Telegraph*.) The hall was bare, decorated with a few union banners and a portrait of Keir Hardie. I sat near the back, recognising no one except the little old man who'd once sold me the *Daily Worker*.

After some dull maundering from the union official, the pacifist lady stood up and introduced the speaker, the Argentine physician Dr Ernesto Lynch. A black-haired, bearded man, about forty, asthmatic, charismatic, apologetic about his cigar-smoking and his English, he brought the audience to their feet and sent me home in a fury.

'You're too gullible,' my father said. 'It's all just Communist propaganda.'

'Hiroshima, Nagasaki, Moscow, Magnitogorsk, Dien Bien Phu, Belgrade, Kinshasa!' I pounded the names with my fist on my palm. 'They happened! Nobody *denies* they happened!'

He lidded his eyes and looked at me through a veil of cigarette smoke. Bare elbows on the kitchen table, mother in the next room, the hiss of water on the iron, the Third Programme concerto in the background.

'If you had seen what I saw in Burma,' he said mildly, 'you wouldn't be so sorry about Hiroshima and Nagasaki. And the men who went into the Vorkuta camps weren't sorry about Moscow, and—'

'And what troops "liberated" Siberia?' I raged. 'The dirty Japs! With their hands still bloody from Vladivostok! Their hands *and* their—'

I stopped myself just in time.

'Look, John,' he said. 'We could go on shouting at each other all night about which side's atrocities are worse. The very fact that we can, that this Argentine johnny can tour the country and half the bloody Empire with his tales of heroic partisans in the Ukraine and sob stories about butchered villagers in Byelorussia, while nobody from our side could possibly do anything remotely similar in the Red territories, shows which side has the least to fear from the truth.'

'Britain didn't let the Nazis speak here during the war—William Joyce was hanged—'

He poured another whisky, and offered me one. I accepted it, ungraciously.

'We listened to Lord Haw-Haw and Tokyo Rose for a *laugh,*' he was saying. 'Then they were decently hanged, or decently jailed.'

'Pity we're on the same side now,' I said. 'Maybe the Yanks should let Tokyo Rose *out.* "Ruthki soldjah, you know what ith happening to you girrfliend? Big niggah boyth ith giving her big niggah—"'

Again, I shut up just in time.

'Your racial prejudices are showing, young man,' Malcolm said. 'I thought Reds were supposed to be against the colour bar.'

'Huh!' I snorted. 'I thought Liberals were!'

'The colour bar will come down in good time,' he said. 'When both whites and coloureds are ready for it. Meanwhile, the Reds will be happy to agitate against it, while out of the other side of their mouths they'll spout the most blatant racialism and national prejudice, just as it suits them—anything to divide the free world.'

'Some free world that includes the American South, South Africa, Spain, Japan, and the Fourth Reich! That holds on to Africa with atom bombs! That relies on the dirty work of Nazi scientists!'

He tapped a cigarette and looked at it meditatively.

'What do you mean by that?'

'The bombers. They're what's made the whole war possible, from Dropshot onwards, and it was the Germans who invented them—to finish what Hitler started!'

He lit up, and shook his head.

'Werner von Braun died a very disappointed man,' he said. 'Unlike the rocket scientists the Russians got. They got to see their infernal researches put to use all right, with dire consequences for our side—mostly civilian targets, I might add, since you seem so upset about bombing civilians. At least our bomber pilots risk their own lives, unlike the Russian missilemen who deal out death from hundreds of miles away.'

I could see what he was doing, deflecting our moral dispute into a purely intellectual, historical debate, and I was having none of it.

'Yeah, I wonder if the Yanks are still sending *children* up to fly the bombers.'

He almost choked on his sip of whisky. Through the open door of the living-room came the sound of the iron crashing to the floor and my mother's shout of annoyance. A moment later she said, sharply: 'James! Margaret! Off to bed!' A faint protest, a scurry, a slam. She bustled through, hot in her pinny, and closed the door and sat down. Her flush paled in seconds. My father glanced at her and said nothing.

They both looked so frightened that I felt scared myself.

'What's—what did—?'

My mother leaned forward and spoke quietly.

'Listen, Johnny,' she said. I bristled; she hadn't called me that for years. She sighed. 'John. You're old enough to do daft things. You could go off and join the Army tomorrow, or you could get married, and there's not a thing we could do about either. And it's the same with listening to Communists and repeating their rubbish. It's a free country. Ruin your prospects if you like. But there's one thing I ask you. Just one thing. Don't ever, ever, *ever* say anything about what you and your father saw in Aird. Don't even drop a hint. Because if you do, you'll ruin us all.'

'You never said this to me before!'

'Never thought we had to,' Malcolm said gruffly. 'You kept your mouth shut when you were a wee boy, as you promised, and good for you, and I thought that maybe over the years you had forgotten all about it.'

'How could I forget that?' I said.

He shrugged one shoulder.

'All right, all right,' I said. 'But I don't understand why it's such a big secret. I mean, surely the age or is it the *size* of the—'

My father leaned across the table and put his hand across my mouth —not as a gesture, as a physical shutting up.

'Not one word,' he said.

I leaned back and made wiping movements.

'OK, OK,' I said. 'Leave that aside. What were we talking about before? Oh yes, you were saying it wasn't the Nazis who invented the flying disc. So who do you think did?'

'Who knows? The Allies had Einstein and Oppenheimer and Turing and a lot of other very clever chaps, and it's all classified anyway, so, as I said—who knows?'

'How do you know it *wasn't* the Germans, then?'

'They weren't working along these lines.'

'Oh, come on!' I said. 'I've seen pictures of the things from during the war.'

'These were experimental circular airframes with entirely conventional propulsion,' he said. 'That doesn't describe the bombers, now does it? Have you ever heard of Nazi research into anti-gravity?'

'Have you ever heard of American?'

He shook his head.

'It's all classified, of course. But it was obviously a bigger breakthrough than the atomic bomb. Consider the Manhattan Project, and all the theory that led up to it.' He paused, to let this sink in. 'What I'd like you to do, John, is to use your head as well as keep your mouth shut. By all means rattle off the standard lefty rant about Nazi scientists, but do bear in mind that you're talking nonsense.'

I was baffled. My mother was looking worried.

'But,' I said, 'the *Americans* say it was German scientists who developed it.'

'They do indeed, John, they do indeed.'

He looked quite jovial; I think he was a little bit drunk.

'I think you've said enough,' my mother told him.

'That I have,' he said. 'Or too much. And you too, John. You have homework to do tonight and school to go to tomorrow. Goodnight.'

The following day I felt rather flat, whether as a result of the unaccustomed glass of whisky or my father's successful deflection of my moral outrage. After school I walked straight to the public library. My parents never worried if I didn't come home from school directly, so long as I phoned if I wasn't going to be home for my tea. The library was a big Georgian-style pile in the town centre. I stepped in and breathed the exhilarating smell of dark polished wood and of old and new paper. It took me only a minute to Dewey-decimal my way around the high stacks to the aviation section. Sheer nostalgia made me reach for the first in the row of tiny, well-worn editions of the *Observer's Book of Aircraft*. I still had that 1960 edition, somewhere at home. Flicking past the familiar silhouettes of Lancaster and Lincoln and MiG, I looked again at the simplest outline of the lot: the circular plan and lenticular profile of the Advanced High Altitude Bomber, Mark 1. The description and specifications were understandably sparse ('outperforms all other aircraft, Allied and enemy') the history routine: first successful test flight, from White Sands to Roswell Army Air Field, New Mexico, July 1947; first combat use, Operation Dropshot, September 1949; extensive use in all theatres since.

I replaced the volume and pulled out the fresh 1970 edition, its cover colour photo of a Brabant still glossy. The AHAB's description, specs, and history were identical, and identically uninformative, but the designation had changed. Checking back a couple of volumes, I found that the AHAB-2 had come into service in 1964.

It didn't take me much longer to find that the biggest military innovation of the previous year had been the Russian MiG-24, capable of reaching a much higher altitude than its predecessors. I sought traces of the AHAB in more detailed works, one of which stated that none had ever been shot down over enemy territory.

All of that got me thinking, but what struck me even more was that after more than twenty years there wasn't a dicky-bird about the machine's development, beyond the obviously (now that it was pointed out) misleading references to wartime German experimental aircraft. Nor were there any civilian or wider military applications of the revolutionary physical principles behind its anti-gravity engine.

I tried looking up anti-gravity, in other stacks: physics, military history, biography. Beyond the obvious fact that it was used in the AHAB, there was nothing. No speculation. No theory. No big names. No obscure names. Nothing. Fuck all.

I walked home with a heavy load of books and a head full of anti-gravity.

'Outer space,' said Ian Boyd, confidently. Four or five of us were sitting out a free period on our blazers on damp grass on the slope of the hill above the playing-field. Below us the fourth-year girls were playing hockey. Now and again a run or swerve would lift the skirt of one of them above her knees. We were here for these moments, and for the more reliable sight of their breasts pushing out their crisp white shirts.

'What d'ye mean, outer space?' asked Daniel Orr.

'Where they came frae. The flying discs.'

'Oh aye. Dan Dare stuff.'

'Don't you Dan Dare me, Dan Orr.'

This variant on a then-popular catch-phrase had us all laughing.

'We know there's life out there,' Ian persisted. 'Astronomers say there's at least lichens on Mars, they can see the vegetation spreading up frae the equator every year. An it's no that far fetched there's life on Venus an a', underneath the cloud cover.'

'No evidence of intelligent life, though,' Daniel said.

'No up there,' said Colin McNicol. 'There is down there.'

'Aye, there's life, but is it intelligent?'

We all laughed and concentrated for a while on the hockey-playing aliens, with their strange bodies and high-pitched cries.

'It's intelligent,' said Ian. 'The problem is, how dae we communicate?'

'No, the *first* problem is, how do we let them know we're friendly?'

'Tell them we come in peace.'

'And we want to come inside.'

'*If*,' I said, mercilessly mimicking our Classics teacher, 'you gentlemen are quite ready to return the conversation to serious matters—'

'This is serious a' right!'

'Future ae the entire human race!'

'Patience, gentlemen, patience. Withhold your ejaculations. Your curiosity on these questions will be soon be fully satisfied. The annual lecture on "Human Reproduction In One Minute" will be prematurely presented to the boys later this year by Mr Hughes, in his class on Anatomy, Physiology, and Stealth. The girls will simultaneously and separately receive a lecture on "Human Reproduction In Nine Months" as part of their Domestic Science course. Boys and girls are not allowed to compare notes until after marriage, or pregnancy, whichever comes sooner. Meanwhile, I understand that Professor Boyd here has a point to make.'

'Oh aye, well, if it wisni the Yanks an' it wisni the Jerries, it must hae come frae somewhere else—'

'The annual prize for Logic—'

'—so it must hae been the Martians.'

'—has just been spectacularly lost at the last moment by Professor Boyd, after a serious objection from Brother William of Ockham—'

'Hey, nae papes in our school!'

'—who presents him, instead, with the conical paper cap inscribed in memory of Duns Scotus, for the *non sequitur* of the year.'

Near the High School was a park with a couple of reservoirs. Around the lower of them ran a rough path, and its circumambulation was a customary means of working off the stodge of school dinner. A day or two after our frivolous conversation, I was doing this unaccompanied when I heard a hurrying step behind me, and turned to see Dan Orr catch me up. He was a slim, dark, intense youth who, though a month or two younger than me, had always seemed more mature. The growth of his limbs, unlike mine, had remained proportionate, and their movements under the control of the motor centres of his brain. His father was, I believe, an engineer at the Thompson yard.

'Hi, Matheson.'

'Greetings, Orr.'

'Whit ye were saying the other day.'

'About the bombers?'

'Naw.' He waved a hand. 'That's no an issue. We'll never find out, anyway, and between you an me I couldni give a flying fuck if they were invented by Hitler himsel, or the Mekon of Mekonta fir that matter.'

'That's a point of view, I suppose.' We laughed. 'So what is the issue?'

'Come on, Matheson, ye know fine well whit the issue is. It isnae where they *came* frae. It's where they *go,* and whit they *dae* to folk.'

'Aye,' I said cautiously.

'Ye were at that meeting, right?'

'How would you know if I was?'

'Yir face is as red as yir hair, ya big teuchter. But not as red as Willie Scott of the AEU, who was on the platform and gave a very full account o the whole thing tae his Party branch.'

'Good God!' I looked sideways at him, genuinely astonished. 'You're in the CP?'

'No,' he said. 'The Human Front.'

'Well kept secret,' I said.

He laughed. 'It's no a secret. I just keep my mouth shut at school for the sake o the old man.'

'Does he know about it?'

'Oh, aye, sure. He's Labour, but kindae a left winger. Anyway, Matheson, what did you think about what Dr Lynch had tae say?'

I told him.

'Well, fine,' he said. 'The question is, d'ye want tae dae something about it?'

'I've already put my name down to raise money for Medical Aid.'

'That's good,' he said. 'But it's no enough.'

We negotiated an awkward corner of the path, leaping a crumbled culvert. Orr ended up ahead of me.

'Dr Lynch,' he said over his shoulder, 'had some other things tae say, about what people can do. And we're discussing them tonight.' He named a cafe. 'Back room, eight sharp. Drop by if ye like. Up tae you.'

He ran on, leaving me to think.

Heaven knows what Orr was thinking of, inviting me to that meeting. The only hypothesis which makes sense is that he had shrewdly observed me over the years of our acquaintance, and knew me to be reliable. I need not describe the discussion here. Suffice it to say that it was in response to a document written by Lin Piao which Dr Lynch had clandestinely distributed during his tour, and which was later published in full as an appendix to various trial records. I was not aware of that at the time, and the actual matters discussed were of a quite elementary, and almost entirely legal, character, quite in keeping with the broad nature of the Front. It was only later that I was introduced to the harsher regimens in Dr Lynch's prescription.

We started small. Over the next few weeks, what time I could spare from studying for my Highers, in evenings, early mornings, and weekends, was taken up with covering the town's East End and most of Port Glasgow with the slogans and symbols of the Front, as well as some creative interpretations of our own.

FREE DUBCEK, we wrote on the walls of the Port Glasgow Municipal Cleansing works, in solidarity with a then-famous Czechoslovak guerrilla leader being held incommunicado by NATO. To the best of my knowledge it is still there, though time has worn the 'B' to a 'P'.

And, our greatest coup, on the enormous wall of the Thompson yard, in blazing white letters and tenacious paint that no amount of scrubbing could entirely erase:

FORGET KING BILLY AND THE POPE
UNCLE JOE'S OUR ONLY HOPE

The Saturday after the last of my Higher exams, I happened to be in the car with my father, returning from a predictably disastrous Morton match at Cappielow, when we passed that slogan. He laughed.

'I must say I agree with the first line,' he said. 'The second line, well, it takes me back. Good old Uncle Joe, eh? I must admit I left "Joe for King" on a few shit-house walls myself. Amazing that people still have faith in the old butcher.'

'But is it really?' I said. I told him of my long-ago (it seemed—seven years, my god!) playground scrap over the memory of Stalin.

'It's fair enough that he killed Germans,' Malcolm said. 'Or even that he killed Americans. The problem some people, you know, have with Stalin is that he killed *Russians,* in large numbers.'

'It was a necessary measure to prevent a counter-revolution,' I said stiffly.

Malcolm guffawed. 'Is that what they're teaching you these days? Well, well. What would have happened in the SU in the 30s if there had been a counter-revolution?'

'It would have been an absolute bloody massacre,' I said hotly. 'Especially of the Communists, and let's face it, they were the most energetic and educated people at the time. They'd have been slaughtered.'

'Damn right,' said Malcolm. 'So we'd expect—oh, let me see, most of the Red Army's generals shot? Entire cohorts of the Central Committee and the Politburo wiped out? Countless thousands of Communists killed, hundreds of thousands sent to concentration camps, along with millions of ordinary citizens? Honest and competent socialist managers and engineers and planners driven from their posts? The economy thrown into chaos by the turncoats and time-servers who replaced them? A brutal labour code imposed on the factory workers? Peasants rack-rented mercilessly? A warm handshake for Hitler? Vast tracts of the country abandoned to the fascist hordes? That the sort of thing you have in mind? That's what a counter-revolution would have been like, yes?'

'Something like that,' I said.

'That's exactly what happened, you dunderheid! Every last bit of it! Under Stalin!'

'How do we know that's not just propaganda from our side?'

'Here we go again,' he sighed. 'It's like arguing with a Free Presbyterian minister.'

'Come on,' I said. 'We know that a lot of what we're told in the press is lies. Look at the rubbish they were writing about how France was pacified, right up until the May Offensive! Look at—'

'Yes, yes,' he said. He pulled the car to a halt in the comfortable avenue where we lived, up by the golf course. He leaned back in his seat, took off his driving gloves and lit a cigarette.

'Look, John, let's not take this argument inside. It upsets your mother.'

'All right,' I said.

'You were saying about the press. Yes, it's quite true that a lot of lies are told about the war. I'll readily admit that, however much I still think the war is just. It was the same in the war with Hitler. Only to be expected. Censorship, misguided patriotism, wishful thinking—truth is the first casualty, and all that. So tell me this—who, in this country, has done the most to expose these lies?'

'Russell, I guess,' I said. After that I could only think of exiles and refugees from the ravaged Continent. 'And there's Sartre, and Camus, and Deutscher—'

'That's the man,' he said. 'Deutscher. Staunch Marxist. Former Communist. Respected alike by the *Daily Worker* and the *Daily Telegraph.* Man of the Left, man of integrity, right?'

'Yes,' I said, suspecting that he was setting me up for another fall. He was. When we went inside he handed me a worn volume from his study's bowed bookshelves.

Deutscher's *Stalin,* published in 1948, was a complete eye-opener to me. I had never before encountered criticism of Stalin or his regime from the Left, nor so measured a judgement and matchless a style. It seemed to come from a vanished world, the world before Dropshot, before the Fall.

'Fuck that,' said Dan Orr. 'Deutscher's a Trotskyite, for all that he's all right on the war. And Trotskyites are *scum.* I don't give a fuck how many o them Stalin killed. He didnae kill *enough.* There were still some alive tae be ministers in the Petrograd puppet government, alang wi all the Nazis and Ukrainian nationalists and NTS trash that the Yanks scraped out o the camps where they belonged.'

I didn't have an answer to that, at the time, so I shelved the matter. In any case we had more urgent decisions to make. Although we had not had our results yet, we both knew we had done well in our Highers, and could have gone straight to University the following September. This would have deferred our National Service until after graduation. Graduates could sign up for officer training. Most of our similarly successful classmates rejoiced at the opportunity to avoid the worst of the hardships and risks. Orr was adamant that we should not take it. It was a principle with him (and with the Front, and with the Young Communist League of which, unknown to me at the time, he was a clandestine member.)

'It's a blatant class privilege,' he said. 'Every working-class laddie has tae go as soon as he turns eighteen. Why should we be allowed tae dodge the column for four mair years? What gies us the right tae a cushy number? And think about it—when we've done our stint that'll be it over, we can get on wi university wi none o that growing worry about what's at the end o it, and in the meantime we'll hae learned to use a rifle and we can look every young worker in the eye, because we'll hae been through the same shit as he has.'

'But,' I said, 'suppose we find ourselves shooting at the freedom fighters?'

Or shot by them, was what was really worrying me.

'Cannae be helped,' said Orr. He laughed. 'I'm told it seldom comes tae that anyway. It's no like in the comics.'

My mother objected, my father took a more fatalistic approach. There was a scene, but I got my way.

We spent the summer working to earn some spending money and hopefully put some by in our National Savings Accounts. In the permanent war economy it was easy enough to walk into a job. Orr, ironically enough, became a hospital porter for a couple of months, while I became a general labourer in the Thompson yard. We joked that we were working for each other's fathers.

The shipyard astounded me, in its gargantuan scale, its danger and din, and its peculiar combination of urgent pace and trivial delay. The unions were strong, management was complacent, work practices were restrictive and work processes were primitive. Parts of it looked like an Arab *souk,* with scores of men tapping copper pipes and sheets with little hammers over braziers. My accent had me marked instantly as a teuchter, a Highlander, which though humiliating was at least better than being written off as middle class. The older men had difficulty understanding me—I thought at first that this was an accent or language problem, and tried to conform to the Clydeside usage to ridiculous effect, until I realised that they were in fact partially deaf and I took to shouting in Standard English, like an ignorant tourist.

The Party branch at the yard must have known I was in the Front, but made no effort to approach me: I think there was a policy, at the time, of keeping students and workers out of each other's way. This backfired rather because it enabled me to encounter my first real live Trotskyist, who rather disappointingly was a second-year student working there for the summer. We had a lot of arguments. I have nothing more to say about that.

Most days after work I'd catch the bus to Nelson Street, slog up through the West End to our house, have a bath and sleep for half an hour before a late tea. If I had any energy left I would go out, ostensibly for a pint or two but more usually for activity for the Front. The next stage in its escalating campaign, after having begun to make its presence both felt and over-estimated, was to discourage collaboration. This included all forms of fraternisation with American service personnel.

Port Glasgow is to the east of Greenock, Gourock to the west. The latter town combines a douce middle-class residential area and a louche seafront playground. Its biggest dance-hall, the Cragburn, a landmark piece of 30s architecture with a famously spring-loaded dance floor, draws people from miles around.

Orr and I met in the Ashton Cafe one Friday night in July. Best suits, Brylcreemed hair; scarves in our pockets. Hip-flask swig and gasper puff on the way along the front. The Firth was in one of its Mediterranean moments, gay-spotted with yachts and dinghies, grey-speckled with warships. Pound notes at the door. A popular beat combo, then a swing band.

We chose our target carefully, and followed her at distance after the dance. Long black hair down her back. She kissed her American sailor goodbye at the pier, waved to him as the liberty-boat pulled away. We caught up with her at a dark stretch of Shore Street, in the vinegar smell of chip-shops. Scarves over our noses and mouths, my hand over her mouth. Bundled her into an alley, up against the wall. We didn't need the masks, not really. She couldn't look away from Orr's open razor.

'Listen, slag,' he said. 'Youse are no tae go out wi anybody but yir ain folk frae now on. Get it? Otherwise we'll cut ye.'

Tears glittered on her thick mascara. She attempted a nod.

'Something tae remind ye,' Orr said. 'And tae explain tae yir friends.'

He clutched her hair and cut it off with the razor, as close to the scalp as he could get. He threw the glistening hank at her feet and we ran before she could get out her first sob.

I threw up on the way home.

Three days later I overheard two lassies at the bus-stop. They were discussing the incident, or one like it. There had been several such, over the weekend, all the work of the Front.

'Looks like you're in deid trouble fae now on,' one of them concluded, 'if ye go out wi coons.'

Call-up papers arrived in August, an unwelcome 18th-birthday present. After nine weeks' basic training I was sent to Northern Ireland, where I spent the rest of my two-year stint guarding barracks, munitions dumps and coastal installations. Belfast, Londonderry, south Armagh: the most peaceful and friendly parts of the British Empire.

Orr was sent to Rhodesia. His grave is in the Imperial War Cemetery in Salisbury.

I was demobilised in September 1974, and went to Glasgow University. My fellow first-year students were all two years younger than me, including those in the Front. The Party line had changed. Young men were being urged to resist the war, to refuse conscription, to take any deferral available, to burn their call-up papers if necessary, to fill the jails. This was not because the Party had become pacifist. It was because the Party, and the Front, now had enough men with military experience for the next step up Lin Piao's ladder.

People's War.

It is necessary to understand the situation at the time. By 1974 the United States, Britain and the white Dominions, Germany, Spain, Portugal and Belgium were almost the only countries in the world without a raging guerrilla war. Although nominally on the Allied side, the governments of France and Italy were paralysed, large tracts of both countries ungovernable or already governed by the Resistance movements. Every colony had its armed independence movement, and every former socialist country had its re-liberated territory and provisional government, even if driven literally underground by round-the-clock bombing.

'The peoples of the anti-imperialist camp long for peace every day,' wrote Lin Piao. 'Why do the peoples of the imperialist camp not long for peace? Unfortunately it is because they have no idea of what horrors are being suffered by the majority of the peoples of the world. It is necessary to bring the real state of affairs sharply to their attention. In order for the masses to irresistibly demand that the troops be brought home, it is necessary for the people's vanguard to bring home the war.'

That later came to be called the Lin Piao 'Left' Deviation. At the time it was called the line. I swallowed it whole.

I lodged in a bed-sitting-room in Glasgow, near the University, and took my laundry home at weekends. During my National Service I had only been able to visit occasionally, and had followed the Front's advice to keep my head down and my mouth shut about politics, on duty or off. It was a habit that I found agreeable, and I kept it. My parents assumed that my National Service had knocked all that nonsense out of me.

Greenock had changed. The younger and tougher and more numerous successors of the likes of Orr and I had shifted their attacks from the sailors' girlfriends to the sailors, and the soldiers. They never attacked British servicemen, or even the police. At least a dozen Americans had been fatally stabbed, and two shot. Relations between the Americans and the town's population, hitherto friendly, had become characterised by suspicion on one side and resentment on the other. The cycle was self-reinforcing. Before long Americans were being attacked in quite non-political brawls, and off-duty Marines were picking fights with surly teenagers. The teenagers' angry parents would seek revenge. Other relatives would be drawn in. Before long an American serviceman couldn't be sure that any sweet-looking lass or little old lady wasn't an enemy.

Armed shore patrols in jeeps became a much more common sight. In the tougher areas, kids would throw stones at them. None of this was covered in the national press, and the *Greenock Telegraph* buried such accounts in brief reports of the proceedings of the Sheriff Court, but the *Daily Worker* reported similar events around US bases right across Britain.

I did not get involved in them. The first petrol-bombing, in January 1975, happened when I was in Glasgow. The first return fire from a group of US naval officers trapped in a stalled and surrounded staff car on the coast road—they'd started going further afield, to the quieter, smaller resort of Largs—took place in February, also mid-week, when I was definitely not in Greenock. I read a brief report of it in the *Glasgow Herald.*

What was going on in Glasgow was political stuff, anti-war agitation, leafleting and picketing, that sort of thing. We took a hundred people from Glasgow to the big autumn demo in London. A hundred thousand or so converged on Grosvenor Square, with a militant contingent of ten thousand people chanting 'We shall fight! We shall win!' (we all agreed on that) and the Front's hotheads following it up with 'Joe! Joe! Joe Sta-lin!' or 'Long live Chairman Lin!' and the Trots trying to drown us out with a roar of 'London! Paris! Rome! Berlin!'

It was fun. I was serious. I knuckled down to the study of chemistry and physics (at Glasgow they still called the latter 'Natural Philosophy') which had always fascinated me. The Officer Training Corps would have been a risky proposition for me—even my very limited public political activity would have exposed me to endless hassles and security checks—but I joined the university's rifle club, which shared a shooting range and an armoury with the OTC. And I was still, of course, in the Reserves. Following the Front's advice, I kept out of trouble and bided my time.

I had seen the diagram a hundred times, and its physical manifestation, the iron filings forming furry field-lines on a sheet of paper with a magnet under it, in my first-year physics class at High School. I had balanced magnets on top of each other, my fingers preventing them from flicking around and clicking together, and had felt the uncanny invisible spring pushing them apart. It was late one night in February 1975 when I was alone in my room, propping my head over an open physics textbook, that I first connected that sensation with my childhood chance observation of the curiously unstable motion of an anti-gravity bomber close to the ground, and with the magnetic field lines.

Was it possible, I wondered, that anti-gravity was a polar opposite of gravity, that keeping it stable was like balancing two magnets one upon the other, and that the field generated by the ship had the same shape as that of a magnet? If so, any missile approaching an AHAB bomber from above or below would be deflected, whereas one directed precisely at its edge, where the two poles of the field balanced, might well get through. The crippled bomber I'd seen had taken a hit edge-on, if that distant memory was reliable. The chance of that happening accidentally, even in a long war, might be slim enough for to have happened only once. Yet the consequences of doing it deliberately were so awesome that this very possibility might well be the secret which the dark-suited security men had been so anxious to maintain. It seemed much more significant than the minor, if grim, detail that the pilots were children or dwarfs.

It was an interesting thought, and I considered whether it might be possible to pass it upward through the Front and thence across to the revolutionary air forces. Come to think of it, to pass on all I knew, and all I'd seen at Aird. The thought made me shiver. I could not get away from the idea, so firmly instilled by my parents, that anything I might say along those lines would be traced back to me, and to them.

The Allied states, and Britain in particular, had at the time a sharp discontinuity in tolerance—their liberal and democratic self-definition almost forced them to put up with radical opposition, and to treat violent opposition as civil disorder rather treason; while at the same time the necessities of the long war inclined them to totalitarian methods of maintaining military and state secrecy. A Front supporter could preach defeatism openly, and would receive at the worst police harassment and mob violence. A spy, or anyone under suspicion of materially aiding the enemy, would disappear and never be heard of again, or be summarily tried and executed. Rumours of torture cells and concentration camps proliferated. To what extent these were true was hard to judge, but irrelevant to their effect.

So I kept my theory to myself, and sought confirmation or refutation of it in war memoirs. Most from the Red side were stilted and turgid. Those from former Allied soldiers were usually better written, even if sensationalised. If these accounts were reliable at all, the AHAB bombers were occasionally used for close air support and even medevac, in situations where (as my careful cross-checking made clear) there was little actual fighting in the vicinity and the weather was too violent for helicopters or other conventional aircraft.

I put my ideas about that on the back burner and got on with my work, until the Front had work for me. I left my studies without regret. It was like another call-up, and another calling.

Davey stopped screaming when the morphine jab kicked in. Blood was still soaking from his trouser-leg all over the back seat of the stolen getaway car. He'd taken a high-velocity bullet just below the knee. Whatever was holding his shin on, it wasn't bone. In the yellow back-street sodium light all our faces looked sick and strange, but his was white. He sprawled, head and trunk in the rear footwell, legs on the back seat. I crouched beside him, holding the tourniquet, only slowing down the blood loss.

Andy, in the driver's seat, looked back over his shoulder.

'Take him tae the hospital?'

It was just up the road—we were parked, engine idling, in a back lane by the sugarhouse. The molasses smell was heavy, the fog damp and smoky.

'We could dump him and run,' Gordon added pointedly, looking out and not looking back.

Save his leg and maybe his life for prison or an internment camp. No chance. But the Front's clandestine field hospitals were already overloaded tonight—we knew that from the news on the car radio alone.

'West End,' I said. 'Top of South Street.'

Andy slid the car into gear and we slewed the corner, drove up past the hospital and the West Station and around the roundabout at a legal speed that had me seething, even though I knew it was necessary. No Army patrols in this part of town, but there was no point in getting pulled by the cops for a traffic offence.

We stopped in a dark spot around the corner from my parents' house. Andy drove off to dump the car and Gordon and I lugged Davey through a door in a wall, past the backs of a couple of gardens, over a fence and into the back porch. I still had the keys. It had been two years since I'd last used them.

Balaclava off, rifle left behind the doorway, into the kitchen, light on. Somebody was already moving upstairs. I heard the sound of a shotgun breech closing.

'Malcolm!' I shouted, past the living-room door. 'It's just me!'

He made some soothing sounds, then said something firmer, and padded downstairs and appeared in the living-room doorway, still knotting his dressing-gown. His face looked drawn in pencil, all grey lines. Charcoal shadows under the eyes. He started towards me.

'You're hurt!'

'It's not my blood,' I said.

His mouth thinned. 'I see,' he said. 'Bring him in. Kitchen floor.'

Gordon and I laid Davey out on the tiles, under the single fluorescent tube. The venetian blind in the window was already closed. My father reappeared, with his black bag. He washed his hands at the sink, stepped aside.

'Kettle,' he said.

I filled it and switched it on. He was scissoring the trouser-leg.

'Jesus Christ,' he said. 'Get this man to a hospital. I'm not a surgeon.'

'No can do,' I said. 'Do what you can.'

'I can stop him going into shock, and I can clean up and bandage.' He looked up at me. 'Top left cupboard. Saline bag, tube, needle.'

I held the saline drip while he inserted the needle. The kettle boiled. He sterilised a scalpel and forceps, tore open a bag of sterile swabs, and got to work quickly. After about five minutes he had Davey's wound cleaned and bandaged, the damaged leg splinted and both legs up on cushions on the floor. A dose of straight heroin topped up the morphine.

'Right,' Malcolm said. 'He'll live. If you want to save the leg, he must get to surgery right away.'

He glared at us. 'Don't you bastards have field hospitals?'

'Overloaded,' I said.

His nose wrinkled. 'Busy night, huh?'

Davey was coming to.

'Take me in,' he said. 'I'll no talk.'

My father looked down at him.

'You'll talk,' he said; then, after a deep breath that pained him somehow: 'But I won't. I'll take him to the Royal, swear I saw him caught in crossfire.' He looked out at the rifles in the back porch, and frowned at me. 'Any powder on him?'

I shook my head, miserably.

'We didn't even get a shot in ourselves.'

'Too bad,' he said dryly. 'Right, you come with me, and you, mister,' he told Gordon, 'get yourself and your guns out of here before I see you, or them.'

Gordon glanced at me. I nodded.

'Through the cemetery,' I said.

I only just remembered to remove the revolver from Davey's jacket pocket. My mother suddenly appeared, gave me a tearful but silent hug, and started mopping the floor.

We straightened out a story on the way down, and I disappeared out of the car while my father went inside and got a couple of orderlies out with a stretcher. Ambulances came and went, sirens blaring, lights flashing. A lot of uniforms about. By this time we were fighting the Brits as well as the Yanks. After a few minutes Malcolm returned, and I stepped out of the shadows and slid into the car.

'They bought it,' he said. He lit a cigarette and coughed horribly. 'Back to the house for a minute? Talk to your mother?'

'Dangerous for us all,' I said. 'If you could drop me off up at Barr's Cottage, I'd appreciate it. Otherwise, I'll hop out now.'

'I'll take you.'

Past the station again, at a more sedate pace.

'Thank you,' I said, belatedly. 'For everything.'

He grinned, keeping his eye on the road. '"First, do no harm",' he said. 'Sort of thing.'

He drove in silence for a minute, around the roundabout and out along Inverkip Road. The walls and high trees of the cemetery passed on the right. Gordon was probably picking his way through the middle of it by now.

'I'll give her your love,' he said. 'Yes?'

'Yes,' I said.

'Won't be seeing you again for another couple of years?'

'If that,' I answered, bleakly if honestly.

He turned off short of Barr's Cottage, into a council estate, and pulled in, under a broken streetlamp. The glow from another cigarette lit his face.

'All right,' he said. 'I have something to tell you.'

Another sigh, another bout of coughing.

'You may not see me again. Your mother doesn't know this yet, but I've got six months. If that.'

'Oh, God,' I said.

'Cancer of the lung,' he said. 'Lot of it about. Filthy air around here.' He crushed out the cigarette. 'Stick to rural guerrilla warfare in future, old chap. It's healthier than the urban variety.'

'I'll fight where I'm—'

His face blurred. I sobbed on his shoulder.

'Enough,' he said. He held me away, gently.

'There's no pain,' he assured me. 'Whisky, tobacco, and heroin, three great blessings. And as the Greek said, nothing is terrible when you know that being nothing is not terrible. I'll know when to ease myself out.'

'Oh, God,' I said again, very inaptly.

His yellow teeth glinted. 'I have no worries about meeting my maker. But, ah, I do have something on my conscience. A monkey on my back, which I want to offload on yours.'

'All right,' I said.

He leaned back and closed his eyes.

'Another time I treated a leg with a very similar injury...' he said. 'You were there then, too. You were much smaller, and so was the patient. You do remember?'

'Of course,' I said. My knees were shaking.

His eyes opened and he stared out through the windscreen.

'The last time we discussed this,' he said, 'I suggested that you look into the origin of the bomber. No doubt you have read some books, given the matter thought, and drawn your own conclusions.'

'Yes,' I said, 'I certainly have, it's a—'

He held up one hand. 'Keep it,' he said. 'I've had a lot longer to think about the origin of the pilot. My first thought was the same as yours, that it was a child. Then, when I got, ah, a closer look, I must confess that my second thought was that I was seeing the work of...another Mengele. The grey skin, the four digits on hands and feet, the huge eyes, the coppery colour of the blood...I thought for years that this was the result of some perverted Nazi science, you know. But, like you, I've read a great deal since. And as a medical man, I know what can and can't be done. No rare syndrome, no surgery, no mutation, no foul tinkering with the germ-plasm could have made that body. It was not a deformed human body. It was a perfectly healthy, normal body, but it was not human.'

He turned to me, shaking his head. 'The memory plays tricks, of course. But in retrospect, and even taking that into account, I believe that the pilot was not only not human, but not mammalian. I'm not even sure that he was a *vertebrate*. The bones in the leg were—'

His cheek twitched. 'Like broken plastic, and hollow. Thin-walled, and filled with rigid tubes and struts rather than spongy bone and marrow.'

I felt like giggling.

'You're saying the pilot was from *another planet?*'

'No,' he said, sharply. 'I'm not. I'm telling you what I *saw.*' He waved a hand, his cigarette tip tracing a jiggly red line. 'For all I know, the pilot may be a specimen of some race of intelligent beings that evolved on Earth and lurks unseen in the depths of the fucking Congo, or the Himalayas, like the Abominable Snowman!'

He laughed, setting off another wheezing cough.

'So there it is, John. A secret I won't be taking to the grave.'

We talked a bit more, and then I got out of the car and watched the tail-lights disappear around a corner.

Scotland is not a good country for rural guerrilla warfare, having been long since stripped of trees and peasants. Without physical or social shelter, any guerrilla band in the hills and glens would be easily spotted and picked off, if they hadn't starved first. The great spaces of the Highlands were militarily irrelevant anyway.

So everybody believed, until the guerrilla war. Night, clouds and rain, gullies, boulders, bracken, isolated clumps of trees, the few real forests, burns and bridges and bothies all provided cover. The relatively sparse population could do little to betray us and—voluntarily or otherwise—much to help, and supplied few targets for enemy reprisals against civilians. Deer, sheep and rabbits abounded, edible wild plants and berries grew everywhere, and vegetables were easily enough bought or stolen. The strategic importance of the coastline and the offshore oilfields, and the vulnerability and propaganda value of the larger towns—Fort William, Inverness, Aberdeen, Thurso—compelled the state's armed forces to hold the entire enormous area: to move troops and armour along the long, narrow moorland roads, through glens ideal for ambush, and to fly low over often-clouded hills; to guard hydroelectric power stations, railways, microwave relay masts, the military's own installations and training-grounds; to patrol hundreds of miles of pipelines and cables.

That was just the Highlands: the area where I was, for obvious reasons, sent. Those who fought in the Borders, the Pentlands, the Southwest, and even the rich farmland of Perthshire all discovered other options, other opportunities. And that is to say nothing of what the English and Welsh comrades were doing. By 1981 the Front was making the country burn. The line had changed—Deng Hsiao-Ping was making cautious advances in the Versailles negotiations—but the fighting continued and we felt proud that we had fulfilled the late Chairman's directive. We had brought home the war.

The Bren was heavy and the pack was heavier. I was almost grateful that I had to move slowly. Moving under cloud cover was frustrating and dangerous. Visibility that October morning was a couple of metres; the clouds were down to about a hundred, and there was a storm on the way. Behind me nine men followed in line, down from the ridge. I found the bed of a burn, just a trickle at that moment, its boulders and pebbles slick and slippery from the rain of a week earlier. We made our way down this treacherous stairway from the invisible skyline we'd crossed. The first *glomach* I slipped into soaked me to the thighs.

I waded out and moved on. My ankle would have hurt if it hadn't been so cold. The light brightened and quite suddenly I was below the cloud layer, looking down at the road and the railway line at the bottom of the glen, and off to my right and to the west, a patch of meadow on the edge of a small loch with a crannog in the middle. Three houses, all widely separated, were visible up and down the glen. We knew who lived there, and they knew we knew. There would be no trouble from them. Just ahead of us was a ruined barn, a rectangle of collapsed drystone walling within which rowans grew and rusty sheets of fallen corrugated iron roofing sheltered nettles and brambles.

We'd come down at the right place. A couple of hundred metres to the left, a railway bridge crossed the road at an awkward zigzag bend. The bridge had been mined the previous night; the detonation cable should be snaking back to the ruined barn. A train was due in an hour and ten minutes. Our job was to bring down the bridge, giving the train just enough time to stop—civilian casualties weren't necessary for this operation. We intended to levy a revolutionary tax on the passengers and any valuable goods in transit before turning them out on the road and sending the empty train over where the bridge had been, thus blocking the road and railway and creating an ambush chokepoint for any soldiers or cops who sent to the scene. Booby-trapping the wreckage would be gravy, if we had the time.

I waved forward next man behind me, and he did likewise, and one by one we all emerged from the fog and hunkered down behind the lip of a shallow gully. Andy and Gordon were there, they'd been with me since the street-fighting days in Greenock. Of the others, three—Sandy and Mike and Neil—were also from Clydeside and four were local (from our point of view—in their own eyes Ian from Strome and Murdo from Torridon and Donald from Ullapool and Norman from Inverness were almost as distinct from each other in their backgounds as they were from ours.)

'Tormod,' I said to Norman, 'you go and check out the bothy there, give us a wave if the electrician has done his job right. Two if he hasn't. Lie low and wait for the signal.'

'There's no signal.'

'The fucking whistle. My whistle.'

'Oh, right you are.'

Crouching, he ran to the ruin, and waved once after a minute. I sent Andy half a mile up the line to the nearest cutting, with a walkie-talkie, ready to confirm that the train had passed, and deployed the others on both sides of the bridge and both sides of the road. Apart from watching for any premature trouble, and being ready to raid the train when it had stopped, they were to stop any civilian vehicles that might chance to go under the bridge at the wrong moment. A light drizzle began to fall, and a front of heavier rain was marching up the glen from the west. Still about five miles distant, but with a good blow behind it, the opening breezes of which were already chilling my wet legs.

I had just settled myself and the Bren and the walkie-talkie behind a boulder on the hillside overlooking the bridge, with half an hour to spare before the train was due to pass at 12.11, when I heard the sound of a train far up the glen to the east. I couldn't see it, none of us could, except maybe Andy. I called him up.

'Passenger train,' he said. 'Wait a minute, it's got a couple of goods wagons at the back—shit, no! It's low-loaders! They've carrying two tanks!'

'Troop train,' I guessed. 'Maybe. Confirm when it passes.'

'I can check it frae here wi the glasses.'

He did, but still couldn't be certain.

Two minutes crawled by. The sound of the train filled the glen, or seemed to, until a sheep bleated nearby, startlingly loud. The radio crackled.

'Confirmed brown job,' said Andy, just as the train emerged from the cutting and into view. It wasn't travelling very fast, maybe just over twenty miles per hour.

I had a choice. I could let this one pass, and continue with the operation, or I could seize this immensely dangerous chance to wreak far more havoc than we'd planned.

I watched the train pass below me, waited until the engine had crossed the bridge, and blew the whistle. Norman didn't hesitate. The blast came when the third carriage of the train was on the bridge. It utterly failed to bring the bridge down, but it threw that carriage upwards and sideways, off the rails. It ploughed through the bridge parapet and its front end crashed on to the road. The remaining four carriages concertina'd into its rear end. One of them rolled on to the embankment, the one behind that was derailed, and the two tank-transporting flatbeds remained on the track.

The engine, and the two front carriages, had by this time travelled a quarter of a mile further down the track, and were accelerating rapidly away. There was nothing that could be done about that. I opened fire at once on the wreck, raking the bursts along the carriage windows. The rest of the squad followed up, then, like myself, they must have ducked down to await return fire.

In the silence that followed the crash and the firing, other noises gradually became audible. Among the screams and yells from the wreckage were the shouts of command. Within seconds a spatter of rifle and pistol fire started up. I raised my head cautiously, watched for the flashes, and directed single shots from the Bren in their direction.

Silence again. Neil and Murdo reported in on the walkie-talkie from the other side of the track, and up ahead a bit. They'd each hit one or two attempts at rescue work or flight. We seemed to have the soldiers on the train pinned down. At the same time it was difficult for us to break cover ourselves. In any sustained exchange of fire we were likely to be the first to run out of ammunition, and then to be picked off as we ran.

This impasse was brought to an end after half an hour by a torrential downpour and a further descent of the clouds. The scheduled train, either cancelled or forewarned, hadn't arrived. Any cars arriving at the scene had backed off and turned away, unmolested by us. We regrouped by the roadside, west of the bridge, well within earshot of the carriage that had crashed on the road.

'This is murder,' said Norman.

I was well aware of the many lives my decision had just ended or wrecked. I had no compunction about that, being even more aware of how many lives we had saved at the troops' destination.

'Seen any white flags, have you?' I snarled. 'Until you do, we're still fighting.'

'Only question is,' said Andy, 'do we pull back now while we're ahead?'

'There'll be rescue and reinforcement coming for sure,' said Murdo. 'The engine could come steaming back any minute, for one thing.'

'They're probably over-estimating us,' I said, thinking aloud in the approved democratic manner. 'I mean, who'd be mad enough to attack a troop train with ten men?'

We laughed, huddled in the pouring rain. The windspeed was increasing by the minute.

'There'll be no air support in this muck,' said Sandy.

'All the same,' I said, 'our best bet is to pull out now, we have the chance and there's nothing more to—wait a minute. What about the tanks?'

'Can't do much damage to them,' said Mike.

'Aye,' I said, 'but think of the damage we can do *with* them.'

It was easy. It was ridiculously, pathetically, trivially easy. Four of us had National Service experience with tanks, so we split into two groups and after firing a few shots to keep the enemy's heads down we knocked the shackles off the chains and commandeered both tanks. They were fuelled and armed, ready for action. We crashed them off the sides of the flatbeds and drove them perilously down the steep slope to the road, shelled the train, drove under the bridge, shelled the train again, then shelled the bridge. Then we drove over the tracks and around the back of the now-collapsed bridge and a couple of miles up the road, and off to one side, and when the relief column arrived—a dozen troop trucks and four armoured cars—we started shelling that.

By mid-afternoon we'd inflicted hundreds of casualties and had the remaining troops and vehicles completely pinned down. Reinforcements from our side began to arrive, pouring fire from the ridges into the glen, raiding more weapons and ammunition from the train and the relief column; and then attacking *its* relief column. The battle of Glen Carron was turning into the biggest engagement of the war in the British Isles. The increasingly appalling weather was entirely to our advantage, although my squad, at least, were on the point of pneumonia from the soaking we'd got earlier.

The first we knew of the bomber's arrival was when we lost contact with the men on the ridge. A minute later, I saw through the periscope the other tank—a few hundred metres away at the time—take a direct hit. That erupting flash of earth and metal told me without a doubt that Gordon was dead, along with Ian, Mike, Sandy and Norman.

'Reverse reverse reverse!' I shouted.

Murdo slammed us into reverse gear and hit the accelerator, throwing me painfully forward as we shot up a slope and into a birch-screened gully. The tank lurched upward as the bomb missed us by about twenty metres, then crashed back down on its tracks.

Blood poured from my brow and lip.

'Everybody all right?' I yelled.

No reply. Silence. I looked down and saw Andy tugging my leg, mouthing and nodding. He pointed to his ears. I grimaced acknowledgement and looked again through the periscope and saw the bomber descend towards the road just across the glen from us, by one of the trapped columns. Five hundred metres away, and exactly level with us.

There was a shell in the chamber. I swivelled the turret and racked the gun as hearing returned through a raging ringing in my ears, just in time to be deafened again as I fired. My aim was by intuition, with no use of the sights, pure Zen like a perfect throw of a stone. I knew it was going to hit, and it did.

The bomber shot upwards, skimmed towards us, then fluttered down to settle athwart the river at the bottom of the glen, just fifty metres away and ten metres below us, lying there like a fucking enormous landmine in our path.

I poked Murdo's shoulder with my foot and he engaged the forward gear. Andy set up a bit of suppressing fire with the machine-gun. We slewed to a halt beside the bomber. I grabbed a Bren, threw open the hatch and clambered through and jumped down. My ears were still ringing. The wind was fierce, the rain an instant skin-soaking, the wind-chill terrible. Water poured off the bomber like sea off a surfacing submarine. There was a smell of peat-bog and metal and crushed myrtle. Smoke drifted from a ragged notch in its edge, similar to the one on the crippled bomber I'd seen all those years ago.

I walked around the bomber, warily leaping past the snouts of machine-guns in its rim. With the Bren's butt I banged the hatch. The thing rang like a bell, even louder than my tinitus.

The hatch opened. I stood back and levelled the Bren. A big visored helmet emerged, then long arms levered up a torso, and then the hips and legs swung up and out. The pilot slid down the side of the bomber and stood in front of me, arms raised high. Very slowly, the hands went to the helmet and lifted it off.

A cascade of blonde hair shook loose. The pilot was incredibly beautiful and she was about seven feet tall.

We left the tank sabotaged and blocking the road about five miles to the west, and took off into the hills. Through the storm and the gathering dusk we struggled to a lonely safe-house, miles from anywhere. Our prisoner was tireless and silent. Her flying-suit was dark green and black, to all appearances standard for an American pilot, right down to the badges. She carried her helmet and knotted her hair deftly at her nape. Her Colt .45 and Bowie knife she surrendered without protest.

The safe house was a gamekeeper's lodge, with a kitchen and a couple of rooms, the larger of which had a fireplace. Dry wood was stacked on the hearth. We started the fire and stripped off our wet clothes—all of our clothes—and hung them about the place, then one by one we retrieved dry clothes from the stash in the back room. The prisoner observed us without a blink, and removed her own flying-suit. Under it she was wearing a closer-fitting garment of what looked like woven aluminium, with tubes running under its surface. It covered a well-proportioned female body. Too well-proportioned, indeed, for the giant she was. She sprawled on the worn armchair by the fire and looked at us, still silent, and carefully untied her wet hair and let it fall down her back.

Murdo, Andy, Neil and Donald huddled in front of the fire. I stood behind them, holding the prisoner's pistol.

'Donald,' I said, 'you take the first look-out. You'll find oilskins in the back. Neil, make some tea, and give it to Donald first.'

'Three sugars, if we have it,' said Donald, getting up and padding through to the other room. Neil disappeared into the kitchen. Sounds of him fiddling with and cursing the little gas stove followed. The prisoner smiled, for the first time. Her pale features were indeed beautiful, but somewhat angular, almost masculine; her eyes were a distinct violet, and very large.

'Talk,' I told her.

'Jodelle Smith,' she said. 'Flight-Lieutenant. Serial number...' She rattled it off.

The voice was deep, for a woman, but soft, the American accent perfect. Donald gave her a baleful glare as he headed for the door and the storm outside it.

'All right,' I said. 'We are not signatories to the Geneva Convention. We do not regard you as a prisoner of war, but as a war criminal, an air pirate. You have one chance of being treated as a prisoner of war, with all the rights that go with that, and that is to answer all our questions. Otherwise, we will turn you over to the nearest revolutionary court. They're pretty biblical around here. They'll probably stone you to death.'

I don't know how the lads kept a straight face through all that. Perhaps it was the anger and grief over the loss of our friends and comrades, the same feeling that came out in my own voice. I could indeed have wished her dead, but otherwise I was bluffing—there were no revolutionary courts in the region, and anyway our policy with prisoners was to disarm them, attempt to interrogate them, and turn them loose as soon as it was safe to do so.

The pilot sat silent for a moment, head cocked slightly to one side, then shrugged and smiled.

'Other bomber pilots have been captured,' she said. 'They've all been recovered unharmed.' She straightened up in the chair, and leaned forward. 'If you're not satisfied with the standard name, rank, and serial number, I'm happy to talk to you about anything other than military secrets. What would you like to know?'

I glanced at the others. I had never shared my father's story, or my own, with any of them, and I was glad of that now because the appearance of this pilot would have discredited it. Compared with what my father had described, she looked human. Compared with most people, she looked very strange.

'Where do you really come from?' I asked.

'Venus,' she said.

The others all laughed. I didn't.

'What happened to the other kind of pilots?' I asked. I held out one hand about a metre above the ground, as though patting a child's head.

'Oh, we took over from the Martians a long time ago,' she told us earnestly. 'They're still involved in the war, of course, but they're not on the front line any more. The Americans found their appearance disconcerting, and concealing them became too much of a hassle.'

I glared down the imminent interruptions from my men.

'You're saying there are two alien species fighting on the American side?'

'Yes,' she said. She laughed suddenly. 'Greys are from Mars, blondes are from Venus.'

'Total fucking *cac,*' said Neil. 'She's a Yank. They're always tall. Better food.'

'Maybe she is,' I said, 'but she is not the kind of pilot I was expecting. And I've seen one of the other kind. My father saw it up close.'

The woman's eyebrows went up.

'The Aird incident? 1964?'

I nodded.

'Ah,' she said. 'Your father must be...Dr Malcolm Donald Matheson, and you are his son, John.'

'How the hell do you know that?'

'I've read the reports.'

'This is insane,' said Andy. 'It's some kind of trick, it's a trap. We shouldnae say another word, or listen tae any.'

'There's eggs and bacon and tatties in the kitchen,' I said. 'See if you can make yourself useful.'

He glowered at me and stalked out.

'But he's right, you know,' I said, loud enough for Andy to overhear. 'We are going to have to send you up a level or two, for interrogation, as soon as the storm passes. Will you still talk then?'

She spread her hands. 'On the same basis as I've spoken to you, yes. No military secrets.'

'Aye, just disinformation,' said Murdo. 'You're not telling us that it wouldn't be a military secret if the Yanks really were getting help from *outer space?* But making people believe it, now, that would be worth something. Christ, it's enough of a job fighting the Americans. Who would fight the fucking Martians?'

He leaned back and laughed harshly.

The woman who called herself Jodelle gazed at him with narrowed, thoughtful eyes.

'There is that argument,' she said. 'There is the other argument, that if the Communists could claim the real enemy was not human they would unite even more people against the Allied side, and that the same knowledge would create all kinds of problems—political, religious, philosophical—for Allied morale. So far, the latter argument has prevailed.'

My grip tightened on the pistol.

'You are talking about psychological warfare,' I said. 'And you are doing it, right here, now. Shut the fuck up.'

She gave us a pert smile and shrug.

'No more talking to her,' I said.

My own curiosity was burning me inside, but I knew that to pursue the conversation—with the mood here as it was—really would be demoralising and confusing. I got everybody busy guarding the prisoner, cleaning weapons, laying the table. Andy brought through plate laden with steaming, fragrant thick bacon and fried eggs and boiled potatoes. I relieved Donald on the outside watch before taking a bite myself, and prowled around in the howling wet dark with my M-16 under the oilskin cape and my belly grumbling. The window blinds were keeping the light in all right, and only the wind-whipped smoke from the chimney could betray our presence. I kept my closest attention to downwind, where someone might smell it. There was no chance of anyone seeing it.

I was looking that way, peering and listening intently through the dark to the east, when I felt a prickle in the back of my neck and smelled something electric.

I turned with a sort of reluctance, as though expecting to see a ghost. What I saw was a bomber, haloed in blue, descending between me and the house. There might have been a fizzing sound, or that may be just a memory of the hissing rain. For a moment I stood as still as the bomber, which floated preternaturally above the ground. Then I raised the rifle. Something flashed out from the bomber, and I was knocked backwards, and senseless.

I woke to voices, and pain. My skin smarted all over; my eyelids hurt to open. I was lying on my side on a slightly yielding smooth grey floor. The light was pearly and sourceless. Moving slightly, I found I had some bruises and what felt like scrapes on my back, but apart from that and the burning feeling everything seemed to be fine. My oilskins were gone, as were my weapons and, curiously enough, my watch. I raised my head, propped myself on one elbow and looked around. The room I lay in was circular, about fifteen metres across. My comrades were lying beside me, unconscious, looking sunburned, but breathing normally and apparently uninjured. There was a sort of bench or shelf around the room, which in one section looped away from the wall to form a seat, at which a tall person with long fair hair sat with their back to me, hands on a pair of knobbed levers. Other parts of the shelf were not padded seating but tables and odd panels. Above the bench was a black screen or window which likewise encircled the room.

Sitting on the bench, on either side of the person I guessed was the pilot, were three similar people—one of them, just then noticing that I was stirring, being the woman we'd captured—and a small creature with a large head, slit mouth, tiny nostrils and enormous black eyes. It skin was grey, but somehow not an unhealthy grey—it had a glow to it, a visible warmth underneath; though hairless it reminded me of the skin of a seal. Its legs were short, its arms long, and its hands—I recalled my father's words, and felt a slight thrill at their confirmation—bore four long digits.

It too noticed me, and it looked directly at me and—it didn't blink, something flicked sideways across its eyes, like an eagle's. The woman stood up and stepped over and stood looking down at me.

'There's no need to be afraid of the Martian,' she said.

'I'm not afraid,' I said, then caught myself. 'John Matheson, unit commander, MB 246.'

She reached down, took my hand and hauled me to my feet, without effort. There was something wrong about my weight. I felt curiously light.

'Your friends will wake up shortly,' she said. 'OK, consider yourself a prisoner of war if you like, but there's no need to not be civil. We have nothing to hide from you any more, and we really don't have anything we want to find out from you.'

I said nothing. She pointed to the bench.

'Relax,' she said, 'sit down, have a coffee.' Then she giggled, in a very disarming way. '"For you, Johnny, the vor iss over."'

Her fake, Ealing-studio German accent was as perfect as her genuine-sounding American one. I couldn't forbear to smile back, and walked over to the seat. On the way I stumbled a little. It was like the top step that isn't there.

'Martian gravity,' Jodelle said, steadying me. The Martian bowed his big head slightly, as though in apology. I sat down beside one of the other people, the 'Venusians' as I perforce mentally labelled them. All except Jodelle were evidently male, though their hair was as long and fair as hers. One of them passed me a mug of coffee; out of the corner of my eye, I noticed a coffee pot and electric kettle on one of the table sections, and some mugs and, banally enough, a kilogramme packet of Tate & Lyle sugar.

'My name is Soren,' the man said. He waved towards the others. 'The pilot is Olaf, and the man next to him is Harold.'

'And my name is Chuck,' said the Martian. His small shoulders shrugged. 'That's what I'm called around here, anyway.' His voice was like that of a tough wee boy, his accent American, but he sounded like he was speaking a learned second language.

I nodded at them all and said nothing, gratefully sipping the coffee. Outside, the view was completely black, though the movements of the pilot's eyes, head, and hands appeared to be responding to some visible exterior environment.

One by one, Neil, Donald, Murdo and Andy came round, and went through the same process of disorientation, astonishment, reassurance and suspicion as I had. We ended up sitting together, not speaking to each other or to our captors, perhaps silently mourning the loss of our comrades and friends in the other tank. The bomber's crew talked amongst themselves in a language I did not recognise, and attended to instruments. None of us was in anything but a hostile mood, and if the aliens had been less unknown in their intentions and capabilities we might have regarded their evident unconcern as an opportunity to try to overwhelm them, rather than—as we tacitly acknowledged—evidence that they had no reason to fear us.

After about half an hour, they relaxed, and all sat down on the long seat.

'Almost there,' Jodelle Smith said.

Before any of us could respond, one side of the encircling window filled with the glare of the sun, instantly dimmed by some property of the display; the other with the light of that same sun reflected on white clouds, of which I glimpsed a dazzling, visibly curved expanse a second before we plunged into them. Moments later we were underneath them, and a green surface spread below us. Looking up, I could see the silvery underside of the clouds. Our rapid descent soon brought the green surface into focus as an apparently endless forest, broken by lakes and rivers, and by plateaus or gentler rises covered with grass. After a few seconds we were low enough for the shadow of the bomber to be visible, skimming across the treetops. The circle of shade enlarged, and then disappeared. I blinked, and saw that we were now stationary above a broad valley bounded by high sandstone cliffs and divided by a wide, meandering river.

Then, with a yawing motion which we could see but not feel—so it seemed that the landscape swayed, and not the ship—we descended, and settled on a grassy plain. Around us, in the middle distance, were rows of Nissen huts; in the farther distance, watchtowers and barbed wire.

'Welcome to Venus,' said the pilot.

The camp held about a thousand people, from all over the world. Most of them were Front soldiers or cadre. There were as many women as there were men, and there were some children. The Front basically ran the camp, through committees of the various national sections, and an international committee for which the main qualification seemed to be fluency in Russian. The only rule that the Venusians enforced was a curfew and blackout between sunset and sunrise. They didn't bother about which hut you spent the night in, so long as you were in a hut.

They gave us no work to do, and watched unconcerned as we practised drill and unarmed combat, sweltering in the heat and humidity. Food and drink were adequate, and in fact more varied and nutritious than the fare to which most of the inmates, including myself, had become accustomed. This is not to say that our confinement was pleasant. The continuous cloud cover felt like a great shining lid pressing down on us, day after day. Every day it seemed to, or perhaps actually did, descend a little lower. The nightly lock-downs were hellish, even though the huts did in fact cool down somewhat. The wire around the camp was almost equally suffocating, one we'd realised that it wasn't so much there to keep us in as to keep the dinosaurs out. The same was true of the guards' strange weapons, which could—if turned to a much higher setting than was ever used against prisoners—fire bolts of electricity or plasma sufficient to turn back even the biggest of the great blundering beasts which flocked to the river every couple of days, their feet making the plain shake. We called them dinosaurs, because they resembled the reconstructions of dinosaurs which most of us had seen in books, but I knew from my scientific education that they could not be dinosaurs—they were too vigorous, too obviously hot-blooded, to be the sluggish reptilian giants of the Triassic and Jurassic eras. Whatever they may have been, their presence certainly discouraged attempts to escape.

The British contingent was in two Nissen huts: twenty men in one, twenty women in the other. They had a committee of three men, three women, and a chairman, and they spent a lot of time trying to regulate sexual relations. It was all very British and messy, uncomfortably between the strict puritanism of the Chinese comrades and the easy-going, if occasionally violent, mores of the Latin Americans and Africans. My unit decided to ignore all that and do what we considered the proper British thing.

We set up an escape committee.

'What the hell are you doing, Matheson?'

I waved my free hand. 'Just a minute—'

It didn't interrupt my counting. When I'd finished, I put the one-metre line and the 250-gramme tin of peas on the table and glanced over my calculations before looking up at Purdie. The young Englishman was on our hut committee and the camp committee, but not the escape committee, which he regarded as a diversion in both senses of the word.

'We're not on Venus,' I said.

He glanced over his shoulder, as if to confirm that we were still alone in the hut, then sat on a corner of the table.

'How d'you figure that out?'

'Pendulum swing,' I said. 'Galileo's experiment. The gravity here is exactly the same as on Earth. Venus has about eighty percent of the mass of Earth.'

'H'mm,' he said. 'Well done. Most people begin by wondering why nothing feels lighter, and then put it down to our muscles adapting to the supposed lower gravity. Still, can't say it's a surprise, old chap. Some of us reckon they keep us in at night because if we went outside we could see the moon through the cloud cover, and even the least educated of us is aware that Venus doesn't *have* a bloody moon.'

'So where are we?' I waved a hand. 'It seems a wee bit out of the way, if this is Earth.'

He crooked one leg over the other and lit a cigarette.

'Well, the camp committee has considered that. The usual explanation is that we're in some unexplored region of a South American jungle, something like what's-his-name's *The Lost World*.'

'Conan Doyle,' I said automatically. I screwed up my eyes against the smoke and the glaring light from the open door of the hut. 'Doesn't seem likely to me.'

'Me neither,' said Purdie cheerfully. 'For one thing, the mid-day sun isn't high enough in the sky for this to be a tropical latitude, but it's *bloody* hot. Any other ideas?'

'What if instead we're in somewhere out of *The Time Machine?* Well, you know...*dinosaurs?'*

Purdie frowned and probed in his ear with a finger.

'That has come up. Our Russian comrades shot it down in flames. Time travel is ruled out by dialectical materialism, I gather. But I must say, this place does strike me as frightfully Cretaceous, the anomaly of hot-blooded dinosaurs aside. My personal theory is that we're on a planet around another star, which resembles Earth in the Cretaceous period.'

He cracked a smile. 'That, however, implies a vastly more advanced civilization which either isn't communist or *is* communist and fights on the side of the imperialists. Neither of which are acceptable speculations to the, ah, leading comrades here, who thus stick with the line that the self-styled Venusians and Martians are the spawn of Nazi medical experiments, or some such.'

'Bollocks,' I said.

Purdie shrugged. 'You may well say that, but I wouldn't. I myself am troubled by the thought that my own theory at least strongly suggests—even if it doesn't, strictly speaking, require—faster-than-light travel, which is ruled out by Einstein—an authority who to me carries more weight on matters of physics than Engels or Lenin, I'm afraid.'

'Relativity doesn't rule out time travel,' I said. 'Even if dialectical materialism does.'

'And no science whatever rules out lost-world relict dinosaur populations,' said Purdie. He shrugged. 'Occam's razor and all that, keeps up morale, so lost-world is the official line.'

'First I've heard of it,' I said. 'Nobody's even suggested we're not on Venus in the two weeks I've been here.'

'Bit of a test, comrade,' he said dryly. He stubbed out his cigarette, hopped off the table and stuck out his right hand for me to shake. 'Congratulations on passing it. Now, how would you like to join the *real* escape committee?'

The official escape committee had long since worked through and discarded the laughable expedients—tunnels, gliders and so on—which I and my mates, perhaps over-influenced by such tales of derring-do as *The Colditz Story* and *The Wooden Horse,* had earnestly evaluated. The only possibility was for a mass break-out, exploiting the only factor of vulnerability we could see in the camp's defences, and one which itself was implicitly part of them: the dinosaur herds. It would also exploit the fact that, as far as we knew, the guards were reluctant to use lethal force on prisoners. So far, at least, they'd only ever turned on us the kind of electrical shock which had knocked out me and my team, and indeed most people here at the time of their capture or subsequent resistance.

The tedious details of how a prison-camp escape attempt is prepared have been often enough recounted in the genre of POW memoirs referred to above, and need not be repeated here. Suffice it to say that about fifty days after my arrival, the preparations were complete. From then on, all those involved in the scheme waited hourly for the approach of a suitably large herd, and on the second day of our readiness, conveniently soon after breakfast, one arrived.

About a score of the great beasts: bulls, cows, and calves, their tree-trunk-thick legs striding across the plain, their tree-top-high heads swaying to sniff and stooping to browse, were marching straight towards the eastern fence of the camp, which lay athwart their route to the river. The guards were just bestirring themselves to rack up the setting on their plasma rifles when the riot started.

At the western end of the camp a couple of Chinese women started screaming, and on this cue scores of other prisoners rushed to surround them and pile in to a highly realistic and noisy fight. Guards from the perimeter patrol raced towards them, and were immediately turned on and overwhelmed by a further crowd that just kept on coming, leaping or stepping over those who'd fallen to the low-level electric blasts. At that the guards from the watchtowers on that side began to descend, some of them firing.

My team was set for the actual escape, not the diversion. I was crouched behind the door of our hut with Murdo, Andy, Neil, Donald and a dozen others, including Purdie. We'd grabbed our stashed supplies and our improvised tools, and now awaited our chance. Another human wave assault, this time a crowd of Russians heading for the fence where the guards were belatedly turning to face the oncoming dinosaurs, thundered past. We dashed out behind them and ran for an empty food-delivery truck, temporarily unguarded. It even had a plasma-rifle, which I instantly commandeered, racked inside.

The Russians swarmed up the wire, standing on each others shoulders like acrobats. The guards, trying to deal with them and the dinosaurs, failed to cope with both. A bull dinosaur brought down the fence and two watchtowers, and by the time he'd been himself laid low with concerted plasma fire, we'd driven over the remains of the fence and hordes of prisoners were fleeing in every direction.

Within minutes the first bombers arrived, skimming low, rounding up the escapees. They missed us, perhaps because they'd mistaken the truck —a very standard US Army Dodge—for one of their own. We abandoned it at the foot of the cliffs, scaled them in half an hour of frantic scrambling up corries and chimneys, and by the time the bombers came looking for us we'd disappeared into the trees.

Heat, damp, thorns, and very large dragonflies. Apart from that last and the small dinosaur-like animals—some, to our astonishment, with feathers—scuttling through the undergrowth, the place didn't look like another planet, or even the remote past. Since my knowledge of what the remote past was supposed to look like was derived entirely from dim memories of *Look and Learn* and slightly fresher memories of a stroll through the geological wing of the Hunterian Museum, Glasgow, this wasn't saying much. I vaguely expected giant ferns and cycads and so forth, and found perfectly recognisable conifers, oaks and maples. The flowers were less instantly recognisable, but didn't look particularly primitive, or exotic.

I shared these thoughts with Purdie, who laughed.

'You're thinking of the Carboniferous, old chap,' he said. 'This is all solidly Cretaceous, so far.'

'Could be modern,' I said.

'Apart from the animals,' he pointed out, as though this wasn't obvious. 'And as I said, it's not tropical, but it's too bloody hot to be a temperate latitude.'

I glanced back. Our little column was plodding along behind us. We were heading in an approximately upward direction, on a reasonably gentle slope.

'I've thought about this,' I said. 'What if this whole area is some kind of artificial reserve in *North* America? If it's possible to genetically…engineer, I suppose would be the word…different kinds of humans, why shouldn't it be possible to do the same with birds and lizards and so on, and make a sort of botched copy of dinosaurs?'

'And keep it all under some vast artificial cloud canopy?' He snorted. 'You over-estimate the imperialists, let alone the Nazi scientists, comrade.'

'Maybe we're under a huge dome,' I said, not entirely seriously. I looked up at the low sky, which seemed barely higher than the tree-tops. It really had become lower since we'd arrived. 'Buckminster Fuller had plans that were less ambitious than that.'

Purdie wiped sweat from his forehead with the back of his hand. 'Now that,' he said, 'is quite a plausible suggestion. It sure *feels* like we're in a bloody greenhouse. Mind you, none of us saw anything like that, from the bomber.'

'That was a screen, not a window.'

'Hmm. A remarkably realistic screen, in that case. Back to implausibly advanced technology.'

We wouldn't have to speculate for long, because our course was taking us directly up to the cloud level, which we reached within an hour or so. I assigned my lads the task of guiding the others, who were quite unfamiliar with the techniques of low-visibility walking, and we all headed on up. First wisps, then dense damp billows, of fog surrounded us. I led the way and moved forward cautiously, whistling signals back and forth. Behind me I could just see Purdie and two of the English women comrades. Underfoot the ground became grassier, and around us the trees became shorter and the bushes more sparse. The only way to follow a particular direction was to go upslope, and that—with a few inevitable wrong turnings that led us into declivities—we did.

The fog thinned. Clutching the plasma rifle, hoping I had correctly figured out how to use it, I walked forward and up and into clear air. A breeze blew refreshingly into my face, and as I glanced back I saw that it had pushed back the fog and revealed all of our straggling party. We were on one of the wide, rounded hilltops I'd seen from the bomber. In the far distance I could see other green islands above the clouds. The sky was blue, the sun was bright.

All around us, people rose out of the long grass, aiming plasma rifles. I dropped mine and raised my hands.

About a hundred metres in front of us was the wire fence of another camp.

We went into the camp without resistance, but without being searched or, in my case, disarmed: I was told to pick up my rifle and sling it over my shoulder. The people were human beings like us, but they were weird. They spoke English, in strange accents and with a lot of unfamiliar words. Several of them were coloured or half-caste, but their accents were as English as those of the rest. I found myself walking beside a young woman with part of her hair dyed violet. I knew it was a dye because it was growing out: the roots were black. She had several rings and studs in her ear, and not just in the earlobe. She was wearing baggy grey trousers with pockets at the thighs, and a silky scarlet sleeveless top with a silver patch shaped like a rabbit. Around her bicep was a tattoo of thorns. Under her tarty make-up her face was quite attractive. Her teeth looked amazingly white and even, like an American's.

'My name's Tracy,' she said. She had some kind of Northern English accent; I couldn't place it more than that. 'You?'

Name, rank, serial number…

'Where you from?'

Name, rank, serial number…

'Forget that,' she said. 'You're not a prisoner.'

A massive gate made from logs and barbed wire was being pushed shut behind us. Nissen huts inside a big square of fence, a bomber parked just outside it.

'Oh no?' I said.

'Keeps the fucking dinosaurs out, dunnit?'

Somebody handed me a tin mug of tea, black with a lot of sugar. I sipped it and looked around. If this was a camp it was one where the prisoners had guns.

Or one run by trusties…I was still suspicious.

'Where are the aliens?' I asked.

'The what?'

'The Venusians, the Martians…' I held my free hand above my head, then at chest height.

Tracy laughed. 'Is that what they told you?'

I nodded. 'Not sure if I believe them, though.'

She was still chuckling. 'You lot must be from Commie World. Never built the rockets, right?'

'The Russians have rockets,' I said, with some indignation. 'The biggest in the world—they have a range of hundreds of kilometres!'

'Exactly. No ICBMs.' She smiled at my frown. 'Inter-Continental Ballistic Missiles. None of them, and no space-probes. Jeez. You could still half believe this might be Venus, with jungles and tall Aryans. And that the Greys are Martians.'

'Well, what are they?' I asked, becoming irritated by her smug teasing.

'Time travellers,' she said. 'From the future.' She shivered slightly. 'From *another* world's future. The ones you call the Venusians are from about half a million years up ahead of the twentieth century, the Greys're from maybe five million. In your world's twentieth century they fly bombers and fight commies. In mine they're just responsible for flying saucers, alien abductions, cattle mutilations and odd sock phenomena.'

I let this incomprehensibility pass.

'So where are we now?'

I meant the camp. I knew where we were in general, but that was what she answered.

'This, Johnny-boy, is the past. They can never go back to the same future, but they can go back to the same place in the past, where they can make no difference. The common past, the past of us all—the Cretaceous.'

She looked at me with a bit more sympathy. My companions were finishing off their tea and gazing around, looking as baffled and edgy as

I felt. The other prisoners, if that was what they were, gathered around us seemed more alien than the bomber pilots.

'Come on,' Tracy said, gesturing towards some rows of seats in front of which a table had been dragged. 'Debriefing time. You have a lot to learn.'

I have learned a lot.

I tug the reins and the big Clydesdale turns, and as I follow the plough around I see a porpoise leap in the choppy water of the Moray Firth. My hands and back are sore but I'm getting used to it, and the black soil here is rich, and arable after the trees have been cut down and their stumps dynamited. The erratic boulders have been cleared away long ago, by the long-dead first farmers of this land, and no glaciers have revisited it since its last farmers passed away. The rougher ground is pasture, grazed by half-wild long-horns, a rugged synthetic species. The village is stockaded on a hilltop nearby. We have no human enemies, but wolves, bears and lions prowl the forests and moors. We are not barbarians—the plough that turns the furrow I walk has an iron blade, and the revolver on my hip was made in Hartford, Connecticut, millenia ago and worlds away. The post-humans settled us—and other colonies—on this empty Earth with machinery and medicines, weapons and tools and libraries, and enough partly-used ball-point pens to keep us all scribbling until our descendants can make their own.

On countless other empty Earths they have done the same. Somewhere unreachable, but close to hand, another man, perhaps another John Matheson, may be tramping a slightly different furrow. I wish him well.

There are many possible worlds, and in almost all of them humanity didn't survive the time from which most of us have been taken. Either the United States and the Soviet Union destroyed each other and the rest of civilization in an atomic war in the fifties or sixties, or they didn't, and the collapse of the socialist states in the late twentieth century so discredited socialism and international co-operation that humanity failed utterly to unite in time to forestall the environmental disasters of the twenty-first.

In a few, a very few possible worlds, enough scattered remnants of humanity survived as savages to eventually—hundreds of thousands of years later—become the ancestors of the post-human species we called the Venusians. Who in turn—millions of years later—themselves gave rise to the post-human clade we called the Martians. It was the latter who discovered time travel, and with it some deep knowledge about the future and past of the universe.

I don't pretend to understand it. As Feynmann said—in a world where he didn't die in jail—it all goes back to the experiment with the light and the two slits, and Feynmann himself didn't pretend to understand *that.*

What we have been told is simply this—that the past of the universe, its very habitability for human beings, depends on its future being one—or rather, many—which contain as many human beings and their successors as possible, until the end of time.

It is not enough for the time-travellers to intervene in histories such as the one from which I come, and by defeating Communism while avoiding atomic war, save a swathe of futures for co-operation and survival. They also have to repopulate the time-lines in which humanity destroyed itself, and detonate new shock-waves of possibility that will spread humanity across time and forward through it, on an ever-expanding, widening front.

The big mare stops and looks at me, and whinnies. The sun is low above the hills to the west, the hills where I once—or many times—fought. Its light is red in the sky. The dust from the last atomic war is no longer dangerous, but it will linger in the high atmosphere for thousands of years to come.

I unharness the horse, heave the plough to the shed at the end of the field, and lead the beast up the hill towards the village. The atomic generator is humming, the lights are coming on, and dinner in the communal kitchen will soon be ready. Tracy will be putting away the day's books in the library, and yawning and stretching herself. Maybe this evening, after we've all eaten, she can be persuaded to tell us some stories. For me she has many fascinations—she's quite unlike any woman I've ever met—and the only one I'm happy for her to share with everybody else is her stories from the world where, I still feel, history turned out almost as it would have done without any meddling at all by the time-travellers: her world, the world where the prototype bomber didn't work; the world where, as she puts it, the Roswell saucer crashed.

A Case of Consilience

'When you say it's Providence that brought you here,' said Qasim, 'what I hear are two things: it's bad luck, and it's not your fault.'

The Rev. Donald MacIntyre, M.A. (Div.), Ph.D., put down his beer can and nodded.

'That's how it sometimes feels,' he said. 'Easy for you to say, of course.'

Qasim snorted. 'Easy for anybody! Even a Muslim would have less difficulty here. Let alone a Buddhist or Hindu.'

'Do tell,' said Donald. 'No, what's really galling is that there are millions of *Christians* who would take all this in their stride. Anglicans. Liberals. Catholics. Mormons, for all I know. And my brethren in the, ah, narrower denominations could come up with a dozen different rationalizations before breakfast, all of them heretical did they but know it—which they don't, thank the Lord and their rigid little minds, so their lapses are no doubt forgiven through their sheer ignorance. So it's given to me to wrestle with. Thus a work of Providence. I think.'

'I still don't understand what your problem is, compared to these other Christians.'

Donald sighed. 'It's a bit hard to explain,' he said. 'Let's put it this way. You were brought up not to believe in God, but I expect you had quite strong views about the God you didn't believe in. Am I right?'

Qasim nodded. 'Of course. Allah was always…' He shrugged. 'Part of the background. The default.'

'Exactly. Now, how did you feel when you first learned about what Christians believe about the Son of God?'

'It was a long time ago,' said Qasim. 'I was about eight or nine. In school in Kirkuk. One of my classmates told me, in the course of…well, I am sorry to say in the course of a fight. I shall pass over the details. Enough to say I was quite shocked. It seemed preposterous and offensive. And then I laughed at myself!'

'I can laugh at myself too,' said Donald. 'But I feel the same way as you did—in my case at the suggestion that the Son was not unique, that He took on other forms, and so forth. I can hardly even say such things. I literally shudder. But I can't accept, either, that He has no meaning beyond Earth. So what are we to make of rational beings who are not men, and who may be sinners?'

'Perhaps they are left outside,' said Qasim. 'Like most people are, if I understand your doctrines.'

Donald flinched. 'That's not what they say, and in any case, such a question is not for me to decide. I'm perplexed.'

He leaned back in the seat and stared gloomily at the empty can, and then at the amused, sympathetic eyes of the friendly scoffer to whom he had found he could open up more than to the believers on the Station.

Qasim stood up. 'Well, thank God I'm an atheist, that's all I can say.'

He had said it often enough.

'God and Bush,' said Donald. This taunt, too, was not on its first outing. Attributing to the late ex-President the escalating decades-long cascade of unintended consequences that had annexed Iraq to the EU and Iran to China was probably unfair, but less so than blaming it on God. Qasim raised a mocking index finger in response.

'God and Bush! And what are you having, Donald?'

'Can of Export.'

'Narrow it down, padre. They're all export here.'

'Aren't we all,' said Donald. 'Tennent's, then. And a shot of single malt on the side, if you don't mind. Whatever's going.'

As Qasim made his way through the crowd to the bar, Donald reflected that his friend was likely no more off-duty than he was. A chaplain and an intelligence officer could both relax in identical olive t-shirts and chinos, but vigilance and habit were less readily shrugged off than dress-codes. The Kurdish colonel still now and again called his service the *mukhabarat*. It was one of his running gags, along with the one about electronics and electrodes. And the one about extra-terrestrial intelligence. And the one about...yes, for running gags Qasim was your man.

As I am for gloomy reflections, Donald thought. Sadness, *tristia,* had been one of the original seven deadly sins. Which probably meant every Scottish presbyterian went straight to hell, or at least to a very damp purgatory, if the Catholics were right. If the Catholics were right! After three hundred and seventeen days in the Extra-Terrestrial Contact Station, this was among the least heretical of the thoughts Donald MacIntyre was willing to countenance.

Qasim came back with the passing cure, and lasting bane, of the Scottish sin; and with what might have been a more dependably cheering mood-lifter: a gripe about his own problems. Problems which, as Donald listened to them, seemed more and more to resemble his own.

'How am I supposed to tell if an underground fungoid a hundred metres across that communicates by chemical gradients is feeding us false information? Or if an operating system written by an ET AI is a trojan? Brussels still expects files on all of them, when we don't even know how many civs we're dealing with. Bloody hell, Donald, pardon my English, there's one of the buggers we only suspect is out there because everyone comes back from its alleged home planet with weird dreams.' Qasim cocked a black eyebrow. 'Maybe I shouldn't be telling you that one.'

'I've heard about the dreams,' said Donald. 'In a different context.' He sighed. 'It's a bit hard to explain to some people that I don't take confession.'

'Confessions are not to be relied upon,' Qasim said, looking somewhere else. 'Anyway...what I would have to confess, myself, is that the Etcetera Station is a bit out of its depth. We are applying concepts outside their context.'

'Now *that,*' said Donald with some bitterness, 'is a suspicion I do my best to resist.'

It was one the Church had always resisted, a temptation dangled in different forms down the ages. As soon as the faith had settled on its view of one challenge, another had come along. In the Carpenter's workshop there were many clue-sticks, and the whacks had seldom ceased for long. In the beginning, right there in the Letters, you could see the struggle against heresies spawned by Greek metaphysics and Roman mysticism. Barely had the books snapped shut on Arius when Rome had crashed. Then the Muslim invasions. The split between the Eastern and Western churches, Christendom cloven on a lemma. Then the discovery of the New World, and a new understanding of the scope and grip of the great, ancient religions of the Old. The Reformation. The racialist heresy. The age of the Earth. Biblical criticism. Darwin. The twentieth century had brought the expanding universe, the gene, the unconscious—how quaint the controversies over these now seemed! Genetic engineering, human-animal chimerae, artificial intelligence: in Donald's own lifetime he'd seen Synods, Assemblies and Curia debate them and come to a Christian near-consensus acceptable to all but the lunatic—no, he must be charitable — the fundamentalist fringe.

And then, once more, just when the dust had settled, along had come —predictable as a planet, unpredicted like a comet—another orb in God's great orrery of education, or shell in the Adversary's arsenal of error-mongery, the greatest challenge of all—alien intelligent life. It was not one that had been altogether unexpected. Scholastics had debated the plurality of worlds. The Anglican C. S. Lewis had considered it in science-fiction; the agnostic Blish had treated it with a literally Jesuitical subtlety. The Christian poet Alice Meynell had speculated on alien gospels; the godless ranter MacDiarmid had hymned the Innumerable Christ. In the controversies over the new great discovery, all these literary precedents had been resurrected and dissected. They pained Donald to the quick. Well-intended, pious, sincere in their seeking they might be; or sceptical and satirical; it mattered not: they were all mockeries. There had been only one Incarnation; only one sufficient sacrifice. If the Reformation had meant anything at all, it meant that. To his ancestors Donald might have seemed heinously pliant in far too much, but like them he was not be moved from the rock. In the matter of theological science-fiction he preferred the honest warning of the secular humanist Harrison. *Tell it not in Gath, publish it not in the streets of Ashkelon...*

Donald left the messroom after his next round and walked to his quarters. The corridor's topology was as weird as anything on the ETC Station. A human-built space habitat parked inside an alien-built wormhole nexus could hardly be otherwise. The station's spin didn't dislodge the wormhole mouths, which remained attached to the same points on the outside of the hull. As a side-effect, the corridor's concave curve felt and looked convex. At the near ends of stubby branch corridors, small groups of scientists and technicians toiled on their night-shift tasks. At the far ends, a few metres away, thick glass plates with embedded airlocks looked out on to planetary surfaces and sub-surfaces, ocean depths, tropospheric layers, habitat interiors, virtual reality interfaces, and apparently vacant spaces backdropped with distant starfields. About the last, it was an open question whether the putatively present alien minds were invisible inhabitants of the adjacent vacuum, or more disturbingly, some vast process going on in and among the stars themselves. The number of portals was uncountable. There were never more than about five hundred, but the total changed with every count. As the station had been designed and built with exactly three hundred interface corridors, this variability was not comfortable to contemplate. But that the station's structure itself had somehow become imbricated with the space-time tangle outside it had become an accepted—if not precisely an acknowledged—fact. It received a back-handed recognition in the station's nickname: the Etcetra Station.

Use of that monicker, like much else, was censored out of messages home. The Station was an EU military outpost, and little more than its existence, out beyond the orbit of Neptune, had been revealed. Donald MacIntyre, in his second year of military service as a conscript chaplain, had been as surprised to find himself here as his new parishioners were to discover his affiliation. His number had come up in the random all ocation of clergy from the list of religions recognised by the EU Act of Toleration—the one that had banned Scientology, the Unification Church, the Wahabi sect and, by some drafting or translation error, Unitarian

Universalism—but to a minister of the Church of Scotland, there could in all conscience be no such thing as chance.

He had been sent here for a purpose.

'The man in black thinks he's on a mission from God,' said Qasim.

'What?' Major Bernstein looked up from her interface, blinking.

'Here.' Qasim tapped the desktop, transferring a file from his finger.

'What's this?'

'His private notes.'

The major frowned. She didn't like Qasim. She didn't like spying on the troops. She didn't care who knew it. Qasim knew all this. So did Brussels. She didn't know that.

'What are your grounds?' she asked.

'He spoke a little wildly in the mess last night.'

'Heaven help us all, in that case,' said the Major.

Qasim said nothing.

'All right.' Bernstein tabbed through the notes, skimming to the first passage Qasim had highlighted.

'"Worst first,"' she read out. '"The undetectable entities. No coherent communication. (Worst case: try exorcism???!) Next: colonial organisms. Mycoidal. Translations speculative. Molecular grammar. Query their concept of personhood. Also of responsibility. If this can be established: rational nature. Fallen nature. If they have a moral code that they do not live up to? Any existing religious concepts? Next: discrete animalia. Opposite danger here: anthropomorphism. (Cf. Dominican AI mission fiasco.) Conclusion: use mycoids as test case to establish consilience."' She blinked the script away, and stared at Qasim. 'Well? What's the harm in that?'

'He's been hanging around the team working on the mycoids. If you read on, you'll find he intends to preach Christianity to them.'

'To the scientists?'

'To the mycoids.'

'Oh!' Major Bernstein laughed. It was a sound that began and ended abruptly, like a fall of broken glass, and felt as cutting. 'If he can get *any* message through to them, he'll be doing better than the scientists. And unless you, my over-zealous mukhabaratchik, can find any evidence that Dr MacIntyre is sowing religious division in the ranks, practicing rituals involving animal cruelty or non-consensual sexual acts, preaching Market Maoism or New Republicanism or otherwise aiding and abetting the Chinks or the Yanks, I warn you most seriously to not waste your time or mine. Do I make myself quite clear?'

'Entirely, ma'am.'

'Dismissed.'

*

I do not what I wish I did.

It was a lot to read into a sequence of successive concentrations of different organic molecules. In the raw transcript it went like this:

Titration	Translation
Indication-marker	THIS
Impulse-summation	MYCOID
Action (general)	DOES
Negation-marker	NOT
Impulse-direction	ACT
Affirmation-marker	[AS] INTENDED [BY]
Impulse-summation	[THIS] MYCOID
Repulsion-marker	[AND THIS] DISGUST[S]
Impulse-summation	[THIS] MYCOID

Donald looked at the print-out and trembled. It was hard not to see it as the first evidence of an alien that knew sin. He well realised, of course, that it could just as well mean something as innocent as *I couldn't help but puke*. But the temptation, if it was a temptation, to read it as an instance of the spirit warring against the flesh—well, against the slime—was almost irresistible. Donald couldn't help but regard it as a case of consilience, and as no coincidence.

'Is there any way we can respond to this?'

Trepper, the mycoid project team leader, shook his head. 'It's very difficult to reproduce the gradients. For us, it's as if…look, suppose a tree could understand human speech. It tries to respond by growing some twigs and branches so that they rub against each other just so, in the wind. And all we hear are some funny scratching and creaking sounds.'

Trees in the wind. Donald gazed past the tables and equipment of the corridor's field lab to the portal that opened on to the mycoids' planet. The view showed a few standing trees, and a lot of fallen logs. The mycoids did something to force the trees' growth and weaken their structure, giving the vast underground mycoid colonies plenty of rotting cellulose to feed on. Far in the distance, across a plain of coppery grass, rose a copse of quite different trees, tall and stately with tapered bulges from the roots to half-way up the trunks. Vane-like projections of stiff leaves sprouted from their sides. Bare branches bristled at their tops. These were the Niven Pines, able to synthesise and store megalitres of volatile and flammable hydrocarbons. At every lightning storm one or other of these trees—the spark carried by some kind of liquid lightning-conductor to a drip of fuel-sap at its foot—would roar into flame and rise skyward. Some of them would make it to orbit. No doubt they bore mycoid travellers, but what these clammy astronauts did in space, and whether this improbable arboreal rocketry was the result of natural selection, or of conscious genetic manipulation by the mycoids—or indeed some other alien—was as yet unclear.

In any case, it had been enough to bring the mycoids a place at the table of whatever Galactic Club had set up the wormhole nexus. Perhaps they too had found a wormhole nexus on the edge of their solar system. Perhaps they too had puzzled over the alien intelligences it connected them to. If so, they showed little sign of having learned much. They pulsed their electrophoretically-controlled molecular gradients into the soil near the Station's portal, but much of it—even assuming the translations were correct—was about strictly parochial matters. It was as if they weren't interested in communicating with the humans.

Donald determined to make them interested. Besides his pastoral duties—social as well as spiritual—he had an allotted time for scholarship and study, and he devoted that time to the work of the mycoid research team. He did not explain his purpose to the scientists. If the mycoids were sinners, he had an obligation to offer them the chance of salvation. He had no obligation to offer the scientists the temptation to scoff.

Time passed.

The airlock door slammed. Donald stepped forward through the portal and on to the surface. He walked forward along an already-beaten track across the floor of the copse. Here and there, mushroom-like structures poked up through the spongy, bluish moss and black leaf-litter. The bulges of their inch-wide caps had a watery transparency that irresistibly suggested that they were the lenses of eyes. No one had as yet dared to pluck a fungus to find out.

A glistening patch of damp mud lay a couple of hundred metres from the station. It occupied a space between the perimeters of two of the underground mycoids, and had become a preferred site for myco-linguistic research. Rainbow ripples of chemical communication between the two sprawling circular beings below stained its surface at regular intervals. Occasional rainstorms washed away the gradients, but they always seeped out again.

Donald stepped up to the edge of the mud and set up the apparatus that the team had devised for a non-intrusive examination of the mycoids' messages: a wide-angle combined digital field microscope and spectroscope. About two metres long, its support frame straddled the patch, above which its camera slowly tracked along. Treading carefully, he planted one trestle, then the other on the far side of the patch, then walked back and laid the tracking rail across them both. He switched on the power pack and the camera began its slow traverse.

There was a small experiment he had been given to perform. It had been done many times before, to no effect. Perhaps this variant would be different. He reached in to his thigh pocket and pulled out a plastic-covered gel disc, about five centimetres across, made from synthesised copies of local mucopolysaccharides. The concentric circles of molecular concentrations that covered it spelled out—the team had hoped—the message: *We wish to communicate please respond.*

Donald peeled off the bottom cover and, one knee on a rock and one hand on a fallen log, leaned out over the multi-coloured mud and laid the gel disc down on a bare dark patch near the middle. He withdrew his hand, peeling back the top cover as he did so, and settled back on his haunches. He stuffed the crumpled wrappings in his pocket and reached in deeper for a second disc: one he'd covertly prepared himself, with a different message.

Resisting the impulse to look over his shoulder, he repeated the operation and stood up.

A voice sounded in his helmet: 'Got you!'

Qasim stood a few metres away, glaring at him.

'I beg your pardon,' said Donald. 'I've done nothing wrong.'

'You've placed an unauthorised message on the mud,' said Qasim.

'What if I have?' said Donald. 'It can do no harm.'

'That's not for you to judge,' said Qasim.

'Nor for you either!'

'It is,' said Qasim. 'We don't want anything...ideological or controversial to affect our contact.' He looked around. 'Come on, Donald, be a sensible chap. There's still time to pick the thing up again. No harm done and no more will be said.'

It had been like this, Donald thought, ever since the East India Company: commercial and military interests using and then restricting missionaries.

'I will not do that,' he said. 'I'll go back with you, but I won't destroy the message.'

'Then I'll have to do it,' said Qasim. 'Please step aside.'

Donald stayed where he was. Qasim stepped forward and caught his shoulder. 'I'm sorry,' he said.

Donald pulled away, and took an involuntary step back. One foot came down in the mud and kept on going down. His leg went in up to the knee. Flailing, he toppled on his back across the tracking rail. The rail cracked in two under the blow from his oxygen tanks. He landed with a huge splash. Both pieces of the rail sank out of sight at once. Donald himself lay, knees crooked, his visor barely above the surface.

'Quicksand,' said Qasim, his voice cutting across the alarmed babble from the watching science team. 'Don't try to stand or struggle, it'll just make things worse. Lie back with your arms out and stay there. I'll get a rope.'

'OK,' said Donald. He peered up through his smeared visor. 'Don't be long.'

Qasim waved. 'Back in seconds, Donald. Hang in there.'

The science team talked Donald through the next minute, as Qasim ran for the portal, stepped into the airlock, and grabbed the rope that had already been placed there.

'OK, Donald, he's just—'

The voice stopped. Static hiss filled the speaker. Donald waited.

'Can anyone hear me?'

No reply.

Five more minutes passed. Nobody was coming. He would have to get himself out. There was no need to panic. He had five hours's worth of air supply, and no interruption to the portals had ever lasted more than an hour.

Donald swept his arms through the mud to his side, raised them above the mud, flung them out again, and repeated this laborious backstroke many times, until his helmet rested on solid ground. It had taken him half an hour to move a couple of metres. He rested for a few minutes, gasping, then reached behind him and scrabbled for something to hold. Digging his fingers into the soil, kicking now with his feet—still deep in the mud—he began to lever himself up and heave his shoulders out of the bog. He got as much as the upper quarter of his body out when the ground turned to liquid under his elbows. His head fell back, and around it the mud splashed again. He made another effort at swimming along the top of the mud on his back. His arms met less resistance. Around him the sludge turned to slurry. Water welled up, and large bubbles of gas popped all across the widening quagmire.

He began to sink. He swung his arms, kicked his legs hard, and the increasingly liquid mass closed over his visor. Writhing, panicking now, he sank into utter darkness. His feet touched bottom. His hands, stretched above his head, were now well below the surface. He leaned forward with an immense effort and tried to place one foot in front of the other. If he had to he would walk out of this. Barely had he completed a step when he found the resistance of the wet soil increase. It set almost solid around him. He was stuck.

Donald took some slow, deep breaths. Less than an hour had passed. Fifty minutes. Fifty-five. At any moment his rescuers would come for him.

They didn't. For four more hours he stood there in the dark. As each hour passed he realised with increasing certainty that the portal had not re-opened. He wondered, almost idly, if that had anything to do with his own intrusion into the bog. He wondered, with some anguish, whether his illicit message had been destroyed, unread, as he fell in on top of it.

The anguish passed. What had happened to the message, and what happened to him, was in a quite ultimate sense not his problem. The parable of the sower was as clear as the great commission itself. He had been in the path of duty. He had proclaimed, to the best of his ability, the truth. This was what he had been sent to do. No guarantee had been given that he would be successful. He would not be the first, nor the last, missionary whose mission was to all human reckoning futile. The thought saddened him, but did not disturb him. In that sense, if none other, his feet were on a rock.

He prayed, he shouted, he thought, he wept, he prayed again, and he died.

At last! The aliens had sent a communications package! After almost a year of low-bandwidth disturbances of the air and the electromagnetic spectrum, from which little sense could be extracted, and many days of dropping tiny messages of blurry resolution and trivial import, they had finally, *finally* sent something one could get one's filaments into!

The mycoid sent long tendrils around the package, infiltrating its pores and cracks. It synthesised acids that worked their way through any weak points in its fabric. Within hours it had penetrated the wrapping and begun a riotous, joyous exploration of the vast library of information within. The mycoid had in its own genetic library billions of years of accumulated experience in absorbing information from organisms of every kind: plant or animal, mycoid or bacterium. It could relate the structure of a central nervous system to any semantic or semiotic content it had associated with the organism. It probed cavities, investigated long transportation tubes, traced networks of neurons and found its way to the approximately globular sub-package where the information was most rich. It dissolved here, embalmed there, dissected and investigated everywhere. In an inner wrapping it found a small object made from multiple mats of cellulose fibre, each layer impregnated with carbon-based markings. The mycoid stored these codes with the rest. Seasons and years passed. A complete transcription of the alien package, of its neural structures and genetic codes, was eventually read off.

Then the work of translation and interpretation, shared out across all the mycoids of the continent, began.

It took a long time, but the mycoids had all the time in the world. They had no more need—for the moment—to communicate with the aliens, now that they had this vast resource of information. They, or their ancestors, had done this many times before, under many suns.

They understood the alien, and they understood the strange story that had shaped so many of the connections in its nervous system. They interpreted the carbon marks on the cellulose mats. In their own vast minds they reconstructed the scenes of alien life, as they had done with everything that fell their way, from the grass and the insects to the trees. They had what a human might have called a vivid imagination. They had, after all, little else.

Some of them found the story to be:

Affirmation-marker	GOOD
Information-marker	NEWS

Spores spread it to the space-going trees, and thence to the wormhole network, and thence to countless worlds.

Not quite all the seeds fell on stony ground.

Con Reports

Whenever I'm a Guest of Honour at a con, or a guest at an event, I feel an obligation to write a con report. The first two were posted to rec.arts.sf.fandom, and were my first sustained efforts at fanwriting. The more recent ones were blogged (http://kenmacleod.blogspot.com/). Going to cons is a rewarding experience, and that goes double for going to cons in countries where the first language isn't English. In Finland and Spain it's taken for granted that SF is part of the general culture. In Poland and Croatia it's the fandoms that are different—they're younger, more ready to rough it, and the written-SF, media and gaming fandoms all sleep on the same floor. There are historical reasons for all that, of course, and it would be silly to urge the English-speaking fandoms to emulate them. But we could learn from them. Travel really does broaden the mind.—K. M.

A Fish Dinner in Helsinki: A report on Millennium Finncon, 18-20 Aug 2000, Helsinki, Finland.

Earlier this year I was invited to be a GoH, along with Steve Baxter and Neil Gaiman, at this convention. It's financed by local public and private sponsorship rather than membership fees, but in other ways it's much the same as the cons we all know and love, as we'll see. The expenses incurred by the con committee on my behalf were met by the British Council, an official organization which promotes British arts and literature outside the United Kingdom. I'd like to thank all involved for inviting me, and for showing me a very good time while I was there. I can honestly say that I liked everybody I met, and that I have nothing but praise for the organisers. Most of the programme items were, of course, in Finnish. This is why I say little about the programme, and a lot about conversations in the bar. *Plus ça change…*

So off I set, early on Wednesday 16 August. Edinburgh to Amsterdam and then on to Helsinki. KLM is actually a very good airline. I arrived at Helsinki and didn't need a card to spot the people waiting for me. Otto, Christina and her boyfriend Pekka looked like classic fannish people—enthusiastic, friendly, and working in IT. Otto Makela was there to look after me; Chris and Pekka were there to be minders for Neil Gaiman, who arrived minutes after I did. We were issued very neat, small Nokia mobile phones and five-day travel cards and whisked to separate hotels. Mine was down at the waterfront and imaginatively called the Seaside Hotel. Small neat rooms, hotel very fine (and genuinely nice). I got a call on the mobile just as I was unpacking, from my Finnish publisher Niko Aula (whom I'd met before—he showed me and Iain Banks the correct way to drink vodka, one night in the Cafe Royal in Edinburgh).

Niko's a great guy, very intelligent and educated and funny, quite tall, and looks very serious most of the time. He was at a table in the street part of the hotel bar with a drink and a copy of the Finnish translation of *The Star Fraction*, which looks way cool and which was launched at the con.

We then met up (liaising by mobile phone across ten metres) with Otto, Chris and Pekka, Neil, Stephen Baxter and his wife Sandra, and went to a Tex-Mex restaurant. I enjoyed the meal and the company, but I was feeling very strange—a combination of jet-lag and hangover, I think—and Neil Gaiman too was up for an early night, so we packed it in about ten. I walked back from the Tex-Mex to the hotel with Kimmo Lehtonen, who lives near the hotel. He's a young Finnish SF writer (and of course website designer, etc.) who has two books published in Finnish by Loki, the same publisher as I have.

He told me he'd made a badge for the con with the hammer-and-sickle-and-4 on it—he'd thought the Fourth International (which plays some part in *The Star Fraction*) was something I had made up :-) (Not many Trots in Finland, y'see—the sixties student radicals joined the official Communist party, so great chunks of business, media and government are now run by 'old Stallies' instead of 'old Trots' like we have running great chunks of the UK.)

As we walked around a corner to the hotel I realised that what I'd thought was an office block with a ship's funnel showing beyond its roof was a ship, a gigantic multi-layered Caribbean cruise liner. This is what the Finnish shipyards make now, instead of icebreakers. We each had a couple of vodka bitters and then I went to bed with a still-splitting headache, because one of the things I'd neglected to pack was Resolve.

I got up just in time to snatch breakfast and then I and the Baxters were scooped up by Otto for a tram ride to the main art museum, the Ateneum, for the opening of a show of comics art (there was a comics festival running jointly with Finncon), and a press conference which resulted in a few interviews (including one on the local cable channel, and one with Pekka Supinen, journalist and publisher of the SF fanzine *Finnzine*).

The exhibition of original comics artwork was fascinating and spectacularly presented, moving from the mid-40s to the present; likewise the press conference was well-organised, and resulted in some serious press coverage. UK con organisers who are fed up with their usual British press treatment ('Weirdos beam down', etc.) might think about, well, having press conferences. After that a fan who works at the museum, Hannele, a very attractive and vivacious young woman, took us all on a tour of Finnish art from the nineteenth century to the 1960s. The XIX stuff is vibrant, original, realistic or romantic, as the Finnish nation, you know, struggles to define itself under the Russian empire. Then after 1918 darkness falls—the stuff from the 20s is very gloomy, things brighten up a little towards the end of the 30s, then it's all decadent and derivative Bad Modern Art. Gee, you'd almost think some dreadful national disaster happened in 1918.

So…after the museum tour and a collective browse of the museum shop, I went off on my own to get some Finn-marks out of the nearest cashpoint, and wandered around the town centre a bit. Helsinki is bloody marvellous—it has a lot of old Tsarist-era buildings, a lot of modern buildings—some of them very good—and is full of glamour and glitz. Almost everybody has a mobile phone. You see people who don't wear watches any more—they check the time by looking at their mobile. Then I hopped on the tram—another great feature is utterly reliable, to-the-minute-like-clockwork public transport—and hopped off one stop from the hotel, at a flea market just around the corner which Kimmo had pointed out the previous night. It was in a big square and was a bit sparse, being on a weekday, but I saw plenty of interesting stuff—cards and cards of old Soviet badges, lots of second-hand clothes and bric-a-brac, tools and weapons. (Oh, all right, bayonets and hunting knives.)

That evening Kimmo took me and the Baxters to dinner with the con committee (the people I've mentioned plus a few others, including Ari, and his girlfriend Maaret). Neil and minders there too, of course. A few quick words about Mr Gaiman. He's a very sound chap, quite unspoiled by the fact that he gets treated like a rockstar. (He looks like one, too.) No side, as they say. He does tend to get listened to when he speaks, but this is more to do with what he says being usually interesting or amusing.

His readings and talks (to anticipate a little) were completely packed out: standing room only in a large auditorium. His signing queues were the stuff of legend. Very long legend, like the Kalevala. The restaurant specialised in Lappish food—I had salmon soup (delicious) and reindeer fillet (also delicious—like venison). Then we had a mad dash to a tram stop to go across town to St Urho's pub, where the Helsinki fans meet fortnightly. The place was packed because of the con and because a big classical music festival was also on. I had a few beers and talked with Maaret and then with a fascinating and very assertive young woman called Joc (pronounced Yok and short for Johanna) who works in Sweden for some media company and also on a feminist popular culture magazine called *Darling*. She told me (and everyone else at the table) about Finland's taboos about the civil war, the 'continuation war' (where after the Winter War they continued fighting the Soviet Union in alliance with the Germans) and the post-war business about keeping the Russians happy. She also said that women in Finland are much less socially inhibited than women in Sweden, which I could well believe.

Kimmo then introduced me to Hannu, a music journalist in his forties who is a huge fan of my books, and we talked for a bit and then walked back to the hotel. This time we didn't fancy having a drink at the bar! The following morning, Steve, Neil and I—along with Kari, the tallest and thinnest member of the con committee—had breakfast with the US Ambassador.

The day before I left I'd got an email from Toni Jerrman (another member of the con committee, a long-haired guy who edits *Tahtivaeltaja*, a well-produced fanzine that has given me some good coverage). He said the GoHs had been invited to breakfast with the US Ambassador, who was a big SF enthusiast, and was that all right with me? It was. I packed a suit, but in the event it looked so shabby and unfashionable that I wore my black jeans, a shirt and tie, and my fancy waistcoat.

The embassy is as you might expect a big building in a posh area, and we were all introduced to people most of whose names I forgot before the handshake was over (a permanent embarrassment to me, and one reason I could never be a diplomat). As well as us there were people from the embassy staff, a real scientist and a couple of executives from the IT and mobile phone industries. Eric Edelman is a charming, courteous and intelligent man, whose career is listed at www.usembassy.fi/usmissio/edelman.phtml. He's also a science-fiction fan and well up on all the science-fictional themes and memes.

The discussion he chaired after we'd eaten was kicked off by a mention of an article in *Wired* by Bill Joy about the dangers of nanotech, robotics and biotech—the dangers including human extinction by mid-century. Also the demographic challenge of longevity, etc. If I'd read it before I might have made some different points, but on the whole I think the contributions made by myself and Neil and Stephen were fairly pertinent, and a good time was had by all. After that (he concluded the discussion at eleven sharp, without once looking at his watch) we (and some embassy staff on their way to a different function) were taken by embassy minibus to the con venue, Lasipalatsi. It's a cinema, with a bar and terrace. You go up a long flight of stairs to the bar and the terrace and the doors of the auditorium.

I then had a long interview with another Johanna, for *Spin*, the fanzine of the Turku SF society. I went to Steve's GoH talk, on the Fermi Paradox, which he pursued with fascinating rigour right up to the final paranoid possibility that the universe we see outside the solar system is a fake.

Then a book signing in Cafe Meteori, an internet cafe and bookshop around the corner, where about five people bought the new Finnish book, and I met the translator, Eevi Kuokkanen (Kimmo's wife), proud owner of the most battered copy of *The Star Fraction* I've ever seen. Niko Aula, the publisher, took me to the office in the 'Arabia' industrial district his company shares with another publishing company, introduced me to his assistant, Soile, and showed off their translations: Amis, Ballard, Banks...good company.

Then we drove out to one of the suburbs that ring Helsinki, which are themselves the three or four next-largest cities in Finland. He bought some food and drink (and I bought some drink) in the food floor of the main department store, Stockmann's. I could not believe the fruit and veg—everything seemed about twice the size and ten times the freshness of anything in our local supermarket. (Same with the produce sold from the back of a lorry at the flea market.)

Niko's house is big and so is their garden—the neighbourhood is sort of like American suburbia, but with lots more trees. He and his family were very hospitable and friendly. Dill-marinated sea-trout and a sauna—wonderful!—and beer and calvados on the porch deck, under the stars. I got a taxi back very late.

By morning I was getting a little anxious about my talk, so I made detailed notes for it, then hopped on the tram in time for an interview with Hannu, I think, and a restoring beer or two. The talk went fine—I talked about SF as congenial to liberalism in a broad sense as well as in the narrower sense of libertarianism, with examples, concluding with a brief discussion of the politics in my own books.

After that there was a kaffeklatch with half a dozen people at the Cafe Meteori, which went well, and then Niko, Kimmo and Hannu took me out to dinner at Kosmos, Helsinki's classic artists' and writers' restaurant. It's the coolest restaurant I've ever been in. Paintings on the walls, an opera singer doing a gig there later, waiters and waitresses who acted with casual dignity, and even the gents' is a work of art! I had fried Baltic herrings, which were fine but not as good as Scottish herring in oatmeal. The cost of the meal, which we split, came to about 25 pounds each including drinks, which is Not Bad.

We walked to the comics festival venue for the Masquerade, which Steve and I had been asked to be among the judges of. Past the Kiasma, the museum of contemporary art (some of it good and none of it Finnish, as Kimmo gleefully told me) and which actually is a chiasma, two different buildings intersecting—one part looks like an office block, the other like an incomplete generation starship—to a long, low brick building known as the Tsar's Stables, which is now an alternative hang-out. We met Steve and Sandra, got beers and went in, through more and more laser-lights, smoke, and loud music ('It's like a descent into hell,' Steve said) to a trestle table. Despite all the Goths and punks running around in perfectly acceptable skiffy/fantasy gear, there were only five items. We all agreed that Kosh was the best costume, but the rest were hard to place. Steve brilliantly suggested 'best bad acting' for Vampirella, 'best scary guy' for the Saint of Killers (a gunman in a long coat, kind of like the Preacher), 'best multi-part act' for the three rocketeers, and 'best single female act' for a girl in striped tights and pigtails. Ari and Kari thought this was fine, and we never heard any more about it because we made a dash for fresh air.

Predictably the bar was inadequate and the queues stretched around the Tsar's Stables and half-way to Russia, so after an hour or two of talking to Shimo, Petra and other members of Turku SF Society and getting drier by the minute I decided to head home about 11.30. If I'd had my wits about me I'd have suggested going to a pub, but it didn't occur to me.

I walked back to the hotel, with only one wrong turning, had an orange juice in the bar and went to bed after a welcome phone-call from home. Sunday I looked around the flea-market again, finding presents for my family, and then walked up to Lasipalatsi. I did a reading from *The Cassini Division*, which took less time than planned, and Gaiman, the next reader, was late. I could see Kimmo looking worried so offered to fill in with some Q&A, which went fine.

The book signing shortly afterwards was the biggest I've ever had—it went on for half an hour.

Then I sat out on the terrace, had another quick cable TV interview with the same guys as before, and talked with Jok and a few of her friends about politics and SF until Kimmo and Hannu dragged me off for dinner. We were joined by Markku Lappalainen and Mikko Pervila, who'd been lured into gofering and tech support. Naturally, the outwardly smooth organisation of the con had been accomplished by the committee and their helpers running themselves ragged, and from that side of the registration table it had seemed one step from chaos. But it had been a big success, with something over 6,000 separate visits over the con.

Dinner started with vodkas at the Café Moscow, which is an impressive postmodern recreation of a Soviet-era bar, all plastic tables and vinyl juke-box and pictures of Lenin. A very good and cheap Chinese dinner across the road, then weheaded for the dead dog party. I had a great time there, talking with lots of people (you know who you are). It was a remarkably well-dressed dead dog party—special mentions for Kimmo (his suit still sharp after a long busy weekend that would have reduced most people's minds, let alone their clothes, to laundry), Hanna (black lace dress, wild black hair and dark make-up on a pale face—she was a dead ringer for Death) and Joc (a knock-out in camo tee-shirt and long ivory satin skirt). I talked some more with the Turku SF society people, said my goodbyes, and found Joc and Hanna and their friends again in the corridor. I stayed for one more drink and a bit of conversation, then said goodbye to them too and got a taxi back to the hotel.

The following morning I packed and did one final trawl of the market, and found a really cute doll which I got for my daughter as soon as I'd found an equivalently cool thing for my son—a cheap but good pair of those new-style neato small binoculars.

The plane journey home went fine.

'I had seen a better world'

I was one of the Guests of Honour at Polcon 2002, (spelled 2pOlcOn2 in the con logo), the Polish national SF convention, held in Krakow from 29 August to 1 September 2002. For (Polish-language) details, see: http://polcon.fandom.art.pl/index.html

Just after I checked in at Edinburgh I realised I'd packed my Targus portable keyboard but not my Handspring, so my plan to keep an electronic diary fell through. This is reconstructed from memory and notes. I'll start with a short account of my arrival, and then—rather than giving a diary—go on to impressions and incidents.

My first glimpse of Poland, as we descended towards Krakow Belice, was of clusters of red-roofed houses among fields that were divided into narrow strips—narrower than the houses. Then, as the plane landed and taxied, I saw something else I'd never seen before: among the green-camouflaged military aircraft lined up along the side of the runway were biplanes. Not old ones, modern ones. Airport security was provided, as far as I could see, by young soldiers.

I was met by Jolanta Pers (Jola), a small, dark-haired woman in her 30s. She works in the IT industry, writing and translating documentation. (Documentation is the stuff that programmers never, ever do properly. Well, some of the stuff.) The car park was busy. The roads were a bit uneven but otherwise good and full of cars, mostly western but with a fair number of Polski Fiats, Star trucks and other vehicles from 'former times'. We drove through villages/suburbs where a lot of building and renovating was going on, and into Krakow. Ringed by the usual factories and apartment blocks, the central part of Krakow is full of beautiful old buildings, the ground floors of most of which were occupied by neon-bright new businesses. The whole effect is of a place which went straight from the nineteenth century to the 21st. As we all know, this impression is sadly illusory.

We passed the massive stone building of the Metallurgical and Mining Institute, which dates from the 1920s and has a post-communist statue of St Barbara on the roof and a communist era sculpture of metal-workers at the entrance. The con was to be held in another of the Institute's buildings, around the back.

On across the Vistula and through to Kazimierz, the old Jewish Quarter, now being renovated and the trendiest part of town. Older buildings, smaller shops. After several turns around a one-way system Jola pulled up outside the Hotel Astoria, a very new and nice hotel (which was currently doing a promotion so aggressive that Polcon was able to put me up there for free).

I left my luggage in a fresh and neat single room, changed into something lighter—the temperature was in the high twenties Celsius—and set off with Jola to the main market square. It's the largest market square in Europe, and at that time of the week was occupied largely with stalls selling tat, but different tat to what I'm used to. People were *carving* tat, right there. Around the square was a large number of very similar arrangements of tables and chairs and awnings and stuff, within which people were consuming beer and coffee and ice-cream.

We sat down and had a beer then walked off to see two churches, the Church of St Francis and the Church of St Ann. One of them had sort of Art Nouveau floral motifs on the interior walls and amazing Modernist stained glass windows—the one of the Creation was particularly fine, especially with the afternoon sun behind it—that reminded me, irreverently, of Marvel Comics covers. The other church (I forget which it was [St Ann]) had the most sumptuous Baroque interior decoration, cupids and flower and leaves in a riot of marble and plaster.

The next street we turned into Jola said was the oldest in the city. How old? Oh, about seven hundred years. And the university building we turned into from that was one where Copernicus had studied. We went through a passageway into a courtyard which had two levels of balconies with pillars and several stairways. It looked like a set for a play by Shakespeare because it was older than any play by Shakespeare.

So—on a bigger scale—did the Renaissance courtyard of the Royal Palace at Wawel Castle, which overlooks the town from a crag above the Vistula. From the castle you can see the Tatra Mountains on a clear day, and the Nowa Huta city of steelworks on a hazy one.

'Nowa Huta was built as a counter-weight to conservative intellectual Krakow,' said Jola. 'In that it was not a success.' (At this point we talked about Wajda's 'Man of Marble', some of which takes place in Nowa Huta. If you haven't seen this film, see it.)

After this Jola took me out for dinner, we had a beer, then I returned to the hotel and she drove home.

And now I'd better talk about the con, which began the following day. It was held in more than one building of the Metallurgical Institute, and it didn't seem to have any central meeting place or bar. The programming was quite largely devoted to fantasy, gaming, and LARP (Live Action Role Playing—'It's like being an actress! But better!' one young woman explained to me) so apart from the opening panel with Russian writer Kyril Jeskow and Polish writer Anna Brezinska, and a GoH interview on the Saturday, I wasn't greatly involved in it. I hung about the corridors and the steps outside, and talked to anyone who wanted to talk to me, and gave one interview for the magazine *Nowa Fantastika* (which is sold in news-agents' kiosks) and one for Jola's website, and the rest of the time I was being taken around sightseeing or out for meals or with a few people in a nearby pizza place which had a beer garden.

Polish fandom is (as Ken Slater and Bridget Wilkinson, who were also there joined me in marvelling at) overwhelmingly young, and most of them look like students, not like fans. They are willing to rough it, to crash, to bring sleeping bags. They are wonderful. They are enthusiastic, welcoming, and most of them speak English. Visit them if you can.

The official closing night of the con involved a masquerade, several awards including the Zajdel Award (the Polish Hugo), and a lot of partying afterwards in and outside the big bar where it was held. It was a warm night and a lot of beer was drunk; but, as with fandom everywhere, no-one behaved as if they were drunk apart from talking a little more loudly.

Speaking of drinking, Kyril was staying in the same hotel, and one night he split a bottle of peppered vodka with me, Russian style. Open bottle, leave the top off, and drink it shot by shot, eating slices of salami in between. His wife kept us company with a bottle of beer. Our discussion covered a great deal of ground, and I wish I could remember more of it.

Back to the sight-seeing. Jola and some of her friends took me to visit a salt-mine (which is full of statues carved from rock salt, and includes three chapels, the largest of which is more like a cathedral with chandeliers, an altar, a statue of the Virgin Mary, a statue of the Pope at the back, and the complete Life of Jesus in bas-relief around the walls, and a smooth patterned floor, all in salt), a Japanese Art Centre on the bank of the Vistula, and in the countryside around Krakow an abbey, a monastery, and lots of castles, many of them built on limestone outcrops with great pillars and buttresses of white rock incorporated into their walls.

In the mornings I did a bit of wandering around on my own, and saw a lot of the old Jewish Quarter—which is, bit by bit, shop by shop, cafe by cafe, becoming something of a new Jewish quarter. The size and number of synagogues in the quarter gives one to think. Two of them at least are functioning.

A bit further afield, just wandering around the centre, it was hard to believe that Poland was in the depths of a recession, with 20% unemployment. There's a huge shopping mall on the edge of town that could have dropped straight out of Western Europe (and more or less did, through a cloud of financial scandal) and is as big and bright and busy as a mall in America. Krakow looks busy and prosperous. The old one-industry towns, I was told, look anything but. The government is leftist—the ex-Communists and their allies. But neither the government nor the people are going back to the old system.

On the Monday evening I sat with Jola and her friends Robert and Derek in Alchemia, a trendy bar: dark, bad art on the walls, old wood, young crowd. Robert reminisced about being a student in the 1980s. On the 13th of every month there would be a Solidarity demo. How did you organise it? They all laughed. It wasn't organised. People knew when and where to gather, and to wear a leather jacket and good boots. The marches would proceed a short distance and then be broken up by the police. You spent the rest of the day and evening running and hiding. On the 13th of next month you did it again.

'It sounds funny now,' Robert said. 'But people were killed.'

He told me how, in the seventies, he'd been to France on a Scout exchange, and how he'd felt returning to a dark and gloomy Warsaw after seeing Paris. 'I had seen a better world.'

When I was walking to the aircraft for the flight home, I saw one of the military biplanes that had just taken off, flying into the morning mist. It was the only thing I saw in Poland that seemed to come from another world.

In conclusion I would like to thank the Polish fans for inviting me, and especially Jola, Krystyna, Robert and Derek for showing me around and looking after me so well. There's more I could say and much I've left out, but take it from me, Poland is a beautiful and surprising country, and its SF scene is lively and its fandom is welcoming. If you've never been there, just think of any mental image you have Eastern Europe and put it right out of your mind. It's nothing like that.

Go there if you can.

Seeing Mars from Uppsala

I've recently returned from Sweden, where I was one of three Guests of Honour at Swecon 2003, held 15-17 August at the Ångströmlaboratoriet, the physics building at Uppsala University. The other writer GoH was Alastair Reynolds, and the fan GoH was P. C. Jørgensen. I travelled with my wife Carol, who joins me in thanking Swecon and the fine SF bookshop SF-Bokhandeln for their generous hospitality. We stayed in the Eklundshof hotel, a very nice place about five hundred metres from the con.

Wednesday 13/8/03

We flew from a warm Edinburgh to a very hot Heathrow, and then on to Sweden: over the North Sea, then over fields, then forests all the way to the edge of the airport, Arlanda. It's a bright, airy, modern airport with great curving metal ribs under the roofs and a control tower that looks like it came from Tracy Island. Maria Jonsson and Sten Thaning met us and drove us to Uppsala. It's a small university town, with few buildings over four storeys; its skyline is dominated by a bulky red castle with dome-topped towers, and the distinctive double spire of the cathedral. We passed through the centre and on to Eklundshof to drop off our luggage, then to Johan Anglemark's house on the edge of town. Johan had prepared dinner for us and for a dozen or so fans. Chili con carne, followed by ice cream with warm cloudberry jam and punch (caloric punch), chilled. Lots of conversation. As one might expect, Johan has an impressive number of books and two cats.

Thursday 14/8/03

Woke in the morning to find the water was off, and that I'd forgotten to pack my shaving gear. Breakfast was self-service, with rolls and rye bread and crispbread, hams and cheese, and pots of pickled herring and caviar as well as cereals, dried fruits, and jams. Walked to the nearby gas station for wipes and razors. The path took me past the Ångströmlaboratoriet, a linked series of large red brick and glass window and metal strut buildings, outside of which shoals of bikes were parked. Back at reception I got an explanation of the water problem—mains broken. It came back on just before we left, at ten.

Walked in to town along the river bank, past houseboats and other boats, turned right at the bridge and then took the second or third left into main shopping street. The first shop we noticed was a thrift shop, where Carol bought a skirt and blouse and I sifted through old books. We had coffee and doughnuts at a pavement cafe, wandered through a mall and bought an umbrella at Stadium, the sports shop, as showers threatened. Met Sten at the station, as arranged, beside a big and rather odd statue of what looks like a couple dancing on top of the heads of much larger naked and priapic figures and various complicated symbolic instuments. He bought the tickets and joined us on the train to Stockholm. Stockholm is much livelier than Uppsala. Maria was waiting for us at the station. Walked up, past the big Lutheran kirk opposite the station, to Cafe Kondittori Bellman where we had coffee and pastries. Then walked down a long shopping street across bridges to the royal palace, guarded by young soldiers doing their military service, and on in to the old town, Gamla Stan. The SF-Bokhandeln, at the sign of the spaceship and dragon, is a fair way down one of Gamla Stan's long and very narrow streets. It's big, well-organised and has a huge English-language section. At the bookshop we met Al Reynolds and his partner, Josette, and the owners and staff. Maths (pronounced Matts), one of the owners, took me and Al through a low door down stone steps to an ancient cellar, where he and a man called Kristian and a woman called Tove interviewed us over a thermos of coffee. Carol and Josette went off with Maria and Sten, shopping. After the interview we had a successful signing session, up at the back of the shop.

After the signing we had drinks in the basement bar of Sally's Place, where one beer and one glass of wine cost 125 SEK (10 pounds). Then the SF-Bokhandeln people took us out to dinner in a very good restaurant, again downstairs. Walked back in the rain showers with Sten, Maria and Therese, who had baked the Tiptree bake sale cookies. Train to Uppsala, where Sten fixed us a taxi to the hotel.

Friday 15/8/03 and onward

Carol and I went into town and had a take-away lunch while people-watching in the mall (it was raining outside.) After finding the Uppsala English Bookshop we crossed a bridge to the town's cathedral, the double-spired Domkyrkan. We walked around it, looking at the tombs of various kings (all of whom seem to be called Gustav Adolf), of the biologist Carl Linne, and of the visionary theologian Emanuel Swedenborg.

The Uppsala English Bookshop has a better SF/fantasy selection than most bookshops in Britain, and the quality of its general stock is likewise high. The signing went well and afterwards we all ducked through rain and piled into cars along with boxes of Al's books and mine and made for the Ångströmlaboratoriet. Registration was on the door, and quick. We walked through halls the size of turbine rooms to the con's central site, a big room with a lot of tables, around which fans were already gathering and drinking beer. All except most of the fans we'd already met, who were on the committee and running themselves ragged, as they did all weekend.

They did a great job of it. Warm thanks to them all. It would be tedious to recount all the panels, but it was far from tedious—in fact, it was a joy—to participate in them. The English-language stream of the con seemed spontaneously to shape itself into a single long conversation about the future, about space and space opera, about the Singularity and alternatives to it. Everybody's English shamed my insularity. We lived for three days on beer and microwaved dinners and Tiptree cookies. It was great.

On the Saturday night, Carol and I were walking back to the hotel with Al and Josette, and I said something about Mars, and looked south and there it was, bright and red and close. A few minutes later, as we walked between trees, Josette pointed up and said, 'There's the space station.' And there it was, a swift spark.

After the con, Carol and I stayed on for a few days. We visited Stockholm again, and then again, and the beautiful island of Vaxholm in the inner archipelago; spent a day in Uppsala going around the ancient burial mounds of Gamla Uppsala, and the garden of Linnaeus where you can see plants labelled in the format *Genus species* L. and realise they were named thus by the man himself, the Adam of science in his own garden; and the Museum Gustavianum with its precipitous and evocative anatomy lecture theatre and its cabinets of curiosities. On our last day we went to the Vasa Museum, built around the great doomed ship, a tall massive bulk surrounded by as conscientious and vivid a reconstruction of its context as could be made. You walk around it, level upon level, you read label upon label, and gradually it makes sense and fills your mind.

Sweden is like nowhere else I've been. You can—literally—set your watch by the trains. Almost everyone looks healthy. Maybe it's the welfare state, maybe it's the ubiquitous bicycling, maybe it's the high price of booze. Whatever, and whether or not it's the future, it works. Visit it if you can.

Eight Days in Zagreb, Saturday, May 08, 2004

Carol and I went to Croatia the week before last. I was a guest of Sferakon, who covered our first four nights in the hotel; my flight was paid for by the British Council, for whom I gave a talk as part of a science festival at Zagreb's Technical Museum.

Vlatko Juric-Kokic met us at the airport, and his friend Goran drove us to the Hotel Dubrovnik. It was a sunny and hot afternoon and after unpacking we went to the nearest pavement cafe, just outside the hotel, and had a couple of beers. The hotel's in a pedestrianised area and it was a good place for people-watching. We then took a walk down Ilica, the longest street in Zagreb, busy with trams. That evening Vlatko took us out for dinner, and then up past the main square to a long street lined with pavement cafes and bars, at one of which we had another couple of beers. The currency is the kuna, of which there are about ten to a British pound. Prices for drinks and eating out are approximately half what you'd pay in Britain.

The centre of Zagreb looks very West European: Austro-Hungarian buildings, red tiled roofs on the houses, and the odd sixties or seventies office block. A few hundred metres in any direction from the centre and it starts to look more like your typical commie downtown, except with brighter neon and better stocked shops. Many of the shops are Western chains, others date back to the Kingdom or the Empire, and some are survivors from the socialist era. Vlatko said it was easy to tell which was which, and I guess a yellow neon sign with black lettering announcing (free translation) Electro-mechanical Devices or Things You Might Wear or Stuff To Eat is something of a clue (by contrast with, say, Miss Selfridge, United Colours of Benneton, or Somebodyic and Sons, Purveyors of Fine Wines and Provisions Since 1789). South of the river is Novi Zagreb, all post WW2 and mostly huge—and not at all identical—apartment blocks many of which seem to have a ground floor of small shops and cafes.

The general feel of the place is pretty laid back. People dress smartly and behave politely and are friendly. You couldn't ask for nicer. Croatia is both Catholic and nationalist, but relaxed about it, in the style of the Irish Republic today rather than in the thirties, or even modern Poland. What Croats primarily disliked about the SRY wasn't the socialism, it was the Serbian dominance.

Vlatko adds:

> Which is not surprising, considering that the original kingdom was created in 1918 as The Kingdom of Slovenes, Croats and Serbs. And then the Serbian king (whom they chose as the head of the state) grabbed all the power into his hands in 1921, installing the people whom he knew into positions of power—ie, Serbs from Serbia. That meant people of other nationalities got a very short shrift for quite a while, up to WWII.
>
> Tito tried to spread the power more evenly, but the state institutions were all in Belgrade.

The successes and failures of Yugoslav socialism were all its own. Dismantling it is a complicated process, including at the level of ownership, where the early wholesale theft and graft has given way to a careful legal unpicking of 'social property rights'. One fan told us that sixty to seventy per cent of people are worse off than they were under socialism, and that what the country really needed was someone like Margaret Thatcher. The average wage is between 300 and 400 UK pounds a month. People don't look that badly off, I said, especially young people in in central Zagreb. Hah! They make a drink last two hours and they live with their parents, he insisted.

Looking at old Yugoslav science fiction is intriguing. A stall at the con had stacks. Futura and other magazines, and the old SF paperbacks, had lurid and lively covers like American and British pulps. A very broad range of contemporary Western SF was available in translation—the only major writer poorly served was Heinlein, and that seems to have been down to a personal distaste on the part of the Grand Old Man of Yugoslav SF, Zoran Zivkovic, rather than official disapproval. SF clubs, like other interest groups, used to apply to the local Cultural Centre for facilities, and get sponsorship from enterprises and municipalities. Charmingly, translators transliterated Western names into Serbo-Croat spelling: Pirs Entoni, Dzejms Balard, Dzems Blis, Artur Klark, Dzon Kembel, Filip Hoze Farmer, Robert Hajnlajn, Mijkl Dzon Herison, Dejvid Lengford, Fric Lejber, Djon Verli, Dzil Vern, Djek Vens, Vernor Vinz are among many listed in Zivovik's massive, loving, dated encyclopaedia (enciklopedija) which I picked up second-hand at the con for 18 pounds (and worth every kuna for the illustrations alone).

Vlatko notes that some of these spellings are incorrect, and adds re transliteration:

> It is the usual linguistic practice in *Serbian*. Croatian leaves names in their original form. It's been like that from...oooh...at least since after WWI, I think. I do have some old Croatian books from 1890s (*The Ghost of Canterville*, frex) and they do have the original forms. OTOH, I also have a *Hamlet* from 1900 and something in Cyrillic and it, of course, has names transliterated.
>
> So I guess it's a remnant of the times when Serbia used only Cyrillic. (They returned to that in 1990s.)
>
> But the practice was present through the Yugoslav era, either the first or Tito's one. One of the differences between Serbian and Croatian.
>
> If the Encyclopaedia was published in Zagreb, and in Croatian, it would have the original names.

The con was held in the ground floor of the Electro-Engineering Faculty of Zagreb University. Hundreds of people attended over the weekend. As usual with this type of con, the average age was younger than you'd expect in Britain, and there was a likewise higher proportion of Trekkies (U.S.S. Croatia), modellers and gamers. Live Action Roleplay (LARP) enthusiasts work-shopped at tables. Making chainmail looks as repetitive and sociable as knitting. The program consisted mostly of talks rather than panels, and film and TV showings. I had four items: being interviewed by Vlatko; a talk about wild AI in global networks, which was followed by an enlightening discussion from the audience about economics and game theory; the launch of the Croatian edition of my YA novella *Cydonia*; and a talk about interstellar travel and life-extension. Otherwise Carol and I hung out, often in the doorway where the smokers gathered. Among other people, we met Milena Benini, who had translated *Cydonia* in a month. That's less time than I took to write it.

My lecture at the Technical Museum was on the Monday morning. Vlatko met us at the hotel and we walked there. The Technical Museum looks dilapidated from the outside—it's wooden, and an old Zagreb Fair stand—but inside it's airy and modern, with good exhibits: aircraft engines, a space probe, a robot football game. About a dozen people turned up for the talk. Most of them sat at the back. I gave an adaptation of my *Sunday Herald* article, then took questions. One guy asked intently about traces of life on Mars. Why were they so strange? I asked him to explain. The Face, he said—why is it so ugly? There were some better questions.

On Tuesday we took a tram to the same area, and explored the Botanic Gardens, which among other things have a pond with turtles. Then Vlatko and his girlfriend showed us around an exhibition of Art Nouveau in Croatia. That was fascinating and included a good deal of early-twentieth-century background material: photographs, advertisements, tableaux of well-displayed dresses, and furniture designed in the New Style. That evening we met up with lots of people from the con committee for a big dinner in a beer hall. The food was meaty in generous portions and the beer was great. Vlatko presented us with a double bottle of local brandy, a gift from the con.

Wednesday we took two tram lines north and west to the mountain that overlooks the city, and then the cable-car to the summit. The cable car holds two people. It zooms up a steep grassy slope to the first pylon, and then the ground drops away beneath you and you are soaring over a small valley, the first of several. Most of the time you're at treetop height. The trees are quite tall. At the top there is a very high television mast, several cafes, and the apparatus of a ski-slope. The air is noticeably thinner and colder. The view is spectacular, though at the time it was hazy.

The following day Goran drove Vlatko and us all the way to the Slovenian border to visit a very impressive castle, simultaneously a fine building and a formidable fortification (never actually attacked). The interior is wonderfully aristocratic, with hidden doors for the servants, massive furniture that smells like honey, libraries full of bound volumes of Sporting Life...The countryside to the north of Zagreb, once you get off the alluvial plain, is all rolling forested hills and small clusters of houses. Fields are generally tiny, and you sometimes see a man ploughing one with a tractor, or a woman weeding one with a mattock. I remarked that there were a lot of new houses. Just because you can see the bricks, Vlatko explained, doesn't mean they're new. They just haven't got round to plastering them. And looking closer, a lot of the apparently new houses had curtains in the windows and lights inside and gardens up to the raw brick. Goran took us to a summer-house that his grandparents had built in the sixties, an entire vintage wooden farmhouse dismantled from the plains and transported and rebuilt in the mountains. You could see the numbers on the beams.

In between all this, we wandered around the centre of Zagreb, taking in the usual sights that you can read all about in the Lonely Planet Guide. The fruit and flower markets, the Stone Gate, Saint Mark's, the Cathedral of the Assumption, the shortest funicular ride in Europe, and the best ice-cream shop (apart from Nardini's in Largs, Ayrshire).

We left with a very warm appreciation of Croatia, and of its fandom. Croatia used to be a popular holiday destination, and is becoming so again. We certainly intend to come back.

Forty Whacks, Sunday, May 23, 2004

Last week I was at the second installment of *Stitch and Split: Selves and Territories in Science Fiction* (http://www.stitch-and-split.org/), in Seville, sponsored by the *Universidad Internacional de Andalucia.* On the plane over I had a window seat. Saw the white cliffs of Dover, the Channel Islands, Britanny, the Bay of Biscay and then a long stretch of Spain. You can tell a country's system of inheritance from the air. Big fields <- primogeniture. A book idea: interesting stuff you can see and figure out from the window seat of an airliner. I can imagine a children's book, but also an adult one.

The University had a taxi waiting for me at the airport. The hotel was in an area called Triana, across the river from the older city and close to the Magic Island of buildings from Expo '92, and to the enormous former monastery in which the university has some rooms, and where the event was taking place.

I freshened up and got there in good time. The university's organizer for the event, Isabel Ojeda Cruz, a very attractive and pleasant young woman, took me through hundreds of metres of architectural marvel to meet Stitch and Split event organisers, the two Belgians I'd met at the earlier gig in Barcelona—Laurence Rassell and her partner Nicolas—as well as other participants and the translator, a bouncy muscular guy who has translated a lot of top-level meetings and is fairly sceptical of the top level as a result.

A Spanish SF writer, Juan Miguel Aguilera was also on the first evening, and he talked about space colonies. I missed some of his talk through not having my translation headphones gadget on the right channel, or something. My talk ('We are one people') was a run-through of the Fall Revo future history and an explanation of what political motives it had (basically a re-work of the Nova Express article from way back)—against identity politics and balkanization. A lot of lively discussion followed.

After that we had a break then watched *Born in Flames* (1983) a film by Lizzie Borden. This film is a cult classic, and deservedly so. Its innovative style and editing stand out and the passion of its creators and actors is evident, and it's a film I intend to see again. As a comment on the earlier discussion it was an inspired piece of programming by Laurence. The premise of this documentary-style film is that ten years after America's peaceful, democratic socialist revolution, women are still oppressed, and a new campaigning movement, the Women's Army, arises to fight this oppression. This would have been a fascinating film if that is what it had been about, but it isn't. It's still fascinating, but in a train-wreck kind of way.

First, we soon find that there has been no socialist revolution. The economy is obviously still capitalist, and not even what a hard-liner might call state capitalist. The new order is called 'social democracy' but it is not even that. Sweden could knock spots off the place. Absolutely no social gains are shown or implied. Not only has nothing changed for women, nothing has changed for anybody, apart from the rhetoric of the rulers. However, this is not a point made strongly in the film. Its whole thrust makes no sense unless it is saying that socialism makes no difference for women, but does for men.

The oppression of women in the future socialist America is in no way subtle. They are forced out of industrial jobs in favour of 'male heads of families'. They are raped in broad daylight in the street. Rape rehabilitation centres are set up to reintegrate rapists into society. Rape victims get nothing. Leave revolutionary or democratic socialism out of it—there is not a Stalinist or Social Democratic bureaucrat in the world who wouldn't jump at the chance to fix women's oppression at that level by pulling women into factories and pushing rapists into labour camps, as formerly existing socialism did. The actual forms of women's oppression in actually or formerly existing socialism didn't get a look-in.

The very best feature of the film was some rap-style singing by a young woman in one of the radical feminist radio stations.

The women's army has a charismatic lesbian black construction-worker leader, who has a charismatic black older feminist mentor behind the scenes. Their first actions are defending women raped in broad daylight in the streets, or hassled by boors on the Metro. Then they escalate to a big demo in New York. This is shown by clips of women's liberation demos of the 1970s, in which unfortunately for the film's thesis the banners and placards of revolutionary socialists are prominent.

The heroine is sacked from her construction job. Women demonstrate in hard hats for union jobs. Nothing happens. The young female editors of Socialist Youth Review, journal of the youth wing of the ruling party, denounce them on television. They, unlike the radical women, wear bouncy styled hair, blouses, and skirts. They mouth absurd lines without conviction. Young white men riot for jobs. Young black men riot for jobs.

Secretaries strike for job advancement prospects. After more of this sort of thing, the women's army gets serious, as only macho New Left Americans can get serious: they pick up the gun.

The heroine is arrested on return from the Saharan republic, where she has been getting military training from disaffected/betrayed Polisario women. She dies in prison in an apparent suicide, but actually a murder. The Socialist Youth Review women see the light, denounce this in their journal, and lose their positions on the editorial board.

Women's Army cadres seize television studios at gunpoint and forcibly broadcast their version of events. Repression hammers down. The radical feminist radio station is blown up. The Women's Army then plants a bomb in the transmission mast at the top of...the World Trade Center. The last frame is of a big explosion at the top of the Twin Towers. Fade to black. Credits roll.

Scattered applause from the audience.

I asked feminist SF critic Catherine Ramirez what she thought of it. She said she found it painful to watch.

The next day I wandered around the centre of Seville, taking in the Cathedral and the Alcazar. For sheer aesthetic overload I've seen nothing like either of them since I stood in front of the wall of the Library of Celsus at Ephesus. I also happened upon the Seville Book Fair, at which I was startled to find a stand of literature from the *Fundacion Frederico Engels* (http://www.engels.org/), associated with the website *In Defence of Marxism* (http://www.marxist.com/). I had a brief and friendly conversation with them, mainly about recent events in Spain.

That evening the British academic and political theorist Salman Sayyid gave a carefully reasoned discourse on how SF was an intrinsically anti-political genre, of which more later, and Catherine Ramirez gave a lecture on slavery and freedom in the SF of Octavia Butler.

I have to say that though I disagreed with it Salman's talk was the high point of the two days I was there, and the discussion that followed was intense. The film that evening was *Tribulation 99: Alien Anomalies Under America* (Craig Baldwin, 1991), a hilarious send-up of the maddest UFO conspiracy theories combined with an account of US interventions in Latin America (explained as its struggle against the aliens).

After each evening we all went out and had dinner around midnight, for 10 euros and 13 euros per head respectively, of some of the best food I've tasted anywhere.

Space Station Hinckley, Sunday, April 03, 2005

I spent the Easter weekend at the Hinckley Island Hotel, as one of the Guests of Honour at Paragon 2, this year's Eastercon or British National Science Fiction Convention. The hotel is outside Hinckley and, as its name suggests, is a bit isolated. But not to worry. Bar the odd trip by supply rocket (£5 inc. tip), it's fairly self-contained. Its reception area is a mirror-ceilinged polygon dominated by a 4-metre plaster statue of Neptune. (The god, not the planet.) This docking pod is at the end of one of the station's long habitation arms, which radiate from a central hub with a glass roof, through which you can observe the universe. These arms are called streets, and are lined with fake shop windows full of real tat, which you can buy at reception. There is one real shop, which sells cigarettes, magazines, and newspapers, except on Easter Sunday and Easter Monday, when by ancient tradition nobody smokes and nothing happens. The whole forms a starfish starship shape half-buried in an artificial mound built by some folk whose rituals required broad expanses of flat tarmac. It faces on to a fake lake containing real fish, on whose bank is a fake museum containing a real stage-coach and a real hackney cab, between the shafts of which are fake horses.

The bar serves real beer, and also by tradition, this ran out by Sunday.

Being an Eastercon GoH was, for me, a real honour, and I was very well looked after by the con committee—for which, many thanks. I took part in several programme events, went to more, and spent some time in the bar. Vivid memories include having a sort of continuing conversation across several panels with Richard Morgan, who heroically volunteered for every panel; longer bar or dinner conversations with Justina Robson, David Langford, Geoff Ryman, Ian Hocking, Frank Wu, Del Cotter, Farah Mendlesohn, Neil Williamson and friends, Charlie and Nojay; watching Dr Who on a big screen in a packed hall; accepting on behalf of the artist Stephan Martiniere the BSFA Award for best artwork, for the US cover of my novel *Newton's Wake;* eating elk salami on rye at the Scandinavian party; and having my brain eaten by Chthulu. Beyond that it's all a bit of a blur.

I came away from the conversations with a few new thoughts, which I intend to return to here over the next few weeks. Here's one for now. SF fandom is an odd community, and one that those outside it tend to lump together with media fans, technology geeks and enthusiastic hobbyists. But it isn't like that at all. The only group I know that is like SF fandom, and which oddly enough barely overlaps with it, is scientists. Scientists, at least the kind I used to know, dress idiosyncratically, drink lots of beer, talk about anything and everything, and *talk in italics.*

About Science Fiction

The first two of these were early, and probably premature, attempts to explicate the political meaning of the Fall Revolution books. They are sincere but confused. I no longer agree with everything I said in them. The third originated as a talk to a Libertarian Alliance conference in England about the libertarianism of SF. The fourth, about *Nineteen Eighty-Four*, originated as a rec.arts.sf.written post (back in the nineties, when a certain Bin Laden was not quite as famous as he is now). The others are reviews and surveys that chart a change and ultimately almost a reversal of my opinions about how SF has developed and what matters in it.—K. M.

Libertarianism, the Loony Left and the Secrets of the Illuminati

"Where do you get your ideas from?"

It may be a cliché but it's true: SF writers do get asked that question, a lot. I've written two SF novels which have had the odd distinction of being described as left-wing, indeed Trotskyist, by some reviewers, and as free-market libertarian by others. At first glance these contradictory assessments come from opposite sides of the Atlantic, but I rather suspect that the libertarian element in my books is more obvious the more familiar the reader is with libertarianism. British libertarians see it just as readily as do Americans; while the Trotskyist allusions are more easily picked up in the UK, a country where hundreds of thousands of people must have been members of Trotskyist organisations—if only for the three years between the freshers' fair and the finals.

A Basically Marxist Analysis of The World

Those hundreds of thousands include me. I was converted to Trotskyism in about 1972, and was active in left-wing politics, off and on, between 1976 and 1991. Even when I got fed up with Trotskyism and became a quite sincere member of the Communist Party—one of the last people to be politically won to the British Road To Socialism—I found that my political reflexes were unchanged: burnt-in like a CD-ROM. These days, well...I still have a basically Marxist analysis of the world and I still think the people who have to work for a living will eventually have little option but to take over the world and run it as a caring sharing co-op. I don't think the existing left will have much to do with making that happen.

Part of the reason why I think so is suggested in *The Star Fraction:* the Left's alliances are all too often opportunistic and counter-productive. There's a slight tinge of personal bitterness in that book, as well as a smidgin of nostalgia, both of which hark back to the time in the late seventies when I lived in an extended household of Trotskyists, feminists, and exiled nationalists collectively known as The Cats. What I came to feel—in a confused, sullen, resentful way—was that the agenda of my political activity was being set by an ever-expanding coalition of minorities, and had nothing to offer the majority of the population and in consequence had nothing to offer me. As Margaret Thatcher, and now Tony Blair, have spectacularly demonstrated, I was not alone in that selfish thought.

The Alternative Bookshop

As well as doing the usual Trotskyist stuff—selling papers, going to meetings and marches, reading perspectives documents, splitting and wrecking, underestimating the peasantry and so forth—I was interested in other political ideas, and particularly in other 'extremist' political ideas. I literally wandered across libertarian political theories by accident. The first time I came across real live libertarians was around 1980, when I delivered a bundle of copies of The Freethinker to the Alternative Bookshop in Covent Garden. Pamphlets from Amnesty International, the Legalise Cannabis Campaign, and an assortment of unrespectable anarchists, dissident socialists, feminists and gay liberationists were displayed next to critiques of socialism and defences of capitalism.

I was intrigued. Up until then, I'd always thought of free-marketeers as Tories—people who might be for one kind of freedom out of sheer self-interest, but who were against all sorts of other freedoms, including the freedom to enjoy sex and drugs and rock and roll. This was different. And, to be honest, I was alienated enough from my own political activity to welcome, at some level, any stick with which to beat it.

Chris Tame and Brian Micklethwait, who ran the shop and still run the Libertarian Alliance, were not at all put out when I told them I was a communist and I wanted to know what they were all about. They told me, politely and at length. I was amazed to learn that *Illuminatus!*, by Robert Shea and Robert Anton Wilson, was (among other things) a satire on the US libertarian movement and its leading personalities. They were intrigued to find that I had an idea for an SF novel set in a society where "the state was privatised", and they told me the name for this arrangement: anarcho-capitalism.

I already agreed with much of what the libertarians had to say, about sex and drugs and rock and roll. I became reluctantly convinced that free speech meant nothing unless it meant free speech for people you regard as utterly mistaken and thoroughly depraved: fascists, holocaust revisionists, tobacco advertisers, etc. As the eighties wore on, I found it increasingly hard to refute what the libertarians had to say about the economic idiocies and political follies of the left. At the same time, I had to disagree with them on other points, and I still do. There's the little matter of capitalism, for example. My enthusiasm for the free market is a great deal more conditional than theirs.

There is also the tricky question of what 'consent' actually means. An indirect, but personal, acquaintance with the issue of sexual abuse—and the disillusioning effect this had on my notion of how much 'bourgeois respectability' was worth—occasioned some painful reflections on this point. This is what lies behind the section in *The Stone Canal* in which two sympathetic characters go on a killing spree, and what (I think) makes it a communist novel about libertarians, in much the same way as *The Star Fraction* is a libertarian novel about communists.

What Is Libertarianism?

So far as the political ideas are concerned, it's easy enough to explain where they came from. They came from thinking about my experiences with the British far left; from thinking about the implications of various libertarian proposals; and from thinking about the implications of the 'non-market socialism' associated with the few but persistent propagandists of the Socialist Party of Great Britain. The conflicting political interpretations of my novels have their roots in the inevitable tensions that result.

What is libertarianism, anyway? 'Libertarianism', like 'freedom', is a contested term. It's used as a synonym—in fact, it was originally a euphemism—for socialist anarchism. It's also used, particularly in the US, to describe an outlook which at its extreme could be called capitalist anarchism. This tends to be regarded as an American import, quite irrelevant to Britain. This is a mistake. Libertarianism is rooted in elements of a political and legal system which America shares with Britain, and which originated in Britain. Its first organised political expression was the radical wing of the English Revolution, the Levellers. Contrary to a labour movement myth, the Levellers weren't pioneer socialists—that honour belongs to the Diggers. The Diggers opposed property, root and branch. The Levellers based their whole political theory on it. They were libertarians of the 'propertarian' persuasion, without a doubt.

The first time I came across the word 'libertarian' was not in a text of political philosophy but in James Blish's *Cities in Flight:* "Under the relentless pressure of competition from the USSR and its associated states, Earth's Western culture had undertaken to support a permanent war economy, under the burden of which its traditional libertarian political institutions were steadily eroded away." (p. 168 of the Arrow 1974 edition). Since the West's traditional institutions are hardly notorious for socialist anarchism, Blish here clearly refers to a political ideology which affirms the rights, however derived, to 'life, liberty and justly acquired property'—the principles of classical liberalism, developed by John Locke, Adam Smith, Lord Macaulay, Lord Acton, Herbert Spencer and John Stuart Mill.

The Truth About the Isolationists

Interestingly enough, the analysis of the 'permanent war economy' and its predicted political effects, to which Blish alludes, was advanced in the US by one wing of American Trotskyism, later influential on the New Left; and at almost the same time by the remnants of what is now called the Old Right, the maligned 'isolationists' who opposed the New Deal and US involvement in World War Two and the Korean War and the Cold War. Most of them, it turns out, were classical liberals. Nowadays this truth about the isolationists has gone down the memory hole: any opponent of Roosevelt's domestic and foreign policies is vaguely assumed to have been some kind of fascist. Dimitrov, who launched this smear at the Seventh Congress of the Comintern, would be proud of its continuing success.

The tradition of liberal anti-imperialism has been carried into the present, most notably by the late Murray N. Rothbard, whose *For a New Liberty* is one of the manifestos of modern anarcho-capitalism. Rothbard's anti-imperialism extended to an attempt to ally with the US New Left against the Vietnam War, not to mention his memorable response to the Falklands/Malvinas campaign: "Finish the American Revolution! Sink the Brits!" Whatever this was, Thatcherism it wasn't.

Interesting Templates for SF

Libertarianism, like SF, has a respectable past and a disreputable present: its roots in the work of people who are conventionally admired, even revered, certainly regarded as mainstream; its leaves and branches populated by obscure pamphleteers and amateur publishers and indigent academics and Internet addicts like us. Just as there are people who will indignantly deny that *Nineteen Eighty-four* and *Brave New World* are SF, there are plenty of people who profess to be shocked at the idea that John Locke and John Stuart Mill and Adam Smith were (ugh!) libertarians.

So I've found, anyway, in discussions on the Internet. I used these discussions, and conversations with some of the friends I made through them, to bring into focus the anarcho-capitalist enclave of Norlonto in *The Star Fraction.* The ideas behind Norlonto derive from Rothbard's *For a New Liberty*. The slightly different anarchy of New Mars, in *The Stone Canal*, owes more to another exposition of anarcho-capitalism,

The Machinery of Freedom by David Friedman. (The court system of New Mars is partly inspired by one of Friedman's real-world models of 'free market anarchy', the Iceland of *Njal's Saga*.) I have no strong views about the likelihood of such societies arising or persisting, but they certainly provide interesting templates for SF—as I'm far from the first to discover.

How Utopian Ideas Bring about Change

What's the political relevance of writing about the extreme implications of a way of political thinking? After all, we all know that—except in extreme circumstances, like Germany in the thirties—extremism loses votes, as the alleged socialists in the Labour Party demonstrated in the eighties and the alleged libertarians in the Tory Party may yet demonstrate in the nineties. The fact is that while utopianism is useless as an electoral strategy, it is very useful indeed as a way of changing people's minds over the long run.

Take the example of socialism. The utopia of *News From Nowhere* has nowhere been achieved, but the idea of it has helped to bring-about changes that were once considered 'socialistic'—although William Morris himself would almost certainly have regarded them as paltry at best and going in completely the wrong direction at worst, i.e. towards state capitalism, albeit democratic welfare-state capitalism. The point is that if people see Morris's vision of socialism—a world-wide classless, stateless, moneyless society—as desirable (and personally I find it difficult to read *News From Nowhere* without desiring it, without indeed feeling something as intense as homesickness or unrequited love for it) and if people believe—as Morris emphatically didn't—that democratic welfare-state capitalism is a stepping stone to socialism, then *News From Nowhere* undoubtedly helped to bring about our present wonderful society. Similarly, the dystopia of *Nineteen Eighty-four* has done a great deal to undermine support for even democratic state socialism, despite the fact that George Orwell actually supported the Labour Party and was a pretty authoritarian democratic state socialist himself.

The threat of a '1984' society is (we may charitably assume) what motivates the 'libertarian' militarism of SF's cold warriors: the Defence of the Free World. There is a case for this: faced with the choice between Stalinism and liberal democracy, tens of millions of people have supported the sort of policies advocated in fiction by Niven and Pournelle. Unfortunately the methods used, from nuclear deterrence through napalm bombing to contra terrorism, actually undermine what you're allegedly trying to defend. To refer back again to Blish, the relentless competition with the Soviet bloc has been won, but the West's traditional libertarian political institutions have been eroded in the process, and are still eroding by the day.

We live in a country where the knee-jerk response to a perceived social problem, or to the misuse of objects—from handguns to hooch—is a hasty, ad hoc law, or the threat of a law; and a world where the knee-jerk response to a national problem is an international intervention, with the new missionaries of the Non-Governmental Organisations softening up the stricken populations for the new colonial marines, the boys in the blue berets. Humanitarianism and peace-keeping have become the new ideologies of imperialism, undermining fragile states of national independence which millions fought, and sometimes died, to achieve.

As a socialist, I have no hesitation whatever in opposing this erosion of the West's traditional libertarian political institutions; and as an SF writer, I have no compunction at indicating the grievous consequences of their loss, and suggesting the glorious consequences of their future recovery.

A Link Between Libertarianism and Socialism

So much for the loony left and libertarianism. What about the secrets of the Illuminati? Most of us who have heard of that mythical conspiracy at all have heard of it via Robert Anton Wilson. (It was quite a surprise to me to find that it actually existed.) Wilson and Shea used it as a deliberately confusing metaphor for both the 'conspiracy' of big capital and the state which makes up the New World Order (the phrase was used by conspiracy theorists long before George [H. W.] Bush—as they see it—incautiously blurted it out) and as a metaphor for the alliance of 'Left' and 'Right' libertarians which their book projects as the last, best hope of defeating it.

It was that idea which inspired the 'Last International' in *The Star Fraction*, and which Wilde plays with in *The Stone Canal*. But I sometimes wonder if there isn't something in it, and I recently stumbled on an intriguing link between libertarianism and socialism, in a series of personal connections between Robert Anton Wilson and one of the founding fathers of socialism. This common ancestry may be as spurious as Piltdown Man, but here it is:

Of all the libertarian writers, Robert Anton Wilson must be the best known and best liked by socialists and anarchists of the left. RAW's individualist anarchist ideas were influenced by his friend Laurance Labadie, whose father Joseph Labadie worked with the great American libertarian Benjamin Tucker. Tucker regarded his venerable friend Josiah Warren (1798-1874) as his 'first source of light'. ('Light'? Another masonic/illuminist allusion? Ha!) Warren founded individualist anarchism after the collapse of a utopian commune founded by his venerable mentor, the English communist Robert Owen.

According to Nesta Webster, the first and probably worst of this century's great conspiracy theorists, Robert Owen was a member of the Illuminati…

I rest my case.

The Falling Rate of Profit, Red Hordes and Green Slime: What the Fall Revolution Books are About

2001. Queensferry, West Lothian, Scotland. I'm halfway through a novel due in six weeks or so. I've rashly agreed to Lawrence Person's offer of A Shameless Opportunity for Self-Aggrandizement: 'I was wondering if you would be interested in writing an article on why you wrote those four books, what you meant to say, and how they fit together.' How can I resist?

The four books in question are *The Star Fraction, The Stone Canal, The Cassini Division* and *The Sky Road,* which I group together as 'the Fall Revolution books'. When I started writing *The Star Fraction,* back in 1987, I had no idea of where it would end up, let alone of making it the start of a series. It still isn't: though they have a future history and some characters in common, the books can be read in any order, and the last two of them —*The Cassini Division* and *The Sky Road*—present alternative possible futures emerging from that mid-21st century world I imagined at the beginning.

The way the books are connected is via a technique with which I began *The Stone Canal:* to take a minor character in one book and make them the central character in another. In a rather similar way, minor ideas and throwaway lines from an earlier book expand into major elements in others. In each book, the main characters are—in the light of the other books—arguably mistaken as to what's going on. The big picture only emerges from all of them, together, and it's only there for readers who like to puzzle out that kind of thing.

The future history which underlies the books wasn't worked out in advance either. Instead it accumulated from details. The premise which ultimately made all—or most—of these details hang together, is this: what if our civilization is in decline, and there are no forces within it to arrest that decline and renew or revolutionize civilization?

A broad analogy may help clarify the point: the Roman Empire rested on a slave population which couldn't reproduce itself, and which therefore had to be renewed by fresh conquests. When imperial expansion reached its limits, the available labour force and with it the whole system went into decline. Marx believed he had detected a similarly limiting factor in the tendency of the rate of profit to decline. Noted by Smith, Ricardo and Mill as well as Marx, it implies that capitalist economies tend towards what the classical economists called 'The Stationary State' and Marx called 'Crisis'. With the growth of constant capital, Marx argued, previously-accumulated capital becomes a growing drag on further accumulation. What if he was right about capitalism, but wrong about socialism?

What follows is a reconstruction of the future history that emerges from the stories. The first future event referred to in any of them is the election of a radical reforming government in Britain in 2015, which abolishes this 'Hanoverian' state's remaining feudal and Royal trappings. The new United Republic confronts instability within and without. Left-wing, nationalist, Green and libertarian-technophile movements keep it busy at home. The Balkan Wars widen as more and more of Eastern and Southern Europe gets sucked into the maelstrom genreated by post-Soviet Russia—the 'Former Union'—as it disintegrates into a patchwork of mafia fiefdoms and socialist statelets ('communistans').

In 2020 the Germans try to restore order by launching the War of European Integration, a military drive to the East and South-East. The conflicts over participation in this war feed into Britain's existing tensions, leading to a fiercely-resisted 'Hanoverian' military coup against the Republic. Europe's war and Britain's incipient revolution are ended when the US comes into the war under the cloak of the UN, using its Israeli client-state to nuke German cities and armies.

Britain, after a brief, brutal and widely popular US/UN occupation, becomes a balkanised Kingdom in a balkanized world under a US/UN hegemony enforced by an American monopoly on nuclear weapons and space-based military force. Potentially destabilising technologies are suppressed or driven underground. This global order confronts a disorderly global resistance. In Britain, the final assembly of the Republic's parliament formally passes its authority to its remaining armed forces, which as the Army of the New Republic (ANR) fight on as the 'legitimate government'. (The precedent and parallel here is with the last all-Irish elected parliament, the Second Dail, whose legitimacy is still claimed by the Army Council of the IRA.) In the far East, China has begun to disintegrate like Russia, and there's a long messy war going on with the Japanese in Siberia and Manchuria. Remnants of the Russian and Chinese armies, and fragments of their border territories, unite in a neo-communist alliance calling itself the Sino-Soviet Union. Meanwhile, the pro-capitalist Vietnam Workers' Party and the Islamic Republic of Thailand are slugging it out with reactionary Green guerrillas, the Khmer Vertes.

The latter are one of many such Luddite movements, referred to in the books as 'the barbarians' or 'the barb' or 'the Green slime'. Their social base is among the growing rural and urban surplus populations thrown off by the system's decadent combination of development and decline: 'Wealth accumulates and men decay,' as the man said. A contradictory progress continues. Lifespans are technologically extended (free rejuve on the NHS by 2020—count me in) but that's no guarantee that an individual's life won't be short. The infrastructure of Space Defense allows a margin for crackpot libertarian and other idealists to try out space colonization, and eventually for actually profitable space industrialization (cf. the development of the Internet.) Militantly extropian posthumanists in the niches of underground 'black tech' and the fringes of the space movement struggle to escape the bonds of Earth and flesh.

By the hot autumn of 2045, policing this mess has become too much for even the US/UN. A successful ANR offensive in Britain, co-ordinated with similar insurrections elsewhere, detonates the worldwide Fall Revolution. Its success in throwing off this new world order leads to attempts to re-unify fragmented nations. But, as one of the characters says, 'What we thought was the revolution was only a moment in the fall.' The civil wars go on. So does the gradual but implacable spread of the Sino-Soviet Union ('the Sheenisov') which brings direct democracy and cybernetic socialism to the communities and countries it conquers. America itself begins to break up, becoming another Former Union: FU2. (Think text message.)

Space Defense spending goes into freefall, but there's a brief flowering of space development as formerly-suppressed technologies come online: nanotech 'diamond ships' and advanced AI carry a new wave of space settlers beyond the reach of barbarian or bureaucrat. Their attempt to seize the Space Defense battlesats in a 'space movement coup' only worsens the situation below. Cut off from Earth, the space settlers split between humanist 'Earth-Tenders' and posthumanist 'Outwarders', the latter of whom flee to Jovian orbit and consummate their transcendence to become the 'fast folk'.

Farther ahead, towards the end of the 21st century, loom even larger and grimmer events: the pandemic know as the Green Death, and the Outwarder viral assault known as the Crash. Civilization on Earth collapses, to be eventually revived—with aid from the humanist space settlers—behind the lines of the Sheenisov's century-long advance to the Atlantic. Beyond that dark 22nd century lies the Solar Union, the Sheenisov-founded utopia whose space-based defense force is the eponymous Cassini Division: egoist communists with attitude, up against posthuman AI with an unknown agenda.

The Sky Road shows the very different world that emerges when Myra, a minor character in *The Stone Canal,* tips a crucial decision the other way. The Sheenisov advance is thrown into disarray, and the space-based progenitors of the posthumans wiped out, in the book's central catastrophe, the Deliverance. Centuries later a society has stabilised where communism and capitalism alike are rejected and abhorred, in a federal quasi-anarchy where Proudhon's mutual banks and Henry George's single tax allow high technology to flourish in Highland towns. The despised barbarians of the previous books have won, and made an arguably better and freer world than either the anarcho-capitalists or the anarcho-communists can offer.

So that's the future history, and that's how the books fit together. The questions that remain are why I wrote them, and what I meant to say. I wrote them out of a fury of political frustration and rage at the balkanization of the world and the fragmentation of the Left. What I meant to say was that the politics of identity gives us the post-civilised world, the world of which post-Soviet Russia is the future, and it doesn't work.

I wrote them for other reasons too, of course, the central one being that the main characters in *The Star Fraction* had haunted my imagination for almost as long as I'd wanted to write science fiction. Likewise, there are other political and philosophical themes, the central one being that there is a deep connection between the AI project of digitizing information, and the capitalist process of commodifying the world. This connection is made quite explicit in the writings of the Extropians, notably Hans Moravec.

Uploaded humans, he says, 'may feel a great economic incentive to streamline their interface to the cyberspace. The streamlining could begin with the elimination of the body-simulation along with the portions of the downloaded mind dedicated to interpreting sense-data. These would be and replaced [sic] with simpler integrated simpler programs [sic] that produced approximately the same net effect in one's consciousness.' (Moravec, 'Pigs in Cyberspace' (Extropy, Vol 3 No.2 (#10)), Winter/Spring 1993).

Underneath this gabble you can hear the tireless nada nada nada natter of the enemy. It's like listening to the Borg, or the IMF. Resistance, I wanted to say, is not useless. Which brings us back to the political ideas. Like the characters, some of them go back a long way.

1972. Greenock, Renfrewshire, Scotland. An industrial town on a beautiful estuary, the Firth of Clyde. From almost every street you can see the river and the hills. I was at Greenock High School, I was a gauche outsider with a few good friends, I was a science fiction reader and a flying saucer believer and a library junkie. I had read Ballard's short story 'The Killing Grounds' and John Brunner's novel *The Jagged Orbit* and *Future Shock* and *Obsolete Communism* and *Chariots of the Gods* and every piece of UFO lore and science fiction science and pseudo-science and politics and sociology I could lay my hands on. It's difficult to convey, now, the intellectual hegemony of the left in the early 1970s. Marxism was merely the extremism of the mainstream consensus.

Working leftward along the shelves I discovered that there were Marxists who had sided with the Hungarian workers of 1956, with the Prague Spring and the Paris May of 1968 and the Polish strikers of 1970; none of which had prevented them siding with Russia against Hitler, and with Korea, Cuba and Vietnam against the US. They were called Trotskyists, and what they said seemed to make sense in a country shaken by a militant unofficial labour movement and a small war in Ireland, and a world whose starkest divisions were flashpointed by the war in Vietnam.

When I read *The Female Eunuch* I instantly added feminism to my eclectic world-view. By my final year at Glasgow University I thought I had socialism and feminism well sussed, that they were walking hand in hand to the barricades of the same revolution. And from what I could see of the women in the left groups, they were feminists, they were socialists, and they were baaad girrls who drank and smoked and fucked and read and wrote and were, like, you know, *liberated*. None of my girlfriends were in left groups but they were all influenced by that feminist and socialist ferment.

In 1976 I went to Brunel University as a post-graduate student, joined a Trotskyist group, and discovered that the movements weren't hand in hand at all. Socialist feminists active in the women's movement were red-baited by radical feminists for being in the same organisations as men. They in turn attacked any women comrades who didn't make the women's movement their main political focus—thus, as I saw it, red-baiting *inside* the party.

I worked on one campaign with a rather nice radical lesbian feminist. At a party I had a long and serious conversation with her, in which she explained that *all* relationships between men and women were oppressive, that there was *nothing* men could do about it, if men wanted to help they would *stop* having relationships with women, and that ideally, men and women should live in separate societies. I decided that if that was what feminism meant, then it actively didn't want any support from me and it wasn't going to get any.

Something like this conversation must have gone on up and down the country, because that is exactly what all too many people now take 'feminism' to mean. Over the years I have met a lot of women, and heard of a lot more, who are feminist in every aspect of their beliefs and attitudes but who firmly insist that they are not feminists. The reason they give is always the same: they don't consider themselves feminists because *they don't hate men.*

Imagine if the left had taken the most hostile caricatures of what socialism was and what being a socialist meant, and proceeded to live up to them. Lots of people would now be saying things like, 'I'm not a socialist, but I think capitalism sucks and should be replaced by a system based on common ownership and democratic control of the means of production and distribution.'

Oh, wait. That happened.

1987. Finsbury Park, Islington, London. A multi-ethnic working-class area. I'm married with two kids and I have a good job, as a programmer. I've finished (at long last) the thesis I started at Brunel, and I want to start writing my book. It's a hot, sultry, thundery summer which has everyone believing in global warming. A big storm flattens millions of trees in Southern England, the stock-market crashes and perestroika takes off. The left is losing its confidence and its grip, fragmenting into identity politics, fascinated by the free market. I'm ahead of the curve on that one: reading Libertarian Alliance literature has been my secret vice for years. The free market is fine by me, but not the identity politics.

The problem, as I saw it, with identity politics was that it implicitly told people that their interests were fundamentally irreconcilable: that the victory of feminism meant a world without men, of gay liberation a world without straights, of anti-racism a world without whites. Few indeed took that logic to its conclusion. What they did instead was act as though it was ideally true, but that action in the real world unfortunately required them to settle for less. What the 'less' amounted to was a share in the control of the repressive state apparatus and the ideological state apparatus, which the various groups then used to torment and harangue the rest of society and each other. In Britain this was called the 'loony left'.

Gens una sumus, I still think, and I still blame the feminist-influenced, Trotskyist-riddled Labour Left for the Labour defeats of the 1980s. I have no patience with Labour's left-wing critics. I'll never forgive the present Labour government for bombing Belgrade, but I'd vote Labour even if they bombed Moscow. There's a misconception that because some of the sympathetic characters in the Fall Revolution books are Trotskyists, I'm sympathetic to Trotskyism. I'm not. One theme of the books is betrayal, which is always associated with Trotskyists (except in *The Cassini Division,* where they're all dead): most explicitly in *The Star Fraction,* most personally in *The Stone Canal* and most bitterly in *The Sky Road,* where Myra is a CIA asset, betrayer and betrayed.

In that I was more accurate than I knew. As a Trot I'd been a CIA asset myself. In October 1999 an episode of the BBC series 'The Spying Game' explained how the left-wing Czech emigre Jan Kavan had used a specially-built van to smuggle thousands of books into Czecheslovakia—books paid for by the CIA.

I knew all about Kavan and his van already, having been on one his smuggling expeditions myself back in 1977. The Trotskyist group I was in at the time ran lots of them. Kavan is now the Foreign Minister of the Czech Republic. The CIA certainly got its money's worth out of him, and me. Don't get me wrong—I'm not sorry I did it, but there is a certain irony in the fact that the only revolution I ever contributed a jot to was a counter-revolution.

By 1987 I could see the counter-revolution coming. I was convinced by von Mises' famous Economic Calculation Argument that private property was essential to industrial civilization: without property, no exchange; no exchange, no prices; no prices, no way of telling whether any given project is worthwhile or a dead loss.

But I was no less convinced by Marx's argument on the tendency of the rate of profit to fall. Unfortunately, there's no reason why the Economic Calculation Argument and the Law of the Falling Rate couldn't both be true. What if capitalism is unsustainable, and socialism is impossible?

We're fucked, that's what.

As Engels said, and as I thought then, capitalism will be replaced by either socialism or barbarism. Socialism, as Mises said, and as I thought then and still think, is impossible.

Barbarism it is, then. That's what's coming down the pike, and the only option is to make it as comfortable and civilised a barbarism as possible. With that cheery perspective in mind, I was ready to start writing.

It was hot on the roof.

Science Fiction, Liberty, and Literature

Why talk about liberty and science fiction specifically, in the first place? Well, I'm sure there are fascinating discussions to be had on issues of liberty in the Western, the crime story, the thriller, the romance...and I'm not kidding about that, actually. But SF and libertarianism have a special relationship, clearly recognised by hostile critics of both.

For example, Andy Robinson, in the British unorthodox-Trotskyist magazine *Workers Liberty* (No 36, Nov. 1996, p. 40) writes about how popular culture promotes capitalism:

> 'Even fantasy, adventure, horror and sci-fi often revolve around procapitalist ideological concepts such as the individual (usually male, white etc) hero, the evil villain, and militarism,' he tells us, and goes on to point the same finger at detective stories, crime thrillers, women's magazines—you know how it goes. But SF is perhaps the worst offender. *Star Trek*, he says, is Cold War in space. *The X-Files*, according to Robinson, 'promotes fear of the power of "big government" which in America can be used to justify welfare cuts and lax laws in areas such as firearms and environmental protection. At the same time, it contains a semi-revolutionary cynicism about politicians, the military, the police and business.'

To some of us this might all sound like a very good idea, but Robinson is on the case:

> 'This is, however, portrayed in such a way as to deny real outlets and present flawed ones. We should seek to change society by exposing the truth, implies the series—not through working-class struggle.'

Well, he said it. The truth is out there!

To understate the obvious, not all libertarians are SF readers, and not all SF readers are libertarians. But I'd hazard a guess that there's more of an overlap than there is between other genres and other political positions. And while libertarianism is very much a minority opinion among SF readers, writers and even fandom, it is at least understood in those circles. They may vehemently disagree with it, but they know roughly what it is. If you're talking about libertarianism to SF readers you have this wonderful automatic shorthand, you can point, you can say the moon colony in Robert Heinlein's *The Moon is a Harsh Mistress* and America in Neal Stephenson's *Snow Crash* have anarchocapitalist institutions, or Annares in *The Dispossessed* by Ursula Le Guin—or better yet, Chronos in James P Hogan's *Voyage From Yesteryear*—has anarchosocialist institutions, or the Spider kingdom in Vinge's new book *A Deepness in the Sky* (Tor Books, NY, 1999) is a minimal state, or whatever. You have a collection of paper models of alternative societies. Another thing that makes SF as a genre unusual is the proportion of its well-known writers, known to almost all readers of the genre, who've been libertarian or have dealt with libertarian themes. Think of Robert Heinlein and Poul Anderson among the big early names, or Neal Stephenson and Vernor Vinge today.

The next interesting question is—what are the reasons for that?

To state the obvious, they're both about the future. You'd have to be rather unimaginative to read the libertarian political philosophers Murray Rothbard or Robert Nozick or David Friedman without some pictures about a possible future society flitting through your mind. In fact, all of them tell little science-fictional tales to illustrate their points, most imaginatively in Nozick, and most explicitly in Friedman, who points his readers to SF stories like Vinge's 'The Ungoverned' and Anderson's 'Margin of Profit' and 'No Truce with Kings'.

Similarly, if you're writing a story about the future and you want to make it interesting, your heroes or heroines might be struggling against an oppressive regime or stuffy bureaucracy or reactionary mob to build their spaceship, raise their robot child, twiddle their DNA and become as gods. Or they're rich, like Heinlein's *Man Who Soldthe Moon,* and how did they become rich, huh? By screwing taxes out of the peasantry? Taking or giving bribes? Well...maybe, but it's so much more sympathetic to present someone who made their pile in some kind of free-market way, and that implies a certain kind of society, for a start one that lets them bloody well keep it.

More fundamentally, as Chris Tame has pointed out, a central theme of SF has been to celebrate the struggle of humanity against the inimical aspects of nature, and by the mere story-telling necessity of focussing on individual striving, it implies that individuals can make a difference in that struggle. I remember Barry MacLeod-Cullinane making that point even more forcefully in conversation, when he tried to persuade me that 'all literature is libertarian'. That may be taking it too far. But even SF's greatest work of collective struggle, Olaf Stapledon's *Star Maker*, in which entire species and civilizations are the 'characters', ultimately returns to this point, to the freedom and reason of the individual striving for 'some portion of lucidity before the ultimate darkness.'

An American SF editor and former political activist pointed out to me recently that particularly in the seventies there was really nowhere else to go politically for fannish people who were keen on space. Mainstream political folks thought all this space stuff was, well, not very important or important for irrelevant reasons, and among the radicals, the socialist left tended to think all this money should be spent solving our problems here on Earth. But the libertarians were their kind of people, in more ways than being keen on space, and often SF fans themselves. Some of these people have gone on to start up private launch companies that actually do get rockets off the ground and attract millions in venture capital; some people now have real jobs designing orbital hotels, just like Brian Micklethwait imagined back in the early 1980s. This whole story of libertarian space activism will make an interesting historical thesis some day, but meanwhile we can read Ed Regis's *Great Mambo Chicken and the Transhuman Condition* (Penguin, 1992) and *Nano!* (Little Brown, 1995), both terrific books.

The spontaneous ideology of SF probably isn't libertarian as such, it's more about whatever gets us into space fastest, so maybe it'll gravitate more to libertarianism if private launch companies seem to be doing a better job than NASA. And of course there are already some SF books with just that scenario, e.g. *Firestar* (Tor, 1996) by Michael Flynn, which I haven't read yet but which looks very good indeed.

I've talked about libertarianism and SF before, and gone through most of the famous titles. This time, I'm not going to do much more than mention in passing some of the books, classic and recent, which are of libertarian interest. Do you really need me to tell you to read Heinlein and Poul Anderson and Cyril Kornbluth's marvellous *The Syndic*? If so, let me do so now, and refer you to Chris Tame's excellent Cultural Note 'Life, Liberty and the Stars' for details.

More recent books of libertarian interest include Vernor Vinge's *A Fire Upon the Deep* and *A Deepness in the Sky*; the British writer Peter Hamilton's Greg Mandel thrillers and his space-opera trilogy 'Night's Dawn'—*The Reality Dysfunction* , *The Neutronium Alchemist* and *The Naked God*; S. M. Stirling's *Island in the Sea of Time* and *Against the Tide of Years* [and the [then] forthcoming *On the Ocean of Eternity*] which are not by a libertarian, in fact by an author who personally despises libertarianism, but which are full of libertarian insights.

And there's great fun to be had with Neal Stephenson's *Snow Crash,* which takes all the bugs of anarcho-capitalism—what about the mafia? what about the right to keep and bear strategic nuclear weapons?—and makes them features, and which gives the state the funniest and best-deserved fate in all fiction.

Instead, I'm going to talk about some books I've read which seem particularly relevant to liberty and which, I think, work better as libertarianism and as literature than a lot of more consciously didactic libertarian science fiction.

The French Marxist or *soi-disant* Marxist philosopher Louis Althusser said somewhere that ideology works by what he called, if I remember right, appellation, or hailing—hey, you! Individualism constitutes the individual, as it were, using the word 'constitute' in an appropriately obscure French philosophical sense. Now we can think of numerous ways in which this could be false but let's dwell for a moment on how it could be true. Because I think that moment of personal appeal, that hailing, is what distinguishes an ideological appeal that actually has an effect from one that is mere didacticism, that distinguishes the living word from the dead letter.

In *The Strange Invaders* by Alun Llewlellyn (1934, NEL paperback 1977, p. 18). the hero, Adun, has just seen one of the ruling class eyeing up the girl Adun is in love with:

> 'He hugged his knees and rocked with the violence of his misery and rage. [. . .] Then his passion had its blinding, sudden lighting.
>
> He was a man! Why should Karasoin have such power over him? He was a man! Why should the Fathers dispose of his body, his very spirit? Why must he give up what he desired, desired with a strength that brought justification from its own intensity? Why should he not love, and chose and take what he loved? He was a man with hands to strive, with a heart to impel him, with a being secret within him that would not be commanded. A man!'

So you see, Ayn Rand wasn't the first to write that sort of thing!

Heinlein's 'If this goes on—' (*The Past Through Tomorrow*, 1967, 1987 Ace Books, NY, 1987 pp. 498–499) deals with a revolt against a future American theocracy. The hero, John Lyle joins the underground revolutionary Cabal (which is, amusingly enough, nothing other than the Freemasons) and gets the chance to read uncensored history for the first time:

> 'I had trouble at first in admitting the possibility of what I read; I think perhaps of all the things a police state can do to its citizens, distorting history is possibly the most pernicious. For

> example, I learned for the first time that the United States had not been ruled by a bloodthirsty emissary of Satan before the First prophet arose in his wrath and cast him out—but had been a community of free men, deciding their own affairs by peaceful consent. I don't mean that the first republic had been a scriptural paradise, but it hadn't been anything like what I had learned in school.'

That's the moment of personal appeal—we're reminded, by this text from an imaginary future, that our present societies in the United States, Britain and other such countries are, in very significant respects, free societies, and we are called on to reflect on what that means. I can't resist adding one of Heinlein's most famous paragraphs of rhetoric:

> 'I began to sense faintly that secrecy is the keystone of all tyranny. Not force, but secrecy—censorship. When any government, or any church for that matter, undertakes to say to its subjects, "This you may not read, this you must not see, this you are forbidden to know," the end result is tyranny and oppression, no matter how holy the motives. Mighty little force is needed to control a man who has been hoodwinked; contrariwise, no amount of force can control a free man, a man whose mind is free. No, not the rack, not fission bombs, not anything—you can't conquer a free man—the most you can do is kill him.'

Here's another such personal reflection, in a passage in Vernor Vinge's *Across Realtime* (Millenium, 1994, p. 383) here the long-lived former statist Della Lu says:

> '"As a government cop, my morality was very different from yours. The long-range goals of the Authority were the basis of that morality. My own interests and the interests of others were secondary—though I truly believed that survival depended on achieving the Authority's goals." [...] "But I grew out of that." Her steepled hands collapsed, and her expression softened. "For a hundred years I lived in a civilization where individuals set their own goals and guarded their own welfare."'

That last sentence may not have quite the force of the Bible's 'every man under his own vine and under his own fig tree, and none shall make them afraid', but it too sums up what living in a free society is all about.

And what's freedom for? Well, for one thing, you can use it to improve your own circumstances in all kinds of ways. In *Cryptonomicon* by Neal Stephenson (Avon Books, NY, 1999), the computer programmer

Randy's arguing against a whole dinner-table of university folks telling him he's a technocrat and part of a scientific power elite—which he, of course, denies (pp. 84–85):

> '"The false consciousness Tomas is speaking of is exactly what makes entrenched power elites so entrenched," Charlene said.
>
> "Well, I don't feel very entrenched," Randy said. "I've worked my ass off to get where I've gotten."
>
> "A lot of people work hard all their lives and get nowhere," someone said accusingly. Look out! The sniping had begun.
>
> "Well, I'm sorry I haven't had the good grace to get nowhere," Randy said, now feeling just a bit surly for the first time, "but I have found that if you work hard, educate yourself, and keep your wits about you, you can find your way in this society."
>
> "But that's just straight out of some nineteenth-century Horatio Alger book," Tomas spluttered.
>
> "So? Just because it's an old idea, doesn't mean it's wrong," Randy said.'

What I've identified in each of these books is a little moment of libertarian epiphany, when a character realises or proclaims what he or she can or can't do, or what someone else is capable of. What these moments do, and why they work, is because they cut through pretension and illusion and make a direct appeal to the reader to examine themselves, examine what they know of others and of how the world works, and decide whether it's true. The experience of reading them is, or can be, itself an example of the exercise of reason and freedom which they illustrate and celebrate. They invite us, incite us, encourage us and enable us to free ourselves.

And by way of one more little epiphany, I'll conclude with a another quote from *Crytonomicon*, where Randy is discussing an old enemy with his comrades in the enterprise of building a data haven, the Crypt, where encrypted information can be kept beyond the reach of governments.

> '"He's been denouncing us," Tom says. "Capitalist roader. Atomizing society. Making the world safe for drug traffickers and Third World kleptocrats."
>
> "Well, at least he got something right," Randy says. He's delighted to have an answer, finally, to the question of why they're building the Crypt.' (p. 253)

So go forth and multiply prime factors, or whatever it is you do.

A Brief Critique of *Nineteen Eighty-Four* as Science Fiction

I really like the idea of a critique of *Nineteen Eighty-Four* as SF, of trying to make 'world-building sense' of it. Can the world be as politically stable as the novel presents? I don't think so. Orwell overestimates the planned economy and underestimates the proles.

He assumes that the economy can go on indefinitely delivering depression-level living-standards to the proles (beer, cigarettes, gambling, porn, films, trashy novels, cinema, an inadequate but acceptable diet, aluminium saucepans, etc) and that the proles will go on accepting all this indefinitely. All of this seems unlikely—at a minimum, the breakdowns of the economy (shortages, admitted in the book) will shift living-standards and work-processes unpredictably and infuriatingly.

No industrial economy can function without intelligence and initiative on the part of the industrial workers. At the very least they will have to bodge, assist managers in covering up plan non-fulfilments, cope with shortages of production goods, and so on. (All quite independently of the thought-control in the Party itself.) The proles (and their immediate supervisors) will have to know that 2 and 2 make 4.

This soon leads to a situation where O'Brien et al are hanging by their heels from lamp-posts (or to reforms to avert that '1956' scenario, which only buys time for the Party until '1981' or '1989'.)

Orwell also underestimates the colonial slaves. Assume as true (and not just more Party propaganda) the picture of three essentially identical competing blocs, with a vast, various 'Fourth World' disputed between them. The armies of Oceania, Eurasia and Eastasia sweep back and forth across this 'Fourth World' like natural disasters. The inhabitants' ideological allegiance is neither asked nor given, but we can assume some passing familiarity on their part with the slogans of Ingsoc, Neobolshevism and Selflessness. (All essentially identical, but each denouncing the others as absurd.) Past ideologies, particularly religion, would persist. And out of all this, no Ho Chi Minh, no Robert Mugabe, no Jonas Savimbi, no Bin Laden emerges? Not bloody likely.

Orwell underestimates natural science, and engineering (and soldiering, come to that).

Sheer accident would be enough to give one or other bloc a scientific-technical (hence military) lead at some point, thus de-stabilising the system by military breakthroughs unexpected on all sides. And once again—the Floating Fortresses, the helicopters (helicopters! think of that!) and so on require constant maintenance by men and women who know that 2 and 2 add up to 4. At a minimum this implies a very large number of people who are impervious to 'reality-control' even if they acquiesce in the Party's political shifts. 'Oceania has always been at war with Eurasia' but when it's suddenly 'always been at war with Eastasia' you have to turn a lot of guns around, replot a lot of bomber flights, change a lot of plans. (And there is a selection pressure for people who don't discard and forget the old plans, but keep them for next time…)

The bottom line is that Orwell (in this book, not in all his very diverse output) projects the characteristics of the social strata with which he was most familiar —the literary intelligentsia and the lumpen-proletariat (the down-and-outs, casual labourers and dossers)—onto the other strata of (in this case) postcapitalist society. As the literary intelligentsia and the lumpen-proletariat are notoriously fickle, feckless, and easily bribed, Orwell's conclusions are unduly pessimistic. The industrial workers, colonial peasants, scientific/technical intelligentsia, soldiers, and industrial managers are more obdurate in their requirements, and in the long run—over decades, not centuries—push postcapitalist society away from totalitarianism.

Trends in Science Fiction, or, SF after the Future Went Away

> 'There is, of course, still a chance that human society will actually have a perfectly tolerable future—but while nobody can quite believe it, there can be no future in, and perhaps for, serious speculative fiction.' (Brian Stableford, 'Traces of a Lost Genre', *Interzone* 133, July 1998)

Science fiction, like society, faces a dark future: unknown, and probably unpleasant. SF writers have responded by focussing on almost everything except a near future of gloom and doom. The most striking expression of this tendency lies outside SF altogether, in the rise of the fantasy genre. Fantasy has its own value and validity, but fundamentally it responds to change by turning to an imaginary past.

Some SF writers, like Peter F. Hamilton, look forward to a resurgent capitalist future beyond the present crisis. Others, like the Australian writer Greg Egan, focus hard on the cutting edge of current science, and take it past a lightly sketched—disastrous—21st century to a brighter world of humanity's AI progeny. Paul J. McCauley's *Fairyland* confronts the near future head-on, but he too turns in his most recent work to a post-human world of conscious machines millions of years hence. Jack Womack's explicitly post-Soviet *Let's Put the Future Behind Us* exemplifies another response—to examine a displaced present rather than a near, or far, future.

Alternate histories and self-conscious pastiche (Stephen Baxter's *The Time Ships*, *Voyage* and others) are a common way of side-stepping the future, however interesting and exciting such tales may be in themselves. Kim Stanley Robinson stands out in that his ambitious Mars trilogy is set in a future which grows out of the present: his long-lived characters, if real, would be already born. The bravura of Iain M. Banks's communist-utopian Culture novels—mostly drafted in the seventies, published in the eighties—has gradually given way to darker, post-human visions as his youthful backlist has cleared.

The idea of the post-human sets the agenda of nineties SF. Whether it's in genetic miscegeny with aliens (Octavia Butler, Gwyneth Jones) or in the emergence of self-aware artificial intelligence (most of the rest of us), posthumanism connotes a continued confidence in technological and scientific progress combined with a scepticism about the capacity of humanity to power it. The torch of progress must be handed on to better minds and stronger hands than ours. It may not be too fanciful to see this as a reflection of a society where technical progress—albeit fitful—coexists uneasily with social stagnation.

To see the depth of the contrast we must look back to when the future seemed bright. What the SF critic John Clute has aptly called 'Agenda SF' flourished from the 1920s to the late 1950s. Although inevitably tracking the vicissitudes of boom, slump, world war and Cold War; including much of counter-current, query, and dissent; and encompassing many developments of literary style and scientific/technological speculation, Agenda SF retained its coherence as an ongoing projection of humanity's—and capitalism's—advance.

The consensus stages of this Future History included first the exploration, then the colonization, of the solar system; the launching of gigantic 'interstellar arks', with generations living and dying en route to Alpha Centuari; until some future Edison/Einstein cracked the intractable problem of the light-speed limit. A great explosion of human pioneers would swarm across the galaxy, and be eventually unified into an Empire which would, inevitably, Decline and Fall...and beyond this Fall, new heights would rise.

It's cheap to laugh. For all its blind spots, Agenda SF's agenda had a grandeur and ambition which can still inspire. John Clute himself dates its decline from Sputnik—the moment when it became apparent that Agenda SF had been telling the wrong story, that the space age had arrived and it was a sight more complicated, messy, and political than its 'prediction' had allowed for. I think the real change came in the 1960s, with what became known as the New Wave.

New Wave SF grew out of the realisation that the 'decadent future societies', glanced at and frowned upon in the backdrops of Agenda SF, had already arrived. Sex and drugs and rock and roll, the Vietnam War, the strange 60s notion that linked the birth-control pill to fears of over-population, all became more important determinants of what went on in SF than the increasingly expensive and bureaucratic manned space programme. Society or psyche became the venues for exploration—'inner space', with outer space as backdrop. Writers like J. G. Ballard, Michael Moorcock, and M. John Harrison consciously despised then-existing SF for what they saw as its unthinking optimism, its cliches, its cardboard characters and, above all, its blindness to what was actually going on around it. How could anyone, in clear conscience, write tales of colonial conquest in space when the US, the very society which was being held up as a model for the whole human future, was bogged down in a long, dirty, losing colonial war in Vietnam?

One of Ballard's short stories, 'The Killing Grounds', sketched a British NLF fighting US occupiers in a world which has become 'a global insurrectionary torch, a world Vietnam'. Moorcock's Jerry Cornelius stories eventually became an exploration of the joys and sorrows of life in the decadent heartlands which, even in its length, weighed in impressively against the Foundation trilogies of yesteryear. Harrison scavenged fantasy, space opera and social realism, and caught the gloom and doom of early-seventies, late-Labour Britain in his finest short story, 'Running Down'. The title says it all.

But the New Wave ran into the same barrier as the old SF—its future arrived. The post-war boom which, in retrospect, suffuses with sunlight even the most entropic and pessimistic tales of that period, faded out. (John Brunner's *Stand on Zanzibar*, published in 1969, set in 2010, brilliantly depicts an appalling world which is actually much better than the one we live in, let alone the one which, 12 years from now, we're likely to get.) The New Wave collapsed in a dribble of exhausted froth.

Other developments—the rise of self-consciously 'hard SF' which didn't fudge the physics—failed to re-ignite the genre's engines. The late seventies and early eighties were pretty dire—in SF, and in the world. Almost as soon as the recession was over, and the destruction of swathes of manufacturing industry 'paid off' in a financial and services boom with its consequent proliferation of computer/communications technology, the SF genre came up with an equivalent response: cyberpunk. William Gibson's *Neuromancer* (1984) is as good a benchmark as any.

Gibson knew almost nothing about computers, but he wrote about them the way their users and programmers thought about them: containing spaces you could get into, problems you could tunnel under, traps you could work around. Inner space joined outer space as backdrop: Gibson's characters, and those of cyberpunk generally, struck an almost sociopathically affectless pose. The real action was inside the computers, in...cyberspace.

'Cyberspace', a word coined in Gibson's novel, is now common currency, and the cyberpunk world a common image: the 'future noir' of *Blade Runner* and *Johnny Mnemonic*, dominated by mega-corporations and policed by their ninja hitmen. Government is irrelevant, the environment a lost cause: 'The sky above the port was the colour of television, tuned to a dead channel' is Neuromancer's first line, and last word on that particular subject.

And cyberpunk, in its turn…but you're ahead of me, right? The world of the Internet, the Web and the fall of the Wall made it, too, a told tale. As William Gibson puts it: 'The best SF of the Nineties is on CNN. Hard to beat that garbage module slamming into space station Mir!' Indeed the cooperation between Russia and the West on the Mir space station may be the perfect symbol for the present state of affairs: actually existing capitalism relying for its life-support on the clapped-out projects of formerly-existing socialism, lurching from one crisis to another and going around in circles.

Which brings us to now. There's no future in post-humanism. The problem in the real world remains one of human agency. There are no saviours from above, no angels or aliens to save us. And, for sure, there are none behind the computer screens. Artificial awareness is where it's been since the 1940s and always will be: 'just twenty years away'. The better minds and stronger hands must be our own; SF still has the capacity to advance—its literary and scientific sophistication is in many respects better than it's ever been. And if it reflects a stalled and fragmented world, it also, as we peer through our own reflections, continues to give us glimpses of the world beyond that wall of glass through which—with hard work and a bit of luck—we may yet break.

Let's not put the future behind us.

Utopias

At this fag-end of the twentieth century, Utopia is something we look down on, rather than forward to. Like the failed real-life states which claimed to be communist, it can only be sold off in small pieces for the nostalgia market. Two new anthologies present it in crumbling fragments glossed with sceptical commentary, like graffiti-daubed bits of the Berlin Wall. How did things come to this, from such a promising start?

Thomas More, Lord Chancellor of England, saint and martyr of the Catholic Church, is Utopia's founding father. He seems a surprising author for such a subversive book. Back in the 'rosy dawn of capitalist accumulation' he denounced the injustices of a society where 'sheep devour men', which turns men into beggars then hangs them when they steal, and which compensates the easiest and most pleasant work more generously than the hardest, most demeaning, and most necessary toil. His Utopia is quite explicitly communist, in a way that no actually existing state has ever been: there's no money, no buying or selling, no rich or poor. All consumer goods are freely available. It's even democratic, though patriarchal. Though its uniformity seems drab to us, and its discipline harsh, it may have looked more appealing—'utopian', even—to its readers, acquainted with poverty and its many civilised penalties: the galley, the stake, the rack and the screw. But even they, I suspect, may have found it lacking in freedom.

It's hardly an original observation that Utopias betray an authoritarian impulse. Not a single human passion has escaped the utopian urge—procrustean rather than promethean—to lop off or stretch. Thomas More's communist island has internal passports. The punishment for being caught outside your district without permission—and for most other crimes—is slavery. There was a gulag already in the garden. Less obviously, Utopias are a product of powerlessness. Machiavelli, writing another slim political classic, did more to realise his ambitions as an exile than the Lord Chancellor could in his pomp. In this, More was at one with the most helplessly-fuming serf who ever dreamed of the Land of Cockayne (where ready-roasted geese fly around), or the later migrant workers who sang of the Big Rock Candy Mountain (where the cigarette trees sway in the breeze).

The democratic struggles of the English Revolution inspired the first scheme for a socialist society brought about not by wise rulers from above, but by common folk from below, acting for themselves. The libertarian, free-market Levellers were outflanked on the left by the Diggers, or True Levellers. Gerard Winstanley's *The Law of Freedom in a Platform* puts the Diggers' anti-capitalist case in biblical language considerably harsher than More's: 'Kingly government governs the earth by that cheating art of buying and selling, and thereby becomes a man of contention, his hand is against every man, and every man's hand is against him; and take this government at the best, it is a diseased government, and the very city Babylon, full of confusion.' The oppressor is the one who makes his brother a hired servant, a wage-worker.

Winstanley projected a Commonwealth that would undo the Conquest, return England to its people, and make the earth a common treasury. In contrast to Utopia's static perfection, Winstanley's new England sponsors science and technology in a spirit of freedom: 'no young wit is to be crushed in his invention'. Unlike all before him and most since, Winstanley took pains to spell out democratic machinery for keeping the elected officials of his commonwealth in line: 'all officers in a commonwealth are to be chosen new ones every year' by popular election. Pages of justification follow—no communist manifesto so explicitly anti-bureaucratic was to be written until Marx's angry elegy on the Paris Commune.

Marx wrote no utopias, but he displayed an uncharacteristic charity to those who did when he described their writings as 'full of the most valuable materials for the enlightenment of the working class'. Unfortunately, as John Carey's anthology makes depressingly clear, they are also full of the most pernicious drivel. Sorting the wheat from the chaff would be the work of centuries. When Marx went on to list approvingly 'the abolition of the distinction between town and country, of the family,' of private enterprise (etc, etc) he couldn't have foreseen that men acting in his name would some day attempt all of these overnight. The morning of Pnomh Penh's evacuation was the beginning of the end for Communist utopianism.

One communist utopia which wouldn't produce an abundance of boat-people is William Morris's *News From Nowhere*. He wrote it in response to Edward Bellamy's *Looking Backward*, a great success in its day. In ours, it's more banal than sinister: the citizens of Bellamy's state-socialist America work for giant corporations! Live in skyscrapers! Spend money with credit cards! Listen to recorded music at home!

Morris revolted at this 'cockney utopia', and wrote his own Home Counties utopia as a rebuttal and alternative. It's in many ways attractive, even seductive, but its engine-rooms are woefully underpowered. As one critic pointed out, for its inhabitants to enjoy the standard of living they do with the technology they have, they'd need to work a four-hundred-hour week. It would never get past the TUC, even under New Labour.

The trouble with most utopias of the literary or political mainstream is that they're static, as places and as stories. The traveller arrives, and is shown around, and goes home, and that's it. End of story. For the professional writer of popular entertainment, however, that can only be the beginning of the story. By turning utopia from a place into a planet, or a period, the science-fiction genre has given it a much needed narrative boost. The famous dystopias of *Brave New World* and *Nineteen Eighty-Four* were written quite independently of the lurid and widely despised pulp-fiction magazines. But it's the rockets-and-rayguns guys and gals who've provided a more encouraging, and perhaps no less influential, atlas of the imaginary. By worrying about the technical details they've given us the only communist utopias which are both attractive and technically feasible, as well as a whole competing shopping-mall of capitalist utopias.

Of the former, the biggest is Iain Banks's Culture, a Galactic society of abundance premised on benevolent artificial intelligences—machines like gods, in which humans live like mice in gliders, or bats in belfrys. Life in a Culture Orbital is like a Caribbean cruise, except that the ship contains its own ocean. Those discontented with this lazy life-style are free to depart or—if they're smart—join in the Machiavellian machinations of Contact Section, which artfully nudges backward planets in the right—or left—direction. Even in their interventions the Culture keeps its scientific cool, selecting certain planets to be left untouched: properly conducted social experiments need control samples. Earth, in case we hadn't guessed, is one such, glanced at in 1977 and hurried away from since, at several multiples of the speed of light.

To his own later surprise, the hard-headed American free-marketeer and engineer James P. Hogan, without reading a line of Marx, reproduced Marx's vision of communism—a stateless, classless, and moneyless society—in his recently-reprinted *Voyage From Yesteryear*. This too relies on robots to do the dirty work, but they aren't conscious robots so we're not relying on their benevolence, just their tolerances. One has the distinct feeling that Hogan has their blueprints, if not (yet) their programmes, in a big drawer in his desk. What makes the story, however, is the fun Hogan's heroes have running rings around the state-capitalist Earthpersons who attempt to repossess them.

Ursula Le Guin, in *The Dispossessed*, has a more dour vision of anarchist communism: something like a particularly fanatical kibbutz or Spanish Civil War collective. Defeated anarchist revolutionaries have been bought off with Annares, a planet that makes Mars look like a botanic garden.

Computers are hand-waved into economic planning, children are discouraged from 'egoizing'—getting possessive about their toys, or their ideas. The conflicts this induces in Shevek, a brilliant physicist with a few too many ideas of his own, are well presented. The rival planet, Urrass, from which the communards have been exiled, is convincingly shown as forbidden and thus appealing fruit. In the end, though, for all her dialectical ambivalence, Le Guin settles for the thin but pure air of Annares.

Leaving Shevek's attempt to bring glasnost to Annares, we turn sharply to the right, into the garish neon glare of the new capitalist order. Top of the list for chutzpah is Cyril Kornbluth's *The Syndic*, in which, far from the State abolishing the family, the Family abolishes the state. Yes, that Family: fortunately, Kornbluth's mafiosi are more interested in supplying mass demand for gambling and cigarettes and whisky and wild, wild women than in muscling out their rivals. In a nicely original touch, the science of psychology becomes completely discredited: with the nanny state out of the way, everybody loses their neuroses. The plot turns on the alarming discovery that the US Navy doesn't (yet) sleep with the fishes…

The dean of science fiction, Robert A. Heinlein, craftily overturns expectations in *The Moon is a Harsh Mistress*. A carefully plotted revolution in a Lunar penal colony—in the name of free trade with Earth—actually succeeds in setting up a democratic state, which destroys the stateless capitalist anarchy which the colonists already enjoyed under the Warden's distant rule. They had utopia, had they but known it, and by the end there's nothing for a good revolutionary to do but move out to the new frontier of the asteroid belt.

Heinlein influenced some American SF writers to write libertarian utopias, but most of them lacked the streak of contrariness which makes Heinlein's didactic wise old men so engaging. His disciples sacrificed far too many trees to long speeches about the evils of environmentalism and paper money. Another inspiration for this sort of thing was Ayn Rand's *Atlas Shrugged*, a thousand-page novel which US opinion pollsters are repeatedly bewildered to find rated right up there with the Bible, despite having smaller print.

Neal Stephenson's *Snow Crash* strikes a refreshingly lighter note. This fastmoving novel is set in a near-enough future where the US government has been reduced to little more than a gang among gangs, printing trillion-dollar bills ('Reagans') as small change. Quite how this big change has happened isn't entirely clear, but with Greater Hong Kong as a chain of motorway service areas, the Mafia as pizza delivery franchise ('You have a friend in the Family') and the whites-only enclaves of New South Africa brandishing their bazookas, who cares? You can only can keep running: happiness, as Hobbes said, is to go forward.

There's plenty of forward momentum in Kim Stanley Robinson's Mars trilogy, where the Red Planet is a literal new world in which new societies tumble over each other in a series of revolutions, even as the landscape is transformed. The books display a very Green awareness of the ecological problems ahead, but don't use that as an excuse to call a halt to progress. Utopia becomes permanent revolution in the solar system.

For a Utopia to inspire us in the 21st century, it'll have to be dynamic as well as sustainable. Science fiction as a whole may be the real utopia of our time. Its most popular form is so familiar that we need to be reminded of its radicalism: *Star Trek*. The Federation is literally a sixties socialist dream: 'Don't tell me,' says the savvy twentieth-century woman to Kirk, 'you don't have money in the future.' Kirk, like Thomas More, has to agree.

On the opposite side of the struggle for hearts and minds, the *Star Wars* universe represents a future where capitalism, republican virtue, and even constitutional monarchies can flourish. Even now, it's hard to say which is the more improbable, the more 'utopian'. Enough that they're there, and fighting.

For as long as they fight, Utopia lives. Its original communist ideals have been discredited, its walls have fallen, and the ruling mafia is fighting dozens of separatist insurgencies for control of the territory. But there's hope for the old republic yet. Its communism may have been repressive, its capitalism may be corrupt, but out in its wastelands and badlands, there's a Baikonur from which rockets still rise.

Review of *The Encyclopaedia of Fantasy*

John Clute and John Grant (editors), Orbit, London, 1997, ISBN 1 85723 368 9.

Why are evil empires almost always in the East?

Leave that question on the back burner for a moment, while we look at another: what is the relevance of fantasy literature to libertarianism? With science fiction, there's no problem—the thought experiments of political and economic theory have had fruitful intercourse with the literature of imagined futures or alternate histories for over a century. But fantasy—SF's older and prettier sister—is different. Tales of swords and sorcery, dungeons and dragons, lords and ladies, ghosts and monsters might seem at best irrelevant, at worst an expression of a reactionary nostalgia for that Old World Order of preindustrial poverty and superstition whose ongoing demolition is capitalism's historic achievement.

So—are Laissez-Faire Books selling the pass when they advertise C. S. Lewis's Narnia series? Is David Friedman indulging a discreditable foible when he swings a sword for the Society for Creative Anachronism? Were such great names of libertarian SF as Poul Anderson, Ursula Le Guin and Robert Heinlein betraying their muse when they turned their hands to *The Merman's Children*, *The Wizard of Earthsea* and *Glory Road?* And is the mass market for Tolkien-clone trilogies pandering to an impulse that, enacted, would leave most of their readers illiterate, reciting tall tales amid the ruins?

A clue to a different answer is suggested by Paul Marks, in his LA Historical Notes No. 21, *The Battle of Marathon and the Spirit of the West*: "There are no slave-owning goodies in *The Lord of the Rings*." The original and unsurpassed Tolkien trilogy, a key text of modern fantasy, is all about individual courage, honour, enterprise—and, crucially, the refusal of power over others. In a deliberate and heroic moral choice, the One Ring to rule them all is consigned to the fiery abyss. Loyalties are freely chosen, and the opposite of loyalty is not freedom but slavery. The good guys and gals in Tolkein, and his lesser imitators, have loyal companions. Their enemy, the Dark Lord, has minions—slaves.

There's a perfect example of this pattern in the film *Krull* (recently shown on Sky). Described in the *Encyclopaedia* as "high fantasy at its best", it features Lysette Anthony as the endangered princess, which for some of us may be recommendation enough. The hero's companions are differentiated individuals. The enemy's troops wear baroque armour, but are as identical as the Galactic Stormtroopers in *Star Wars*. The enemy himself, the Beast, interestingly enough can take many forms, can *mimic* individuality, but his dead eyes are a dead giveaway in all of them.

At the crassest political level, what this type of fantasy counterposes to an idealised feudalism is not capitalism but despotism—the Asiatic mode of production! Ever since Sumer, civilizations have arisen, degenerated into slave empires, and fallen. For geographical reasons the only escape from them has been westward. (And that's why evil empires are almost always in the east.) By now, as Robert Anton Wilson has pointed out, the marathon westward flight has fetched up on the Pacific shore. Some libertarians feel that the minions of the evil empire, in the form of the black-uniformed, jack-booted storm-troopers of the BATF and the DEA, are closing in. From that westward shore there's nowhere to run but the ocean, or the sky. But that's science fiction, and another story.

Although not expressed in the above terms, the polarity of freedom and slavery is one of many thoroughly explored in *The Encyclopaedia of Fantasy*, edited by John Clute and John Grant. With over 4,000 entries, over a thousand pages and over a million words, this book is an impressive labour of love and scholarship, unified by extensive thematic entries and thorough cross-referencing, and by a prescriptive definition of fantasy itself.

Fantasy is seen here as a coherent story of impossible events. This broad, yet focussed, definition overcomes one major prejudice that confronts any serious discussion of fantasy—what I came to think of as the 'Not My Cup of Tea syndrome'. Anyone who thinks fantasy is all pastel-jacketed Tolkien-clone trilogies will find this book eye-opening, covering as it does the works of H. P. Lovecraft and C. S. Lewis, Robert E. Howard and Robert Louis Stevenson, Neil Gaiman and Jorge Luis Borges, Fritz Leiber and Stephen King, Michael Moorcock and William Morris, and many, many more. Film, television, and graphic novels are given the same careful attention as written texts. I have to admit I was surprised to find how much of what I liked *was* fantasy.

Some mainstream critics infuriate SF fans in the manner memorably summed up in the epigraph to *Spectrum 2*, an SF anthology edited by Kingsley Amis and Robert Conquest:

'SF's no good,' they bellow till we're deaf.
'But this looks good.'—'Well then, it's not SF.'

Like many a despised minority, SF fans have sometimes responded by picking on an even more despised group, and the fantasy genre and its readership is their chosen target. Any fantasy literature that they, the SF fans, happen to like is defined out of fantasy and into horror or planetary adventure or, for that matter, SF. *Mea culpa*, too.

Serious writers and readers have little time for this kind of snobbery. The names of the *Encyclopaedia*'s editors and contributors are almost a checklist of the best current critics of fantastic literature, and they can be proud of their work. Their awesome breadth (and depth) of coverage is matched by a coherence - though by no means uniformity - of approach, which is ably articulated in several thematic contributions by John Clute.

The fully-developed fantasy tale, Clute argues, is the story of a difficult journey ("an earned passage") from a damaged or blocked condition ("bondage") signalled by a sense of "wrongness" and an attrition ("thinning") of self or world, via recognition and transformation, to healing. Discrete stages of this trajectory define cognate genres: the "supernatural fiction" such as the ghost story deals with the intrusion of wrongness into an otherwise untransformed world; and an almost exclusive focus on an often literal attrition of body or soul (or world) is the province of horror. It's no disparagement of these genres to point out that the questions they raise are not, within the context of the story, finally settled: the ghost may be laid, the demon exorcised, the vampire buried with a stake through his heart—but we as the story ends, we remain in a world where they can walk again. In the fully-developed fantasy, the outcome is a true resolution. The Dark Lord is defeated (never to rise again). The land is healed.

This model—here demonstrated on a literally encyclopaedic scale—suggests that the individualistic appeal of fantasy goes deeper than any simple mapping of the political structures of good kingdoms and evil empires. Its hold on our imaginations may be rooted in the necessary struggle and self-transformation that is prosaically known as *growing up*. One need not subscribe to any psychological theory to agree with this. Fantasy tells us truths about ourselves, but—as I think is pointed out, somewhere on one of these thousand pages—the deepest truth it tells us is that we are the kind of people who enjoy this kind of story.

And that's enough.

Review of *Whole Wide World*

Paul McAuley has worked his way through a succession of SF's sub-genres: space opera, alternate history, cyberpunk, the Mars novel, the far-future apparently-fantasy-but-really-sf Gene Wolfe sort of thing…Now, with *Whole Wide World* (Voyager, 2001, 388 p., £16.99) he has turned to crime; in his case, an indication of confidence rather than desperation. As a crime novel it conforms to genre expectations and tropes, perhaps too well—the cynical cop with a conscience in conflict with his superiors and with the new intake of young graduate whippersnappers is a stock figure, for all the originality of the inevitable shadow of the past, the haunting, career-ruining failure that dogs his steps. The career-ruined relationship, now mediated at long distance by Eurostar and mobile, is likewise familiar. But the moves, the revelations and concealments, are all fair. Ian Rankin doesn't tell us the content of all of Rebus's phone calls either.

So, it works as a crime novel. What about as SF? Here, too, it plays fair in that it's not a crime story which just happens to be set in the future—without the near-future technology and society, the crime could not exist.

In London, an unstated ten years or so into the present century, it's a bright hot day in June and the watches are reading thirty-one degrees centigrade. There's a permanent background-radiation state of war and the "metal shoeboxes" of surveillance cameras are everywhere in the streets. What's watching you is ADESS, the Autonomous Distributed Expert Surveillance System. It is to Big Brother as New Labour is to IngSoc: smarter, smarmier, and much more effective at controlling the proles. Virtual reality affords no escape: half the Home Office's crime budget is spent on policing cyberspace. The only jarring note in this picture's plausibility is the pro-censorship Decency League: in a society in which stability is based on atomisation and anxiety rather than mobilisation and terror, such organizations are neither needed nor wanted by the authorities.

The motivation for this panoptic regime is no transparent pretext. Its immediate occasion, in the novel's recent past, is the InfoWar: a real and devastating assault on the City of London by an alliance of rogue states, terrorists and anti-capitalist rioters. Its continuing justification is that there really are enemies within and without, just as there is some very nasty stuff out there on the Net. Coming between the consumers and the producers of images of actual violence and violation committed for the very purpose of being distributed can be seen as crime prevention rather than censorship, and so it is. The line between preventing real crime in a virtual environment and policing fantasies in the real world is, however, dangerously faint, and it's one the police (in the real world, and in this novel) have never hesitated to scuff as they step over it.

The crime that McAuley's hero and narrator investigates is to initial appearances an instance of snuff porn as webcam performance art. Its portrayal is quite disturbing enough to drive home the point that cunning schemes of cryptography and anonymity have a downside little regarded by some of their advocates. This is not necessarily to damn these advocates—widespread availability of strong encryption may well be a necessary defence against worse enemies than terrorists and rapists, but the case has to be argued because there is no doubt now, if there ever was, that terrorists and rapists are real and deadly enemies of the rest of us. The data havens celebrated by cyber-libertarians are shown here not as offshore oil platforms or convenient enlightened island monarchies but much more believably as radical rogue states—an apparently post-Castro but still-Communist Cuba being the refuge of choice for the hacker backpackers, tax-exiles and pornographers. You can leave London, sweating in the global greenhouse, but you'll find Havana even hotter. Sovereignty is a game for serious players.

The flashbacks of the InfoWar don't include a scene of a cruise missile hitting Canary Wharf, but somehow left me with the impression that they do, even before I'd been imprinted with repeated video imagery of the atrocity of September 11 2001. The world which is likely to result from that attack (assuming the present war doesn't escalate to a point which renders such speculation irrelevant) is already emerging like the image in a developing photograph, and its lines and shadows are clear enough. Increased surveillance of people's physical movements and virtual connections is inevitable, at least in the short term. Whether it should be evaded and/or resisted is a serious question, and in posing it McAuley lifts the book above the technothriller genre in which it should, for marketing reasons alone, be placed.

If *Whole Wide World* had been written as a technothriller—out of Tom Clancy's Op-Center, say—the battle lines would have been drawn in a highly predictable manner. The terrorists, criminals, pornographers, hackers and Cubans would all be aspects of the same enemy. The cops and spooks and censors would be the good guys. If the rising heat in the real world is anything to go by, it's a very good thing that science fiction, here as elsewhere, draws different lines.

Singularity Skies

New space opera is twenty-eight years old. It began, and almost ended, in 1975, when M. John Harrison's *The Centauri Device* took a British New Wave sensibility to the stars. Its cover claimed it as a galaxy-spanning space adventure in the great tradition, that stood comparison with the classic works of E. E. 'Doc' Smith and A. E. Van Vogt. Anyone who bought it under that misapprehension was likely to hurl it across the room. Its hero would have been, to Smith and Van Vogt, at best a villain: 'he had sung revolutionary songs and pushed meta-amphetamines to the all-night workers on Morpheus—not because he was in any way committed to the insurrection that finally blew the planet apart, but because he was stuck there and broke'. For its author, it was intended to terminate space opera, not to expand it. Mike Harrison wanted to knot its legs behind its neck and to walk away, brushing his palms. He did the same to the post-catastrophe novel with *The Committed Men*, and to heroic fantasy with *The Pastel City*. Then he walked away, brushing his palms.

Yet for some of his naive readers, like me, *The Centauri Device* was exactly the sort of thing we wanted to see more of. We had grown up on *Analog* and we were reading *New Worlds Quarterly*. We enjoyed the scale and ambition of classical space opera, but disliked the cardboard characters and the American chauvinism. We admired the freight and density of New Wave writing, but despaired of the unsympathetic characters and the British pessimism. In some mercifully lost notebook or diary of mine from the time, I describe how it felt reading a collection called *The New SF* and then reading a current issue of *Analog:* 'The new SF gives me a baffled urge to emulate. The other lot gives me a frustrated urge to refute.' We wanted to see *this* done, like *that.*

There weren't enough of us to look like a market. Iain M. Banks wrote four full-scale works of new space opera and collected numerous rejections on all of them before slipping under the radar as a mainstream writer and then exploding on to the SF scene with *Consider Phlebas*, the fourth to be written. It found and made a market for the other three. They were new then, and they will endure as SF, but their prolonged gestation made them subtly dated before they were published, in the second half of the

1980s. There is no nanotech in them. Their great AIs, the Minds, are essentially mainframes. The personal access devices are even *called* terminals. There are no networks. (These deficiencies are more than made up in Banks's later work, notably the data-dense, baroque *Excession*.)

Colin Greenland eased space opera's limbs out of the contorted shape in which Harrison had left them, visibly drawing on while lightening his tone, in *Take Back Plenty*. Its title adumbrates its cheerful, brazen reappropriation of the Golden Age Solar system: Greenland's Venus has jungles, his Mars has canals, but his characters are space truckers and musicians who could have reeled out of any of Harrison's dives into a cold Camden morning. Meanwhile Gregory Benford, Stephen Baxter, and other writers of a new hard SF—too serious in intent and execution to be called space opera—were showing that a knowledge of the universe informed by contemporary astronomy and physics was far more exciting and interesting than that inspired, if that's the word, by a nodding acquaintance with the Hertzsprung-Russell Diagram and a token black hole. Paul McAuley gave us a taste of—and for—this new plenitude, with *A Hundred Billion Stars* and *Eternal Light*.

If the first phase of new space opera applied a British New Wave (and, as John Clute has pointed out, a British scientific romance) sensibility to traditional tropes, the second applied a cyberpunk and hard-SF sensibility to what the first had made space for. (These divisions are of course arbitrary—there are entire sentences in *The Centauri Device* that read as if cyberpunk was already a done deal: 'She was mainlining adrenochrome activators cut with the ribosomes of a local breed of bat,' its hero is told, of his mother.) The agenda-setting text of the second phase was Vernor Vinge's *A Fire Upon the Deep*. This was space opera for people who'd read *Neuromancer* and who posted to Usenet. It was anarcho-capitalist, rather than (like much of the old SF) imperialist or (like some of the new) socialist or liberal. Its galactic community was modelled on the Internet.

It gave one answer to a question Vinge himself had raised: how is space opera possible in a post-Singularity universe? That is to say, how can we write about human beings adventuring out there in the Galaxy, if the not so distant future (as Vinge had elsewhere argued) belongs to humanity's incomprehensible successors? Vinge's computer-conscious answer was to partition the great hard disk of the Galaxy between the zones in which posthumanity and AI were possible, and those in which they were not. In Greg Bear's *Blood Music* - not space opera, but with its cosmic scale and escalating speed—the Singularity *is* the human adventure: 'Nothing is lost.'

For British writers there was an additional challenge: the Americans had raised the stakes again. Their stock characters were no longer competent engineers with slide-rules at their belts like swords, but complex personalities with computers in their blood. There was no hostility in this emulation: British new space opera could be described as British SF written by people who like American SF, for people who like American SF. Or, more provocatively, left-wing SF by and for people who like right-wing SF. (This is on a spectrum where Peter F. Hamilton would have to be located towards the red end, fractionally to the right of Iain M. Banks.)

I didn't start off writing space opera—my emulation text was Neal Stephenson's *Snow Crash*—but the Vingean question of the Singularity was there in *The Star Fraction*, and more explicitly in *The Stone Canal*. When I got around to writing full-length space opera, with *The Cassini Division*, the notion of Singularity had been taken up by intellects small, cold and unsympathetic, who flaunt their contempt for the human species from behind a squid-ink discourse of rights that, they fancy, compels the rest of us to leave them alone while they work on the extinction agenda. I pillaged Max Stirner and Marx for a rhetoric more ruthless than their Social Darwinism. (You think you can outmegadeath *us*? Bring it on, frat boy, bring it on. Daddy's lawyers, guns and money won't get you out of this.)

That was one possible answer to Vinge's question: the posthumans will come, and the humans will kill them. I played variations on this in my first four books. In my next three, the wholly space-operatic Engines of Light series, the godlike niche is already occupied by naturally evolved intelligences (who, if the posthumans come, will kill them). In *Newton's Wake*, the space opera I'm currently writing (that, if truth be told, I should be working on at this minute) a remnant of humanity survives the Singularity to expand into a universe from which the most advanced posthumans have absconded, but which has been altered by their passage.

Others give different and diverse answers. Peter F. Hamilton, in his 'Night's Dawn' trilogy and related texts, shows enhanced humans in symbiosis with superhuman intelligences, but avoids the Vingean Singularity by foregrounding other and perhaps more plausible future techological paths. At an antipodean pole Greg Egan takes the opposite course, boldly conjecturing what a posthuman POV might be like: his *Schild's Ladder* is simultaneously intellectually rigorous and physically adventurous, a genuine space opera with a bibliography. Charles Stross, in various short stories and in *Singularity Sky* (forthcoming) adroitly contrives the coexistence of baroque interstellar empires with a broad spectrum of post-Singularity intelligences. (In other stories, notably the astonishing series that began with 'Lobsters', he makes living through the Singularity look like perilous but enormous fun.) Alastair Reynolds makes ingenious use of hard-SF rigour: in his Einsteinian universe, astronomical scale, deep time, and slower-than-light travel ensure that any Singularities are local incidents, and episodes in his characters' long lives within which successive and sometimes grotesque transformations of body and mind take the subject beyond the human condition without angst or even, necessarily, their noticing. Justina Robson, in *Natural History*, does something quite other, and just as unflinching.

Most radically of all, M. John Harrison has returned to space opera with *Light*, a book that projects an astronomical singularity beyond the Singularity, and that confronts, most painfully, the darkness of the *desire* to be posthuman, as well as its splendour. The physics has insight, the psychoanalysis is calculated, and it is difficult to say which equations are colder: 'All the drives worked.' It is a hard act to follow. It may come to be seen as the final flowering of new space opera, or as the seed-pod for many more to come. The future is up to us.

Does Science Fiction Have to be About the Present?

In articles and interviews which I've ruthlessly recycled as talks at SF conventions, I've put forward a by no means original thesis that SF can be more illuminating about the time of its writing than about that of its imagined future. In an interview or Q&A session at Swecon 2003, Alastair Reynolds pointed out that while there may be some truth in this, there are a great number of stories that aren't—even unconsciously—about the present, but quite straightforward and conscientious attempts to imagine what the real future might be like. He mentioned Arthur C. Clarke's *The City and the Stars*.

Good point, I thought, and stole it at once. It was about time I came up with another topic for SF convention talks. Especially as the next one I was due to give was at P-Con in Dublin, and too many people there might well have heard me rambling on about SF-as-contemporary-reference before. (As it happened, I didn't have to give a talk, because Charlie Stross interviewed me instead.)

Besides, that whole argument gets uncomfortably close to a capitulation to the oft-heard claim (which deserves to become known as the Atwood Defence) that what is really interesting and important about SF just *is* its contemporary reference; that some novel that might superficially *appear* to be SF (because it's, say, set in the future after a genetically engineered plague has wiped out most of the human race) isn't *really* SF but satire, and really about the present, and not related to that vulgar stuff about rockets and rayguns and talking squids in outer space, and therefore may deserve serious consideration and can be safely opened without risk of releasing *alien germs* to which normal Earth readers have no natural immunity and which could sweep through the entire literary community and all die, oh, the embarrassment.

So, with space helmets on, brass bras brightly polished, and phasers set to stun, let's boldly go in search of SF that really is about the future, and whose contemporary reference is reduced to as close to a trace element as humanly possible.

Interestingly enough, the division between what I'll boldly call pure SF and SF-as-satire cuts across, rather than between, a lot of the themes and tropes and subject areas of SF. Let's start with the most obvious: stories set in the far future. Clarke's *The City and the Stars*, already mentioned, or Olaf Stapledon's *Star Maker* are undoubtedly novels which, while inevitably of their time, are not fundamentally interested in or secretly about their time. They are about the far future of humanity and the universe. Michael Moorcock's 'Dancers at the End of Time' stories, however, aren't. They are about an opulent, irresponsible decadence, about ennui, about fin de siecle, rather than the literal end of time.

On to the second most obvious: post-apocalypse stories. It seems to me that Walter Miller's *A Canticle for Leibowitz* is a story that can be understood without much reference to the time in which it was written, and gains little from applying a knowledge of that time to it. It looks at a post-catastrophe recovery of civilization *sub specie aeternatis*. The closest it comes to contemporary comment is in its final section, set a thousand or so years in the future, and in the eerie sense that section conveys that *our* civilization is a post-catastrophe recovery civilization, as indeed it is.

Robert Heinlein's *Farnham's Freehold*, on the other hand, is so embarrassingly about contemporary concerns, as refracted through the siltier layers of Heinlein's mind, that to discuss it is to push at the fallout shelter's open door and let in all kinds of toxic and radioactive stuff. In this novel the descendants of Black Americans have come out on top after a nuclear war, and become slave-holding (and slave-castrating) cannibals. If that doesn't reflect racial and sexual fears I don't know what does. Whether you cut the Dean of Science Fiction some slack (as Farah Mendlesohn has pointed out to me, Heinlein's other works are clearly anti-racist) and read it in the spirit of Swift's *A Modest Proposal*, or read it (as I certainly did when I first read it) as a racist tract maybe one notch above *The Turner Diaries*, it has to be thrown out of court as a serious attempt to examine what a post-nuclear world might be like.

A like distinction can be made between (almost) entire bodies of work that are otherwise closely affiliated: contrast, for example, that of William Gibson with that of Bruce Sterling; or J. G. Ballard with Keith Roberts. In Neal Stephenson's *Snow Crash*, anarcho-capitalism is a satirical device; in most of the work of Vernor Vinge, it's a serious thought experiment. Many more examples could be given, and could be argued over (as I'm sure these could be).

For now, though, I want to raise the possibility that the (British) New Wave might be the source of all that was wrong with British SF for thirty years. What was good in the New Wave was the literary quality of some of its writing, and the exacting quality—and polemical verve—of most of its criticism. What was wrong with it was its content. It marked a turn from rationality to irrationality, from outer space to inner, from exploring the universe to inspecting navel fluff, and from popularity to respectability. Yes, 90% of Trad SF was crap. 90% of New Wave SF was crap, and boring, miserabilist, depressing crap at that. It was an abandonment of everything that justifies SF as a genre, in favour of what is acceptable to mundanes.

What is it that distinguishes, and justifies, SF as a genre?

For thousands of years, people have been huddled around the campfire, telling stories. The stories were about what went on around the campfire (who was sleeping with whom, who had become king and who had plotted to depose him, etc) and about the figures that were seen in the enormous distorted human shadows that the campfire projected onto the surrounding darkness: gods and demons, ghosts and monsters.

Then, some time around the seventeenth century, the sun came up.

> 'Nature, and Nature's laws, lay hid in night.
> *God said "Let Newton be!" and all was light.'*

Science fiction is the stories we tell about the surrounding landscape that then became visible, the world seen in Newton's light. As Swedish SF critic John-Henri Holmberg has said, it's the literary expression of the Enlightenment.

It's often not a very *good* literary expression. I'm not defending cardboard characters, clunky plots, chunky exposition or any other literary sins of SF. What I want to take issue with is the criterion of judging SF by its degree of closeness to 'realistic' or 'fantastic' literature, the literature of the campfire and the dark.

One of the most insidious ways of doing that is to privilege SF that deals imaginatively with social and political issues. Speculative political fancies have been respectable since Plato, who is more or less the Form of Respectability in the Western canon. Thomas More could write an approving speculative fiction about communism and remain respectable, not only canon but canonized. The most respectable work of recent SF is very likely Ursula Le Guin's *The Dispossessed*. To outflank any unwanted agreement, let me say right away that this isn't because it's feminist, because it isn't—it's Mills & Boon monogamist to the bone, as well as subtly homophobic and biological-sex-essentialist; and nor is it because it's communist or anarchist. James P. Hogan gave a much more attractive and indeed more plausible depiction of a communist anarchy in *Voyage From Yesteryear*, and I don't see that book on academic SF courses.

No, *The Dispossessed* is respectable because it's an SF book that people with no interest in SF can read comfortably. Its sole real SF content, the theory of the ansible, can whizz right over their heads. It might as well be talking about radio. The real focus of interest is all the cosy familiar campfire stuff about the Individual versus Society, and Society versus Society, which plugs it neatly into the Great Tradition. In short, it's SF for people who don't like SF.

SF isn't fundamentally about that. Getting that right is good, don't get me wrong. Do for heaven's sake have some understanding of human beings before writing about them, at least to the extent that you do write about them. But what SF is fundamentally about is not the Individual versus Society, or Society versus Society, but humanity in the universe.

SF needn't thereby lose in human relevance and universality, because the situation it posits is both objectively true and universal to the human being, as a knowing subject confronting a knowable object. If SF about that is despised and rejected, rather than criticised and improved *in terms of its own project*, then both the Individual and Society are, in the long run, in deeper shit than any dystopia.

And that, comrades, is the real social relevance of SF.

The Inhabitants of the Planets and the Bottom of the Sea

The first book I read *about* SF was *The Disappearing Future*, edited by George Hay, circa 1970. I still have a copy of it, somewhere under the shifting stacks. It contained essays, a story or two and, I think, a poem. It was published as a mass-market paperback. (As, some years later, was a similarly fine volume of SF criticism, *Explorations of the Marvellous*, edited by Peter Nicholls.)

One essay, by James Blish, asked what the social justification of SF was. He began by demolishing some familiar codicils of the Gernsbackian contract. I don't have the issue to hand, so to speak, but here's how I recollect its general thrust.

SF helps us to foresee the future! No, it does not. SF's record of failed predictions, unforeseen events, and overlooked trends was already long when Blish wrote, and has lengthened since.

SF painlessly teaches science! No, it does not. SF painlessly teaches pseudoscience, misinformation and imaginary science. Conscientiously worked out hard SF that actually teaches science is as rare as archaeopteryx teeth. SF has been a coruscating tractor beam for psi powers, FTL, race memory, the prevalence of alien intelligence, evolution as a purposeful process, and many more scientific howlers. Today we can add the ease and imminence of the construction of AIs, uploads, and brain-computer interfaces to the dustbin of disrepute.

Nowadays, of course, anyone who wants to learn about real science without reading boring textbooks can find in any good bookshop a heady stack of well-written, well-informed, up-to-date books, often by practicing scientists, as well as a wealth of information on the Web.

I don't know if Blish mentioned this one:

SF encourages kids to study science and engineering! No, it does not. It encourages kids to wool-gather, daydream, write SF stories, and draw anatomically optimistic figures and kinetically implausible weapons on the covers of their exercise-books. To the extent that it does encourage kids into a scientific or technological career, it's often enough *the wrong kids*, setting them up for disappointment and, with luck and hard work, a job in IT. In ten or so years studying and researching in biological sciences, I don't recall meeting one colleague—student or scientist—who was a science fiction reader. As soon as I got into programming I was swapping SF paperbacks around the office like floppy disks, often with people who had irrelevant science degrees.

Blish went on to argue that the real value of SF was in dramatizing to people that the world is changing because of science and its application. I wouldn't disagree with that, but by now anyone not aware of this in their bones is probably beyond the reach of SF.

Closer to the mark, I suspect, was George Orwell in his essay 'Wells, Hitler, and the World State' (1941), in which he says:

> "Back in the nineteen-hundreds it was a wonderful experience for a boy to discover H. G. Wells. There you were, in a world of pedants, clergymen and golfers, with your future employers exhorting you to 'get on or get out', your parents systematically warping your sexual life, and your dull-witted schoolmasters sniggering over their Latin tags; and here was this wonderful man who could tell you about the inhabitants of the planets and the bottom of the sea, and who *knew* that the future was not going to be what respectable people imagined."—*The Penguin Essays of George Orwell*, 1984, 1994 ed., page 192.

This was true for me word for word back in the nineteen-seventies, and I suspect for many it still is in the twenty-hundreds. SF, I felt then, was about something other than all this crap, and it was about something real and important that put all this crap into perspective. The way I'd express it now is that SF is not fundamentally about human-to-human, or human-to-supernatural, but about human-to-nature, and that this is what makes it both appealing (to some) and unique as literature.

The great advantage of this explanation of the importance of SF is that it resonates with the experience of the reader, who certainly hasn't opened a book with spaceships on the cover in order to learn science, or to discover that the future will be different from the present. They want to read stories set in the universe *outside* the world of human relationships, because (a) if they're a typical new reader, i.e. an adolescent, they already have the world of human relationships ringing in their ears *all the fucking time*, and (b) they know that universe to be full of interest and wonder. They may read fantasy too, but the special kick of SF comes from the fact that it's *not* fantasy. It's set in a universe as scientifically credible as the writer can make it, and as long as this clause is honored, the rest of the Gernsbackian small print can go hang. This incidentally is why it's possible to read scientifically dated SF with the same pleasure as reading contemporary SF, and why SF that was scientifically sloppy or dated when it was written can't.

This explanation neatly entails other familiar consequences. One is the distinction between fans and mundanes. However petty and divided fandom may sometimes be, it's at least a social milieu where you can meet other people who share a sense of the importance of something outside human affairs, and who therefore bring a peculiar perspective to bear on human affairs, at its best a certain experimental open-mindedness. (I once met a fan who told me she'd been asked in her twenties 'Is sex the same with mundanes?' and had to admit she didn't know, and wasn't exactly panting to find out.) It also explains why real scientists are usually not much interested in SF. They get their extra-human fix from their daily working lives, and they get their fannish common interests from their colleagues. The science community itself can sometimes curiously resemble SF fandom in its toleration of unconventionality in appearance and behavior, to say nothing of beards, beer and feuds.

Another is the frequency with which the habit of SF reading is outgrown. 'I used to read a lot of it in my teens,' people tell you, 'but not for a long time now.' I did that too. As soon as I was out of my teens I became bitterly hostile to SF, not because I'd sorted out all the employers and parents and clergymen and warped sexual life stuff but because I felt reading SF was an active impediment to doing so. Maybe it was, because in my twenties I did sort it out, more or less. It was only in my thirties that I became interested in SF again.

Even now, I'd say that in some respects it *is* good to outgrow SF, if what you grow into is to read novels and learn about human relationships. But it is also worthwhile to reconsider that outgrowing, to look outside the campfire of humanity at the surrounding stars, and to ask yourself whether you're ready to read again about the inhabitants of the planets and the bottom of the sea.

(December 2003)

Not a Good Word to Say, Monday, April 18, 2005

A fixture of SF conventions is the Dealers' Room. It's mostly books, of course, and these mostly second-hand, but you can also find craftwork, from real deadly daggers to dragon-patterned hairclips; jewellery and embroidery, t-shirts and tiaras. But it's mostly books. Usually I buy one serious critical work, new. This year I bought a funny critical work, David Langford's *The Complete Critical Assembly*, and a load of old paperbacks. Six of these were issues of *New Worlds*, the 1970s paperback series that succeeded the SF magazine of the same name. Specifically, they were *New Worlds* numbers 1, 4, 5, 6, 8, and 10. I read them all as they came out.

They contain some of my favourite stories from the time, and many that I loathed, but the main thing that has stuck in my mind from them is the criticism, largely by John Clute and M. John Harrison. At the time I enjoyed it. I still do, in a way. But what strikes me, on re-reading, is how negative it was. Harrison, in particular, has with very rare exceptions (Norman Spinrad's *Bug Jack Barron*, Arthur Sellings' *Junk Day*) not a good word to say about anything published as SF. It's a tellingly selective range that he targets. Most of the books he notices are now forgotten, and were marginal at the time. (Colin Wilson's *The Black Room*, anyone?) Those that weren't (e.g. *Tau Zero*) are lined up to have their cardboard characters kicked and their clunky dialogue ridiculed. Their specifically science-fictional strengths—and come on, a competent book about travelling at relativistic velocities to the end of the universe has to have *some* science-fictional strengths—are passed over with a yawn. It's like reading SF criticism by someone who despised SF; who just didn't see the point of SF's existence in the first place.

(Clute's a different story. No matter how harsh he was, you always got the feeling he thought there was something there worth worrying at. He has gone on to become the field's most erudite, exacting and comprehending critic. Harrison's strengths were and are as a fiction writer, and his early exercises in criticism may have been just that, exercises: wrestling with the genre and building his muscles for other feats entirely. And they are great feats.)

Now you could say that Harrison—and the New Wave generally—was just railing at SF's failure to live up to its possibilities, its lazy contentment with life in a literary slum, its windows steamed up with potboilers. But what rather tells against that is this: in the whole of that series, I can't remember—I may have missed it, but the point is there's nothing that sticks in the memory—*anything at all* about the good stuff that was coming out at the time. I owe this recognition to a conversation at the con with Farah Mendlesohn: when I ventured that the New Wave's critical negativity could be explained by the fact that the early 70s in SF were a bad period anyway, she pointed out that, on the contrary, it was a period of immense vigour: some of the best work of Robert Silverberg, Joe Haldeman's debut, the first wave of feminist SF…I've just checked the half-decade's details in (where else) John Clute's *Science Fiction: The Illustrated Encyclopaedia*, and here they are:

The *New Worlds* paperback series series came out between 1971 and 1976. Let's allow a year for publication lag, and look at some notable titles of 1970 to 1975: Larry Niven's *Ringworld*, Robert Silverberg's *Dying Inside*, Ian Watson's *The Embedding*, Ursula Le Guin's *The Dispossessed*, Joe Haldeman's *The Forever War*, Joanna Russ's *The Female Man*, John Brunner's *The Sheep Look Up* and *The Shockwave Rider*, Gene Wolfe's *The Fifth Head of Cerberus*, Suzy McKee Charnas's *Walk to the End of the World*, Bob Shaw's *Orbitsville*, Samuel Delany's *Dahlgren*…there was a lot of SF being written that just didn't fit the neat New Wave classification of on the one hand *boring rightwing mechaporn militarist nerdwank* and on the other *bold experimental fiction that really is vastly superior to all that.*

What that left out was the gripping hand. (That's an American SF joke. Never mind.)

Now, I knew all this. I'd read most of these books at or soon after publication. I'd also and likewise read, of the major books that came out between 1976 and 1983: *The Alteration* (Kingsley Amis), *The Malacia Tapestry* (Aldiss), *If the Stars are Gods* (Benford and Eklund), *Gateway*, *JEM*, *Beyond the Blue Event Horizon* (Pohl), *The Ophiuchi Hotline* (Varley), *The Martian Inca* (Watson), *Timescape* (Benford), *The Book of the New Sun* (Wolfe), *Star Songs of an Old Primate* (Tiptree), *Worlds* (Haldeman), *Helliconia Spring* (Aldiss), *The Anubis Gates* (Powers), *Golden Witchbreed* (Mary Gentle).

And yet I've said, of that period between the end of the New Wave and the beginning of cyberpunk:

The New Wave collapsed in a dribble of exhausted froth.

Other developments—the rise of self-consciously 'hard SF' which didn't fudge the physics—failed to re-ignite the genre's engines. The late seventies and early eighties were pretty dire—in SF, and in the world.

What rubbish! How completely, embarrassingly, crushingly wrong! I don't even have the excuse of ignorance. I've thought, and said and written, that I didn't read much SF at that time. Yet it's obvious now, looking at those titles, that I did read them more less as they were published. And it's not that I didn't *like* them. In almost all cases I enjoyed them, admired them enormously, and enthused about them. And there's the rub. At that time my enthusiasm met a cold blast of indifference or hostility from most of the people I talked to about it. When I wasn't struggling vainly to be a scientist, I was working at crap jobs. When I wasn't active in the most philistine of the Trot sects, I was hanging out in its milieu. Then, in the mid-80s, just as cyberpunk came along, I got a job as a computer programmer and walked away from the sects and finished my thesis, and within a short time was organising an SF club at work and writing *The Star Fraction*. No wonder, then, that many years later my backward glance at the period between the end of *New Worlds* and the publication of *Neuromancer* was bleak. It wasn't dire in SF, or fallow in my own reading of SF, but in the *response I got to my talking about SF*, and this darkened my [retrospective] view.

I've also attributed the New Space Opera and the British boom to the application of 'a British New Wave [...] sensibility to traditional tropes'. The Americans, I've suggested, supplied the big ideas, and the Brits came along with the literary sophistication and political complexity. This is just *insultingly* wrong, as well being as an unconscious, and thus all the more galling, echo of that British declining-imperialist conceit of being Athens to the new Rome. For the books I've listed above, and many that I haven't, are quite clearly among the true ancestors and inspirations for New Space Opera and the British boom. They're certainly not lacking in political and literary sophistication. In Britain SF was, with some shining exceptions, indeed in the doldrums in the late 70s and early 80s, but in the US it was flourishing, and branching out in all kinds of new directions. Its contribution, in terms of style and subject-matter and challenge, has proved far more lasting and fruitful than that of most of the British New Wave.

There remains the interesting question of why one of its consequences is, at the moment, a specifically *British* boom, but that was the subject of another conversation, with Charlie Stross, and for another time.

About Science Fact

Two jobs I'd now and again idly prefer to being a science fiction writer are: a scientist, and a science writer. The three pieces here contain very little evidence that I missed my calling. For my M. Phil. thesis I invented an original theory of the action of bone cells based on market economics, which adequately accounted for certain long-etablished and paradoxical observations but which failed to predict any new ones and served in no way to illuminate the tediously obtained results I actually got. Its subsequent influence has, to the best of my knowledge, been nil. In the first talk below, originally given at the Crichton Campus of Glasgow University, I came up with an original illustration of Ricardo's theory of comparative advantage based on the relationship between Victor Frankenstein and Igor. It too has not been taken up. At least Chris Tame said it was sound. The second article, written in haste for the *Sunday Herald*, is—in its commissioning and in its execution—a testimony to the delusion that being an SF writer is a qualification to comment on space policy. One of my earliest pieces of original research, recounted in the third piece below, had a fate that should have warned me of what my scientific career was going to be like.

But I enjoyed doing science. My very first piece of original research began when, on holiday, I noticed how barnacles on a sun-dried rock would open up as soon as the first or second drop from the rising tide splashed on them. I wondered if they also opened up to rain. The following semester I had a marine biology course at Millport, on the Isle of Cumbrae, and seized the chance to find out. I spent hours clambering on a steep, rocky shore, with measuring-rod, notebook, jars of water—salt and fresh—and a pipette, and eventually established a relationship between the time a barnacle spent out of water and its sensitivity to salt water. (And that it was only salt water they responded to.) The only really awkward part was measuring the precise height above sea level of the rocks on the shore. I tested the results for statistical significance, wrote them up and made a presentation at the end of the course. I think I called it 'The Psychology of Barnacles', for a laugh.

A day or two later, as the ferry pulled out of Millport, I noticed the tide table and clock displayed on the quay, and the wooden piers, some with ladders fixed conveniently beside them, all completely encrusted in barnacles.—K. M.

Rewriting Humanity: Reflections on the Possibility and Desirability of Genetic Engineering

I'm a science fiction writer. My only other qualification for talking about genetic engineering is that I have a zoology degree from Glasgow University. Unfortunately, when I was studying for it, in the early 1970s, genetic engineering really was science fiction. Even more unfortunately for my qualifications to talk about this, the effect of science fiction on public discussion of genetic engineering has been rather unhelpful. From *Frankenstein* to those 1950s horror movies which ended with a priest saying, above the smouldering ruins of a laboratory, "There are things which Man was not meant to know", SF and its mutant offspring have lurched and stumbled through popular consciousness, leaving a trail of broken glassware and misconception, suspicion and superstition about science behind them.

What I'd like to do is look at three questions about the genetic engineering of human beings:

1 — Can we do it?

2 — If we can, should we do it?

3 — If we do it, what consequences can we expect?

It can be done

OK, first, can we do it? It's traditional at occasions like this for authors to plug a book, and the book I want to plug is not my one of my own but Matt Ridley's *Genome* (which is a lucid, up-todate and readable explanation of what the human genome actually is and how we might be able to make changes to it.) The answer, as far as I can see from this book and a lay person's reading of *New Scientist* and so forth, is yes, we can.

As Ridley explains (pp. 243-257) retroviruses can have genes spliced into them, and some of their own genes edited out. The resulting modified retrovirus can then be used to infect a patient, and it proceeds to insert the new gene in the patient's cells. This has actually been used for gene therapy for rare and obscure immune deficiency disorders.

But this—somatic gene therapy—only modifies the body of one individual. It doesn't affect the germ cells, and produces no inherited changes. Changes that could be inherited are not only be possible but easier—instead of changing billions of cells, you need only change one or a few, in the early embryo. You can literally stick the genes in with a pipette. Transgenic mice already exist, and are used in research.

So in principle, yes, it can be done. We could have transgenic people if we wanted to. Doing this to change anything other than conditions where one or a few genes are missing or have gone wrong would be complicated, but we can throw computing power at complexity. Computing power halves in price every eighteen months or so, and will go on doing so for quite some time.

Of course at the moment it seems we don't want to. Germline gene therapy on human beings is effectively banned, and nobody in the business is proposing it.

The human genome is not sacred

Which brings me to the second question, which is: given that we can do it, should we do it?

There are two kinds of possible objections: ethical and prudential.

Is it ethical to pass on genetic changes to future individuals, without their choice? Well, we already do, unintentionally. If it's not unethical to have children who inherit your own existing genes for susceptibility to heart disease or cancer or whatever, it can hardly be unethical to pass on modified genes which confer a *reduced* susceptibility. Any change that isn't socially understood as an impairment or, let's say, an embarrassment—anything that is an actual improvement—would seem on the face of it to be well worth inheriting.

But is tampering with the human genome in itself ethically unacceptable?

I think we're in a rather unusual situation here in that we have a new science and technology to which the major traditional religions and philosophies in the advanced countries have no major moral objection in principle. Some Christians, particularly but of course not only Catholics, have moral objections to destroying or discarding human embryos in research. But suppose there was a technical way around that, that human genetic engineering could be done without damaging or destroying human embryos. If that were the case, would Christianity, Judaism, Islam or the secular humanism which for so many of us is a default option have any objection to human genetic engineering as such?

As far as I can see, the answer is no, they wouldn't. Human life may be sacred but the human genome is not. Whatever the image of God may be, it isn't a long skein of DNA molecules. It isn't chromosomes and genes, and most particularly it is not the genes for cancer, Alzheimer's, Tay-Sachs and cystic fibrosis. The human genome is a part of nature, however it came into existence. I think the evidence is overwhelming that it came into existence by natural selection, and many religious believers of course would agree. But, whether they take Genesis literally or symbolically, the religions which include Genesis among their scriptures acknowledge that we have a duty—indeed, a mission from God—to change nature for human benefit. No teacher of these religions should really say, of any question about the natural world, that "There are some things that Man was not meant to know."

"The sacred depths of nature"

But of course there are other religions and philosophies in our societies, whose adherents might strongly object to that view. Deep ecology, paganism, some forms of pantheism all regard nature as sacred, and might regard the genome itself as part of "the sacred depths of nature"—to use the title of a book by Ursula Goodenough which I haven't read. She's a biologist, and I don't know what her views are on the subject of genetic engineering. But I think the phrase itself captures an attitude very well, and some expressions of that attitude are indeed quite opposed to tampering with the genome.

So we have this interesting situation where the established traditional religions may be more open to human genetic engineering than some new—or revitalised old—religions and philosophies, and where these new views are a minority but a minority which is growing in influence. In fact their influence meshes well with much more widespread and prudential worries about the whole thing—not just genetic engineering, but even the mapping of the human genome.

How could mere knowledge be harmful? Here's one way—knowing in sufficient detail what genes individual people carry could make these individuals uninsurable—a 'genetic underclass'. With some genes—like those for Huntington's chorea—the time of onset can be predicted almost to the year. Less spectacularly, if genetic screening became cheap and easy for lots of genes predicting various illnesses, insurance companies could start asking if you'd ever been screened, or asking for the results. Their interest in tailoring the policy as precisely as possible to your predicted risks—a policy as unique as yourself! as they might advertise it—would conflict with your interest in pooling your risks with those of others.

Another area of justifiable public concern is the notion of patenting gene sequences and claiming intellectual property in genes, which is part of the wider problem of the business interests which are driving a large part of the whole endeavour. However, both the insurance and the intellectual property problems are of a kind which is eminently fixable by passing appropriate laws, or tweaking existing laws.

Justifiable concerns

What's much less easily dealt with are unintended consequences, and here we have two levels of possible concern. One is that because of the BSE disaster, people in Britain are inclined to be suspicious of assurances from scientists and governments and agro-industrial companies. So we have a situation where genetically modified crops that have been used on a huge scale in America get torn up and trampled by protesters here, to the bemusement of Americans.

But even without that arguably irrational fear, there would still be justifiable concerns because there *will* be unintended consequences which no amount of computing power can predict. To justify this I can only handwave about chaos theory, complexity theory and so on, but I'm sure the point is fairly evident: small changes in complex systems can have large and unpredictable effects. Besides that, there are lots of things we still don't understand. This is all very new. It's only in the last hundred and fifty years that we've known about natural selection; only a century since Mendelian genetics was rediscovered; half a century since the structure and function of DNA was understood; a decade or so of genetic engineering; and the first rough draft of the human genome was published this year.

However, I think human genetic engineering will be done, if only because somebody, somewhere, will try it regardless. Better it were done in the open, in free societies and not in secret laboratories.

An awareness that trade is better than conquest

Which brings me to my final question, which is what consequences we can expect.

The most immediate consequence of mapping the human genome will be better—and better targeted—medical treatments, as explained in a recent issue of *New Scientist* (number 2263, 4 November 2000). More long-term, somatic gene therapy will be applied to a wider range of illnesses and conditions. Somatic gene therapy will remain necessary even if germline gene therapy ever becomes universal, because genes will always mutate.

Suppose that human genetic engineering, in the sense of heritable changes to the genome, became widely practised. Suppose, for example, that suddenly there's a generation of Japanese schoolchildren with IQs of 200. Or suppose rich people could suddenly afford to make their children, and all their descendants, highly intelligent. Would this be a problem for the rest of us?

Not necessarily. It might seem unfair, but the better-off already transmit many advantages to their children—in social connections, in education, and in inherited wealth. And this is not necessarily unjust, or to the disadvantage of anyone else.

People of ordinary intelligence can *benefit* from the existence and activities of people of superior intelligence or ability, if their relationship with these people is peaceful, productive, and profitable. And such relationships can always potentially exist.

Take, for example, an all-round genius called Victor, and an ordinary bloke called Igor. Victor can do *everything* better than Igor. He can wash his laboratory glassware twice as fast as Igor can. But, because the time Victor spends washing the glassware would be much more profitably spent doing something else, such as designing experiments and deciding which green, bubbling chemicals he's going to put in the glassware today, it pays Victor to pay Igor to wash his glassware. And if Igor gets better pay as a bottle-washer up at the castle than as a labourer down in the village, then they both benefit.

A lot of our worries about a 'master race' and so on quite understandably come from the history of Nazism. But the ideas on politics and economics that the Nazis shared with a lot of other people in their time were as crude and mistaken as their understanding of genetics. Which is to say, they were distorted by envy, greed, hatred, pseudo-science and superstition. These are still with us, of course, but they are a lot less intellectually and socially respectable than they were in the 1930s and 1940s. I think there's more of an awareness now that trade is more profitable in the long run than conquest and enslavement.

The technology is new but the arguments are not

I suppose what I'm saying is that the genetic revolution doesn't raise any new ethical issues, it just sharpens our awareness of old ones.

For example, suppose it was possible to engineer a retrovirus to be highly infectious and which carried a permanent, inheritable fix for, say, susceptibility to heart disease. Would it be wrong to release it on the world, thus in effect giving people a preventive medicine whether they wanted it or not? We don't ask people's permission to drop emergency food aid to them, why should we ask their permission to unilaterally improve their life expectancy?

Is it the genetic engineering aspect of this suggestion that makes us uneasy? Well, suppose we could do the same by releasing a gas into the atmosphere? Would this be any different from releasing a benign retrovirus? Or—moving in the other direction on the same slippery slope—how about putting a mineral in the drinking-water supply that reduces the incidence of dental caries?

The genetic technology is new, but the ethical and political principles by which we can decide how to use it aren't. They'll continue to be argued about, and that's one aspect of human nature which genetic engineering is unlikely to change.

Space

Space is back in the headlines. Beagle 2, the Hubble Space Telescope, the Mars rovers Spirit and Opportunity, and President George W. Bush's sketchy outline of a bold space programme have all received recent wide coverage. More important is that it's back in our minds. The idea of space exploration seems to have got under many people's skins in the past few months, in a way that even last year's Space Shuttle tragedy didn't. The recent discovery of a tenth planet, Sedna, even made the evening papers. One reason for this new interest and engagement may have been a natural event. Last autumn Mars burned bright and low in the evening skies, almost impossible to overlook. The last time the planet was this close was fifty thousand years ago. The last people to see Mars like this—though far brighter, in unpolluted skies—shared the view with the Neanderthals. This time around, millions of people were able to actually recognise and point to Mars for the first time in their lives. The flotilla of probes that landed —or, in Beagle 2's case, crashed—in December and January were therefore not doing so on some random dot of light but on a place that had recently been almost as familiar a celestial object as the Moon.

Space travel has been part of my mind almost as long as I can remember. One of my earliest memories is of hearing about Sputnik, the first artificial satellite, launched by the USSR in 1957. I can still see a Giles cartoon in the *Daily Express*, of his distinctive kids and tykes peering at a spiky object in a smouldering hole in the ground. The only thing I don't remember is the caption, but then I couldn't read. I was three years old, and a little worried about it all. Might Sputnik land in that cold shadow behind the back door, and *bleep* at me? A few years later, I puzzled over the clippings on the school notice-board of Yuri Gagarin smiling and waving at crowds in London. He was a *Russian*, wasn't he? One of the *enemy*? Why wasn't everybody shooting at him?

(Not long ago ago I wondered why—with such vivid memories of the time—I had no memory of the Cuban missile crisis, and also wondered why I had a strong, distinct childhood memory of a day of fear of rockets bringing apocalyptic death from the sky. Well, *duh*,...but yes, it took me a while to put the two together.)

When I was about ten, my mother told me just before I set off for school that Russian scientists had detected signals which they thought might come from a 'super-civilization' in space. All day I kept an eye on the skies, and when I came home I picked up the *Daily Express* and carefully checked every inside page for the story. (Even then, I knew that science got short shrift in the press.) Nothing. Then I noticed the front page headline, so huge that I'd missed it: SIGNALS FROM SPACE?

False alarm, sadly. But it didn't dim my interest. I followed the US and Soviet space programmes with an even-handed enthusiasm, and only missed seeing the first Moon landing live on television because (a) we didn't have a television and (b) going to see it at the neighbours' house in the wee hours of a Monday morning would have implicitly connived at their Sabbath-breaking. (But I saw the Apollo 11 splashdown, live on television, OK? Nixon and all. How many can say *that*, eh? Defensive? Me? Come outside and say that.)

Recently I re-read *Space Cadet*, one of a series of novels for young readers written by the great American SF author Robert A. Heinlein in the 1950s. I was struck by a scene where the heroes are approaching an asteroid and notice its layered appearance. One of them remarks that it could be sedimentary rock, and might contain fossils. Sedimentary rock, of course, is laid down in water. For an asteroid to be made of sedimentary rock it would have to have once been part of planet with rivers and oceans. For Heinlein, even in the 1950s, the speculation that the asteroid belt could be the rubble of a blown-up planet between Mars and Jupiter was not far-fetched. Nor, indeed, were his assumptions in the same series that Mars has artificial canals and that Venus has humid jungles under its cloud canopy. The only reason we know better today is because unmanned space probes have revolutionised our knowledge of the Solar System. That revolution continues. Cassini, now a few months away from Saturn, is sending back postcards of unprecedented clarity. ESA's spacecraft Rosetta was launched earlier this year on a ten-year chase after comet Chury. Mars Express, the ESA orbiter that deployed the ill-fated Beagle 2, is photographing Mars at 2-metre resolution. It has shown us a landscape more alien and astonishing than ever: a 3000-metre 'dustfall' over the lip of the gigantic Albor Tholus caldera; valleys and gullies that look shaped by water and smoothed by lava; and water ice at the south pole.

A recent issue of *New Scientist* ran NASA's claim that the latest data from the rovers clinched the case for liquid water on the Martian surface at some time in the past. It was illustrated with a photograph of the rocks in question, and—although layered rocks are common on Mars and not necessarily sedimentary—it's hard to look at them without seeing their layered appearance as a hint that they were laid down in water. They look as sedimentary as the sandstones I walk past near the Hawes Pier in South Queensferry. Now NASA's quad-bike-sized robot geologists are probing for ripple marks. Gusev Crater, being explored by Spirit, might be a lake-bed, and on the opposite side of the planet Opportunity's landing-site, the Meridiani Planum, the bottom of a vast ocean. Traces of waves and currents would really clinch it; and would, I think, be almost as weird as Heinlein's imaginary and impossible asteroid. Sedimentary rocks in space! And where water was, life may have been. Life on Mars!

Some of us while looking at Mars last year must also have noticed for the first time an object less constant and higher in the sky, but just as bright, moving swiftly, fading as it passed into Earth's shadow: the International Space Station. It's unlike anything else—you can't mistake it for an aircraft, or for another satellite - and there's something a little uncanny about it. It looks solid, it looks *big*, and it is. But its purpose seems as dim as its presence is bright. When machines can tell us so much, what's the point of putting people up there? It's a good question.

Manned space travel marked two dates last year. On February 1 the Space Shuttle *Columbia* disintegrated on re-entry; the lessons of the *Challenger* crash (when engineers worry, listen to them) still apparently unlearned by NASA's unwieldy management. On 16 October China became a new space-going power, and added a word to the world's languages, as *taikonaut* Yang Liwei took a Shenzhou-5 capsule through fourteen orbits of the Earth. This January, President Bush announced a new US manned space programme. Complete the space station, replace the Shuttle, return to the Moon, build a Moon base, learn more stuff, go to Mars...and worlds beyond. It would be 'a journey, not a race,' he insisted; a human adventure, with no prospect of an end: 'Human beings are headed out into the cosmos'. Bush is thus the first head of state to project the vision of open-ended human space exploration—never articulated even by Kennedy or Krushchev in the Space Age of the sixties, but a familar theme of science fiction's Golden Age in the 1950s.

Sometimes my interests as a science fiction writer conflict with my duties as a citizen. For most people outside of the science fiction readership, space is what is what science fiction is all about, and—along with flying saucers, little grey aliens, and other such embarrassing associations—it's one more reason why they think we're nuts. Almost any SF writer is bound to feel at least a touch of vindication from any public acknowlegement of the importance of space, no matter how ill-conceived. My first reaction to the speech was, I must admit, enthusiastic, but sober reflection soon set in.

Bush's programme sounded good, but critics were quick to point to its weaknesses and evasions. The additional funding proposed for NASA was so meagre that the programme's ambitious goals could only be met by deep cuts in the immensely productive unmanned space exploration and Earth observation satellite programmes. The announcement, days later, that NASA had cancelled next year's repair mission to the Hubble Space Telescope, dooming it well before the end of its useful life, seemed to confirm this gloomy view. NASA argues that in fact the cancellation had more to do with a new post-*Columbia* caution than cost. Meanwhile, the Pentagon's far-reaching plans for the militarization of space exposed a darker side of the sky. Competition—perhaps eventually confrontation—with China and other powers may be the real bottom line, and 'full spectrum dominance' the real thrust towards a more lasting human presence in space. Even without that sinister prospect, the argument for manned space flight is complex.

Sending people to Mars presents risks and challenges far greater than going to the Moon. Protecting astronauts, cosmonauts or even taikonauts from the effects of many months of cosmic radiation and microgravity remains a serious problem. The cost could run into trillions of dollars. The benefits would be likewise great. Much of what has been discovered over the past months by the Mars rovers could have been learned in five minutes by an astronaut with a geological hammer and a magnifying glass. The frustrations and ambiguities of even the best photographs and experiments could be resolved by simply going and having a look. And no robot yet made, or yet designed, has the flexibility, adaptability and eye for the unusual that comes as standard with the human frame. But the counter-argument is straightforward: it would *still* be cheaper to just throw more robots at it. Cleaner, too: with robots you can be much more confident that any life found on Mars wasn't, a few months earlier, life on Earth.

It's important to disentangle the goal from the means. If human space travel is desirable in itself, bigger and more expensive rockets are not necessarily the way to go. Advances in materials science are making such apparently outlandish—but in fact seriously considered—proposals as a space elevator look increasingly feasible. A space elevator is, literally, a lift that travels up and down a cable suspended from a geostationary satellite. At first glance it looks ridiculous, but the physics is sound, and so is the economics. All you need is a strong enough cable; we're not there yet, but work is already underway in the labs. The first person to stand on the surface of Mars may step out of a lift. Even without space elevators, it's possible that entrepreneurs and enthusiasts may yet undercut NASA's Soviet-scale bureaucratic planners. There's money in it, too. Space tourism is a surprisingly well-costed venture, awaiting its venture capitalists.

Within decades, a week in orbit could be the holiday of a lifetime; a generation later, perhaps, a weekend break.

Solutions to the problems of living in space might likewise be found by more creative and indirect approaches. It's very easy to see outer space as the ultimate hostile environment: a hard vacuum awash with hard radiation. What is less easy to see is that we are already in that environment, protected from outer space only by a few tens of kilometres of gas and a feeble, though immense, magnetic field. The American futurist Marshall T. Savage, in *The Millennial Project*, has argued that space habitats could be radiation-proofed by pressurised shells of water and a very thin layer of gold. To prevent the microgravity of free fall from sapping the strength of our bones and muscles, he suggests a direct attack on that problem through artificial stimulation of the muscles, electrical stimulation of bone growth, and regular exercise in localised artificial gravity centrifugal wheels—rather than spinning the entire ship, or the entire colony. Some of his suggestions seem to me far-fetched—I have, a long time ago, done real research on how bones adapt to loading, and it's not a simple matter. But his ideas do stimulate original thought, and that's what we need to make progress.

It's also important to clarify the goal. Ultimately, if civilization survives, people will go to Mars 'and worlds beyond' not because they must, but because they want to. It's not that it's necessary for the sake of studying Mars, but that it's vital for the sake of enriching Earth. The universe may or may not be crying out to be filled with life. It is crying out to be filled with meaning, to be reflected in a mind, to be transformed from a thing in itself into a thing for us. To that, our own minds have to go out there, and the only way they can go is in human brains and bodies. The human beings who go out into the Solar system will make the Solar system part of the human home and the human story. They'll make it real to us. And in doing so, they'll help civilization to survive and expand. The real justification is spiritual, not scientific. As the prophet wrote: 'Where there is no vision, the people perish.' Vision, especially television, isn't enough. We need to do more than see—we need to reach out and touch it. On that point Bush is right. There's no guarantee that it's his project that'll take us there. But one way or another, humanity is headed out into the cosmos. The Space Age, far from being over, is only beginning.

The Scientist's Apprentice

The Jurassic marine crocodile Metriorhynchus was a lithe and elegant beast. We know a fair bit about it, including that it sometimes suffered from arthritis. You can see the fossilised femora, one of which has a rough knob at the end, where there should be a smooth one. I've held these stone bones, or a pair very like them, and grimaced at that ancient agony myself. For a few months in 1976 I knew almost all there is to know about Metriorhynchus; I had read the textbook references, looked up the articles on which they were based, and looked at many of the specimens on which the articles were based; I saw the original display-drawer of laid-out bones of the beast's hind foot in the very arrangement that I'd seen drawn in a dozen places. And I found, or thought I found, that the standard drawing was wrong, and with it much that we think we know about the Jurassic marine crocodile.

The question I was trying to answer, for a final year Zoology undergraduate dissertation, was this. Crocodiles spend most of their time in water but can walk, indeed run, on land. Turtles have a laborious trek up the beach. Most marine reptiles couldn't mange even that. A Mososaur or an Ichthyosaur is as marine-adapted as a dolphin. And like a dolphin, they gave birth to live young. They still laid eggs, but the eggs hatched inside. One famous fossil is of an ichthyosaur at moment of giving birth.

Now, your Jurassic marine crocodile, right, is sort of betwixt and between. Its legs look like flimsy flippers, very unlike the sturdy hind leg of a modern croc. On the other hand, or leg, their foot bones aren't the almost undifferentiated platter of tarsals that you see in the old ichthyosaur. You can tell them apart and fit them together. They articulate, but (you might think) a bit pointlessly, because the whole palm or foot was completely flat. And, *and*, there is no evidence at all that Metriorhynchus laid its eggs anywhere but on land. But looking at that floppy foot, you fancy Metriorhychus mums-to-be had a hard time of it up on the mud-flat.

So, with the telling vagueness that's the dead give-away of a bad extinction story, a just-was story you might say, this amphibious condition was hand-waved to as their fatal flaw. Perhaps because my tutor had a doubt about this, and certainly because the Hunterian Museum contained a good few specimens, I chose to investigate just how far the marine adaptations of Metriorhynchus had actually gone. In particular, I looked at whether there might be more to the articulation of the foot than met the eye.

The Hunterian Museum is quiet, with the sort of hum that might be an aural hallucination. The smell is of locusts and wild honey, like John the Baptist's menu. The windows are like in a church. There is armour and parchment. There are vases and mummies. Every length and lath of wood is polished to a force-field sheen. Around the hall are galleries where minerals and fossils lie under sloping glass. And under these displays are drawers that glide out, in memory, as if on wheels. They are full of detritus and shards labelled in india ink and held together with varnish and Sellotape.

In a corner of one of these galleries I had a table and a chair, and on that table I laid out bones taken from the drawers, and looked at them and puzzled over them, and doodled them, and fiddled with suspending them from bits of thread, and read all about Metriorhynchus when I wasn't skiving off and reading about something more exciting, like the Portuguese Revolution or *The Outcasts of Foolgarah* (by Frank Hardy. It's a great book.) I took more than one girlfriend to see that table. Come up and see my fossils. It wasn't much, but it hardened them for the experience of seeing my bedsit. (Mouse footprints in the frying pan lard. Trace fossils! No, they weren't impressed either.)

Anyway, I checked all the specimens I could find, including in the basement of the Natural History Museum where they keep the stuff not on public view: the dragon's egg, the Woking Martian, the Piltdown skull; and, more excitingly, the above mentioned bones of the arthritic crocodile and the original reconstruction of the hind foot, in a little tray lined with indented baize. I drew it and made notes. All the bones were flat, and the foot was a flat paddle.

Then, back at the Hunterian, I started pulling out the drawers and rummaging through the bits. Ribs mostly, teeth, bits of jaw. In among all the rubbish I found a calcaneus—a heel-bone. It wasn't flat, like every other Metriorhynchus calcaneus. It was the same shape as the calcaneus of a modern crocodile. I think I may have found an astragalus as well—the next bone down—but that doesn't matter, because…

The heel-bone is connected to the foot bone, and these bones lived. Because they weren't flattened, you could see the planes where they articulated, like facets. And when I looked again at the other bones, I could see that they were all flatter than they should have been, and they all had lots of tiny cracks, just as if…just as if…they'd all been crushed under tons and tons of mud.

The Jurassic marine crocodile hadn't had a flat foot after all. It's just that the bones of the standard specimens had all been flattened.

So, with black thread, black cards, and Blu-Tac, I and the Museum supervisor (who was keen, and helpful, and a fine photographer) I put together a new reconstruction of the hind foot and photographed it. The new view of the foot was of a proper foot, not a paddle. It was a foot that could push, not just flap. And in the nick of time I typed the whole thing up and got it to the office on the dot of five on the final day. And my dissertation passed, and was filed in the vaults of the Zoology Department, where it probably remains to this day.

Every picture of Metriorhynchus is still wrong.

http://www.bbc.co.uk/science/seamonsters/factfiles/metriorhynchus.shtml
http://www.gtj.org.uk/en/item1/26414

The Land Shall Not Be Sold Forever

Scotland is where America comes from. Not, of course, in all or even most of its people or traditions, but in its revolution and constitution, and in their historical precursors and preconditions. There's a relic of one of them in my local museum:

It's on vellum. You can still see the shape of the lamb. It's hard to read: the orthography, if not the language, has changed since 1638. It's harder yet to grasp its significance: the rant against the Roman Antichrist, the intolerance to all outside God's true church, the professed loyalty to the King's Majesty are now alien. But some phrases still leap out: 'a free monarchy', 'the fundamental laws, ancient privileges, offices and liberties of this kingdom', 'the people's security of their lands, livings, rights, offices, liberties, and dignities preserved'. The cramped signatures at the foot, of the lord, the councillors, the burgesses and the ministers of Queensferry. I looked at it today, in the museum that was once the town hall. It's behind a small pair of red curtains; you are asked to pull them back after looking at it. Its ink cannot bear the light.

Philosophers have imagined a Social Contract. Scotland actually had one; or rather, two. This is the original of this town's copy of the first, the National Covenant, signed in Greyfriars Kirk and then in local copies in most of the towns of the kingdom. Quaintly loyal as it seems to us, to Charles I it was provocation enough to raise an army. He neglected to ask Parliament's leave for its supply, and the English Revolution began.

The English Revolution was detonated by the Scots; the Glorious Revolution was defended against its most pressing peril by the Scottish Covenanters, singing their psalms and firing their muskets amid the burning, falling ruins of Dunkeld. The Scottish Enlightenment explained the whole process and foresaw its future with a then unmatched lucidity. Between 1688 and 1776 lay an event whose significance has long been as obscure as its surface has been famous: the Jacobite rising of 1745 and its defeat at Culloden. My friend Neil Davidson's pioneering interpretation of that event is reviewed in the second and third pieces below.

The first piece was requested some time in the late 90s by the *Sunday Herald* and never published. It was some time after the establishment of the Scottish parliament, a development for which I voted and now regret. The others originated as blog posts and deal with aspects of Scottish history and politics.—K. M.

Scotland and Europe

'Scotland' and 'Europe' have become codewords of confusion: the country, and the continent, identified with their political representation at Holyrood and Brussels respectively. The once-new SNP slogan, 'Scotland in Europe' has now become part of a fuzzy consensus for a (more) separated Scotland, in a (more) integrated European Union. To oppose it may seem eccentric and backward-looking, a position only upheld by Old Labour and the Tory Right. I stand with neither of these traditions. My internationalism has made me oppose every war—including the current one—fought by the United Kingdom in my entire adult life. But—if talked down from that high ledge, and forced to make a choice of national arrangements on national ground—I'd prefer to have Scotland remain in the UK, and the UK get out of the EU.

Let's start with Scotland. Scotland is a nation, but not an oppressed nation. No soldiers' boots crash through doors in Glasgow, and Maclean and Macdiarmid did not perish in the ruins of Edinburgh's General Post Office in Waterloo Place. Galling as that lack may be to nationalist romantics, it is no loss to Scotland the nation. It has its sovereignty already, which it exercises through the parliament at Westminster. No amount of grumbling over parcels of rogues and English gold can alter the fact that the Union was voluntary and remains so—the odd half-forgotten doomed uprising notwithstanding, no movement for separation has won the allegiance of the Scottish majority. Every radical force in Scotland—from the Covenanters, through the Chartists, to the Communists and beyond—has sought power on a national scale: by which they meant, a British scale. Whatever may be thought of their aims, they had the right target in their sights.

The Union parliament is the current embodiment of the sovereignty of the Scottish people. It's as revolutionary in its way as the Dail in Dublin, even if was won by the people's sword and gun in the seventeenth century rather than the twentieth. For all its ancient and arcane flummery, Westminster has not blocked a single progressive and popular measure since the one disastrous exception of Irish Home Rule. Complaining about the Constitution was not long ago the preserve of cranks, and it still would be if the British labour, liberal and progressive movements hadn't gone a bit cranky in the Thatcher decades.

Unable to formulate a popular programme that could unite a big enough minority to dislodge the compact minority in favour of Thatcher, let alone win a majority, they decided that the problem was in the details of the political system. First-past-the-post, the Lords, even the monarchy began to loom large as great reactionary obstacles. This, of course, was piffle, making mountains out of the molehills that every Labour leader from Keir Hardie to Callaghan had stepped over with ease. As Marx and Engels remarked on different occasions, if the British workers couldn't get measures in their interest passed at Westminster—up to and including socialism itself, if they were that way inclined—it would be entirely their own fault. How right they were about that!—but that's another story.

After the Tories self-destructed, the landslide Labour government, elected by a smaller percentage of the electorate than any previous Labour government, found itself in power with an economic policy of Thatcherism with a human face and a political programme of cranky constitutional tinkering. The Atlantic course remained unchanged, but the temptation to fiddle with the valves and gauges has proved irresistible. What explosions they are preparing in the boilerroom, heaven only knows.

And now to Europe, and 'Scotland in Europe'. Away with the remote mastery of Westminster! Forward to the popular, responsive democracy of Brussels! What are they talking about?

The democratic or even nationalist point of transferring a shared but real sovereignty to bodies on which there is even less democratic control, if any at all, frankly escapes me. And a democratic Europe is a long way off. The difficulties of forming democratic polities across the vast differences of legal and political culture, not to speak of material interest, between the European nations are immense.

Europe isn't a nation, and we the Europeans aren't a people. It would take a revolution to make us one, and a revolution that big wouldn't be just European. It'll happen, no doubt—the falling rate of profit will, some day, reach the end of its run, and Wall Street will fall like the Berlin Wall —but I'm old enough to know that no sect knows the secret of what number the countdown has reached. At least until the day when that 'old mole' of capitalism's self-undermining shakes all foundations, and makes 'all Europe start from its seat'.

So let's go out on a limb and suppose there isn't going to be a democratic socialist world revolutionary upsurge any time soon. In that case, an increasingly federal Europe is what the EU must become. It's too late to hope that it'll be the Common Market we were promised when Britain joined. A common market would work, and wouldn't lead to endless national bickering over budgets and regulations. The attempt to 'harmonise' the conditions of doing business across Europe is something else. Almost inevitably the unelected bureaucrats will have their way. Equally inevitably, given the scale of their tasks, the principle of subsidiarity comes into play, and detailed implementation of the latest regulation about the price of fish and the permitted sizes of commercial paper gets devolved to regional sub-bureaucracies.

And there you have it: 'Scotland in Europe' is just the local station on a branch line of the gravy train. It's already a far from original remark that it's likely to deliver us a new parcel of rogues. So many jobs for the boys and girls are on offer in the arrangement, that it seems almost churlish to turn it down. I would gently point out, however, that the genius of the Scots has been manifested in many fields, but not in that of Scottish politics. The possibilities of escalating irritations between Holyrood and Westminster, and increasing aggravations within Scotland itself, are all too evident.

What annoys me is the presumption that anyone who is sceptical of either 'Scotland' or 'Europe' as political entities is assumed to be hostile to their nonpolitical characteristics. In my case, and I'm sure in the case of many like me, this is simply not true. The Scotland and Europe of cultures and countries are the air I breathe. Scotland in Europe, the real places this time, is where I'm from. But I also love England, and I honour the English Revolution which a Scottish invasion long ago detonated and which in its turn and in the long run made Scotland free. English liberty and English Labour have done Scottish liberty and Labour a power of good. I don't think We The People of Scotland should turn our backs on that England for any amount of easy EC money.

The Scottish Revolution

Last Saturday evening I went to the well-attended launch of Neil Davidson's *Discovering the Scottish Revolution 1692–1746* published by Pluto Press. Well over a hundred people were there, including historians, journalists, and political activists. This is in quantity and quality an impressive audience for a book written by an active socialist with a full-time job and no full-time academic position.

A few years ago, when Neil said he was writing a book on the Scottish bourgeois revolution, my first question was: 'When was it?' It wasn't a bad question, because it's easy to think of several mistaken answers: that it happened in one or other bloody episode of the Scottish Reformation, that it was accomplished as part of or in tandem with the English Revolution (including the Glorious Revolution), or that it never happened at all.

I'd more or less taken for granted the fairly common view that the bourgeois revolution in Lowland Scotland was completed by 1692, and that its decisive military victory was at Dunkeld. The subsequent Jacobite risings are on this view the assault of the remaining feudal/tribal Highlands, supported by foreign feudal/absolutist reaction, against an already consolidated bourgeois state.

In his talk introducing the book, Neil challenged this view. He argued that Scotland, still feudal in the 1690s, underwent a bourgeois revolution from above in the first half of the 18th century, and one whose results were decisive for the future of the world.

After the Glorious Revolution feudal relations persisted in Lowland Scotland as well as in the Highlands. Feudal rent, military tenure, and hereditary jurisdictions thwarted the development of capitalism. (A feudal lord is *A Man You Don't Meet Every Day*: 'I have acres of land, I have men I command, I have always a shilling to spare…') The Scottish bourgeoisie, such as it was, gambled its all—up to half the capital of the kingdom—not on agricultural improvement or manufacturing, but on the disastrous Darien Scheme. In the absence of agricultural improvement, food production was insufficient to prevent famine in the1690s.

The incorporating Union of 1707, far from extending the gains of the Revolution to Scotland, extended Scotland's vulnerability to counter-revolution to Britain as a whole. Any Jacobite restoration had to aim for the national capital: London. In the context of the world-wide struggle between the empires of capitalist England and absolutist France, this was a real threat. A restored Stuart monarchy would have made Britain a vassal state of France.

Between 1707 and 1745 reforms and improvements were made, but not enough. Only a few of the greatest lords, notably Argyle, could go over to capitalist relations on their estates, and even for them it was a partial and difficult process. Others simply racked-rented their tenants and/or racked up their debts. It was the most indebted 'lesser lairds', Highland and Lowland, who threw in their lot with Charles Stuart.

It was only the defeat of the Jacobite rising of 1745, and the subsequent smashing of Highland society and the abolition throughout Scotland of the hereditary jurisdictions and feudal or military tenures, that made capitalist development finally and fully possible in Scotland and irreversible in Britain as a whole. If the counter-revolution had succeeded, capitalist development could well have been blocked even in England, and absolutism strengthened in France, for an indeterminate but quite possibly historic period: perhaps no American independence, no French Revolution, no Industrial Revolution in the early 19th century.

The world we know was won at Culloden.

Their Snuff-filled Rooms, and A' That

I've just finished reading Neil Davidson's *Discovering the Scottish Revolution 1692–1746*, whose launch I refer to and whose thesis I sketched in the last but one post below. Having read it I can heartily recommend it. The writing is excellent: cool, witty, free from rancour. Davidson is sparing in his approbation (for Fletcher of Saltoun) and his condemnation (for the atrocities after Culloden) and partisan only for progress and for its victims among the poor. For the rest, the strongest emotion he permits himself to display is scorn. The narrative grips like a thriller. We are shown the undead ogre that was Scottish feudalism, and the feeble forces of progress arrayed—or disarrayed—against it, and we want to know how it was slain. Even though we know the outcome, the story is a page-turner.

How did Scotland go from being the armpit of the universe to the Athens of the North in a generation? How did a country that burned its last witch when Hume and Smith were boys become one in which these men and others could ignite the Enlightenment? How did a capitalist class whose international debut was the Darien Disaster rise to the top ranks of the industrial and financial masters of the world? How did landowners hitherto notorious for their backwardness become a byword for Improvement?

There are two popular answers. One is the 'Kirk to Enterprise' theory that the Scottish church promoted certain democratic and capitalist virtues. To an extent it did, but not enough to account for the take-off (quite apart from all the burning witches and stuff). Another is the 'Long Live the Glorious Fraternal Assistance of the English Revolution' (or 'Beam me up, Scotty') theory, which attributes the advance to the Treaty of Union. The killer fact for this beautiful theory is that the Treaty of Union quite explicitly left Scottish feudalism intact, just as the revolutionary struggles of the seventeenth century had.

What followed the Union was a protracted struggle, a decades-long situation of dual power that was only finally resolved when the counter-revolution lashed out in 1745. Within months of the military defeat of the rising the hereditary jurisdictions and military tenures that made the Scottish nobility a state within the state were abolished lock, stock and barrel: lords Highland and Lowland, Whig and Jacobite alike were stripped of their private courts and armies. This outcome, Davidson argues, was the climax of the Scottish, and completion of the British, bourgeois revolution.

As he points out, Scotland's revolution is a peculiar one, that does not lend itself to populist, socialist, or nationalist inspiration. There was no Bastille to storm, no tyrant to behead: only 'deals struck in snuff-filled rooms' and thousands of poor peasants butchered on the heather. It was no less real, and no less progressive, for all that.

Islands, Funerals, and the Footnotes of Buckle

Last Easter my wife and I took a cruise on the *Maid of the Forth* to Inchcolm Island. This island, a couple of hillocks joined by a short strip of strand, is in the middle of the Firth of Forth. Like all the other Inches it's cluttered with rusted and ruined fortifications from two World Wars (Inchgarvie and Inchmickery look like stone battleships, not coincidentally wasting more than one German bomb). It also has an abbey, which unlike most in this area is only partially demolished. Its lawns and garden, its cloisters and some of its rooms, are intact, and it's used for weddings. (All denominations and none—it belongs to the Scottish History trust, not to any of the churches.) The chapter house, where the monks met daily for abbey business, is a polygonal structure with a stone vaulted roof, with stone benches around the walls and three arched seat-niches for the abbott, the prior and the sub-prior. Standing in the middle of the floor and imagining the monks lining the benches I realised what it reminded me off. 'It's a locker room!' I said. It probably smelled like one, too, when full of seldom washed men in often wet clothes.

The island's main pull, however, is its bird life and sea views, which you get to via pathways, stairways, tunnels and dangerous cliff edges. I saw my first puffins, a flock swimming in the sea, small birds with big triangular rainbow beaks that look as if they're held on with elastic, like clown noses. Lots of gulls, making ready to nest and already noisy in defence of their territories. A nearby rock, the Haystack, has a colony of seals, of which you can see a dozen or so at low tide.

I didn't read up the history, but the abbey's been there in one form or another for almost a thousand years, during half of which it was in use. What happened? Well, the Reformation happened. 'The best way tae prevent the black corbies fae returning,' said Knox, 'is *tae pull doon their nests*.'

In the third volume of Henry Thomas Buckle's *Introduction to the History of Civilization in England* he deals with Scotland. This was by way of comparison and contrast to (Vol 2) the history of Spain, which in turn was to point up the peculiarities of the history of France, which in its turn was to show how different it was from the (Vol 1) history of England, which was in Buckle's opinion the ideal country in which to observe the undisturbed and natural course of Civilization, what with its being an island and all (except for its attachment to Scotland and Wales, which introduced minor disturbing factors). So Buckle, in preparation for a scientific study of history, wrote in succession introductions to the history of England, France, Spain and Scotland, and—just when he was getting to what he thought was the main point—died. (In Damascus.) Bummer. But he left us one of the most entertaining and indeed enchanting hard-core rationalist and libertarian histories of these countries ever penned.

This is especially true of Scotland. Buckle sought to explain the paradox that the Scots were liberal in politics, and bigoted in religion. Loyalty, Buckle owned, was not one of their faults. 'The Scotch have made war upon most of their kings,' he wrote with barely concealed approval, 'and put to death many.' How were so rebellious a people so craven before their clergy? It was the association of the Church with, first the king against the nobles, and then the people against the king, that explained its ascendancy. That ascendancy, upon victory, it turned rapidly to a tyranny of its own, a spiritual Cheka complete with its very own people's courts, the Kirk Sessions.

The Scottish Presbyterian clergy of the seventeenth century did more to inculcate superstition, gloom, asceticism, fear of hell, and dread of evil spirits than perhaps any religious establishment outside of Spain or Tibet. Not even the Puritans, not even in their godly pomp during the Reign of the Saints, could hold a candle to the ministers of the Kirk. They told of themselves and each other self-serving miracle stories of the sort that, told elsewhere of Catholic saints, make Protestants scoff and Jesuits blush. (I myself have been in all sincerity shown the footprints of a renowned preacher from centuries past, still there in the top of a rock.) If a class of men is given power they will abuse it, Buckle said. 'The entire history of the world affords no instance to the contrary.'

It is no exaggeration to say that the reputation of the Scotch Kirk has never recovered from the merciless kicking it received from the footnotes of Buckle. And it *is* the footnotes you have to read: in his chapter on the seventeenth century their small print occupies more space than the main text, page after page. He trawled every hell-fire sermon, every seditious screed, every tormenting self-tormented twisting of the conscience of the elect, every relevant Act of the Parliament of Scotland, every witch trial and heresy hunt and ludicrous hagiography and miracle-mongering memoir, and came up with the goods. He documented the clergy's savage misanthropy and refuted it in a stirring defence and justification of physical pleasure and worldly gain that echoes that of Spinoza, and is all the more touching in that Buckle (again like Spinoza) was himself among the most abstemious and studious of men.

Buckle has a clear explanation of how the Scotch clergy gained their power, and how long they kept it, and how slowly they began to lose it, but he misses—or lived barely long enough to see—how they acquired, in the second half of the nineteenth century, a somewhat more liberal and enlightened hegemony. The Free Kirk's theological college—still called New College, on the Mound in Edinburgh - was the pioneer of German-influenced biblical criticism in the English-speaking world, and some of its clergy and laity (Hugh Miller, for instance) were intellectuals, patriots and philanthropists of the first degree. They did it by siding, once again, with the people.

The story is peculiar and contorted. The Highland clansfolk, smashed and demoralised by the post-Culloden culminating terrors of the Scottish Revolution-from-above (*vide* Neil Davidson), lapsed from Episcopalianism or a nominal Presbyterianism almost into their ancient and never entirely abandoned paganism. They were re-evangelised and re-moralised by the Church of Scotland. In Ireland, after a later and greater catastrophe, another feckless Gaelic peasantry pulled themselves together in the Catholic church, and became in a generation or two the canny kulaks who defeated the British empire. The Scottish Gaels had a less fraught destiny. They stopped—or became remorseful about—their hard drinking and promiscuous dancing, and became respectable hard-working on-the-make Scots. (Not that the pagan trace has entirely departed. There's one island, to all appearances devout, of whose people I've heard a minister complain: '[These] folk are so heathen they're not even afraid of dying.') And strangely enough, they identified not with the contemporary Moderate, moralising, ministers of Enlightenment Scotland, but with the persecuted, radical, King-hating, bishop-stabbing, hell-raising evangelists of the seventeenth-century conventicles. The Highland Presbyterians took as their heroes and saints people to whom the Highlanders were known only and hated as a terrorist and terrifying horde of lickspittle, servile, counter-revolutionary, savage, Papist, cattle-thieving, bare-arsed mujahedin.

Soon enough, the tame preachers of the capitalist landlords who had (often in the same person, or that of their sons) replaced the patriarchal petty-tyrant chieftains of the clans, came into conflict with those favoured by their tenants, tenants whom the aforementioned landlords were busy shipping to Canada (and earlier, the Indies) to replace with sheep. The popular preachers, for the most part, and to their credit be it said, stood with their congregations against the Clearances. Little worldly good this did them—the benefice was in the gift of the landlord, not the congregation. Hence the Great Disruption of 1843, over that very issue of patronage, which across the Highlands emptied the churches and manses of the Church of Scotland and filled those of the new Free Kirk.

('What do you understand by "the invisible church"?' a Free Kirk elder is said to have asked an aspirant to the communion. Came the hesitant reply: 'The Established Church?')

Predictably, as the century wore on, some of the fervent Highlanders began to call into question the liberal theological drift of the now hegemonic Free Church, and some few of them—a savoury remnant, as the old phrase goes—separated from it in 1893 to establish, with less than a handful of ministers, the Free Presbyterian Church.

In that church I was raised. It retains faint but discernible traces of some of the faults excoriated by Buckle, and has added a few more. It was also the first church in the British Isles to denounce apartheid, and the first whose secular head—its Moderator, an annual post—was a black man. The majority of its adherents are now African. There were not many fundamentalist denominations in the white world of the 1960s where (literally) red-necked farmers listened with reverence to a black reverend from Zimbabwe (I still remember staring at the holes in his earlobes) or to an English Jewish convert, enthusiastically and knowledgeably expounding the Hebrew text that underlies King James.

Last year I attended the funeral of a relative of mine, a member of that church, in Skye. The rain was terrible. The church was packed. There was no sermon, only a singing of the 23rd Psalm, and two prayers. It is a peculiarity of that peculiar people that they have no funeral service; there is a dread of even the appearance of prayers for the dead, that Papist innovation. So the worship on the day of the funeral does not mention the deceased by name; the coffin stays outside, in the hearse, in the rain; and at the graveside the minister does not pray. The burial was miles away, in Glendale. A slow procession of cars followed the hearse. On the hillside above the cemetery is a memorial to 'the Glendale martyrs', one of whom—John MacPherson—was an ancestor of the woman we buried. His sword is in her attic. Another of the 'martyrs' was a minister. These men were arrested and jailed for leading a confrontation of 600 Skye crofters with the Sheriff's men who had come to enforce an eviction. Their victory is visible in the houses and crofts that still spread across the hills of the glen and the dale.

There have been moments when I thought my family's funerals resembled the Mafia's as depicted in movies. Businessmen in black suits, conferring quietly, smoking by their big cars outside the graveyard. This time, standing in the mud outside the drystone wall, on the land our fathers fought for, I was suddenly reminded of pictures of funerals on another island not far away. The religion and politics could hardly be more different, but something in the shape of the faces and the landscape was the same, and the same rain.

For his great, long, flawed poem *Island Funeral* Hugh MacDiarmid stole an entire chunk of text word for word from Haldane's essay on materialism. I have no compunction in stealing it back:

Yet if the nature of the mind is determined
by that of the body, as I believe,
It follows that every type of human mind
Has existed an infinite number of times
And will do so. Materialism promises something
Hardly to be distinguished from eternal life.
Minds or souls with the properties I love
—The minds or souls of these old islanders—
Have existed during an eternal time in the past
And will exist for an eternal time in the future.
A time broken up of course
By enormous intervals of non-existence
But an infinite time.

I don't believe that, either, but not to believe is not the same as to scoff.

The Strange Death of Socialist Scotland, November 2004

Socialism, in its modern sense, was born in Scotland. Before Owen there were millennarians and utopians, prophets and putschists. After him there was A New View of Society. New Lanark is where it all began.

(I'll come back to that.)

Not that Scotland has had a natural inclination toward socialism. This is the country that literally rationalised capitalism, by explaining to the English the new world they had stumbled into, and repeating in practice with great consciousness and purpose what the English had done first in their wonted empirical way. The effect was lasting. In the 1950s half the popular vote went to the Tories. The Clyde shipyards and the Fife coalfield produced the bedrock Labour vote and a thin but hard stratum of Communism, and most of the few British Communists whose names became household words: John Maclean, Willie Gallagher M.P., Jimmy Reid, Mick McGahey. Labour, the Liberals and the Nationalists slowly colonised the raised beaches left by the Tories' long decline, and proved tough as *machair* grass. For all that, Scotland in the 60s and 70s wasn't a particularly left-wing country. At the level of credible political vision, 1979 clobbered Old Labour and 1989 despatched Communism, here as everywhere else. Other socialist traditions less wedded to the state, though deeply rooted, were as obscure and obscured here as everywhere else. So why did Scotland become ever more left-wing in the 80s and 90s?

What gave Scottish socialism a second life was Margaret Thatcher. For nearly two decades Scots voted Labour and got the Tories. Scottish heavy industry—mines, shipbuilding, steel—withered in the blast. To add insult to injury, the Poll Tax was introduced in Scotland a year ahead of England, rather as dangerous weapons are tested off the coast of Mull. Thatcherism never caught on north of the Border. It wasn't just a question of policies. The woman was detested. Something about her rubbed most Scots the wrong way. It wasn't just the working and middle classes she failed to charm. I know a man who in the course of his work met many pillars of the Scottish establishment—captains of industry, distinguished scholars, princes of the church, retired Army officers, lairds so conservative they were spiritually Jacobites—who loathed her with a passion. Some apparent exceptions—Michael Forsyth, Malcolm Rifkind, Lord Mackay spring to mind—all came from outside the establishment. (Mackay of Clashfern's title is not inherited. His father was a railway worker. He was probably the first presbyterian Lord Chancellor since the Revolution.)

Although it was old Labour that had, in 1978, dashed the hopes of devolution, the Scottish left and intelligentsia responded to the Thatcher years with a devolution of the mind: 'Work as if you lived in the early days of a better nation', and all that. The results were brilliant. The art was magic. A left-wing nationalism became the common sense of the age. Its left fringe became the Scottish Socialist Party. Tommy Sheridan, now Scotland's best-known Socialist MSP, first became famous for leading popular resistance to the Poll Tax, and for winning a council seat from the prison his resistance had put him in. Later, he spoke for many who were left out by New Labour: those with no hope, and those with much.

The SSP is much more important in Scottish politics than its 6% of the vote would suggest. The political editor of a Sunday newspaper a few months ago explained it like this: By its permanent potential to take disillusioned left-wing votes from Labour, the SNP and the Liberal Democrats, it acts as a sheet-anchor keeping the whole system from shifting to starboard. It's the main reason why the Scottish Parliament seems to have five left-of-centre parties and one right-of-centre party. The right-of-centre party, the Tories, are almost embarrassed to exist. Now this is all about to change.

In Scotland socialism died this month. It was killed by two Executives: the Executive of the Scottish Parliament, when they decided to ban smoking in all enclosed public (and many private) spaces; and the Executive of the Scottish Socialist Party, when they voted to ditch Tommy Sheridan as Convener. Laugh if you like, but if some day there's a book with the above title, November 2004 will have a chapter to itself. Here's why.

First, the smoking ban. Of course I'm against it, but that isn't why I think it's a nail in the coffin of Scottish socialism. Plenty of decisions made by Scottish Labour have been a lot worse. This one, however, is the first time since the Poll Tax when they've decided to go after their own constituents. It's a huge attack on traditional Labour-voting working-class culture, and a huge attack on traditional Labour-voting bohemian culture. Of course its proponents don't see it that way. They see it as protecting the workers, and (as one of them put it) 'saving the dying Scotsman from himself'. They really think it will be popular. The most prominent left-wing journalists agree. They have some sad awakenings coming.

Another Executive setting itself up for a fall is that of the Scottish Socialist Party. Rumours about Tommy Sheridan's personal life had reached the press. The executive were dissatisfied with how Sheridan handled them. They demanded that he either say nothing to the press, or speak to a sympathetic newspaper, or face an open press conference. He insisted he would sue the newspaper retailing the allegations. The executive refused to back him or back down, and thus (it would seem) forced him to resign. When he spun his resignation as the result of a need to genuinely spend more time with his wife, other stories promptly emerged in print.

The SSP executive had no standing to put Sheridan's personal life on its agenda. Nothing had been alleged that affected the public interest, or the working-class interest. If he was reckless to insist on his day in court, that was his business.

I have no inside information. Perhaps having it would make a difference. That's beside the point. For everyone outside a party, its public actions *are* its actions. I can only go by what I see, and what I see is a train-wreck.

The SSP executive's political ineptitude in this matter is staggering. None of the other five SSP MSPs have a sixth of Tommy Sheridan's nous and charisma. I don't know him personally, but I've seen him speak in quiet rooms and noisy streets. I've by chance seen him convey to an individual a most personal sympathy. The man is an authentic working-class hero, the SSP's only household name, and its greatest asset.

That this should matter to the SSP is a sign of its weakness. It has many strengths. It has flaunted its republicanism. It has stood firm for the legalisation of cannabis, and the decriminalization of heroin addiction. It has opposed the imperialist war. It has stood up for persecuted asylum-seekers. It has stood by beleaguered trade unionists. It has sunk roots that extend far beyond the far left. But one thing it has not done is produce a credible and coherent socialist programme. By quite deliberately setting out to straddle nationalism and internationalism, reform and revolution, state-socialism and left-libertarianism, the party as such has had nothing very convincing to say. There is no conversation of socialism in Scotland. The SSP—as a party, not necessarily in all its parts and certainly not in all its members—is culturally philistine and economically incoherent. It's a tax-and-spend party with a nationalist tinge and more than a touch of political correctitude.

I've always respected the SSP's strengths, but I've never agreed with its statism and its nationalism. Its successes have been very inconvenient to the powerful and privileged. It has been the backbone of the anti-war movement in many parts of Scotland. That movement has now extended to some military families. It can be only a matter of time before it reaches the military itself. The SSP, and Sheridan personally, have been central to this very recent development, which has caused deep concern at the highest levels of the British state. For those in power the SSP's crisis couldn't have come at a more convenient moment.

Back to New Lanark, where it all began.

Robert Owen's enlightened capitalism succeeded. His communist experiments, inspired by that success, failed. His syndicalist and mutualist union failed. He then threw his great energy and ability into the co-operative movement. This voluntary and everyday socialism was a global success. There are now 800 million members of co-operatives. Engels counted Owen with the utopians, but the workers' co-operative has outlived the workers' parties and the workers' states. Which is not to say that Engels was altogether wrong. We still need the commonwealth as well as the co-operative. If it were to re-examine its libertarian and radical roots, a socialism that began again in Scotland might yet have the last laugh.

The Earth Question

Is seems a little unlikely that answers to most of the burning questions of our time could be found in the works of a bearded Victorian philosopher who wrote a controversial book on economics, inspired and led radical, popular and working-class movements, met global fame, faced derision from orthodox economists, and is now almost forgotten. Surprising as it may seem, though, a small but growing number of libertarians (some in the Democratic Party), as well as less partisan reformers, have taken to applying and popularising the ideas of Henry George.

Well, I was surprised. I was even more surprised to find that they have an office and bookshop near Haymarket Station in Edinburgh. Georgists in Edinburgh! It gave me an inkling of how E. P. Thompson must have felt when he met a Muggletonian in Nottingham. So I rang them up, checked their opening hours (10 to 6, weekdays) and set off to find them. I'd read *Protection and Free Trade* and *Progress and Poverty* about twenty years ago, in editions printed thirty years earlier. I fully expected, as I walked along Haymarket Terrace, to alight upon a dusty, fly-specked shopfront window display of yellowing pamphlets brown at the edges and curled at the corners.

Not a bit of it! 58 Haymarket Terrace is a bright, airy bookshop. Two guys were busy in the back. They left me to browse in peace. If the bookshop looked new, their library along the corridor to the back looked old, wide-ranging and well-used. The shop's stock included the standard books by George himself, lots of more recent Georgist economic books, a whole lot of green-and-global-related stuff and a new series of slim books about particular issues, from a Georgist perspective, by people involved in the issues—hence the marvellous result of a London property developer and landlord advocating a tax on land value, and a Fife farmer advocating the end of farm subsidies. Also, a good deal of scholarly conference procedures and policy wonk stuff.

After I'd decided what I wanted to buy a young Danish guy called Lars sold me the pamphlet, gave me a back issue of *Land and Liberty*, and told me what they were all about. He quickly sussed that I was the author of *The Sky Road*, and I as quickly admitted that I'd stolen 'single tax and funny money' (as one character puts it) from the Georgists, as the principles of the society depicted therein. (Well, the single tax, anyway. The funny money I stole from the Proudhonists. The Georgists aren't currency cranks.)

The basic argument of Henry George (in common with many of the classical liberals) is that land is in principle common property, and should not be owned but be rented from the community. The practical proposal is that essentially all tax should be shifted onto land value—i.e. that all ground rent is taxed at 100%. (Same, in principle, with minerals and other natural resources.) A big political obstacle in Britain would be that so many of us (including me) are land speculators—we may say we've 'invested in bricks and mortar' but have in fact invested in the rising land/location value of our houses. Hence, I guess, the fiddly policy wonkery.

But it's the broader ramifications of the idea that I find intriguing. Global debt, environmental and ecological issues, transport policy, town planning, rural development, intellectual property, bio-patents, the price of fish...the Georgists have a distinctive take on all of them, and one that has attracted growing interest from campaigners in these areas. *Land and Liberty* has something of the look and feel of *New Internationalist*, without the hand-wringing and guilt-tripping.

What it all reminded me of was the first time I wandered in to the Alternative Bookshop, run by the Libertarian Alliance back in the early eighties. Two idealistic chaps running a place stocked with classical economics texts, policy proposals picked over, unexpected connections and outreaches made, an unusual combination of radical principle and pragmatic practice...

The Libertarian Alliance, of course, had some crazy ambitions, like privatising British Rail and bringing down the Soviet Union—as well as some more moderate ones, such as legalising cannabis and bringing down agricultural tariffs. I expected to see some of the latter attained in the foreseeable future.

But seriously—the issues raised and questions asked by the Georgists are central to the history and problems of the past decade and a half. The impoverishment of many, and the enrichment of a few, in the post-Soviet states are in large part due to the privatisation, not so much of capital, but of (what in the Georgist view should be) common wealth: gas, oil, timber and gold. What makes it all the more galling is that the burdens and the windfalls respectively have fallen on precisely those who did least to deserve them. On a broader scale, the scramble to monopolise land and mineral resources is arguably at the root of many recent wars, in which millions of helpless and innocent people have died—as in the Congo holocaust, about which hardly anybody gives a damn. The unresolved land question (and that other evil the Georgists have targetted, protectionism) is probably killing twenty million people *a year*. Even in the relatively comfortable West, free-market reforms have given us plenty of cool kit at the expense of chilling insecurity and growing inequality and indebtedness.

In a sense, we're back where we were a century ago. Freedom and progress on the one hand, justice and security on the other, seem poles apart with the gap ever widening. Those who offer us the one pole without the other—the neo-liberals and the communists—as well as those who essay a mish-mashed 'Third Way' or (on the political fringe) a downright sinister 'Third Position', arouse nothing but suspicion and indifference. That all of this could be set straight by revisiting and applying the classical liberal view of land and natural resources seems, as I said, a little unlikely on the face of it. But, you know, maybe worth looking into. Another century of booms, slumps, wars and revolutions would make a great subject for science fiction, but living through it is something we could live without.

See also:

http://geolib.pair.com
http://members.aol.com/_ht_a/tma68/geolib.htm
http://www.progress.org/dfc/index.html
http://www.cooperativeindividualism.org/
http://www.landvaluetax.org/
http://www.landandliberty.net/
http://www.henrygeorge.org
http://www.progress.org/books/george.htm
http://www.henrygeorgefoundation.org/

Scottish Politics

'It's a disgrace,' Margaret said. 'All this about one man!'

'He was a great man,' I said.

She gave me a look of pitying scorn: 'He was a *Tory*.'

We were talking about the death of Winston Churchill. We were ten years old. I had read a *Reader's Digest* collection of adulatory articles about the great man. It honoured his finest hour, of course. It lavished attention on his bulldog recklessness—turning up with a tommy-gun at the Seige of Sydney Street! What a guy!—and his common touch—saving his cigar butts for his chauffeur to smoke in his pipe! What a gent! I can't swear they weren't mentioned, but the names of Tonypandy, the Dardanelles, Gallipoli and Dieppe weren't ones the book left burning in my mind. I doubt they were on Margaret's mind either.

Some months earlier a Labour canvasser had driven into the village, stopped where a gang of us were playing, rolled down the window, handed a sheaf of election leaflets to us, and driven on to the next village. He didn't need to knock on doors. In our house, I suspect, the Labour leaflet went straight in the trash. My parents may have voted Liberal, which was something of a tradition in the areas where they came from.

'They couldn't vote for the Tories,' my mother said, decades later, 'because the Tories took their land.'

No Highland minister ever turned down a poacher's gift of salmon or venison. They would never have touched anything stolen. They respected property. They just had the Highland theory of it.

'The land shall not be sold for ever; for the land is mine; for ye are stranger and sojourners with me.' *Leviticus 25, 23.*

In classical political economy there were three factors of production: land, labour, and capital; which begat three sources of income: rent, wages, and profit; upon which subsisted three classes: landlords, labourers and capitalists; which in the fullness of time give rise to three parties: Tory, Labour and Liberal; and then the Tarriff Question arose, and tempted Churchill, and he crossed the floor, and he did eat; and poor Adam Smith was driven from his garden, and had live by Labour.

Well, something like that. Enough like it to put steel in the voice of a little old lady, and a sharp little girl.

A Hope of Peace is as Good as Any

> "If these are the early days of a better nation, there must be hope, and a hope of peace is as good as any, and far better than a hollow hoarding greed or the dry lies of an aweless god."
> —Graydon Saunders

I adopted that as the slogan of my weblog, 'The Early Days of a Better Nation', for which I wrote all but the first two of the pieces below. (These two are late 90s newsgroup posts.) Like many people I began blogging out of anger, and it shows. In a post to a newsgroup in March 2003 and a little later to my blog I wrote:

> "The rulers of the world should be regarded and resisted as if they were giant lizards from another star, which as far as humanity is concerned they might as well be.
>
> I oppose this war regardless of its course and outcome. The only support I give to the UK and US troops is to agitate for their immediate and unconditional return home."

Nothing that has happened since has seemed to me any reason to revise that. Nor have the arguments, patient, courteous and well-informed though they were, with which Norman Geras and the bloggers of 'Socialism in an Age of Waiting' responded to my piece on 'The Pro-War Left and the Anti-War Right' and other posts. As far as I know these arguments are all still out there on the net.—K. M.

Another View of Russian Capitalism

I have no idea what description of 'capitalism' people in what is now the Former Soviet Union learned about in school, but those who had any influence on shaping the post-counter-revolution state structures would have probably dozed through lectures on the official theory of 'state monopoly capitalism' which while tendentious and dogmatic was by no means some Dickensian caricature of Victorian England.

It described actually existing capitalism as a system with its own crises and contradictions, to be sure, but one where state regulation brought some public benefits as well as opportunities for political corruption, and where workingclass and popular movements had some influence on policy. It was not far removed from some libertarian descriptions of actually existing capitalism—though, naturally, with some of its phenomena evaluated differently. It was very far removed from a description of the kind of 'capitalism' they've actually got now: elements of capitalism without a capitalist state or civil society or bourgeois legality.

Part of the reason for this is that the only people with any experience of commercial relationships were those who operated illegally in the cracks of the bureaucratically planned economy. This was not the case in China or the Eastern European states (and to the extent that it was, could be overcome by assimilation and osmosis). Another part of the reason is that the ex-Soviet populations are reluctant to die off in sufficient numbers to make post-Soviet industry competitive in the world market. Hence production can drop by about half but unemployment only rise by about five per cent. They're still dying off—ten million more deaths in the 1990s than would have occurred if the conditions of the late 1980s had continued, according to a recent UN World Development Report. Still—can't make an omelette without breaking eggs, eh?

The Joy of Sects

The book I would actually like to write about all this isn't about the left per se but about the milieu from which groups like the British & Irish Communist Organisation (a small group from a mainly Irish nationalist background which claimed to be Stalinist, but concluded that democratic socialism was the correct shining path for the West, and eventually quantum-tunnelled their way out of Marxism altogether) and the Socialist Party of Great Britain (which was founded in 1903 and is still labouring to convince a majority of the workers of the world to vote for nothing less than the immediate establishment of non-market, non-state socialism) and the Freedom Group and odd individuals like Tommy Jackson and George Walford and Sid Parker emerge: working-class intellectual London, where (this is my speculation, my research proposal) there is a sprawling underground network of political and philosophical debate, quite independent from that of mainstream society, which goes all the way back to the English Revolution. Chris Tame told me of one discussion club, the Old Cogers (as in 'cogitate', not 'codger') which has met in the same pub every week since the 1640s.

The smaller the political meeting in London, the greater the chance that some retired building worker at the back has read Hegel and speaks Esperanto like a native. Every so often someone from the academic left would stumble across the pamphlets and journals of the B&ICO in the back room of Collet's and be intrigued. Attending a meeting of the B&ICO usually sent them reeling back to the security of a world where a left-wing piety might be questioned, might even be 'interrogated', but not picked up, held upside down, and shaken to see what fell out of its pockets.

Brendan Clifford, the leading light of the B&ICO, wrote a long pamphlet called *Against Ulster Nationalism* while working as a bus conductor in the mid-seventies. In it, he took on Tom Nairn, the British intellectual left's most sophisticated analyst of the nature of nationality. Clifford's interpretation of Irish history may be completely wrong—I have no idea—but on the point at issue he left Nairn without a thread of a shred of a rag of credibility. He also explained what he thought was going on in the world, which was this:

The process of turning traditional people into modern freewheeling individuals is a bloody business. You have to beat your ploughboys into swordsmen. People who never expected to do anything other than what has always been done are hurled into factories and cities and armies, get some uniform ideology drilled into them with Bibles or Shorter Catechisms or Short Courses or Little Red Books, and the survivors or their descendants suddenly find themselves thinking for themselves. (You can read about this in heart-rending detail in Jung Chang's *Wild Swans*.)

Back in the seventies, the Russians saw their ideology being taken up with genuine and terrifying enthusiasm in Ethiopia, the last surviving fragment of classical antiquity, and thought this was an indication that Marxism-Leninism was the vanguard of human progress. Clifford saw it as evidence that Marxism-Leninism had almost run out places to be progressive in.

Two consequences: one, there's no point in deploring or despising the process. Those who don't go through it will be trampled over by those who do. Two, once it's done, it's done. You are all individuals, and you won't be told What Is to Be Done.

The Pro-War Left and the Anti-War Right, Sunday, December 07, 2003

I want her to be happy
I want her to be free
I want her to be everything
She couldn't be with me.
—Warren Zevon, *She's Too Good For Me*, The Wind, 2003.

The pro-war left is smaller and more isolated than it has been in some recent wars, but it exists. What follows is an argument with a (literally) synthetic pro-war left position. No one person puts forward all these points. There are dangers in this, of posing strawman arguments, but I've included enough links for my sceptical readers (most, I hope) to check out for themselves.

One group for whose general position and tone I have a lot of sympathy claims that the antiwar left is 'Marching into Oblivion'[1]. Over at *Harry's Place*[2], you can find any amount of links to—and arguments in support of the general case made by—left-wing intellectuals, some of whose intellects were formed by Marxism, who support the war. Christopher Hitchens, David Aaronovitch, Norman Geras, Johann Hari and others[3] have a straightforward argument as to why socialists, democrats, and liberals should stand shoulder to shoulder with Bush and Blair: the enemies these men are fighting in the war against terrorism are much, much worse than they are, and implacable enemies of everything the left has historically stood for.

Despite the left's differences with some, or much, or even—for the sake of the argument, comrades—*all* of their domestic policies, the world Bush and Blair stand for, hope for, and fight for is vastly preferable to that dreamed of—and, to the extent of their power, accomplished—by Saddam Hussein, let alone Osama Bin Laden. American and British imperialism—yes, comrades, let's call it that, if it makes you happy—is the projection of the power of bourgeois democracies—yes, comrades, let's call them

1. http://www .marxist.org.uk/htm_docs/comm11.htm
2. http://hurryupharry.bloghouse.net/
3. http://www.marxist.org.uk/

that, if it makes you happy—and that means, if one is not to be a fool or a nihilist, that they can be an instrument for progressive purposes, or at least have a progressive effect regardless of the subjective purposes of those in charge of them. And in the case of the war on terrorism, and the war on Iraq, an agency of progress is exactly what the imperialist democracies are.

They have accomplished the overthrow of the monstrous Ba'athist regime and thereby—whatever the ongoing blunders and brutalities of the occupation—brought a great and genuine liberation to the people of Iraq. No other prospect of their early relief than foreign arms existed. The left has a moral and political blind spot if it ignores this, and ignores along with it the plain views of, for example, the Iraqi Communist Party, not to mention the ordinary people of Iraq. However quickly they think the occupation should end, however critical or even hostile they may be towards the actions of Coalition troops, most Iraqis are glad the tyrant is gone, and grateful to the forces that removed him. There are no torture chambers operating in Iraq today (though, I would interject, there are still political prisoners; and torture, albeit much less barbaric, goes on). There are independent political parties, trade unions, and a vastly freer press. Beside the enormous reality of this liberation, all the lies and half-truths brought forward by governments to justify the war—imminent threat, WMD, etc—fade into irrelevance. Bringing freedom and democracy or—at a minimum—regime change to Iraq is, and all along should have been, the justification of the war. And if you think the Coalition's proclaimed intention to leave a democracy behind them before they leave is a fraud, look at northern Iraq, where a Kurdish democracy has existed for ten years under Allied protection.

As to the wider war on terrorism, the threat from Al-Qaeda terrorism is not some bogeyman brandished by the imperialists. There is no doubt at all that Al-Qaeda will use the most powerful weapons they can get their hands on, and use them to maximum effect. Apart from the innocent victims, a terrorist WMD strike on America, or on the UK, could mean the swift curtailing of many democratic rights, or even—General Franks expects as much—outright military rule:

It means the potential of a weapon of mass destruction and a terrorist, massive, casualty-producing event somewhere in the Western world—it may be in the United States of America - that causes our population to question our own Constitution and to begin to militarize our country in order to avoid a repeat of another mass, casualty-producing event. Which in fact, then begins to unravel the fabric of our Constitution. Two steps, very, very important.[4]

In the US and the UK, we may be one disaster away from mass arrests and the complete shutting down of inconvenient civil liberties for

4. http://www.infoshop.org/inews/stories.php?story=03/11/22/2385330

the duration. We are faced, say the pro-war left, with a worldwide movement that even if it doesn't have the industrial resources and territorial base of classical fascism, has the potential for doing almost equivalent damage, and has aims that if anything are *more* reactionary than those of fascism.

The argument, depending on who's making it and to whom they're making it, can be back-stopped with unimpeachable socialist historical precedent. Didn't Marx and Engels support the British Empire, with all its brutalities in India and stupidities in the Crimea, against Tsarist Russia? Didn't they wholeheartedly back the United States—with all its hesitations, hypocrisies, faults and evils—against the Southern slaveholders' rebellion? Didn't almost the entire left—not just the liberals and Social Democrats and (Stalinist) Communists, but in their own inimitably contorted way most Trotskyists and even some anarchists—fundamentally, and however critically, support the world war waged by the imperialist democracies and Stalinist Russia against German fascism? Didn't Trotsky execrate those who claimed to believe there was nothing to choose between democracy and fascism? Didn't Lenin himself, that unflinching revolutionary defeatist as far as imperialist and colonial wars are concerned, say that we (the left, the socialists, the revolutionaries, the Marxists) do not in any circumstances support 'the uprisings of the reactionary classes against imperialism'? And are not the Ba'athist torturers, the jihadist terrorists, the mujahedin throat-cutters the upraised arm and mailed fist of the reactionary classes *par excellence*? And don't they want us (the liberals, the feminists, the left, the socialists, the revolutionaries, the Marxists), *us above all*, dead?

To those who splutter, at this point if not sooner, 'But what about—!' (make your own list: Vietnam, Greece, the Congo, Chile, Guatemala; the death squads armed, the torturers trained, the tyrants embraced—'Somoza is a son of a bitch, but he's *our* son of a bitch'—the arming of the muj and the contras and Renamo and the FNLA, the seating of Pol Pot's justly overthrown regime at the UN and the knighting of Sir Nicholas Caucescu; in Iraq itself the support for Saddam Hussein until his unexpected invasion of 'all of Kuwait', etc, et bloody cetera—the list is long) the pro-war left has a suitably materialist answer.

Yes, they'll freely admit, *back then*, during the Cold War, the US and UK ruling classes had an *objective material interest* in supporting any dictator or insurgent, any tyrant or terrorist no matter how vile, who supported capitalism against Communism or who—if a Communist—supported the Western alliance against the Soviet bloc, or could be used by the former to weaken the latter, no matter what the cost to the populations concerned. *But now*, things have changed. Imperialism—yes, comrades, we're still calling it that, if it makes you happy—has an *objective material interest* in ending tyrannies like Iraq and anarchies like Afghanistan, because bitter experience if nothing else has taught even the thickest right-wingers that tyrannies and anarchies are sponsors of, or havens for, terrorists who can bring the world down about our ears. And democracies, you know, generally speaking, are not.

So *this time*, we're told, the spokesmen of capital really mean it, when they mouth again all those worn-thin words we've heard so often and so falsely before about human rights and freedom and democracy. No longer are hapless peoples to be left under the lash or floundering in a bloody welter of chaos just as long as it suits the suits, with their cynical geopolitical calculations and their beady eye on the balance sheets of multinational corporations. Because *this time*, this time for sure, the calculations and the balance sheets are in the black for the 'red' of democracy and freedom. *This time* even George W. Bush really does genuinely need the bourgeois revolution in the House of Saud, if only—if we must be cynical, comrades—to save his own selfish skin. *This time*—for a change, yes; this once, if you insist—the interests of the masters of the world and the workers of the world and, not least and let's not forget, the wretched of the earth, are at last in synch.

And anyone (the pro-war left insists) who claims to be on the left and who fails to recognise this new and changed reality is at best someone who stopped thinking in the 1960s, or 1970s, or 1980s, or 1990s, or in any case some time before September 11 2001; at worst a cynic, a nihilist who 'sees no difference' between democracy and tyranny, between the bikini and the burkha, between elected leaders and self-anointed saviours; a calculating totalitarian schemer or ultra-leftist dolt; or a dupe of any or all of the above. Just *listen* to the chants that echo on antiwar demos:

'Bush! Blair! CIA! How many kids have you killed today?'

'George Bush! We know you! Your daddy was a killer too!'

How peurile, how unjust, how derivative, how bloody *unhistorical* can you *get*?

And, comrades (the pro-war left will say) do for heaven's sake spare us your new-found fervour for humanitarian pseudo-pacifist hand-wringing, muck-raking and atrocity-mongering. *Western Trots! We know you! Your Old Man was a killer too!* Even liberals can be ruthless if reluctant supporters of lesser-evil empires, in their usual wishy-washy way. Let's take Afghanistan (again). *Guardian* journalist Jonathan Steele has recently revisited Red Kabul:

I was no supporter of the Soviet invasion. Although nominally a response to an invitation from Afghan leaders, the despatch of Soviet troops in December 1979 was foolish and illegal, as I vigorously argued against an official from the Soviet embassy at a protest meeting at the LSE a few days later. But what I saw in 1981, and on three other visits to several cities over the 14 years that the People's Democratic Party of Afghanistan (PDPA) was in charge, convinced me that it was a much less bad option than the regime on offer from the western-supported mujahedin.

It's a view that surfaces continually. "Those were the best times," said Latif Anwari, a translator with an NGO in Mazar. Now in his late 30s, he studied engineering in Odessa from 1985 to 1991. "There was no fighting, everything was calm, the factories were working," he said. I asked him about Mohammed Najibullah, the PDPA leader who ruled for more than three years after Soviet troops withdrew. He's universally known as "Dr Najib". "He's still popular. If Dr Najib were a candidate in the presidential elections, he would easily win. No one likes the mujahedin," Latif said.[5]

Dr Najib won't be a candidate in any elections. He was lynched by the Taliban. We know that. We of the left may suspect that (at however many deniable removes and behind however many financial firewalls) as Christie Moore sang of another progressive doctor, Allende: *'And the good doctor dies/ with blood in his eyes/ and bullets/ from the CIA.'* But, taking the most intransigent among us as well as some of the more moderate, those of us who thought—rightly or wrongly—that, in Afghanistan at least, Soviet occupation and progressive dictatorship with all its inhumanities was preferable to the rule of the mujahedin and then the tyranny of the Taliban, surely *we* can admit in principle that progress can come literally from without and from above, can come even out of the barrel of a machine-gun mounted on a helicopter gunship, can result even from the policiesof the venal and self-seeking and short-sighted leadership of a superpower with rivers of unjustifiably shed blood still drying on its hands?

I trust this is an accurate and left-rhetorically persuasive, if sometimes sarcastic, statement of a case that could be put by a pro-war leftist with a Marxist background. It seems so to me. As I read over it I could almost believe it myself.

(When I wrote the above I feared I might be constructing a pro-war Marxist strawman, but apparently not:

Marx and Engels had no difficulty in supporting Polish nationalists against Prussia and the Russian empire, or Irish nationalists against Britain, despite their abhorrence of nationalism, nor in recognising the progressive effects of Bismarck's activities in helping to overthrow Napoleon III and unifying Germany, despite their awareness of Bismarck's reactionary policies. Why do contemporary 'Marxists' find it so very difficult to make the elementary distinction that Marx and Engels always made, between the motives of political actors and the effects of their actions?)[6]

5. http://www.guardian.co.uk/comment/story/0,3604,1083742,00.html

6. http://www.marxist.org.uk/htm_docs/princip5.htm

Ethically, I don't have a problem with this position. The argument from progressive effect doesn't trump every other consideration for me, but it trumps a lot—not in terms of personal behaviour or emotional identification, but in terms of historical evaluation and political calculation. No one who has more than a smidgin of sympathy with Cromwell and William of Orange, with Lincoln and Lenin (to say nothing of more controversial contenders like, say, Kemal Ataturk or Leonid Brezhnev) has any standing to deplore, however much they may regret, the cost of progress. No one who feels in their bones the uncounted cost of backwardness and regress—the dead babies, the dimmed minds, the thwarted lives, the shit and flies—can weigh it light in the balance.

There are, however, those who can. They are on the anti-war right.

At Antiwar.com, along with an unrivalled selection of links to relevant articles in the world press, you can find the arguments of the anti-war right. These are in some ways a mirror image of those of the pro-war left: they agree that Bush and Blair want to bring democracy to Iraq and the Middle East, and that this is a revolutionary project—and they oppose it. It's none of our business what goes on in Iraq or anywhere else so long as it doesn't threaten our national security. We should get the hell out[7], now, and let the Iraqis fight things out among themselves. Whoever comes out on top will have to sell us oil. That some neo-cons are former Trotskyists is, for the anti-war right, a telling point against neo-con plans. These neo-cons may call themselves conservatives, but they're still dedicated to the world revolution, albeit this time a democratic rather than a socialist one. And turning the world upside down is still a dangerous, hubristic aim. The rights of Iraqis or Afghans or Saudis are not worth the bones of one US Marine. The backward peoples are not ready for democracy, and even if they were it's not possible to impose it by force.

Needless to say, such arguments aren't handily available to the anti-war left. Some, however, most definitely are:

The fate of thousands of Iraqis is in your hands. Americans, and West Europeans, as residents of the aggressor nations (or, rather, subjects of the aggressor governments), have a particular moral responsibility to act before it is too late. [...] We must raise the issue of Iraq, before our elected officials, and in public forums, oppose the war plans of this administration, and expose the criminal sanctions that are killing Iraqi children. Whatever the crimes of Saddam Hussein, he will have to answer to his own people, and to history, not to some judicial or political authority acting in the name of a "New World Order." Our concern is with the crimes of our own governments, who bomb and starve children in the name of "international law"—and use war as a rationale to expand their own power over our lives.[8]

7. http://www.canoe.ca/Columnists/margolis_nov23.html

8. http://www.antiwar.com/justin/j112803.html

But the anti-war left does have arguments of its own, and nothing I've seen from the pro-war left has refuted them. There is no need to indulge in conspiracy theories, or to seize on instances—inevitable in the nature of the case—of crony capitalism in the sharing out of reconstruction contracts, to characterise the attack on Iraq as imperialist.

As some intransigiently anti-Baathist and anti-Islamic leftists from the region point out:

The US war is not about Saddam's Weapons of Mass Destruction as supporters claim, nor is it for the sake of the liberation of the Iraqi people from the yoke of a despotic regime or to establish freedom and justice in Iraq as defenders claim. Nor is it primarily about oil, as some 'anti-American' protesters repeat. Instead it displays the need and greed of the far-right Bush administration to impose, by military means, US supremacy on the world and to make US military intervention everywhere into the "norm" of future international relations. It is a sharp warning to Europe, Japan, Russia and China that after the Cold War the US will no longer allow a bi-polar or multi-polar world order. It will have the last word. Other powers, whether or not they have been "convinced" in the UN Security Council, have to be subordinate to the US as the lone super-power for the years or even decades ahead.[9]

The strengthening of imperialism, of the New World Order, is no small thing. It is to enhance the moral authority and material power of a force that has been, and will be, used against far more hopeful and progressive uprisings, movement and states than those it is now deployed to crush. In even the opposition to it in Europe and Russia, we can see the heat lightning of worse storms to come; of, in the words of Gabriel Kolko, another century of war.

But might not even that be a risk worth taking, if the alternative were to be the triumph of the Islamist reaction?

Yes. I'll give you that. If the fight were really one of Jihad versus McWorld, I'd take McWorld every time. But Al-Qaeda and its ilk are not just a reaction against McWorld, they're a product of it. They are distinctly postmodern movements, whose actual aims (as distinct from their fantasies) are ultimately compatible with Western interests. The West consistently supported them against more enlightened adversaries: the nationalists against the communists, then the Islamists against the nationalists, from Afghanistan to the West Bank.

And the invasions of Afghanistan and Iraq aren't exactly helping the actual fight against terrorism, says *Newsweek* Dec 1 2003:

Administration officials insist that they have not been robbing Peter to pay Paul in the war on terror. Much of what the CIA knows about Al Qaeda and other Islamic extremists comes from other intelligence services. The Egyptians

9. http://www.wpiran.org/Why%20people%20should%20say%20no%20to%20US%20war.htm

or Jordanians are much more likely to get inside an Islamic terror network than the Americans. Countries that don't always observe democratic niceties sometimes have more effective interrogation methods (the Egyptians have been known to closely question a suspect's family members). The CIA has a pipeline, lubricated by large amounts of cash, to the secret police in various Middle Eastern countries.

Still, the war in Iraq has not helped foster these special relationships. The security services of Middle Eastern despots are not enthusiastic about promises of democratic change coming from Bush, who made clear in his speech last week in England that America would push even its allies to become more democratic. After 9/11, Syrian intelligence began working with the CIA against a common enemy, the Syrian Muslim Brotherhood, which wanted to both overthrow the Assad regime and help Al Qaeda attack the United States. But, intelligence sources tell NEWSWEEK, the neocons in the Pentagon have been undermining that relationship by accusing (without much proof) the Syrians of encouraging jihadists to cross into Iraq and of hiding Saddam's WMD inside Syria.[10]

All the tough-minded arguments for liberal imperialism are ones that could have been—and were—used to justify wars that today's liberal imperialists retroactively deplore. The USSR's progressive intervention in Afghanistan didn't turn out too well, all things considered. It's difficult to think off-hand of any future war or intervention in the Second or Third Worlds that couldn't be justified on the grounds of stopping slaughters, freeing prisoners, ending torture. These practices are sufficiently rife that a pretext could always be found for any intervention. Meanwhile, the our-son-of-a-bitch defence is being applied to a new cohort of tyrants whose tortures can be conveniently overlooked, as in Uzbekistan. Nor is it at all likely that anything like a stable democracy could be constructed in Iraq under the Coalition, even if the fighters were to stop, or even if they were defeated (not that they will be).

That the US and UK's present enemies on the ground in the occupied countries are led, where they are led at all, by some nasty pieces of work is not contested by anyone. That there are follies and fallacies on the antiwar side I wouldn't dispute. That the left, notably its older contingents, has a lot of growing up to do I would heartily agree. It is true that the biggest demonstration in British history was politically the weakest and least effectual. It is also true that the reasons authoritatively given for the wars, as opposed to those concocted by their left-wing supporters, were a tissue of lies. The very circumstances in which the present wars are possible at all virtually guarantees that they be fought on the shoddiest of pretexts, against

10. http://www.msnbc.com/news/997146.asp?0cv=KB10

the most disreputable and insupportable of enemies, and opposed by the broadest and thinnest of coalitions.

For what are these circumstances? Overwhelmingly, they are—still, and for the foreseeable future—those created by the end of the Cold War. As was written as long ago as 1991, in The Gory Dawn of the New World Order:

The collapse of the East meant also the demise of the West as its opposite pole, as a defined economic, political, military and ideological entity forged to contain and defeat the Soviet bloc after the Second World War. The old West, both as a concept and as a politico-economic reality, was erected on the basis of the hegemony, or the so-called 'leading role', of the United States. The preservation of this role, or even its extension, in the radically transformed world of post-Cold War politics, is the essence of the American vision of the 'New World Order'.[11]

The Cold War shaped and polarised the world more deeply than we knew. The confrontation between the Free World and Communism, or between imperialism and socialism (as the other side would have it) formed and energised every political difference within the opposed camps. Every needle, every iron filing was lined up, quivering, by that field of force. In the West, the entire left, not just the official Communists but every liberal and social democrat, every Trot and Maoist, every anarchist and impossibilist —however anti-Soviet—stood cloaked in the credibility of the alternative to the East. Whatever names the near or far left called it, however fervently they dissociated themselves from it and its crimes, the mere fact that a nuclear superpower called *itself* the 'Union of Soviet Socialist Republics' lent throw-weight and real-world resonance to their similar-sounding words. The jibe 'Go back to Russia!' snarled or sneered at every leftist agitator was itself a back-handed recognition of the first and so far only revolution won by the working class itself. In Britain the SWP may have cheered the fall of what it called 'state capitalism', but inwardly, on the days and nights of that mighty crash, it trembled too.

(Don't let anyone tell you different. Don't let the party's press from August 1991 deceive you. I was in a branch meeting the night the statues fell.)

The SWP survived the fall all right, and may even have increased in numbers, but that's not the point. During the Cold War the Communist Party had, as was often remarked, an influence out of all proportion to its size. The same could be said today of the Socialist Workers Party, but in reverse. Its influence is smaller than its membership.

OK. Back to the real world. So what happens after the Cold War? Well, in the former Third World there are a lot of ramshackle tyrannies whose former position as key players in the great contest has been forgotten even

11. http://www.m-hekmat.com/en/2270en.html

by themselves. The US has lost a role and not yet found an empire. Maintaining hegemony means taking down any of an embarrassingly rich array of malefactors, and (partly by this means) dissuading the emergence of any military rival among the metropolitan countries. New American Century. Full spectrum dominance. Sole superpower. You know the drill.

In this situation it is absolutely inevitable that the targets of choice should be (a) no great threat to anyone outside their borders and (b) a bloody menace to people inside them and (c) completely uninspiring to, if not downright detested by, anyone on the left in the West. Vietnam without Vietcong. It's hardly a surprise that their overthrow should improve matters in the countries concerned, at least in the short run. Whether it's a good thing for the world and for the long run is another matter entirely. I don't know where all this is heading, but I have a very bad feeling about it.

It is also absolutely inevitable that a left that has lost its main real-world reference point and is only slowly realising that it had better offer some more exciting prospect for the glorious future of humanity than wage labour in nationalised industries (or worse, in co-operatives) with or without workers' control etc etc should flounder and flail in its opposition, dream up silly slogans and daft stunts, believe in conspiracies, and all the rest. But, you know, so bloody what? We just have to thole it.

Thin and wide as an oil-slick the 'No Blood for Oil' opposition may be, but in its inevitably inchoate way it expresses a healthy suspicion of the military machines of the great powers. The movement is better than it knows itself to be, and more vital. At each new war it revives, stronger and bigger than before. We can only hope and work for the day it is big enough to swamp the build-up to the next great war, the war that is sure to come.

Well, I'm sure of it, anyway. I could well be wrong about that, and I hope so, but the thought does tend to haunt one a little. Even the possibility makes me very wary of lending an ounce of support to any war, no matter what the immediate effect.

This is why no argument so far presented could convince me to take the position of the pro-war left. I admit to being one of those boring old ex-Trots whose thinking on war and peace was shaped, not only by the 1960s and 1970s and 1980s and 1990s, but by the oft-invoked historical memory of the 4th of August 1914, when the War to End All Wars began, and a world ended. As my oldest surviving uncle once said: 'I haven't believed in God since the First World War.' Most of the left, Marxist and liberal and anarchist, backed one side or another in that war too.

'And the flood came, and destroyed them all.'

Conspiracy in the Shadow of Hierarchy, Saturday, November 15, 2003

Despite some recent indulgences, I'm not much of a one for conspiracy theories. In general they hinge on misapplications of the principle of *cui bono*. Who shot JFK? Lee Harvey Oswald must surely top the list of suspects. Who benefitted from the shooting of JFK? The list is as long as your arm, but the beneficiaries may have been as surprised as anyone else. The term 'conspiracy theory' is sometimes used as a dismissal, but this usage is odd.

For instance, to say that the 9/11 attacks were the work of a small team whose members were part of a vast clandestine network of terrorists led or inspired by Osama Bin Laden is not usually called a 'conspiracy theory', although that is exactly what it is: it attributes the events to a conspiracy. It is also almost certainly true. Nobody doubts that conspiracies, sometimes on a large scale, exist. What is loosely called a 'conspiracy theory' is any theory that purports to explain an event or events by some kind of covert action, or a motivation other than those admitted publicly.

The respectability of conspiracy theories in that sense (leaving aside sheer insanities) is surprisingly relative. In the 1920s Nesta Webster's theory that the Bolshevik Revolution was the work of the Illuminati was quite respectable, but is now taken seriously only by cranks. In the 1930s the theory that Trotsky, Bukharin, and other Bolsheviks conspired with certain Red Army officers, themselves in contact with the Germans, to overthrow Stalin was considered quite respectable. It was believed by, among others, the US ambassador to Moscow (Joseph Davies) and the New York Times. Today the respectable conspiracy theory is that Stalin contrived the murder of Kirov, and invented out of whole cloth the previously mentioned conspiracy, to get rid of his Bolshevik rivals, who were innocent of anything but peaceful (though clandestine and illegal) opposition. Some recent historians dispute both conspiracy theories, and suggest instead that the whole ghastly bloodbath may have been the unintended outcome of an intelligence snafu.

The theory that Roosevelt allowed Pearl Harbour to happen in order to bring the US into the war is unrespectable, but not beyond the pale of respectable discussion. Likewise the theory that the nuclear bombing of Japanese cities had more to do with warning off the Soviet Union than defeating Japan. The theory that Stalin held back the Red Army at the gates of Warsaw to allow the Germans to destroy the anti-Communist Polish Home Army (and with it much of Warsaw) is highly respectable. Soviet historians always denied it, claiming (e.g.) that the Red Army was too exhausted of men and materiel to help the Polish insurgents. The theory that the same Home Army, for highly discreditable reasons, had previously stood by and done nothing much to help the heroic Jewish uprising in the Warsaw Ghetto was respectable when Leon Uris wrote *Exodus*, but may no longer be.

Likewise, the theory that Clinton tried to kill Osama Bin Laden to distract attention from his own domestic woes is now less respectable than it was.

In short, the respectability of a conspiracy or hidden-hand theory—sheer insanities always excepted—is variable, and largely a matter of political prejudice. That Mossad agents in the US spied on Islamic extremists who happened to include the 9/11 hijackers is plausible enough, whether or not it's true (and, as I've said, it's quite possibly not). That some consequences of the attacks—e.g. the invasion and occupation of Iraq—were to the perceived advantage of Israel is hard to dispute. That they also advanced the agendas of people in and around the US government who had long sought to settle accounts with Iraq and had wider plans for the region is likewise true. The idea that elements within the US or Israeli state apparatuses had some foreknowledge of the attacks (if not necessarily their exact nature) but allowed them to proceed is a highly unrespectable conspiracy theory, and one that goes beyond any evidence I've seen, but not, I think, a sheer insanity. To attempt to refute it by lumping it in with crackpot and/or malevolent theories (of which, of course, there are plenty) only muddies the waters. The real problems with it are deeper.

One problem with it is that from the point of view of opponents of the Reptilian Party and critics of the War on Terra, it's too good to be true. Smoking Gun Found. We Name the Guilty Men. Dream on. Another problem is that conspiratorial explanations may seriously overestimate the abilities of the best and the brightest. Gabriel Kolko, in a review of some recent memoirs on intelligence and the Vietnam War, persuasively depicts a situation where time after time, the intelligence apparatuses simply get it wrong, and those within them who get it right are ignored when they aren't crushed underfoot like bugs. Policy decisions shape intelligence, not the other way round. It reads like something straight out of the works of Robert Anton Wilson. Not his conspiracy theory spoofs, but his account of the effect of hierarchical structures on information. Far from concentrating raw data into usable intelligence, they degrade the data. The farther up you are, the less you know. According to Kolko, towards the end of the war in Vietnam this applied as much to the Communists as to the US and the Saigon regime. The NVA left as much heavy equipment behind them in their unexpectedly rapid advance as the ARVN dropped in their retreat. Luckily for Hanoi, they had a general who knew how to wing it.

It's possible, then, that even if some people in the security agencies did have some idea that something like 9/11 was in the pipeline, their information was ignored or passed over for entirely bureaucratic reasons rather than a Machiavellian plan. The same line of argument works on the other side of the war. I've sometimes speculated that Osama Bin Laden set up the attacks precisely to draw the US empire into a quagmire. Create two, three, many Afghanistans! This would attribute to him a better understanding of the US than he seems to display. He clearly believes that a culture that permits women and homosexuals to run around freely, just like normal people, is on the verge of collapse from sheer moral degeneracy. Being bombed out of Tora Bora was probably not part of his cunning plan. He may not be a bureaucrat, but like anyone at the top of a hierarchy he has the problem of being told what people who defer to him think he wants to hear.

Hierarchy was invented to regulate human relations with imaginary beings, and it still performs that function quite admirably. In the shadow of that pyramid, conspiracy theories are little grassy knolls.

The Midnight Fathers, Sunday, May 02, 2004

It's late. Your wife, or husband perhaps, is out or away somewhere or gone to bed before you. The kids are in bed, or out, or away. For now, you're alone. There may be a small glass of whisky on the table. Tobacco, or some stronger leaf, smoulders in the ashtray. Some voice that speaks to your darker or quieter moments plays low on the sound system. The television is off. Definitely off. The newspaper is crumpled, the novel has no savour. You prowl the bookshelves, hunker down, run your finger over the dust of forgotten corners. Your glance alights on a lean volume or skinny pamphlet; your fingertip tugs it out. Blow the dust, sneeze, flick over pages that once seemed cogent.

It could be anything of many, that text. The dry statistical tables of Lenin's *Imperialism*; the scathing prose of Rosa's *Junius Pamphlet*: 'German social democracy is a stinking corpse.' Jim Cannon in the dock at Minneapolis, as Japan's fleet slipped its harbours: 'Wherever capitalism penetrated, its laws followed it like a shadow.' The glare of Vietnam burning through pages in *Imperialism and Revolution*, by David Horowitz. (Whatever became of him?) The grim prescriptions of Guevara: 'It is necessary to prevent him from having a moment of peace, a quiet moment outside his barracks or even inside...Then his moral fiber shall begin to decline. He will become even more beastly, but we shall notice how the signs of decadence begin to appear.' You look away from that page, to the blank television, and your neck hairs prickle as the guerrilla's ghost walks. You reach for something lighter: the Yiddish commonsense of Cliff at his best, the unquenchable optimism of Mandel, who as a lad argued his guards into letting him off that eastbound train...these men too felt the shadow that paces the laws.

Their words, or those of others like (or unlike) them, shook up your life for a year or three, a decade or three ago. You settle back, sip the whisky, take a reminiscent draw. It did you no harm, that early fervour. The skills of small-group politics transferred easily enough to bigger organizations;

experience in sticking your ground was character-forming; a rudimentary grasp of the sales pitch and the public spiel didn't go amiss; and an abiding interest in the bigger picture and the longer view you parlayed into some success that surprised yourself. The room is comfortable, the kit is recent, the job is interesting, the credit cards can be juggled at each month's end.

You never really repudiated these words. Not like some. If the subject ever comes up, and it seldom does, you know the exact shrug, the right ironic half-smile, to distance yourself just enough. Thought we had all the answers. Interesting times. It was the big strike. The dole. The war. The nukes. Everything seemed a bit, you know, urgent. Impatient youth. Went a little too far. Not all regretted, mind. But you know how it is. Matters not so black and white. Bit off more than we could chew. You grow up.

You had a call the other day, out of the blue. Just catching up. No, really? Well done. Or bumped into someone at a conference. Shared a half-indulgent, half-embarrassed reference back, an in-joke. Nobody overhearing would ever get it. And now? A sideways glance at a headline, a shrug of one shoulder, a grimace, a gesture of the hand. You're still on the same wavelength, you and him, or you and her. For a moment it sparks the gap between you, an anger neither of you have felt or shown since… that other time. But what can you do?

And it strikes you, quite suddenly, what you *have* been doing. It's not good. You've been doing more for the system than the clamant renegades or blatant sell-outs you despise. You've transmitted a small portion of its weight downward. It's subtle, this ideology and hegemony business that Gramsci used to go on about. You may not be suborned, but you function as one of the subaltern intellectuals. The most conservative and deadening and discouraging response to new impatient youth is yes, that's how it all works, but…what can you do?

The question ceases to be rhetorical. What *can* you do? You are certainly not going to get into *all that* again. (If you've been with me so far, you know just what I mean by *all that*.) Christ, no. What else? Letters to the editor? To your elected representative? There are liberals enough.

Something within you has become harder and colder this week. You've glimpsed the bestiality and the decadence, in the system's nerves like a venereal disease. It's sick, and there *is* something sexual in its sickness, something warped beyond therapy. The oiled skin of a gladiator, the lusty roar of the arena. A line from Cornford, whom you haven't read for years, slides beneath the surface of your mind. 'The painted boy in the praetorian's bed.' Camphor and pincers, piss and blood. You're in this rotting system, you're part of it. You pay the soldiers. *Civis Romanus sum.*

But you know how it all works, how the small actions add up. And you now see how you can start to stack them up differently. The helpful suggestion upward, not made. The confidential memo leaked downward, or out. The book recommended to an inquiring student. No longer on the curriculum, but you might find it interesting—a different angle. The conversational concessions withdrawn. The conventional civility dropped. The hard stare back, the harder line held. The slack not cut. Elsewhere, the warmer smile. The word of encouragement. The grant approved. The link forwarded. The cartoon tacked up. The dues paid. The paper bought, the extra coin passed, the minute spent in friendly chat before you hurry for the train. The firm nod to your own kid's tentative query.

There are more of you than you know. You're in deep in the system, in its fouled blood, in its creaking bones, in its edgy nerves. In its schools and universities, its bureaucracies and businesses, its studios and offices, its factories and homes. You're under its skin. The midnight fathers. The summer of love mothers. Thousands of you, tens of thousands, in Britain alone. You have the numbers. You know the drill.

A Canticle for Wojtyla, Saturday, April 02, 2005

I have conflicting emotions about the Pope, which go beyond the compassion anyone must feel for an old man in his last hours. His dignity abashes disagreement. To the end he is living the meaning of his life. But here is the conflict. On the one hand he is a reactionary. The contrast with the last pope to be popular beyond the RC church, John XXIII, is striking. He has beatified and canonised some of the most sinister and pathetic figures of recent times. He contributed quite significantly to, not the collapse of the Soviet bloc, but the depth of regression that followed. He has stuck to a doctrine that's contributed directly to the spread of AIDS. The Catholic theologian Hans Kung has recently written a scathing analysis of *The Pope's Contradictions*[1], which goes into these and other dark aspects of Wojtyla's papacy in detail. (Via[2]).

The other side is that he has stood for peace and human rights in a way that set his face against not only Communism but certain aspects of imperialism and neoliberalism. He condemned the attack on Iraq. He moved the church to a greater acceptance of modern science. He has been more open to other religions than previous popes. He began a repentance toward the Jewish people. He rehabilitated Galileo and apologised for the Crusades.

Like the Dalai Lama and Nelson Mandela, he became a figurehead of an inchoate global humanism that has little to do with what he (and the others) specifically stand for. Fidel Castro is an awkward fourth in that company, but—like it or not—he belongs in it. All four of these old men have their roots in the Cold War, of which they are the last men standing. It's a measure of the strangeness of the New World Order that they all, in very contradictory ways, have become icons of its discontents.

1. http://service.spiegel.de/cache/international/spiegel/0,1518,348471,00.html
2. http://nielsenhayden.com/electrolite/archives/006200.html#77922

Squibs

2001 and All That (or, Life before and after the End of History), Sunday, May 18, 2003

'Events, events, events.' — Ted Grant

'In the early morning in 11 September 2001 four Plaines were hitchiked from American Airports.'— a first-year University student essay

Introduction

This slim volume (well, page, really) has two notable predecessors (or precedents), *1066 and All That* by Sellar and Yeatman, and *1984 and All That* by Paul Manning. The latter brought the story begun by Sellar and Yeatman up to the eponymous date. Much history, including the End of it, has happened since. Even after the End of History, many events have taken place. In the spirit of my distinguished precursors, and at least one distinguished President, I think it important that they should not be remembered.

First (and Last) Chapter: HOW HISTORY ENDED AND WHAT HAPPENED AFTERWARDS.

Karl Marx said that communist society would bear the birthmarks of the old, and Mikhail Gorbachev bore one of them on top of his head. Gorbachev rose to power as a result of the Chernobyl Reaction, which came about because the Russians discovered that their previous two leaders—Brezhnev, Andropov, and Chernenko (these are three, but the third does not count)—were dead but still standing. They had been propped up every May Day on the Leaning Mausoleum, reviewing the workers

and soldiers who marched past. The workers and soldiers carried large pictures of the leaders to help them remember who they were, and for many years, they did. Fortunately for them, President Reagan had by then forgotten who he was too.

Gorbachev attempted two important things. The first was to abolish the Leading Roll of the Party. Without its Leading Roll the Party did not know what to do, and it lost the elections. Afterwards it won elections again, but without its Leading Roll it could do nothing, except sit in Parliament, which was soon abolished to save democracy (see under Yeltsin). Because it was abolished with artillery it became known as an Empty Shell.

The second thing Gorbachev did was to introduce Russia to the market. The problem was that Russia did not have bourgeois civility, so after it was introduced to the market it did not know what to say to it. Instead it stood about with its hands in its pockets, until it found that its pockets were empty. Its pockets had been picked by the Russian Mafia, which is just like the Sicilian one, except it is not Roman Catholic so does not have a Godfather at its head. Instead it has Ministers, like Protestants.

The outcome of this was the Restoration of Capitalism, which was a Good Thing. Francis Fukayama wrote that it meant the End of History. The whole world would become like Switzerland, because people no longer had anything important to fight over. Saddam Hussein read this in April, and misunderstood it, so he invaded Kuwait, which is like Switzerland, except that it is flat and sandy and it has votes for women. A great Collision had to be brought together to drive him out. In the end his troops surrendered to CNN and were killed by the Collision, on the Highway of Death.

This was the beginning of the New Word Order. It is what we used to have instead of History. Many important events happened in it, notably the Destruction of Yugoslavia and the Death of Diana. Yugoslavia had to be destroyed because the Serbs lived all over it and practised ethnic cleansing. This was stopped by another Collision and the Serbs now live only in Serbia. Serbia has been a democracy ever since its elected government was overthrown by policemen driving tractors. Diana died because of yet another Collision. The car she was being driven in was driven into a Parisian tunnel support pillar, known as a paparazzo. People still lay flowers at the pillar.

The New Word Order lasted until September 11 2001, when hitchhikers took over four airliners with box-cutters and flew them into the Twin Towers and the Pentagram (and Pennsylvania). After that it was generally understood that the whole world would not ever become like Switzerland, and Swiss Army knives were banned from airliners. This has prevented any more hitchhiking.

Afghanistan was bombed to get rid of Osama Bin Laden. He now no longer lives in Afghanistan but in the hearts of millions of devoted followers. Iraq was bombed to kill Saddam Hussein and to get rid of his Weapons of Mass Destruction, which are now in the hands of the people of Iraq.

America is still Top Nation.

Vietnam War Hero Disappoints War Hawks, Tuesday, May 11, 2004

HANOI, May 1–Vietnam war hero General Vo Nguyen Giap, who sent first the French then the Americans out of his country with their sorry asses in a sling, refused to be drawn on possible parallels with the current war in Iraq. 'Any country that wants to impose its will on another nation will certainly fail and all nations fighting for their own independence will be victorious,' he said enigmatically. 'Everyone in the world should acknowledge that each country has the right to independence and sovereignty. Nothing is more precious than independence and freedom.' The obscurity of his views deepened as he blew a smoke-ring from a vintage Marlboro and added: 'I haven't had a chance to go to Iraq and to study the specific tactics there.'

The veteran revolutionary's comments drew immediate fire from left-wing and liberal war-hawks. 'It's disappointing that Comrade Giap should express himself in this cryptic manner,' coughed Cristoforo Hitching. 'We had hoped for a clearer differentiation between the noble struggle of the Vietcong and the dead-end Islamofascist jihad in Iraq. Still, if he won't make the distinction, there are plenty of veteran freedom fighters who will, right here on the front lines in Washington.'

In London, too, Giap's remarks went down like a dud cluster-bomb. 'There are no conceivable parallels between Vietnam and Iraq,' said experienced liberal war promoter John Harry (17), who remembers the time vividly from a previous life. 'It's not like the Vietcong were some kind of violent authoritarian movement, or anything. They never harmed any Vietnamese civilians, or targeted any other Vietnamese socialists or nationalists. It was, like, peace and love, man. Anyway, opinion polls showed a consistent majority of Vietnamese opposed to the US presence. If they hadn't, it would have been perfectly proper to wait until several years of intensive bombing had swung their opinions before taking a stand.'

His older colleague, Dafydd Harrumfovitch (51), was sharper in his condemnation. 'You only have to compare the people opposed to this war with those who opposed the war in Vietnam. Today you see Socialist

Worker readers joining hands with pacifists, religious nutters and unreconstructed Stalinists, and people like Noam Chomsky and John Pilger writing hysterical screeds about US imperialism. The contrast with the movement against the war in Vietnam couldn't be more stark.'

A spokesman for the influential website MIAW (Marxism Inflicted by American Warplanes) added crossly: 'Countries want independence, nations want liberation and peoples want revolution, do they? Well, tough shit. The next wave of world revolution will eliminate these small counter-revolutionary peoples down to their very names. Except Albania, Kosova and Bosnia-Hercegovina, heroic vanguards of liberated humanity.'

http://www.johnlacny.com/archives/000030.html

Molvania Calls, Monday, May 10, 2004

Molvania is one of those little-known places about which we all have too much information. Even the most casual browser of the international and medical pages of the broadsheet newspapers is aware of its key position as a mutation site for new influenza strains heading west from China. Microsoft users are wearily familiar with the ingenuity of Molvania's computer virus designers. As a staging post in a major smuggling route for heroin, cigarettes, and bonded labourers, Molvania is familiar even to the readers of *The Sun*. Molvania's political transition has featured in Channel 4 documentaries and long flame-wars on soc.history.what-if.

The country has moved slowly and painfully from a grotesque parody of socialism to a no less offensive caricature of free market capitalism. Its first and so far only free elections have seen a rigid one-party (formally, a two-party) state replaced by a democratic coalition of National Conservative, Progressive Liberal and Religious Obscurantist parties, all of whose leaders are united by their Communist past and divided by business interests and clan feuds. The parliamentary opposition consists of the Social Democrats-Democratic Socialists (Reformed) and the Agrarian Unity Party. The AUP, ironically, is the only party which is not ex-Communist and which was legal—indeed, part of the governing Popular Patriotic Front—throughout the Communist period. Its origins are in the electoral wing of the inter-war nationalist and militarist movement, the Steel Toecaps, which was spared the taint of collaboration with the Axis puppet government by qualms about its 'extreme racism' and 'excessive violence' privately expressed by local units of the SS, and which joined the Anti-Fascist Committee of National Salvation hours before Soviet troops liberated the capital. Extra-parliamentary opposition is confined to small, under-heated cells and to clandestine branches of the Democratic Socialists (Unreformed) who retain a certain base of support among cement workers and (in an older age bracket) the White Lung (Silicosis) Compensation Campaign.

Unemployment remains high, following the loss of major export markets and the collapse of the agro-industrial complex that supplied axle grease and margarine in differently labelled tins to the Soviet Army. Molvania's five brands of cigarette—Patriot, Peasant, Partisan, Proletarian and Partinost—once as popular as they were indistinguishable in all the barracks of the Warsaw Pact—have lost market share to ex-GI Marlboros and Camels illegally imported from Vietnam. The exchange rate of its currency, the *khunta*, is shown on hourly updated boards of intermittently flashing red lights in the major cities. Visitors should be aware that at other times these figures show the date (in the Gregorian calender, adopted as a concession to the Religious Obscurantist party) or the background radiation in millicuries.

Health services, once spartan but adequate, are now supplied by Christian Aid, Medicins Sans Frontieres, and (for Molvania's often overlooked Muslim population) the Bin Laden Mercy Fund and Cross-Border Community Bank.

All of the above, of course, is merely what I know off the top of my head, and is perhaps a little impressionistic and dated. More recent and reliable information about Molvania, this forgotten aphid in the rose garden of post-post-capitalism, is available here: http://www.molvania.com/

Free-Market Think-Tanks Out-sourced

Callers to the Intellect Foundation, the Caesar Institute and other libertarian think-tanks will from today be surprised to hear a pause, a click, and an answer in a flawless but distinctly Indian-accented English. The free-market foundations' entire staffs have been sacked and replaced by eager graduates in the Bombay-based Kali Call-Centre, dedicated to the Hindu goddess of creative destruction.

'If you really want passionate denunciation of an over-regulated economy, and paens to the glory of the free market, there's no better place to come than India,' explains its owner, self-styled 'intellectual entrepreneur' Saresh Ramakrishnan (19), as he proudly oversees a small back room full of two hundred fast-talking, keyboard-tapping, headset-wearing men, women, *hijras* and children. 'Here we know what strangling red tape and mass poverty are really like. As for religious interference in politics and private morals, we're up against the world's worst serial offenders outside of Iran. We can undercut American ideologues any day. We're English-literate, hip, and nobody can accuse us of being a bunch of fat white men.'

Jonathan Wilde, *eminence grise* of the Deforestation Alliance, England's 'premier free-market and anti-environmentalist think-tank', gloomily agrees but is holding out against the tide. 'Here in Britain we have libertarians who will work for nothing,' he says. 'I know, to our American friends it seems incredible, if not immoral, but that's the way it is. And it gives us a chance to hang in there until the Indians are in turn undercut by the Fr—the Fr... the frigging Chinese.'

The New England Science Fiction Association (NESFA) and NESFA Press

Selected books from NESFA Press:

- *Once Upon a Time (She Said)* by Jane Yolen $26
- *Dimensions of Sheckley* by Robert Sheckley $29
- *Once More* With Footnotes* by Terry Pratchett $25
- *Dancing Naked* by William Tenn $29
- *Immodest Proposals* (Vol. 1) by William Tenn $29
- *Here Comes Civilization* (Vol. 2) by William Tenn $29
- *With Stars in My Eyes* by Peter Weston $23
- *Fancestral Voices* by Jack Speer $17
- *A Star Above It* by Chad Oliver (Vol. 1) $24
- *Far From This Earth* by Chad Oliver (Vol. 2) $24
- *The Rediscovery of Man* by Cordwainer Smith $25
- *Nostrilia* by Cordwainer Smith $22
- *Silverlock* by John Myers Myers $26
- *Ingathering: The Complete People Stories* by Zenna Henderson $25
- *Homecalling and Other Stories* by Judith Merril $29
- *Years in the Making* by L. Sprague de Camp $25

Details and many more books available online at: www.nesfa.org/press

Books may be ordered online or by writing to:

NESFA Press
PO Box 809
Framingham, MA 01701

We accept checks, Visa, or MasterCard. Please add $3 postage and handling per order.

The New England Science Fiction Association:

NESFA is an all-volunteer, non-profit organization of science fiction and fantasy fans. Besides publishing, our activities include running Boskone (New England's oldest SF convention) in February each year, producing a semi-monthly newsletter, holding discussion groups relating to the field, and hosting a variety of social events. If you are interested in learning more about us, we'd like to hear from you. Write to our address above!

Acknowledgments

Thanks to Ken MacLeod, Donato Giancola, Jo Walton, Alice Lewis, Pan Fremon, Tony Lewis, Mark and Priscilla Olson, Dave Grubbs, Sharon Sbarsky, Dave and Claire Anderson, Geri Sullivan, David Dyer-Bennet, and Patrick Nielsen Hayden, the Boskone committee, and NESFA, without whom this book could not have been made. Any infelicities that remain are mine.

—Sheila Perry
December, 2005